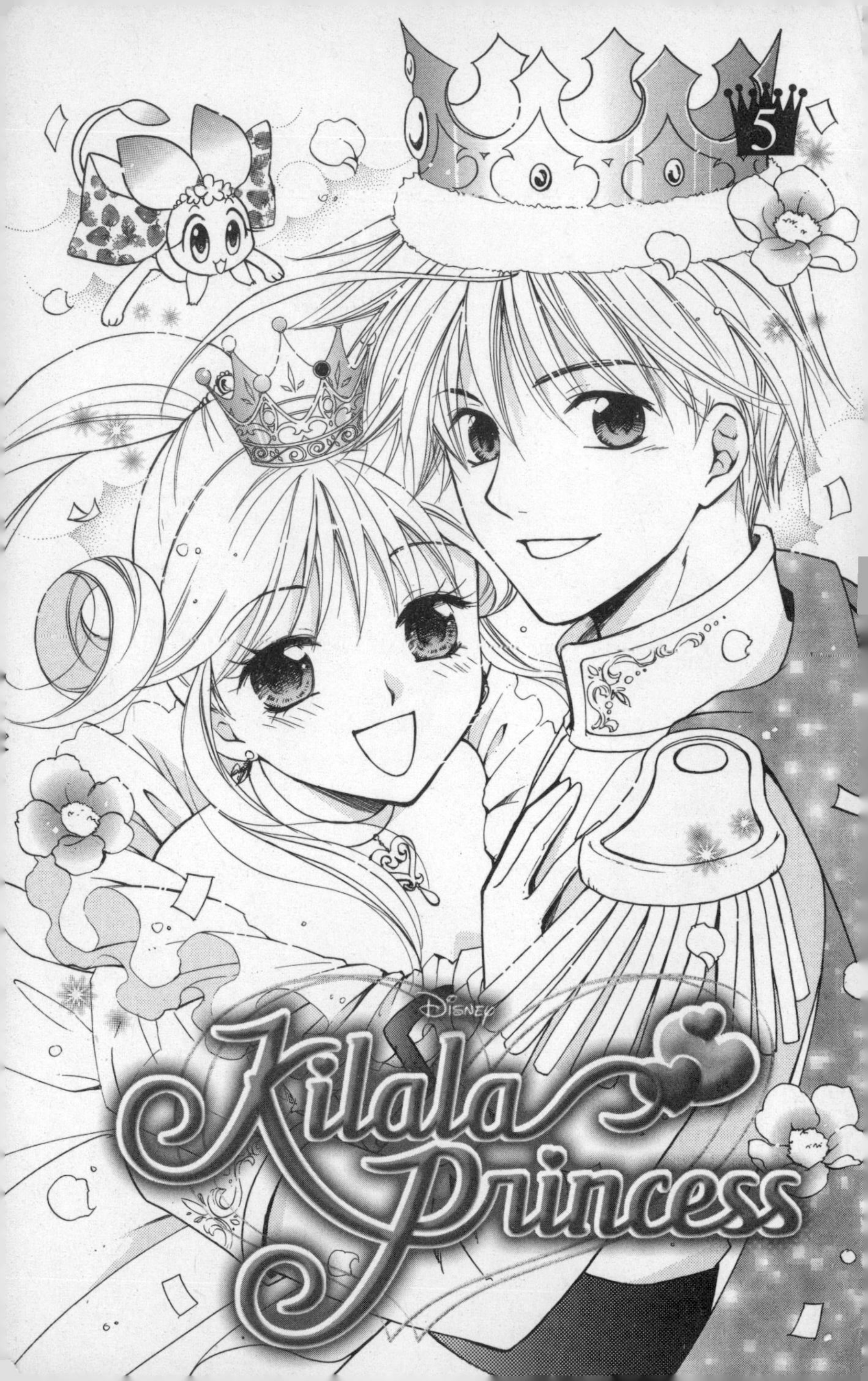
5
Disney
Kilala Princess

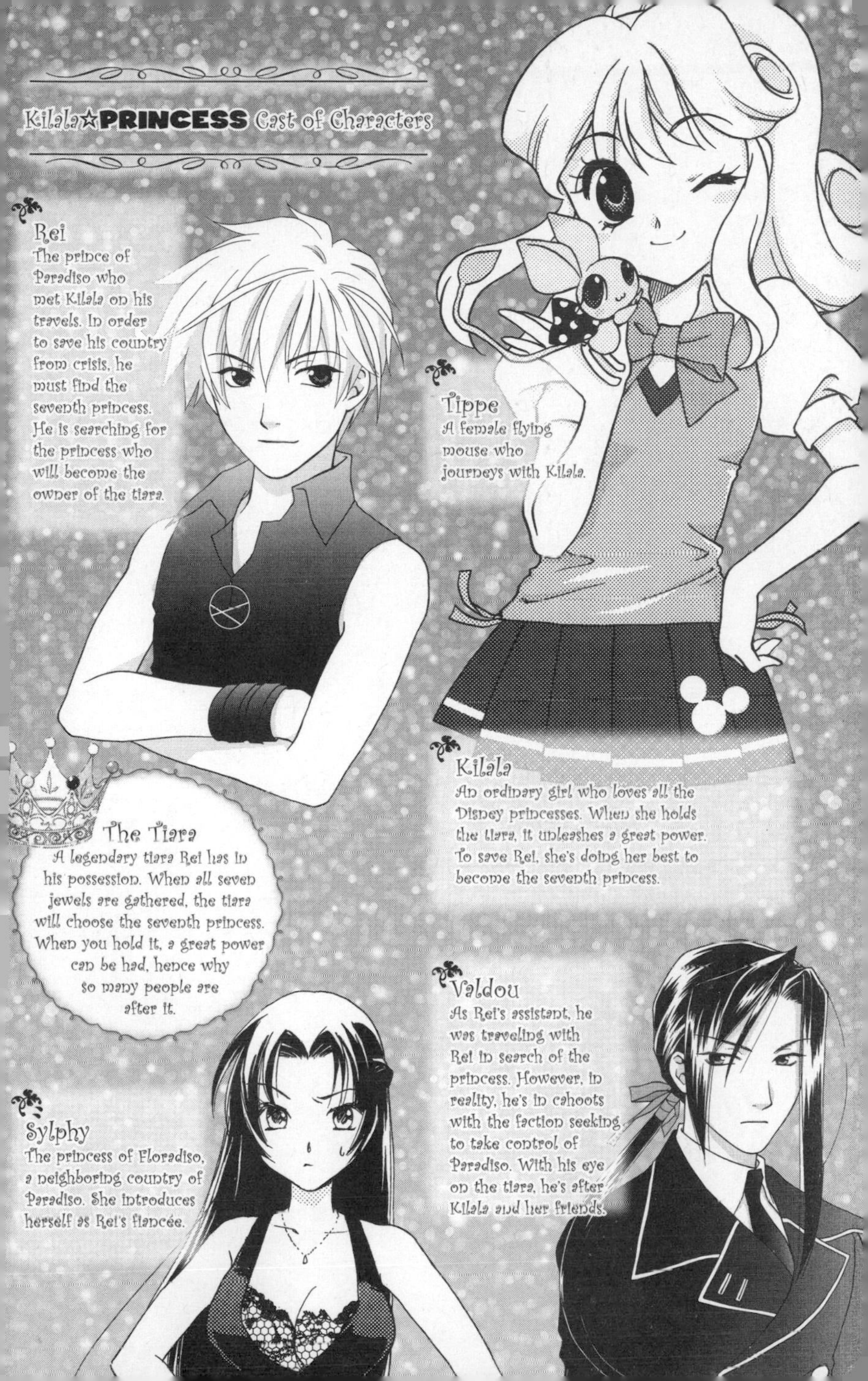
Kilala☆PRINCESS Cast of Characters
Rei
The prince of Paradiso who met Kilala on his travels. In order to save his country from crisis, he must find the seventh princess. He is searching for the princess who will become the owner of the tiara.
Tippe
A female flying mouse who journeys with Kilala.
Kilala
An ordinary girl who loves all the Disney princesses. When she holds the tiara, it unleashes a great power. To save Rei, she's doing her best to become the seventh princess.
The Tiara
A legendary tiara Rei has in his possession. When all seven jewels are gathered, the tiara will choose the seventh princess. When you hold it, a great power can be had, hence why so many people are after it.
Valdou
As Rei's assistant, he was traveling with Rei in search of the princess. However, in reality, he's in cahoots with the faction seeking to take control of Paradiso. With his eye on the tiara, he's after Kilala and her friends.
Sylphy
The princess of Floradiso, a neighboring country of Paradiso. She introduces herself as Rei's fiancée.

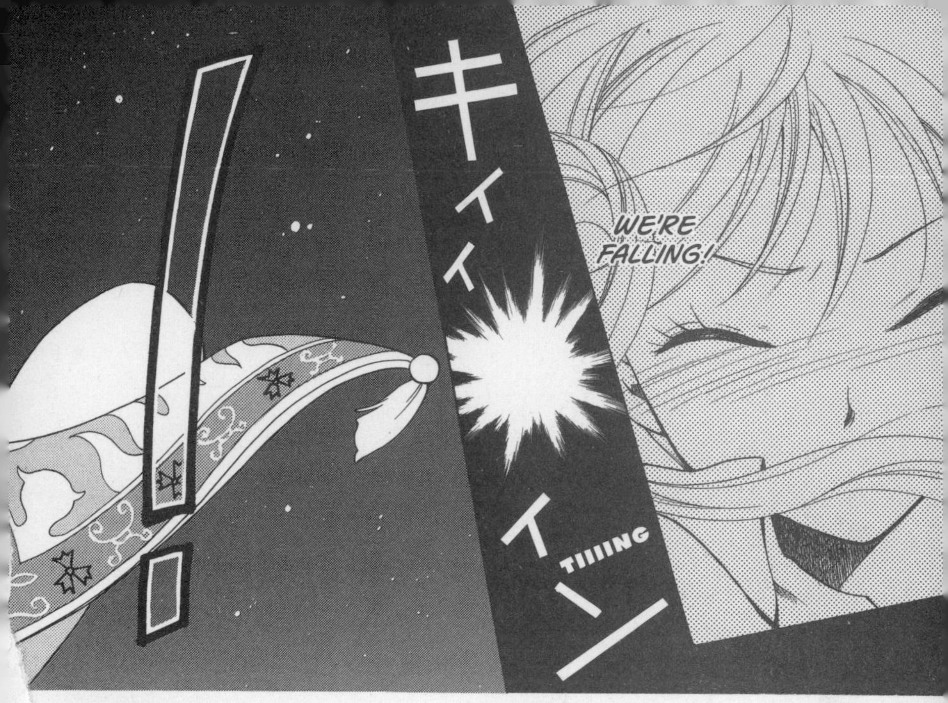
WE'RE FALLING!
キイイイン
TIIIING
!
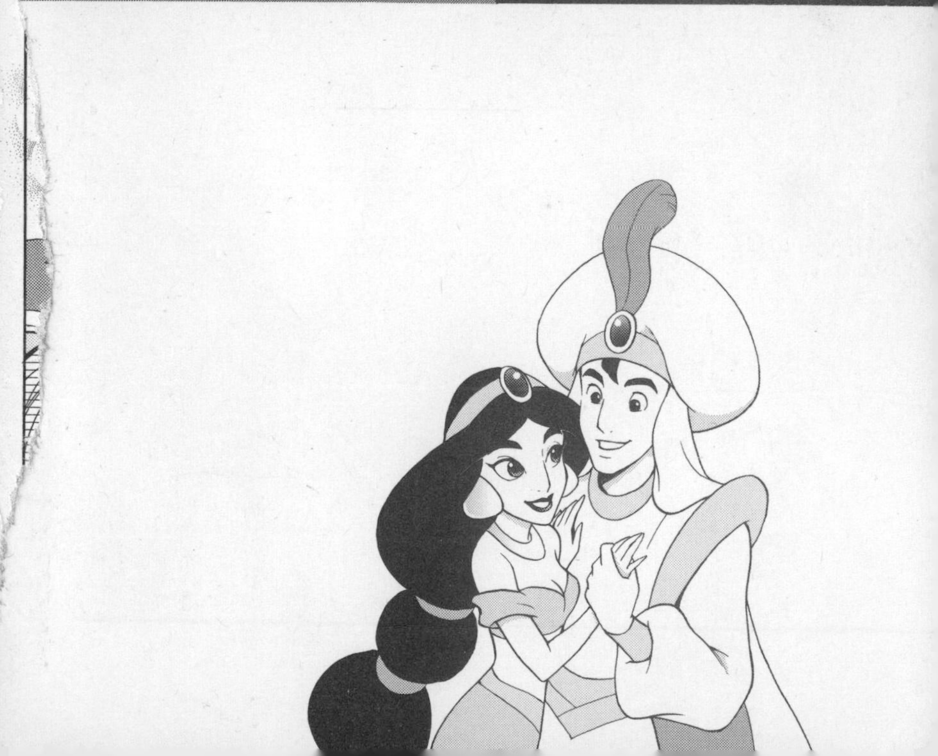

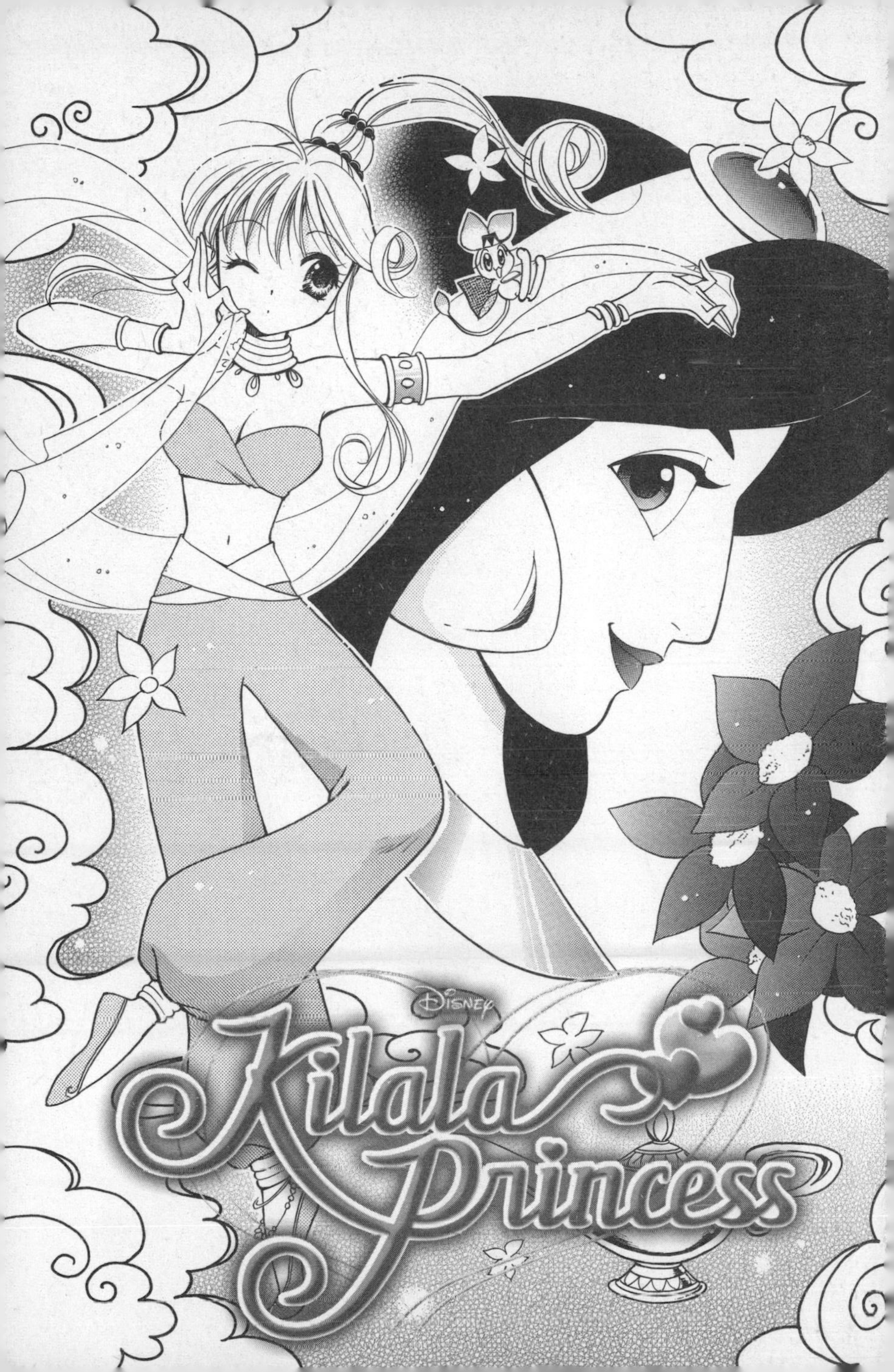
Disney
Kilala Princess

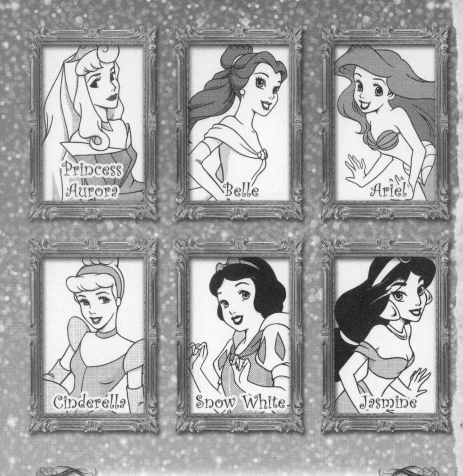

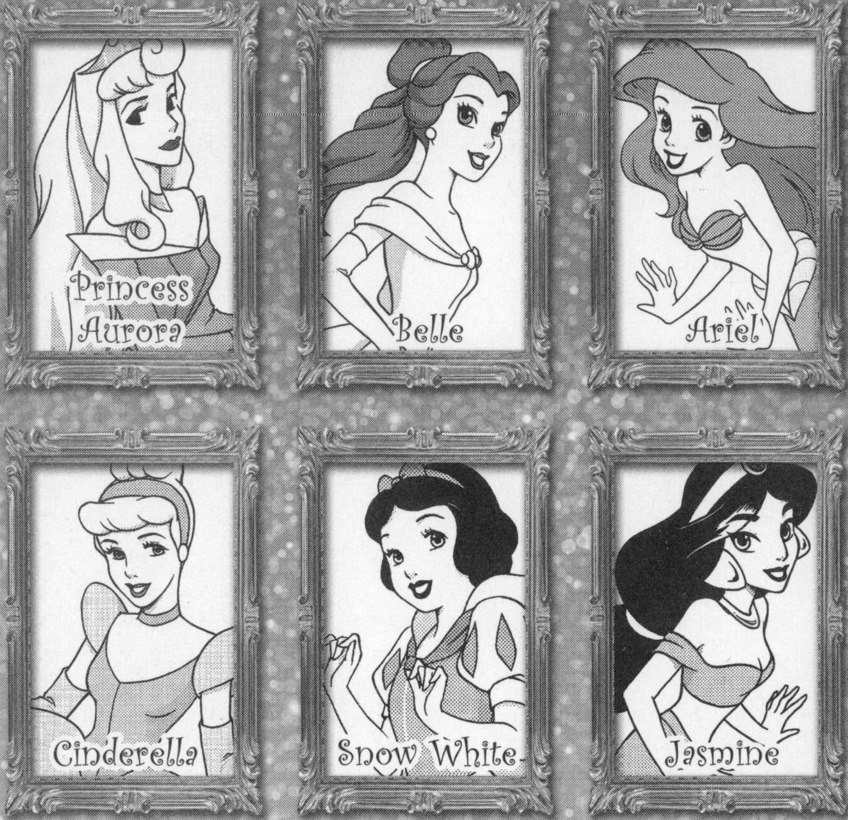
Princess Aurora
Belle
Ariel
Cinderella
Snow White
Jasmine

Story so far:

♦Kilala, a young girl who idolizes princesses, meets Rei and instantly her destiny awakens in a big way. Led by the mysterious tiara Rei possesses, Kilala finds herself in the worlds of the Disney princesses!

♦She saves Snow White, finds Rei with Ariel's help, gets back the tiara when it's stolen in the world of Cinderella, patches things up between Beauty and The Beast, and saves Aurora from her deep slumber once more. Throughout all these adventures, Kilala receives jewels for the tiara from each princess.

♦But there are other villains who have their eye on the mysterious powers the tiara possesses. Kilala resolves to become the seventh princess and save the world but when Valdou tracks her down, she finds herself in a pinch. Will she ever meet the sixth princess...?

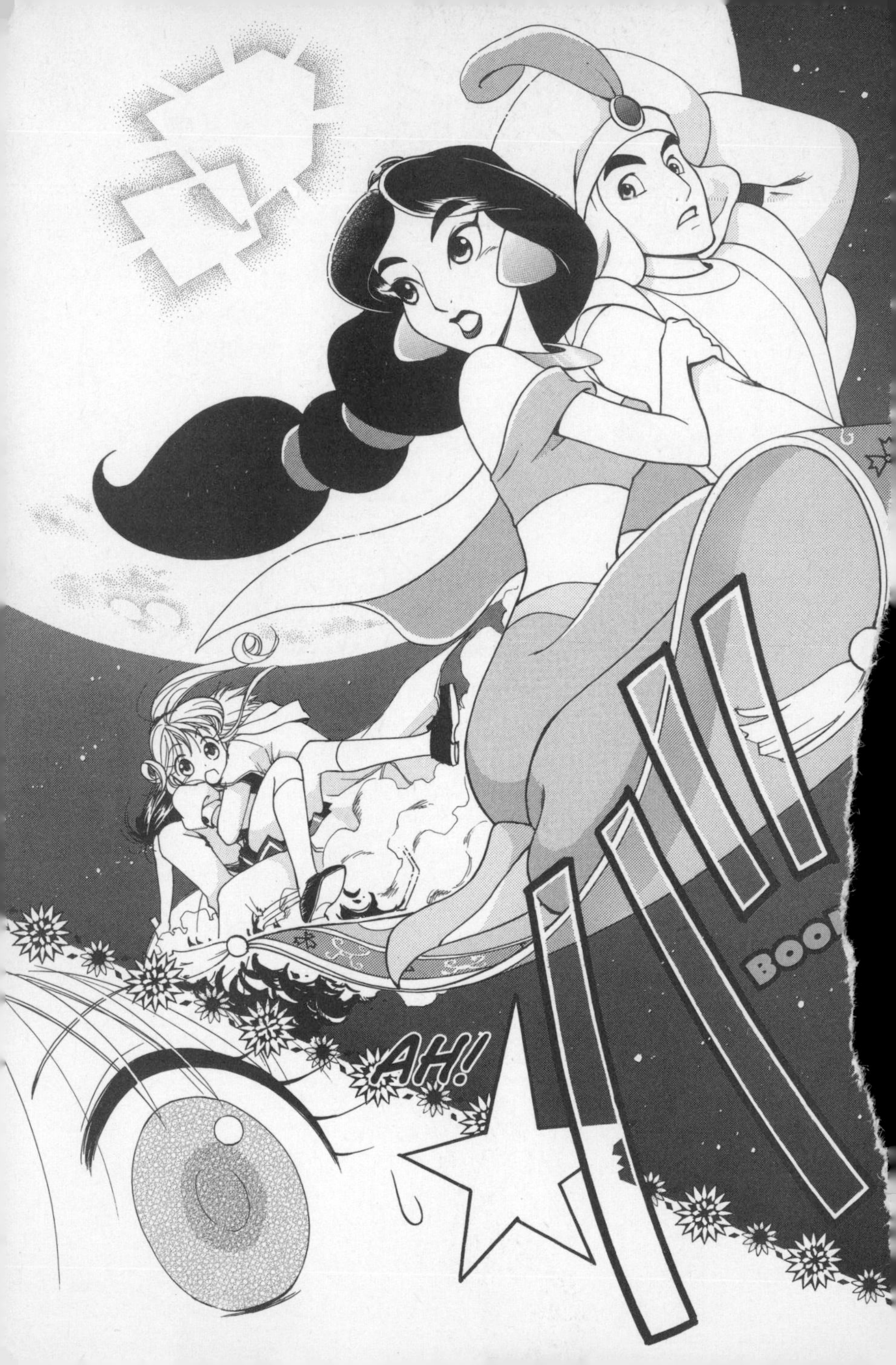
BOO
AH!

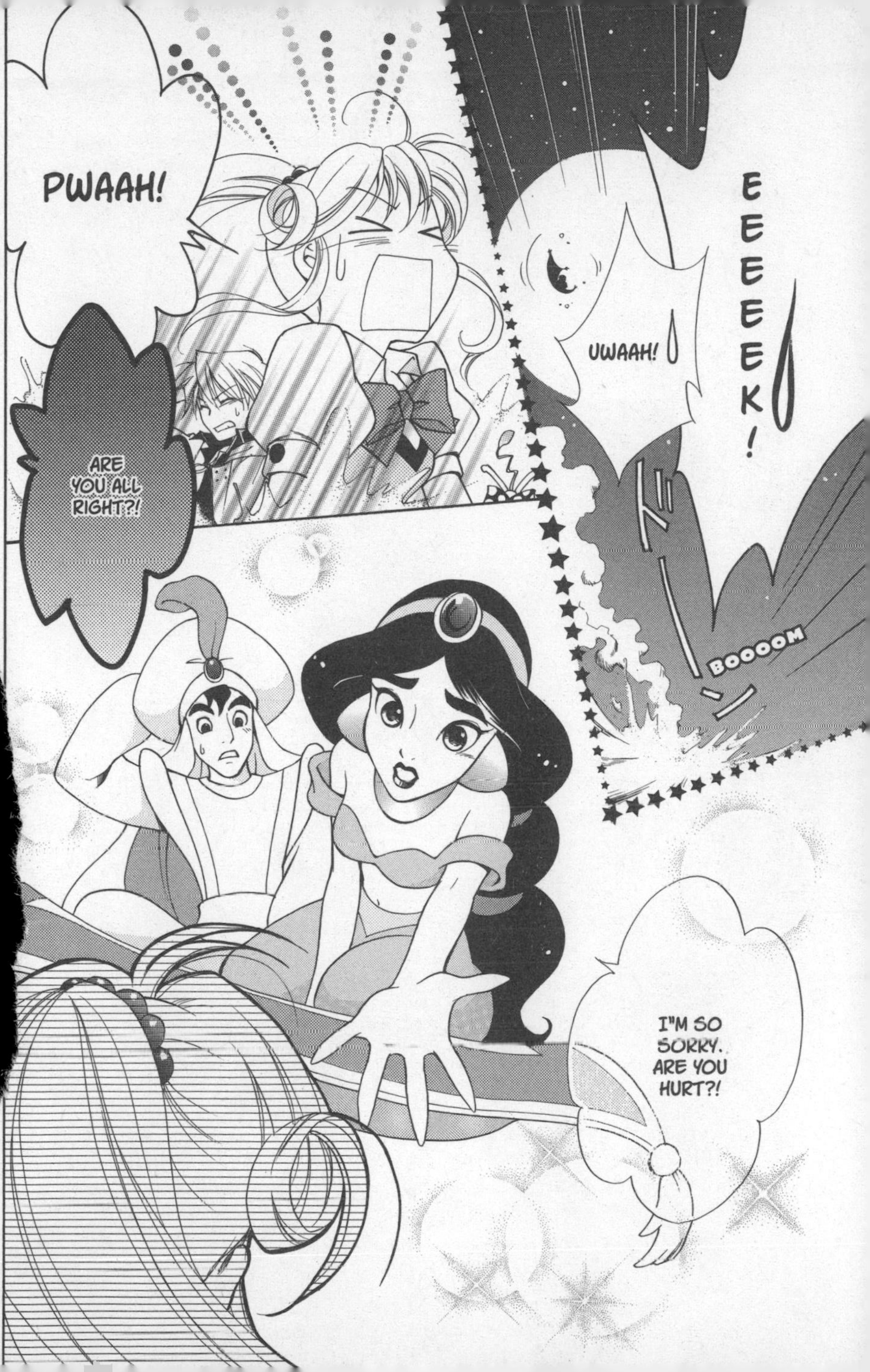
EEEEK!
UWAAH!
ドーン
BOOOOM
PWAAH!
ARE YOU ALL RIGHT?!
I'M SO SORRY. ARE YOU HURT?!

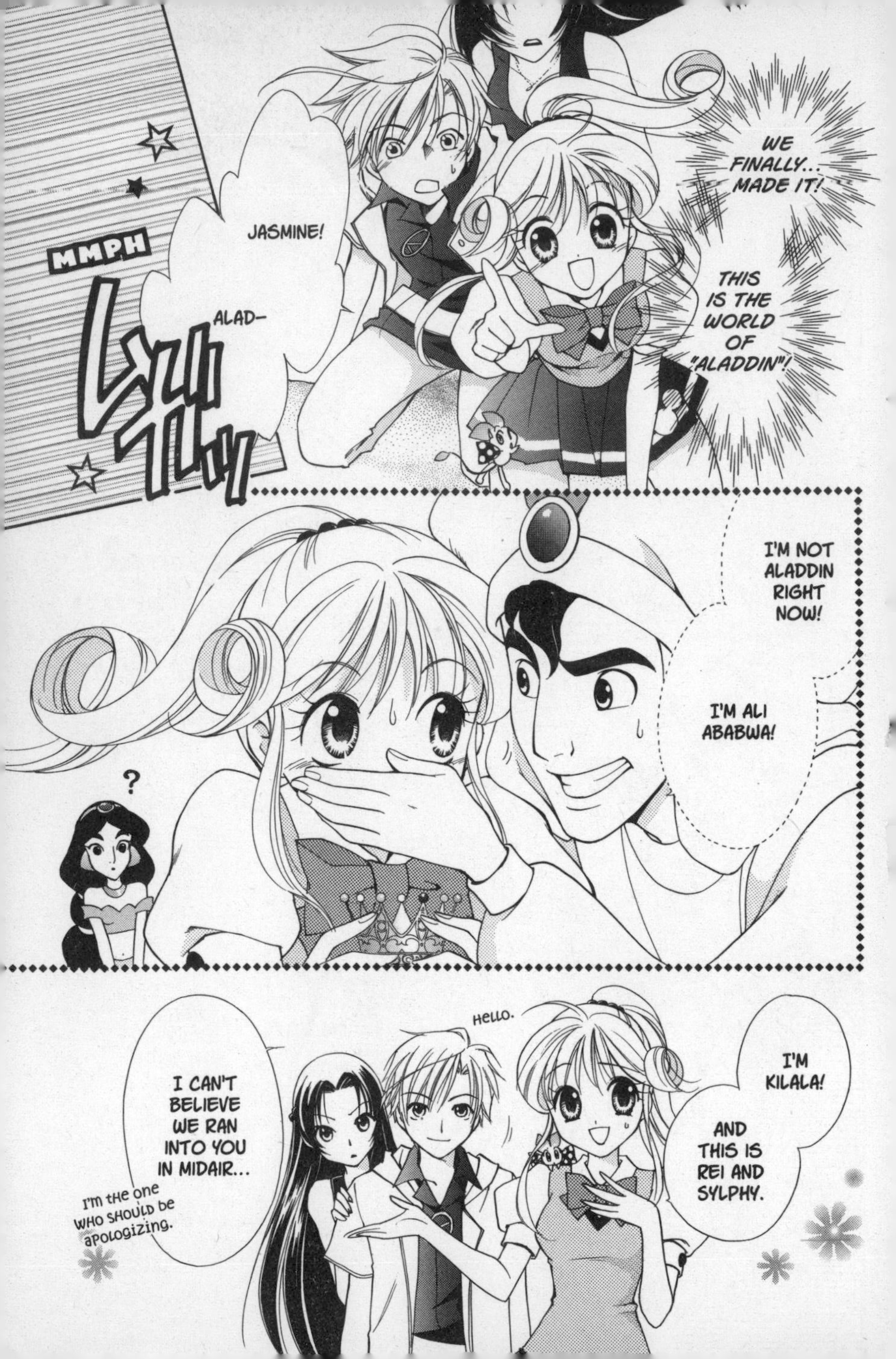
WE FINALLY... MADE IT!
THIS IS THE WORLD OF "ALADDIN"!
JASMINE!
ALAD-
MMPH
I'M NOT ALADDIN RIGHT NOW!
I'M ALI ABABWA!
?
I'M KILALA!
AND THIS IS REI AND SYLPHY.
HELLO.
I CAN'T BELIEVE WE RAN INTO YOU IN MIDAIR...
I'm the one who should be apologizing.

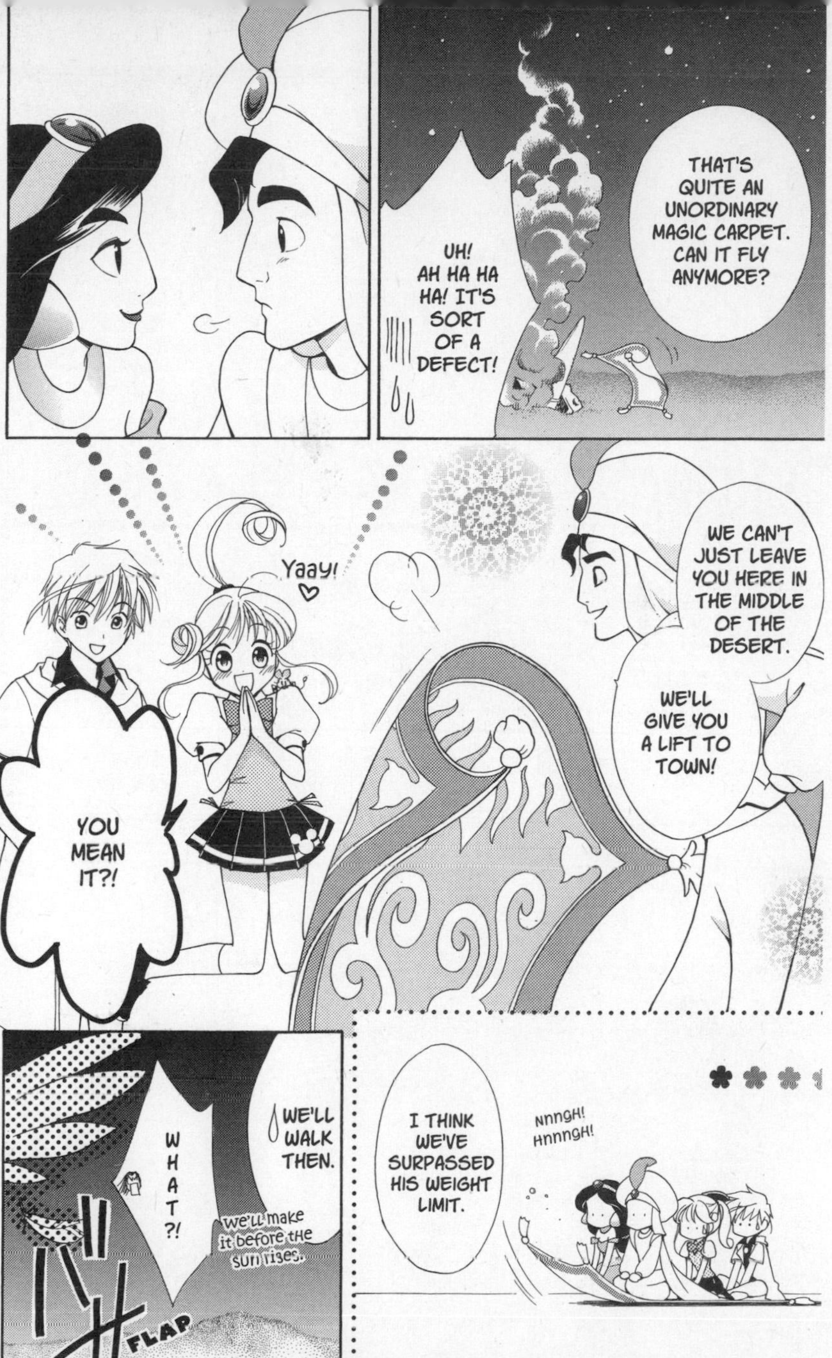
THAT'S QUITE AN UNORDINARY MAGIC CARPET. CAN IT FLY ANYMORE?
UH! AH HA HA HA! IT'S SORT OF A DEFECT!
WE CAN'T JUST LEAVE YOU HERE IN THE MIDDLE OF THE DESERT.
WE'LL GIVE YOU A LIFT TO TOWN!
Yaay!
YOU MEAN IT?!
NNNGH! HNNNGH!
I THINK WE'VE SURPASSED HIS WEIGHT LIMIT.
WE'LL WALK THEN.
WHAT?!
We'll make it before the sun rises.
FLAP

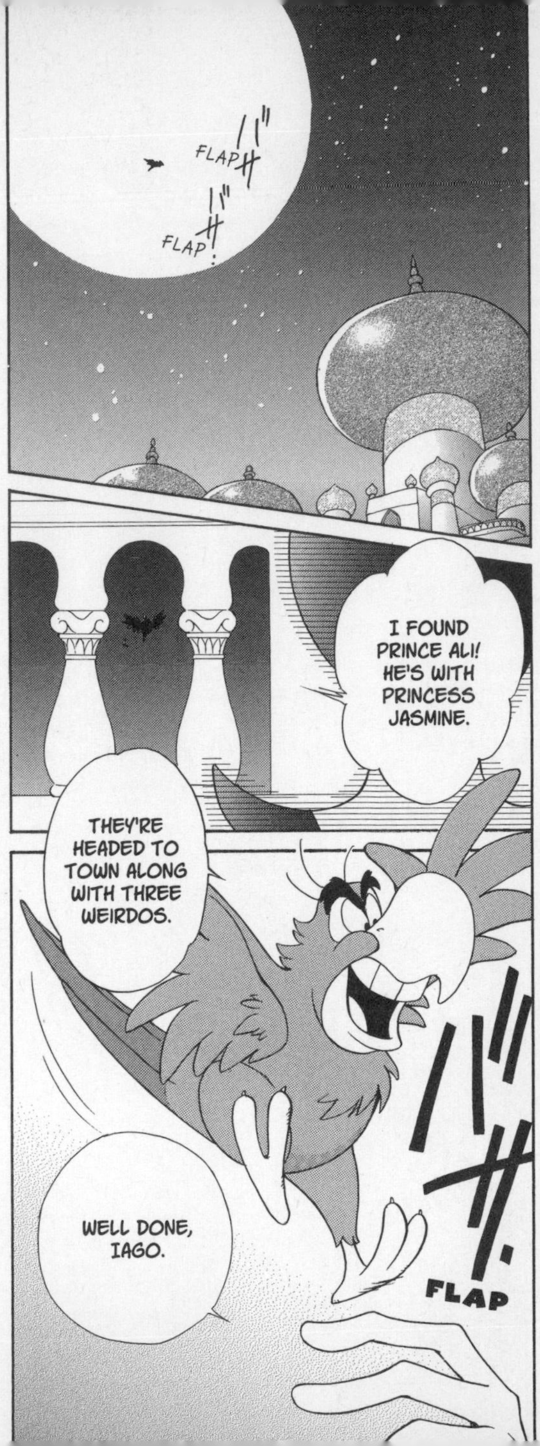
FLAP
FLAP!
I FOUND PRINCE ALI! HE'S WITH PRINCESS JASMINE.
THEY'RE HEADED TO TOWN ALONG WITH THREE WEIRDOS.
FLAP
WELL DONE, IAGO.

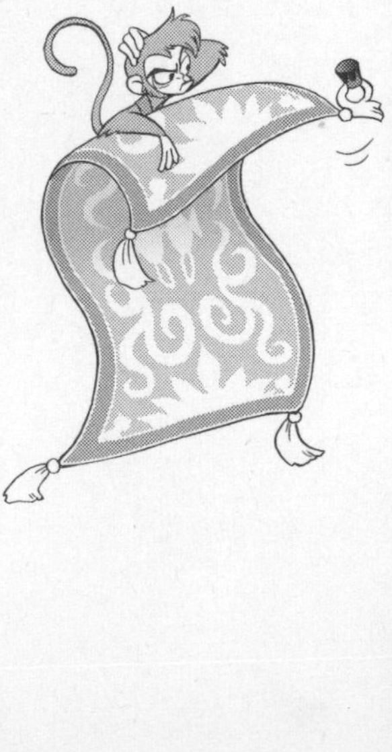

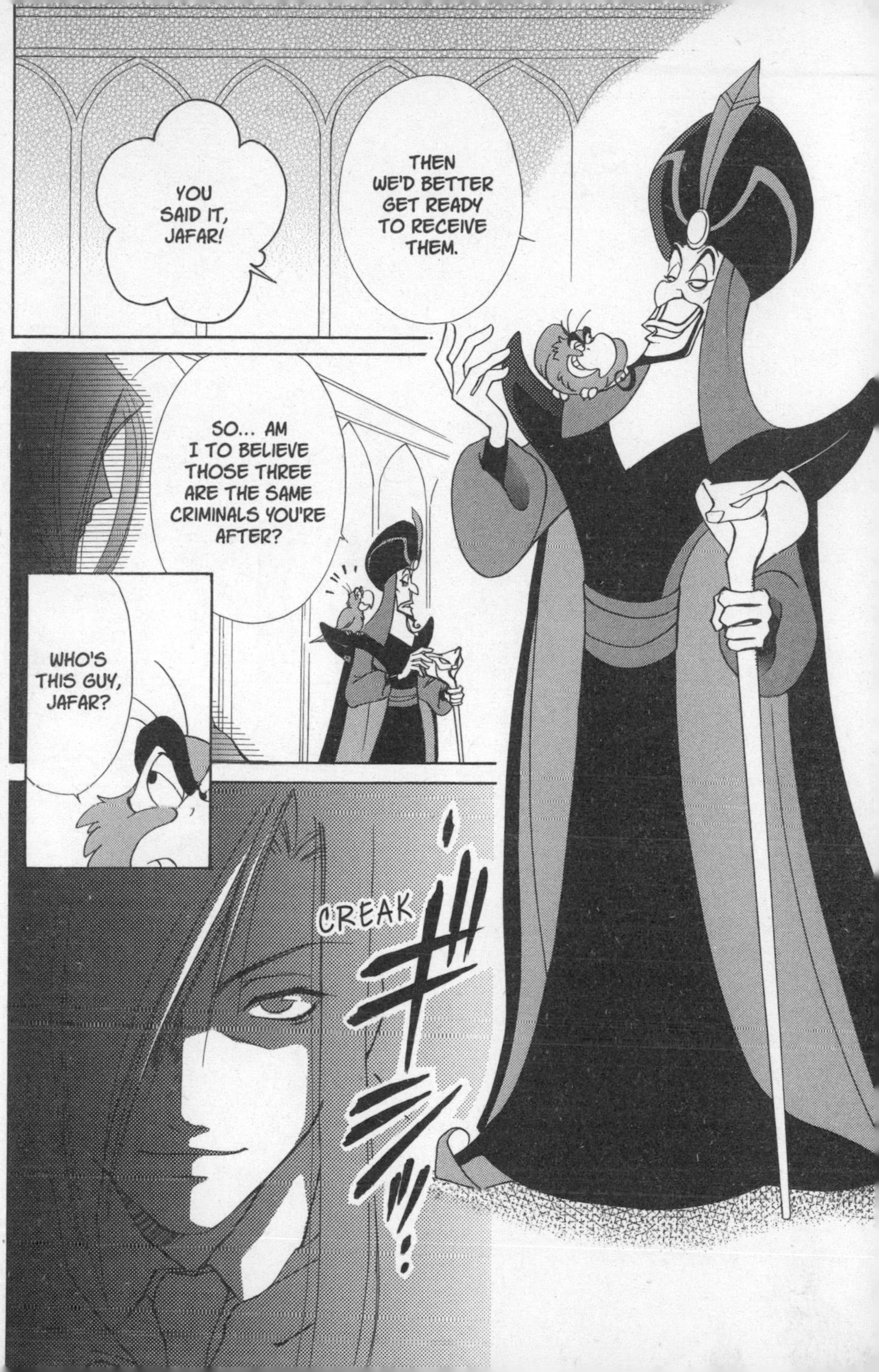
THEN WE'D BETTER GET READY TO RECEIVE THEM.
YOU SAID IT, JAFAR!
SO... AM I TO BELIEVE THOSE THREE ARE THE SAME CRIMINALS YOU'RE AFTER?
WHO'S THIS GUY, JAFAR?
CREAK

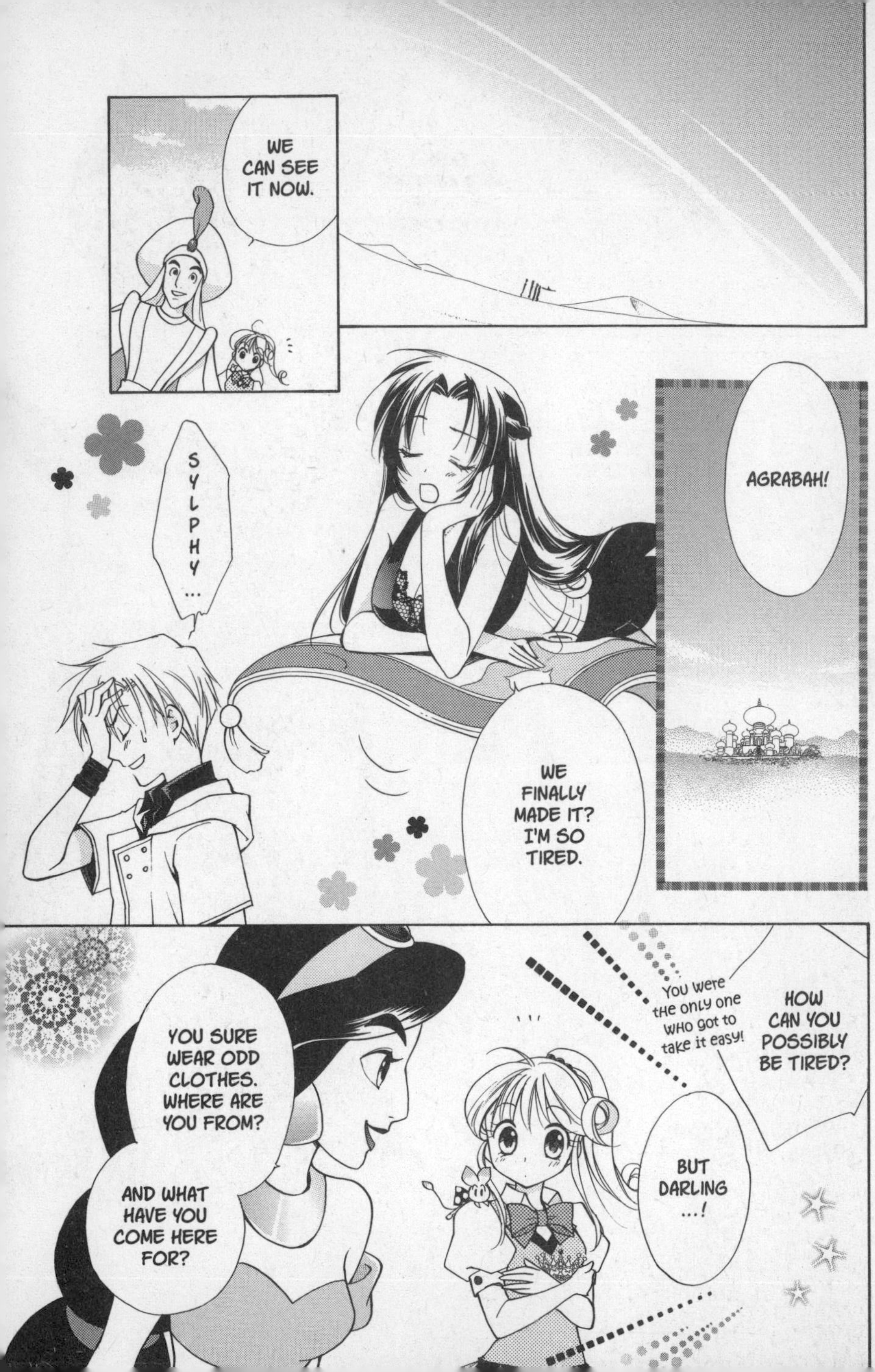
WE CAN SEE IT NOW.
AGRABAH!
WE FINALLY MADE IT? I'M SO TIRED.
SYLPHY...
HOW CAN YOU POSSIBLY BE TIRED?
You were the only one who got to take it easy!
BUT DARLING...!
YOU SURE WEAR ODD CLOTHES. WHERE ARE YOU FROM?
AND WHAT HAVE YOU COME HERE FOR?

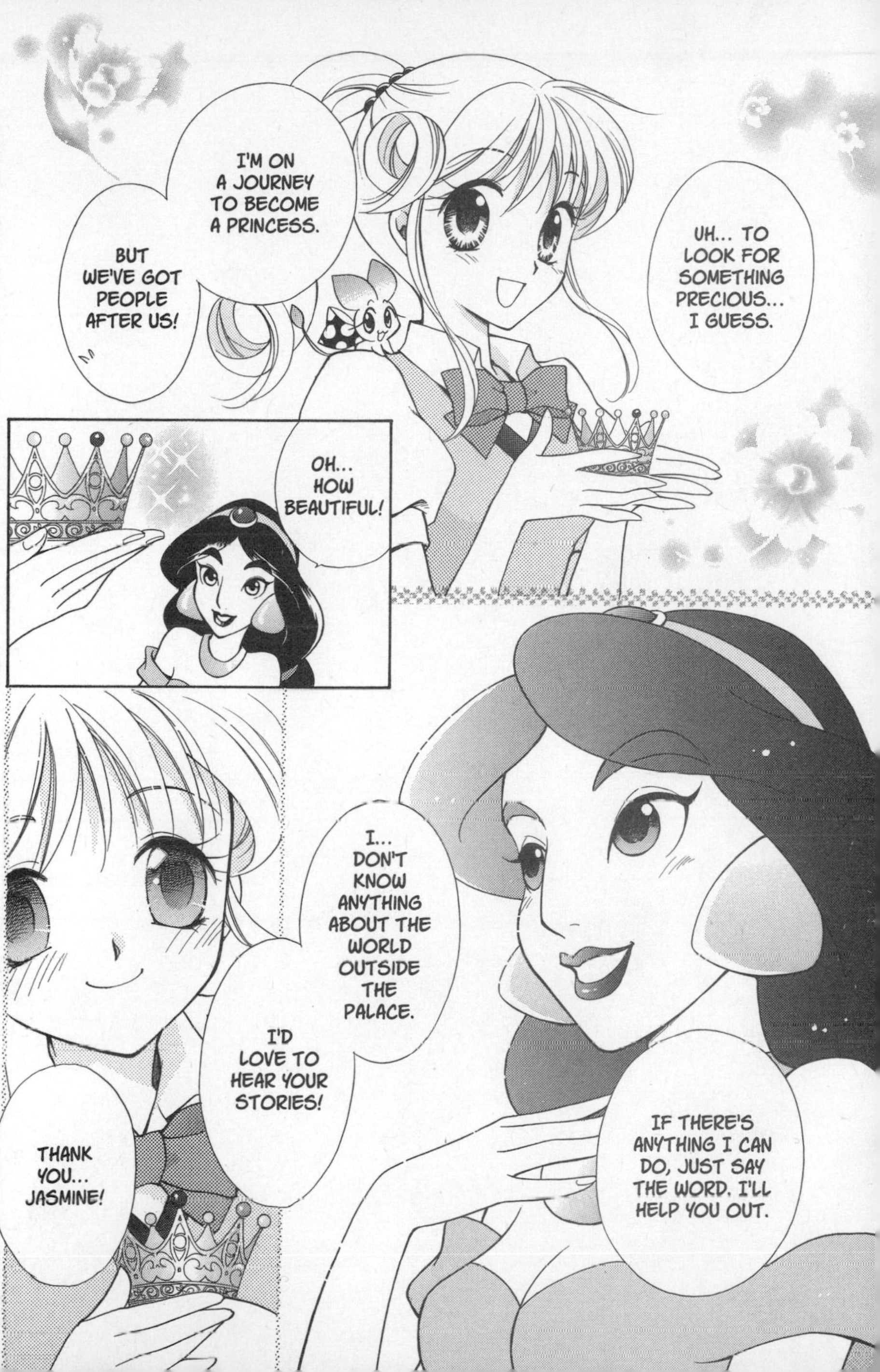
UH... TO LOOK FOR SOMETHING PRECIOUS... I GUESS.
I'M ON A JOURNEY TO BECOME A PRINCESS.
BUT WE'VE GOT PEOPLE AFTER US!
OH... HOW BEAUTIFUL!
I... DON'T KNOW ANYTHING ABOUT THE WORLD OUTSIDE THE PALACE.
I'D LOVE TO HEAR YOUR STORIES!
IF THERE'S ANYTHING I CAN DO, JUST SAY THE WORD. I'LL HELP YOU OUT.
THANK YOU... JASMINE!

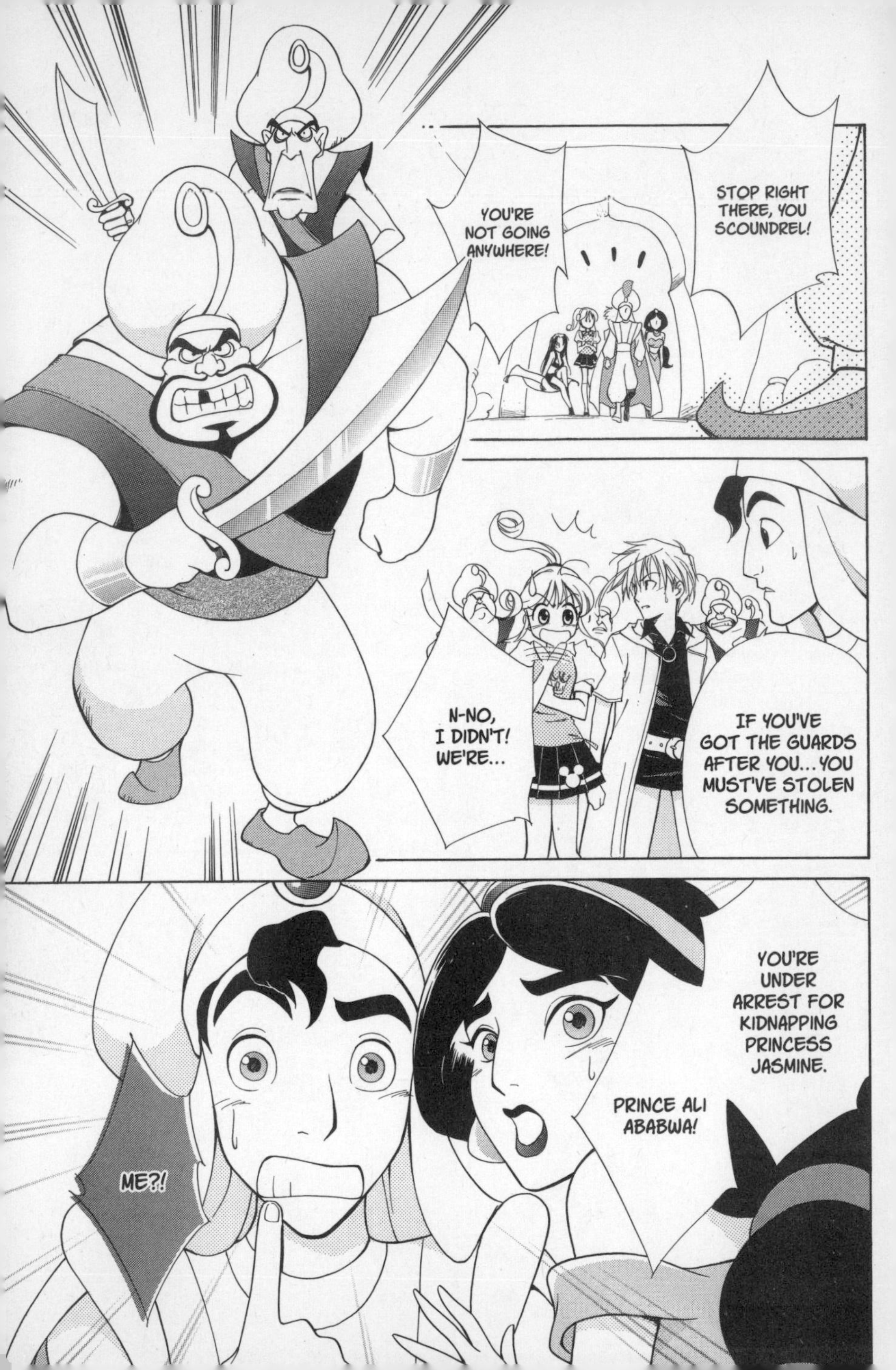
STOP RIGHT THERE, YOU SCOUNDREL!
YOU'RE NOT GOING ANYWHERE!
IF YOU'VE GOT THE GUARDS AFTER YOU... YOU MUST'VE STOLEN SOMETHING.
N-NO, I DIDN'T! WE'RE...
YOU'RE UNDER ARREST FOR KIDNAPPING PRINCESS JASMINE.
PRINCE ALI ABABWA!
ME?!

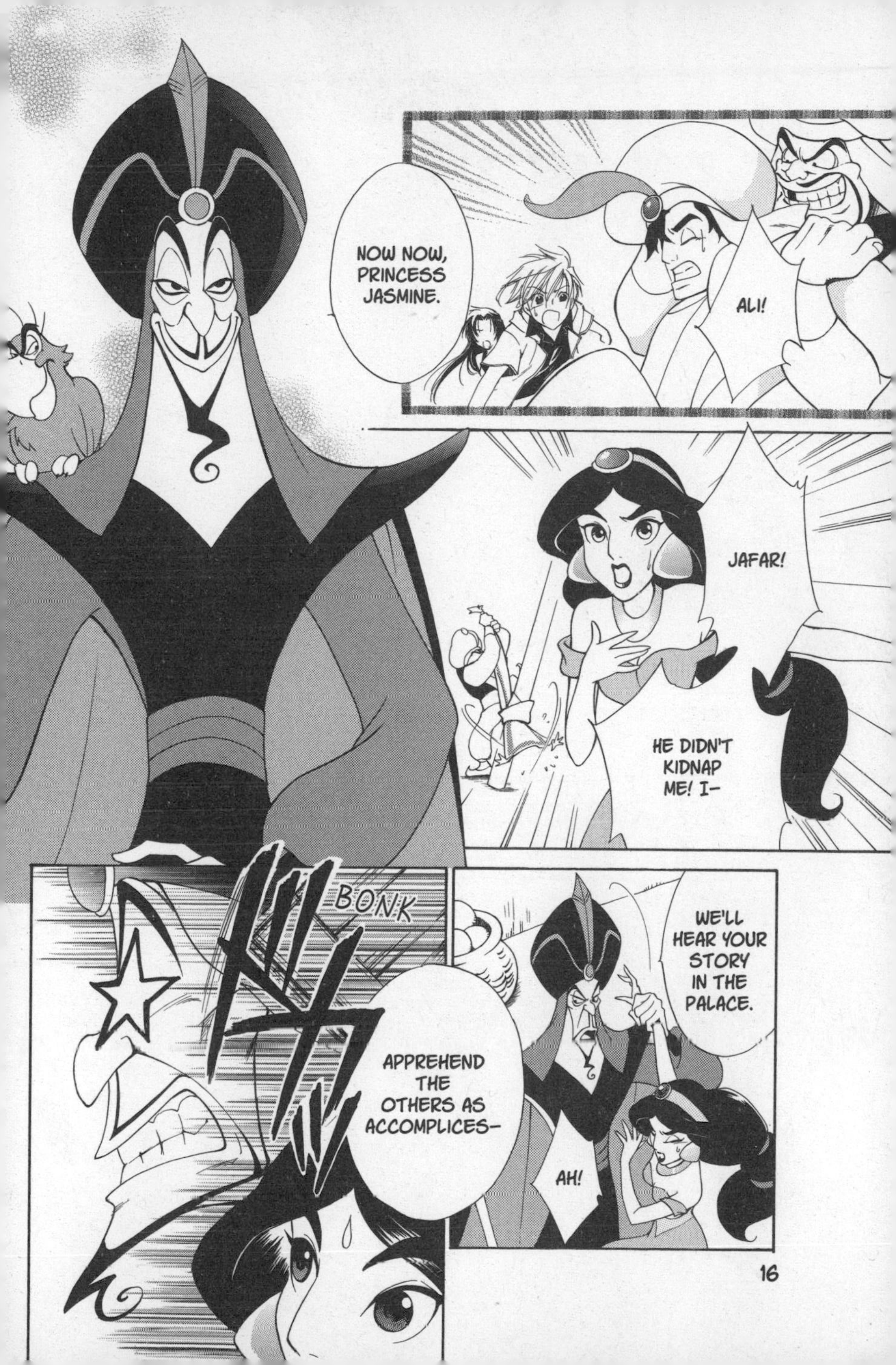
ALI!
NOW NOW, PRINCESS JASMINE.
JAFAR!
HE DIDN'T KIDNAP ME! I–
WE'LL HEAR YOUR STORY IN THE PALACE.
AH!
APPREHEND THE OTHERS AS ACCOMPLICES–
BONK

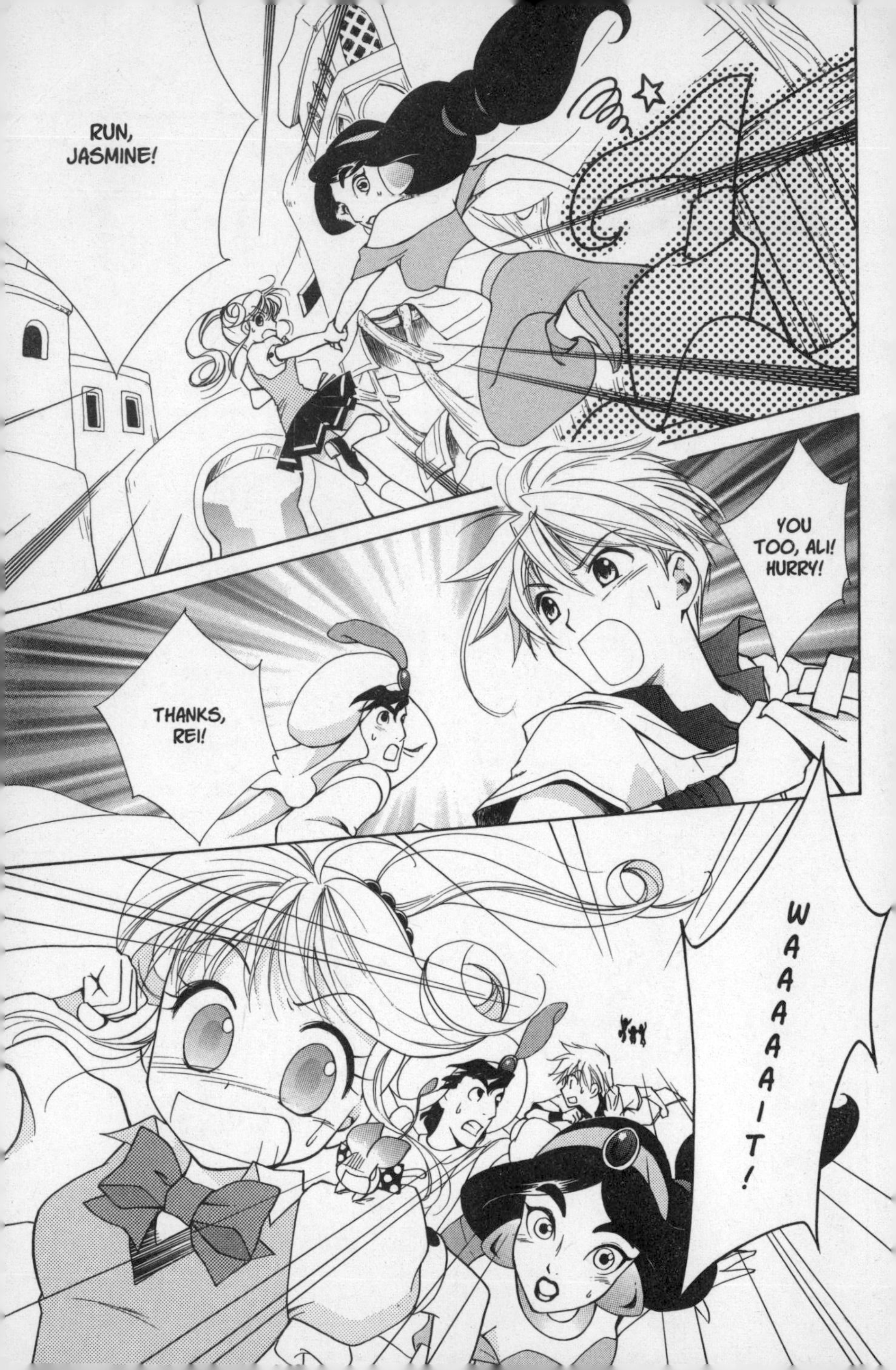
RUN, JASMINE!
YOU TOO, ALI! HURRY!
THANKS, REI!
WAAAAAIT!

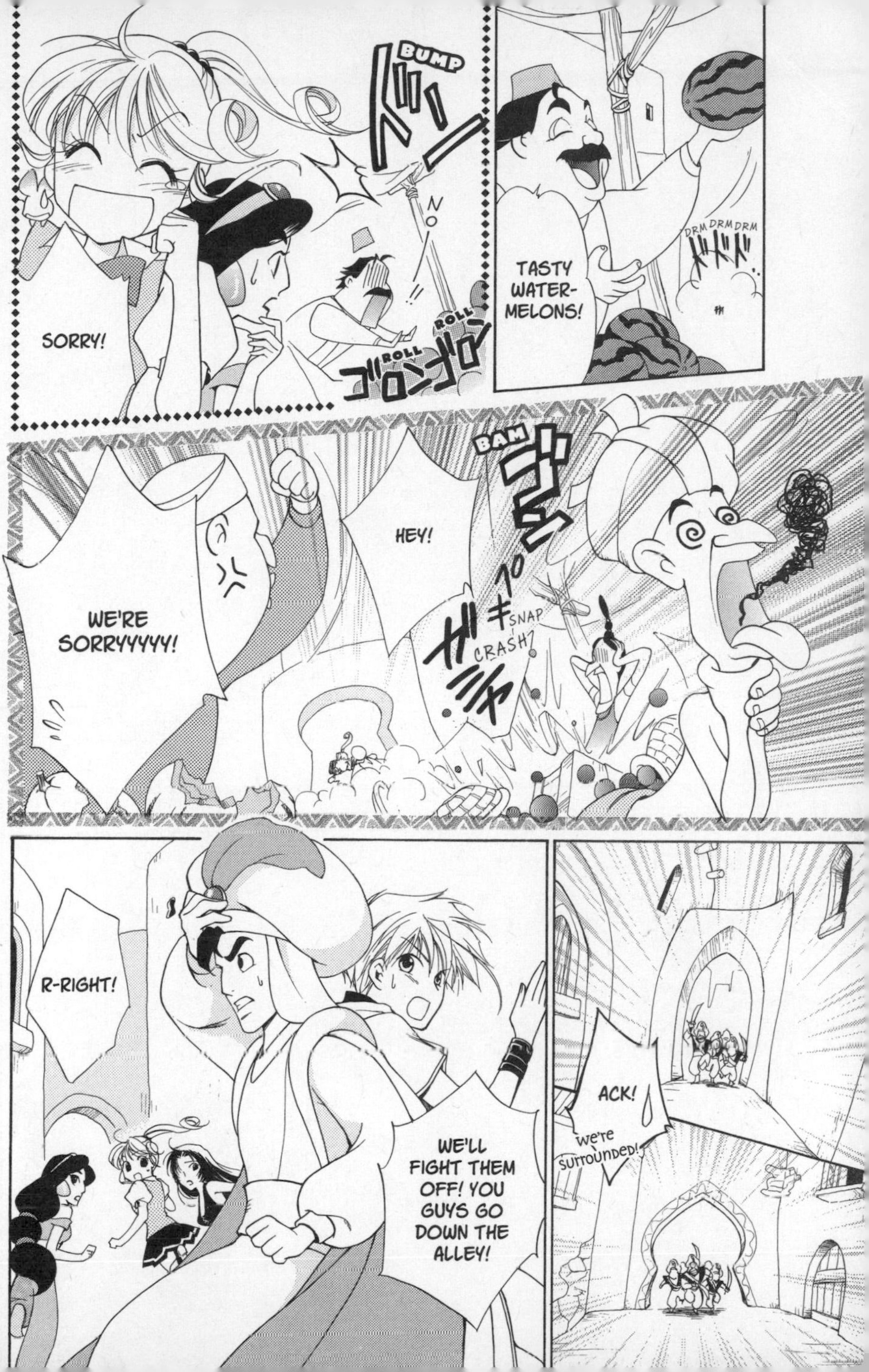
TASTY WATER-MELONS!
DRM DRM DRM
BUMP
ROLL ROLL
SORRY!
BAM
SNAP
CRASH
HEY!
WE'RE SORRYYYYY!
ACK!
We're surrounded!
WE'LL FIGHT THEM OFF! YOU GUYS GO DOWN THE ALLEY!
R-RIGHT!

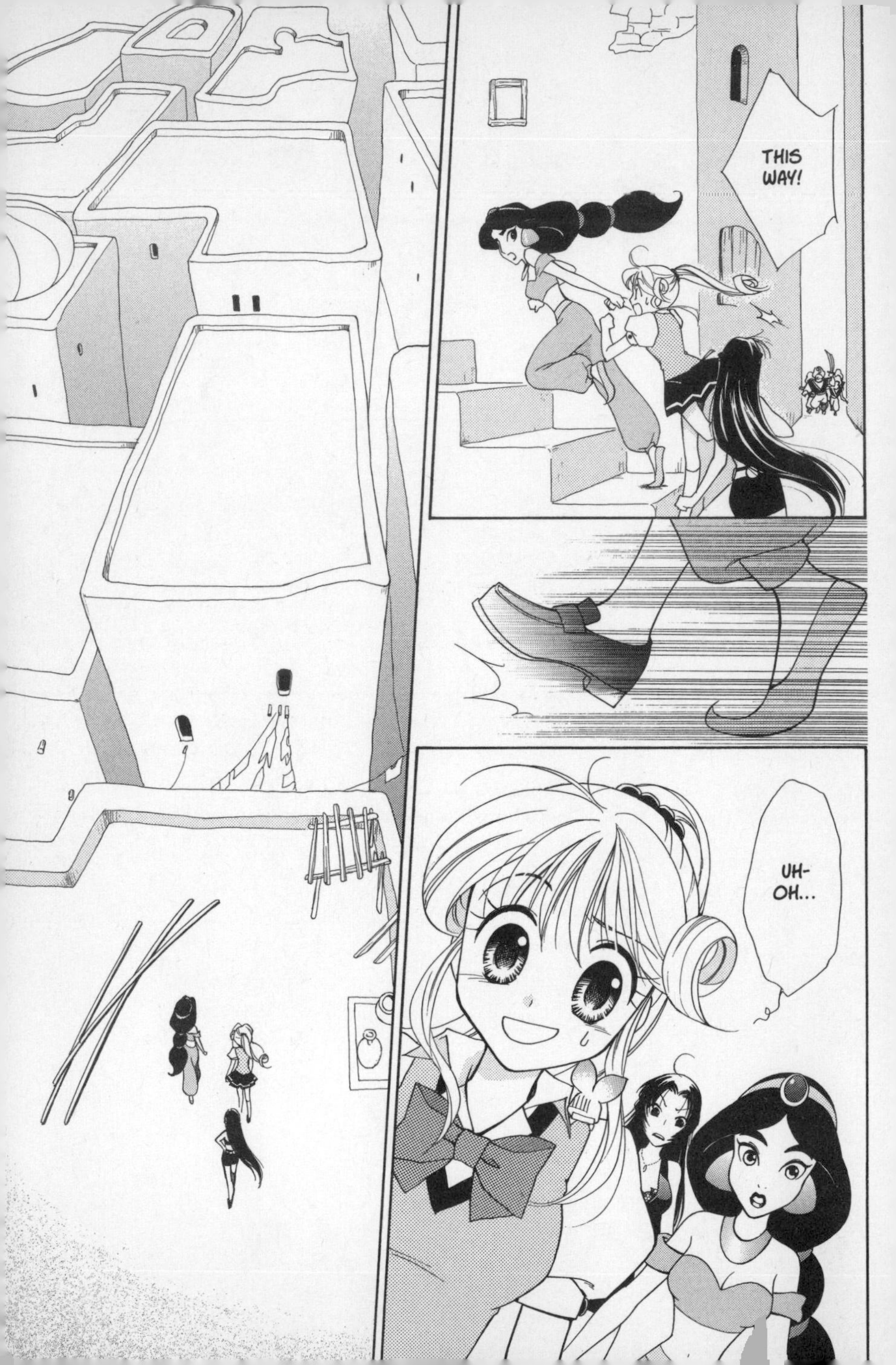
THIS WAY!
UH-OH...

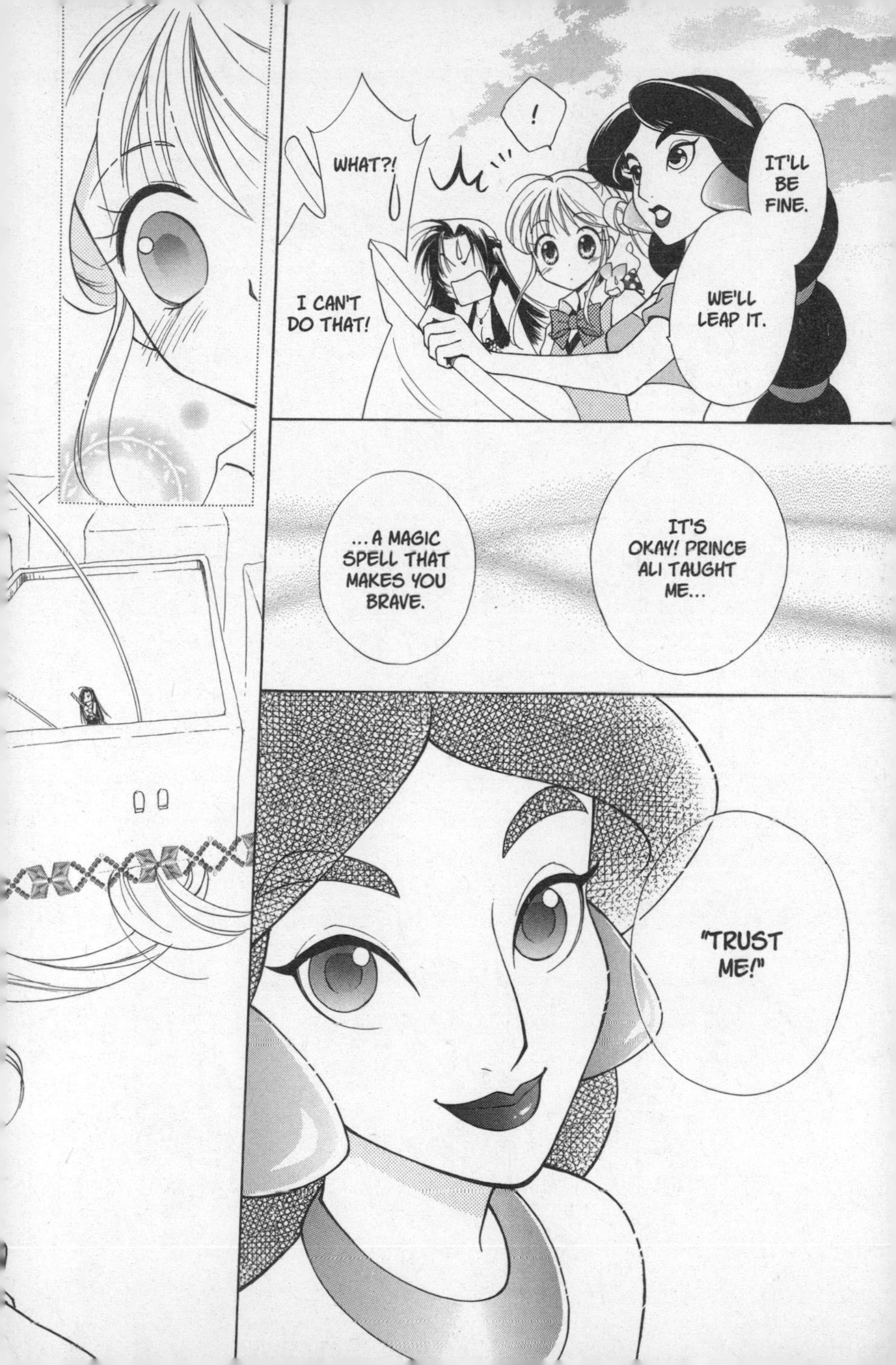
IT'LL BE FINE.
WE'LL LEAP IT.
!
WHAT?!
I CAN'T DO THAT!
IT'S OKAY! PRINCE ALI TAUGHT ME...
...A MAGIC SPELL THAT MAKES YOU BRAVE.
"TRUST ME!"

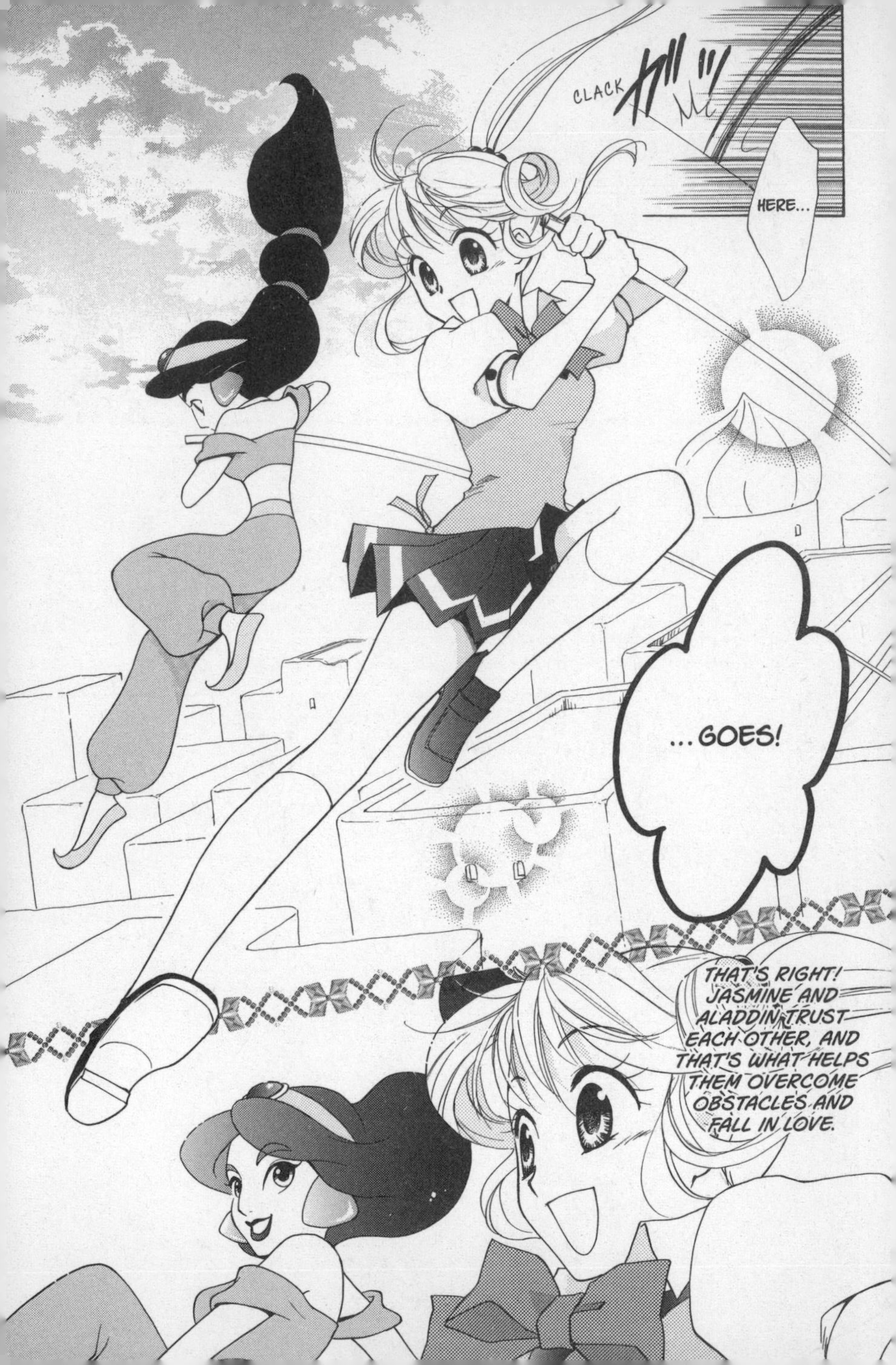
CLACK
HERE...
...GOES!
THAT'S RIGHT! JASMINE AND ALADDIN TRUST EACH OTHER, AND THAT'S WHAT HELPS THEM OVERCOME OBSTACLES AND FALL IN LOVE.

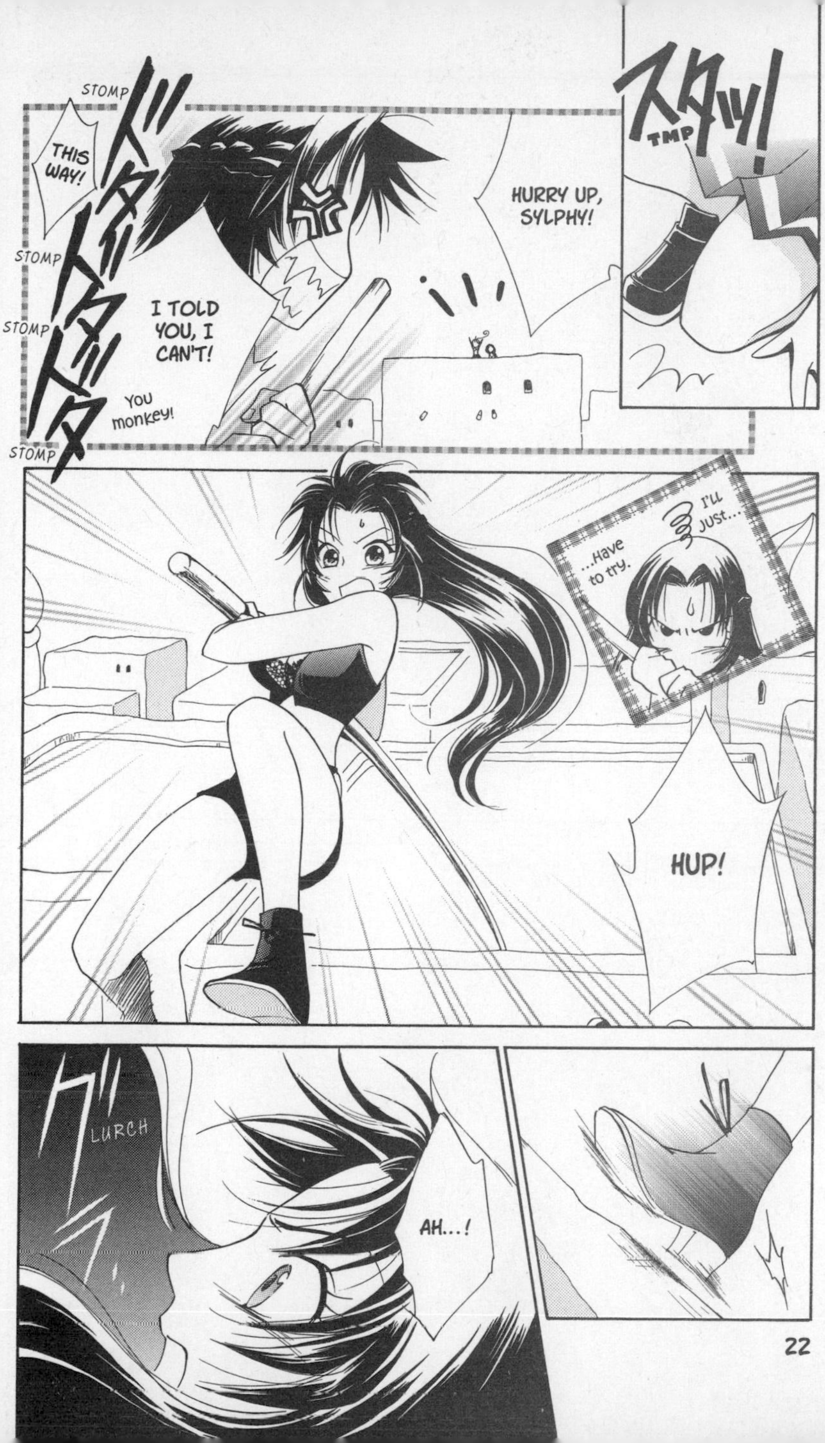

スタッ!
TMP
HURRY UP, SYLPHY!
THIS WAY!
STOMP
STOMP
STOMP
STOMP
ドタドタドタ
I TOLD YOU, I CAN'T!
You monkey!
I'll JUST...
...Have to try.
HUP!
LURCH
AH...!

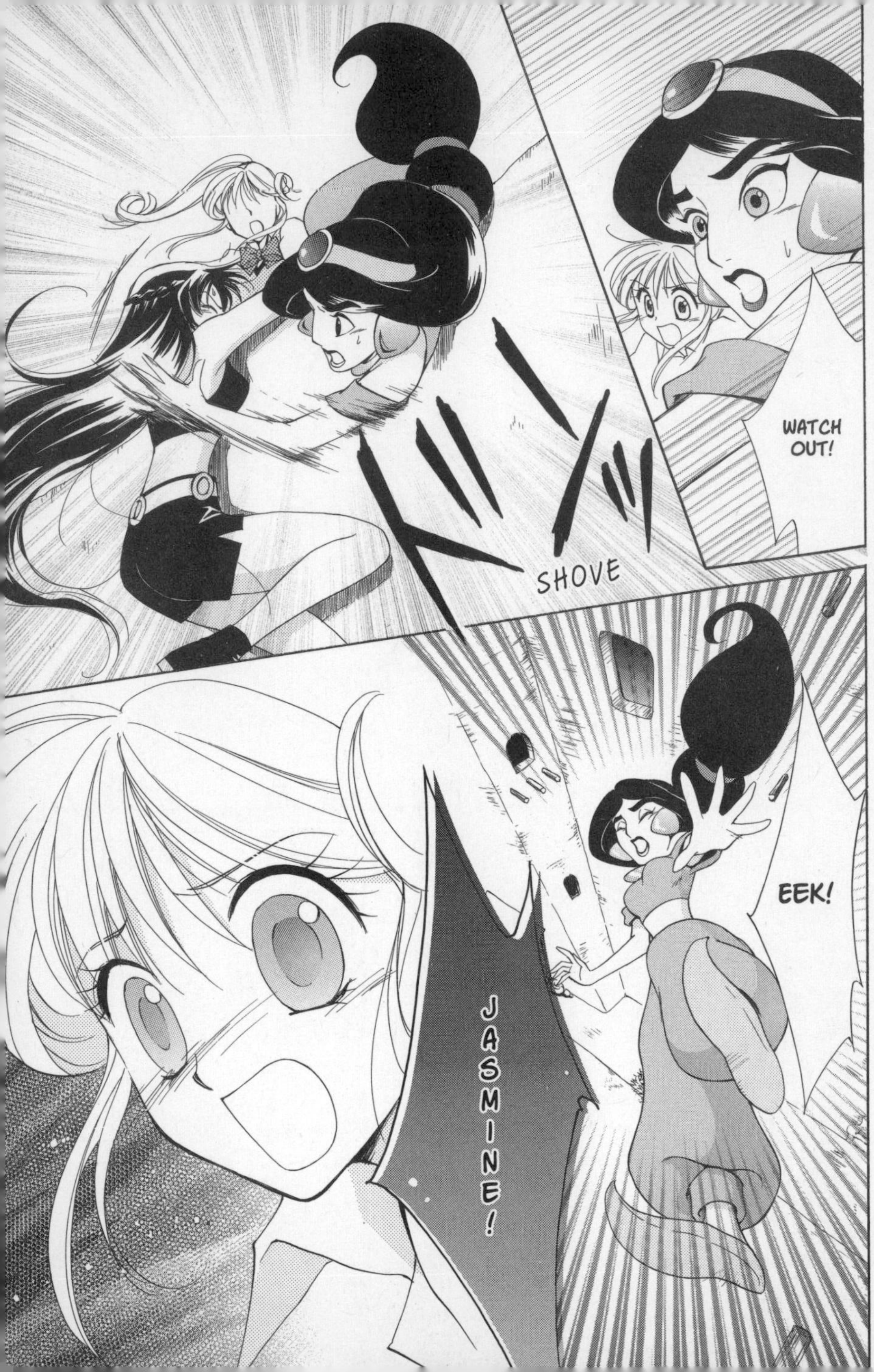
WATCH OUT!
SHOVE
EEK!
JASMINE!

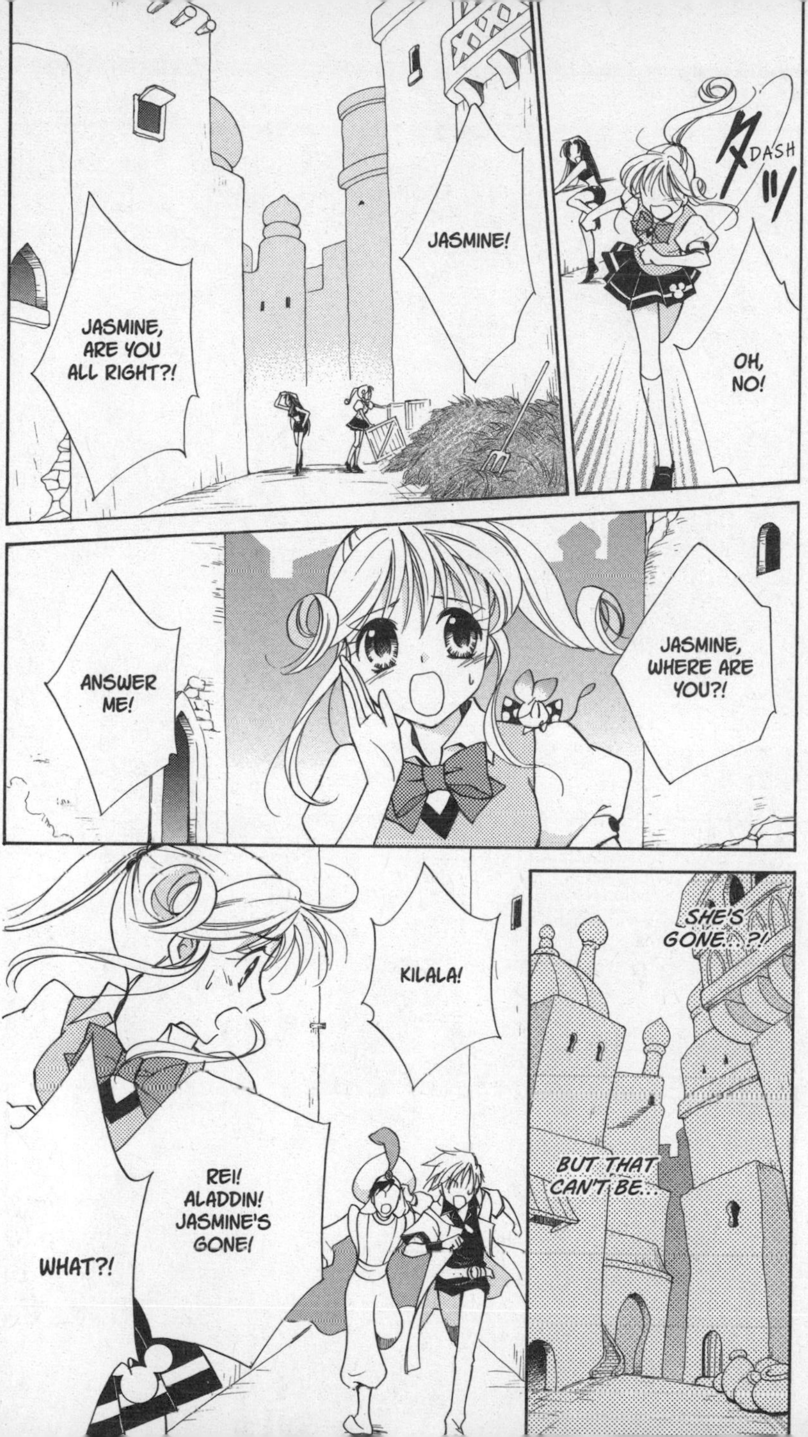
DASH
OH, NO!
JASMINE!
JASMINE, ARE YOU ALL RIGHT?!
JASMINE, WHERE ARE YOU?!
ANSWER ME!
SHE'S GONE...?!
BUT THAT CAN'T BE...
KILALA!
REI! ALADDIN! JASMINE'S GONE!
WHAT?!

READ THIS WAY

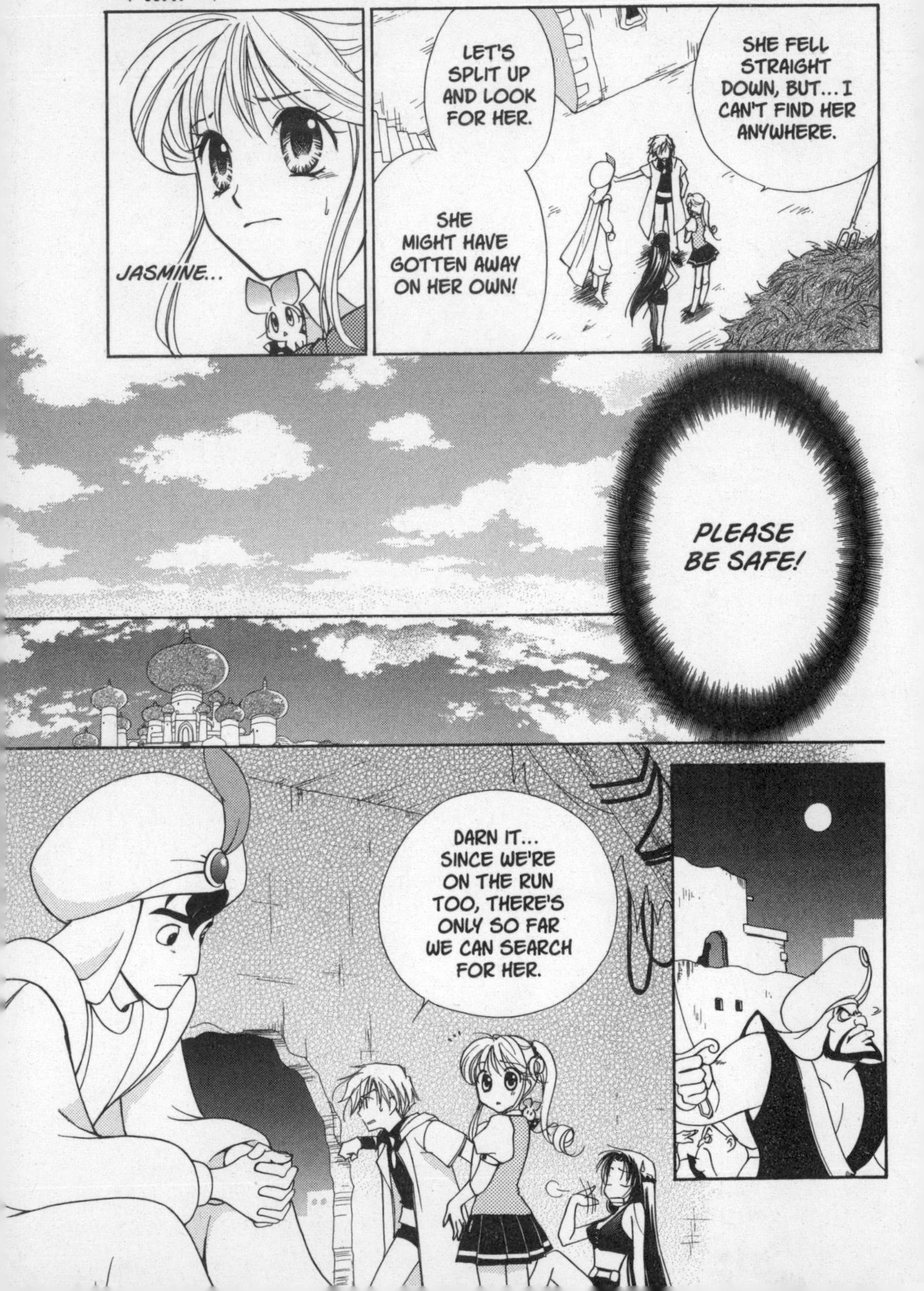

SHE FELL STRAIGHT DOWN, BUT... I CAN'T FIND HER ANYWHERE.
LET'S SPLIT UP AND LOOK FOR HER.
SHE MIGHT HAVE GOTTEN AWAY ON HER OWN!
JASMINE...
PLEASE BE SAFE!
DARN IT... SINCE WE'RE ON THE RUN TOO, THERE'S ONLY SO FAR WE CAN SEARCH FOR HER.

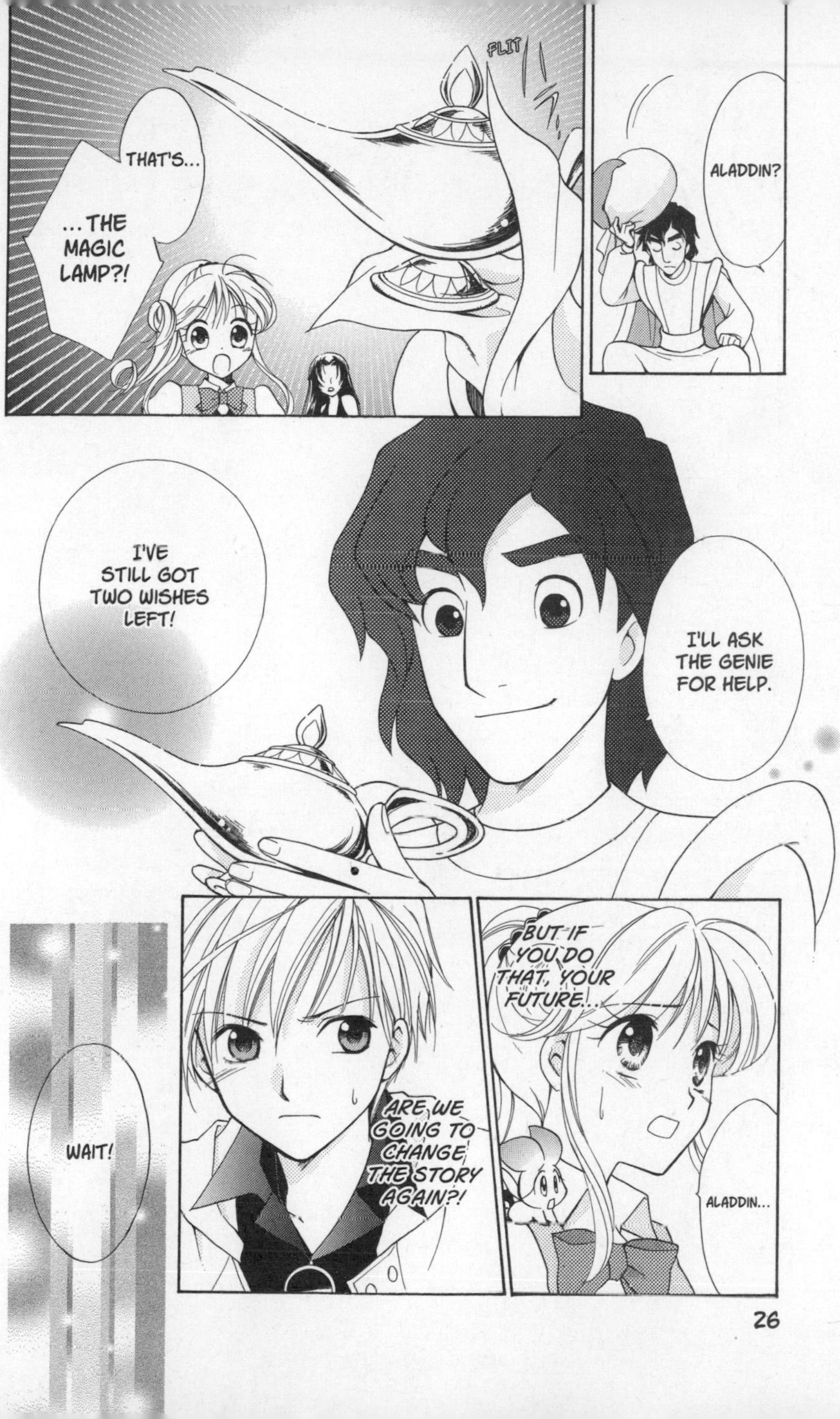
ALADDIN?
FLIT
THAT'S...
... THE MAGIC LAMP?!
I'VE STILL GOT TWO WISHES LEFT!
I'LL ASK THE GENIE FOR HELP.
ALADDIN...
BUT IF YOU DO THAT, YOUR FUTURE...
ARE WE GOING TO CHANGE THE STORY AGAIN?!
WAIT!

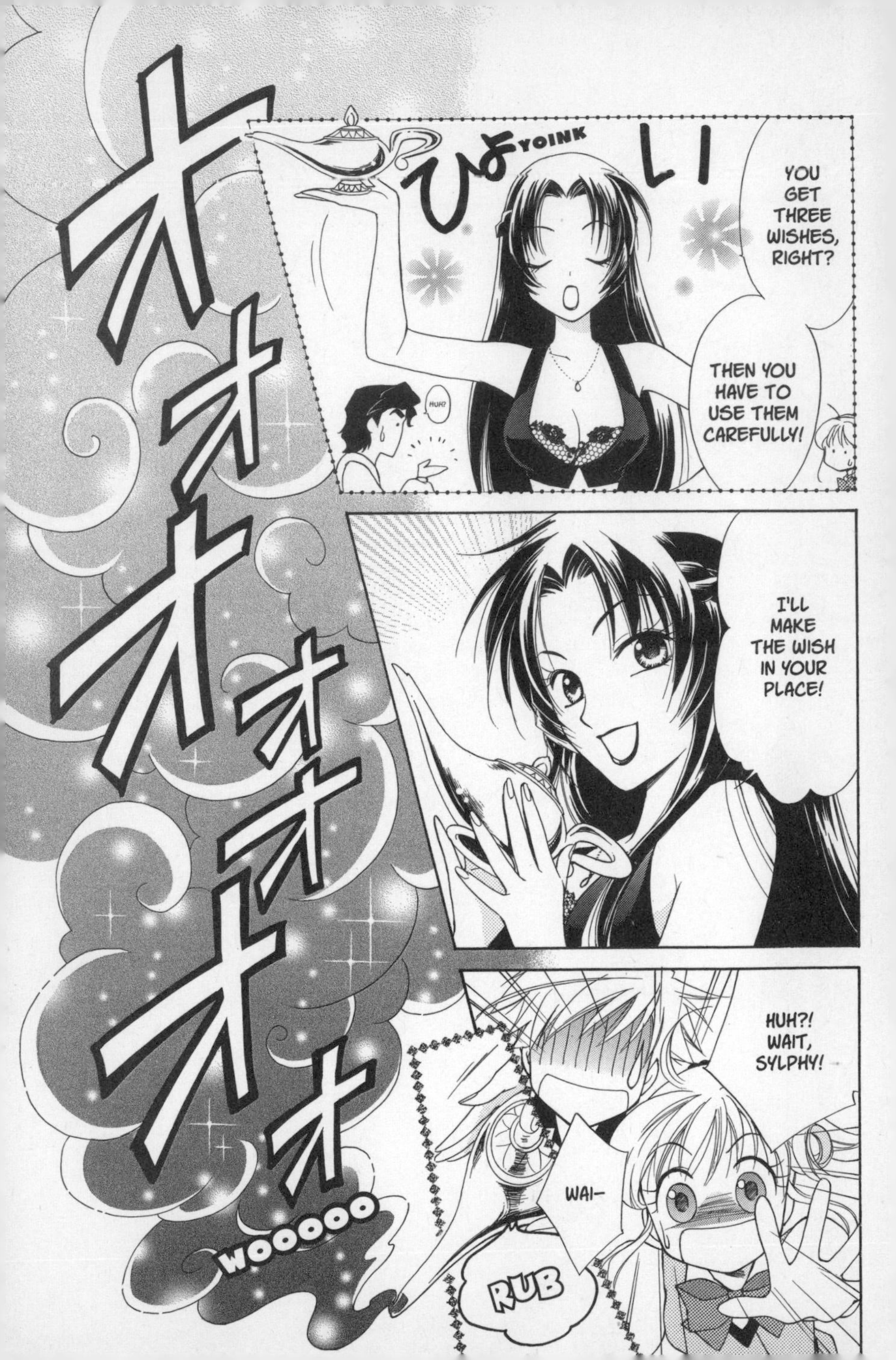
YOU GET THREE WISHES, RIGHT?
THEN YOU HAVE TO USE THEM CAREFULLY!
ひょい YOINK
HUH?
I'LL MAKE THE WISH IN YOUR PLACE!
HUH?! WAIT, SYLPHY!
WAI-
RUB
オオオオオオォ
WOOOOO

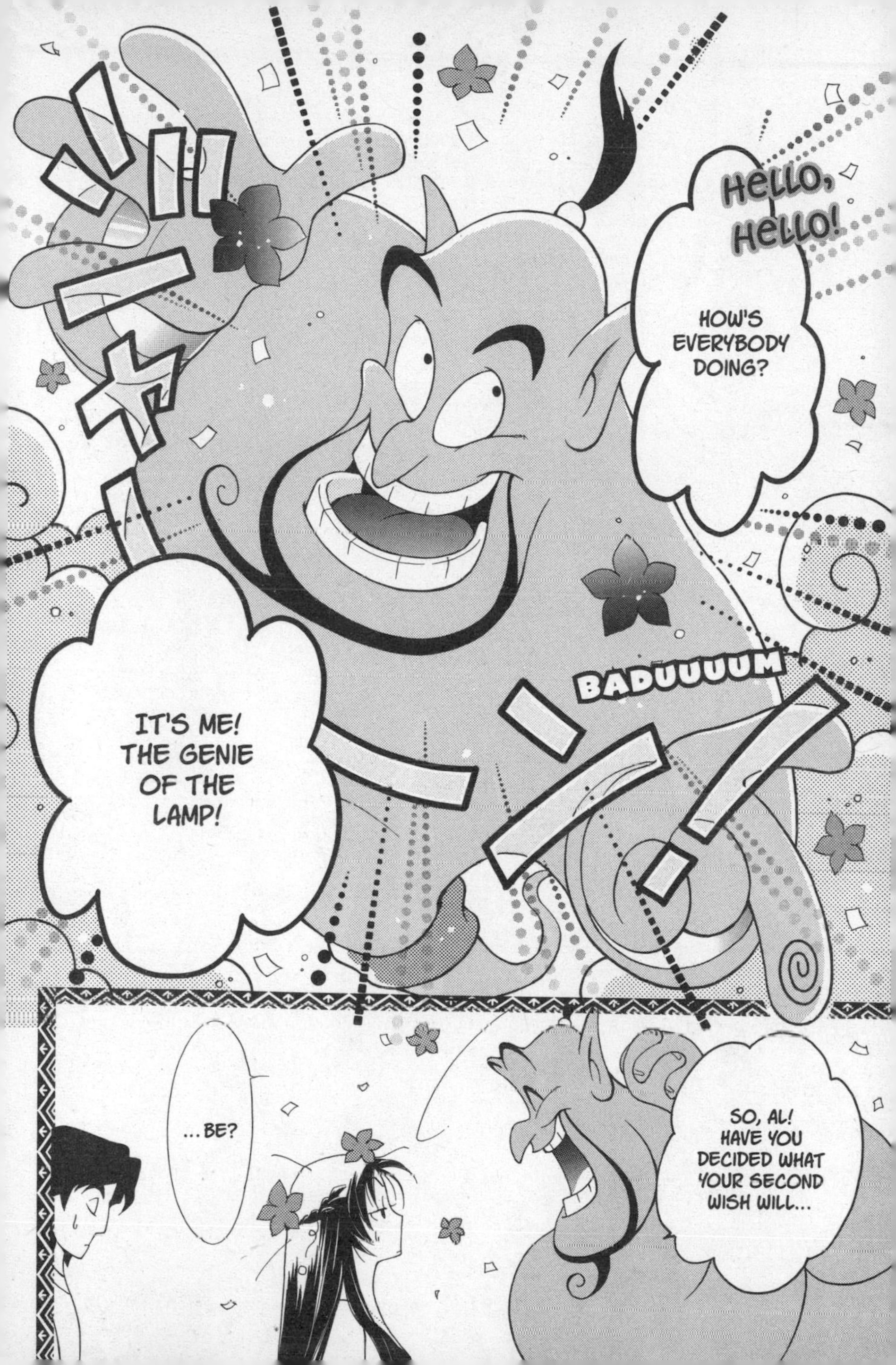
HELLO, HELLO!
HOW'S EVERYBODY DOING?
BADUUUUM
IT'S ME! THE GENIE OF THE LAMP!
SO, AL! HAVE YOU DECIDED WHAT YOUR SECOND WISH WILL...
...BE?

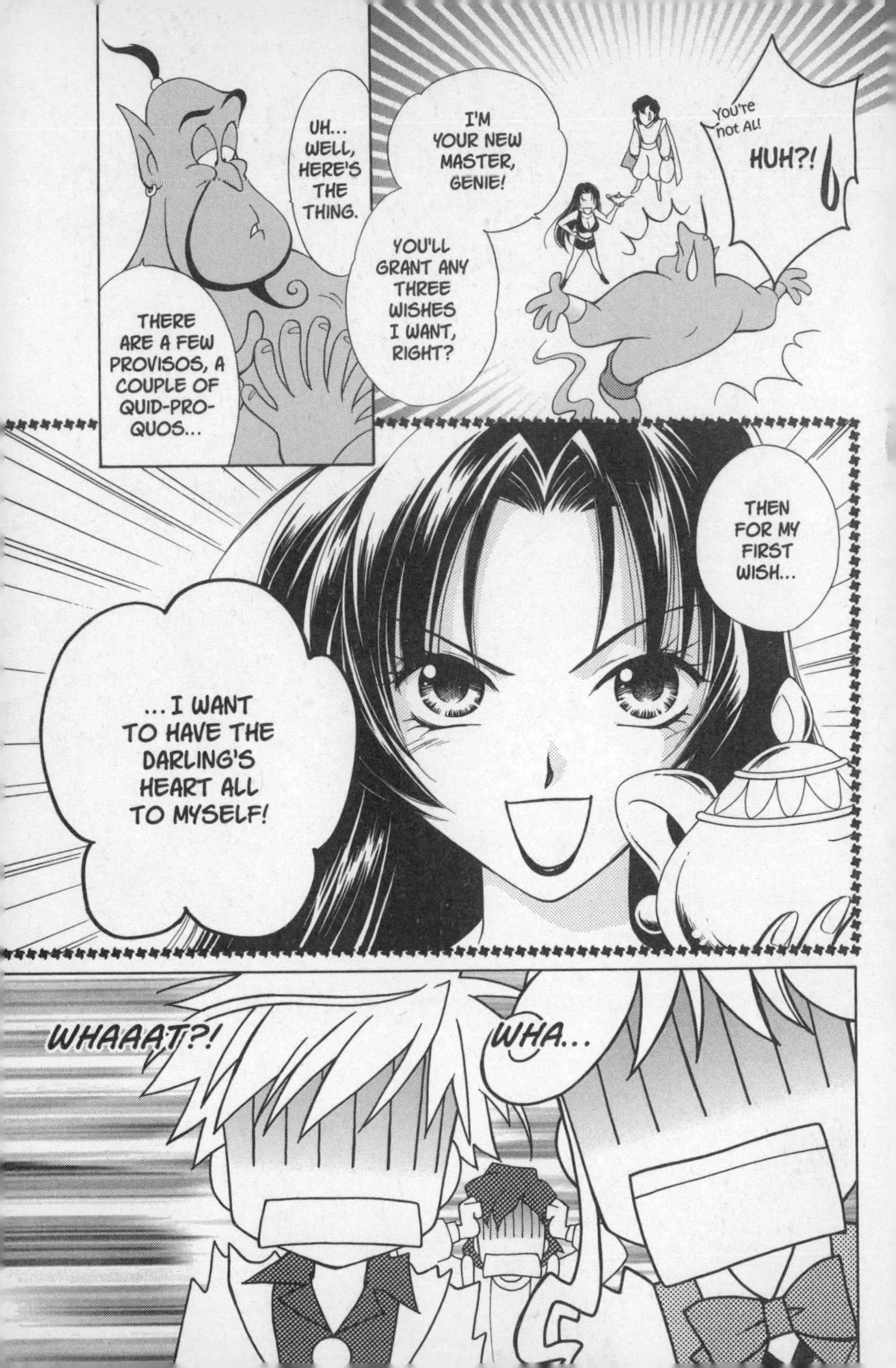
You're not Al!
HUH?!
I'M YOUR NEW MASTER, GENIE!
YOU'LL GRANT ANY THREE WISHES I WANT, RIGHT?
UH... WELL, HERE'S THE THING.
THERE ARE A FEW PROVISOS, A COUPLE OF QUID-PRO-QUOS...
THEN FOR MY FIRST WISH...
...I WANT TO HAVE THE DARLING'S HEART ALL TO MYSELF!
WHA...
WHAAAT?!

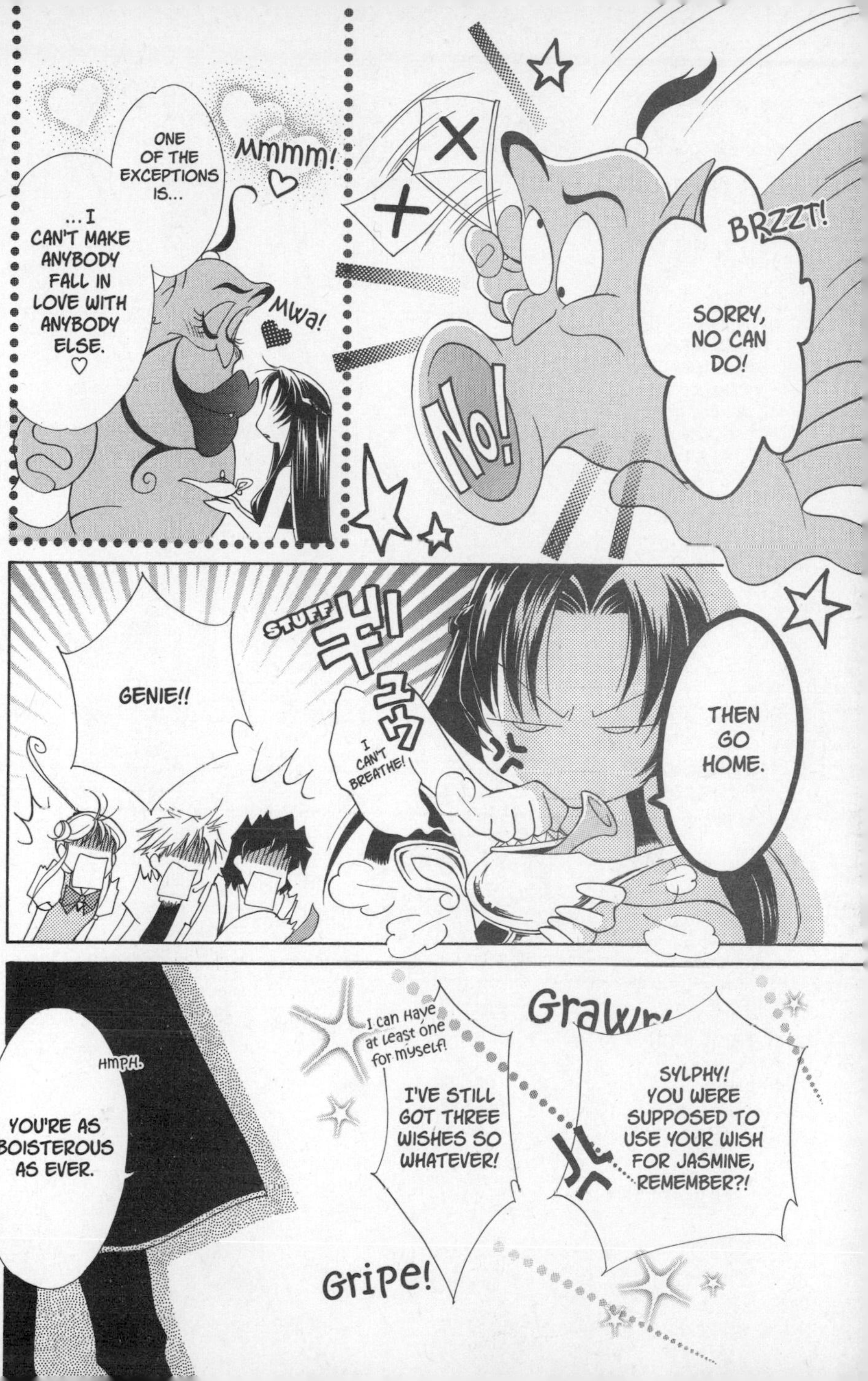
BRZZT!
SORRY, NO CAN DO!
No!
ONE OF THE EXCEPTIONS IS...
Mmmm!
...I CAN'T MAKE ANYBODY FALL IN LOVE WITH ANYBODY ELSE.
Mwa!
THEN GO HOME.
STUFF
ギュウ
I CAN'T BREATHE!
GENIE!!
SYLPHY! YOU WERE SUPPOSED TO USE YOUR WISH FOR JASMINE, REMEMBER?!
Grawr
I can have at least one for myself!
I'VE STILL GOT THREE WISHES SO WHATEVER!
Gripe!
HMPH.
YOU'RE AS BOISTEROUS AS EVER.

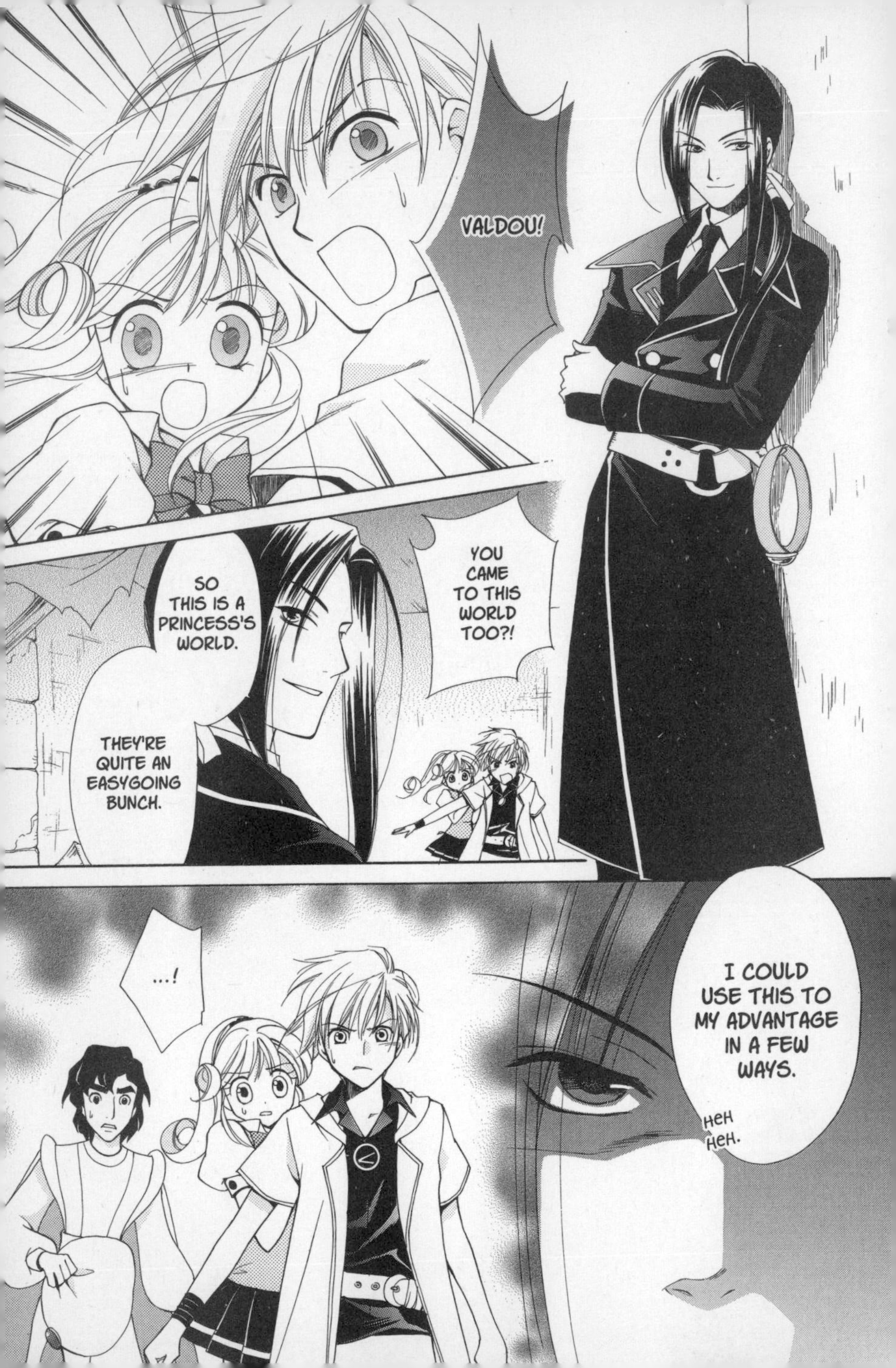
VALDOU!
YOU CAME TO THIS WORLD TOO?!
SO THIS IS A PRINCESS'S WORLD.
THEY'RE QUITE AN EASYGOING BUNCH.
I COULD USE THIS TO MY ADVANTAGE IN A FEW WAYS.
HEH HEH.
...!

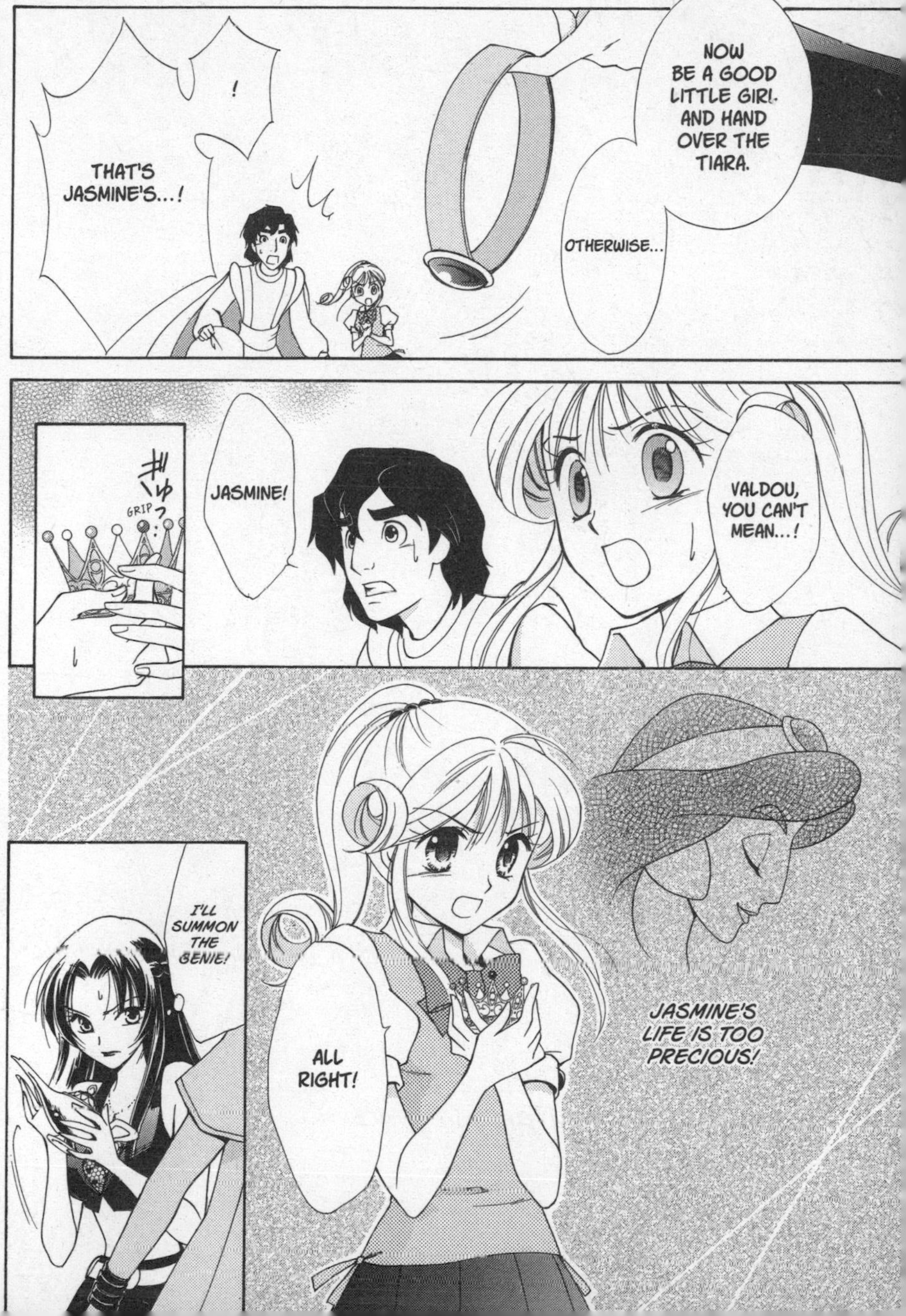
NOW BE A GOOD LITTLE GIRL AND HAND OVER THE TIARA.
OTHERWISE...
!
THAT'S JASMINE'S...!
VALDOU, YOU CAN'T MEAN...!
JASMINE!
ギゅっ
GRIP
JASMINE'S LIFE IS TOO PRECIOUS!
ALL RIGHT!
I'LL SUMMON THE GENIE!

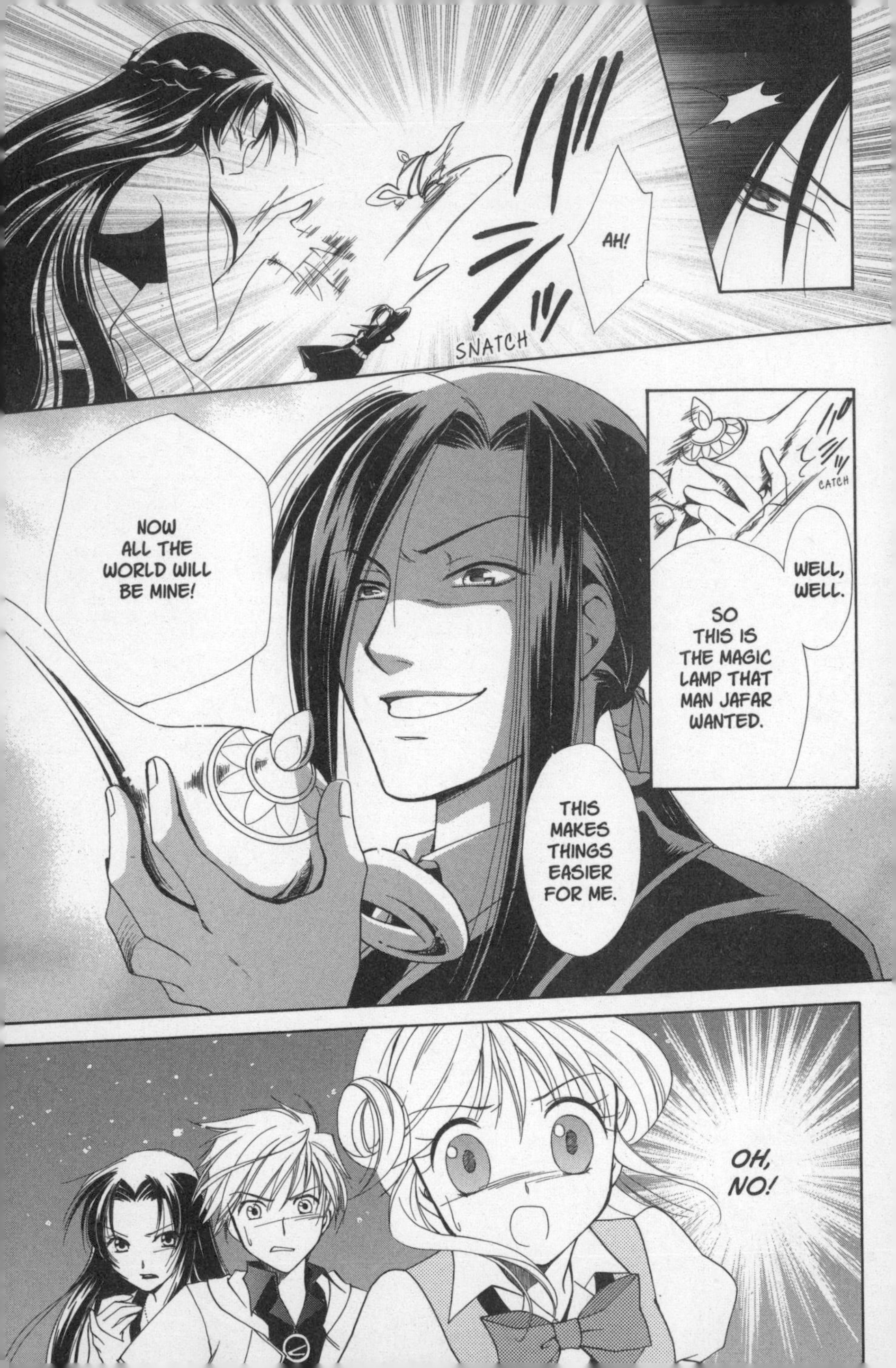
AH!
SNATCH
CATCH
WELL, WELL.
SO THIS IS THE MAGIC LAMP THAT MAN JAFAR WANTED.
THIS MAKES THINGS EASIER FOR ME.
NOW ALL THE WORLD WILL BE MINE!
OH, NO!

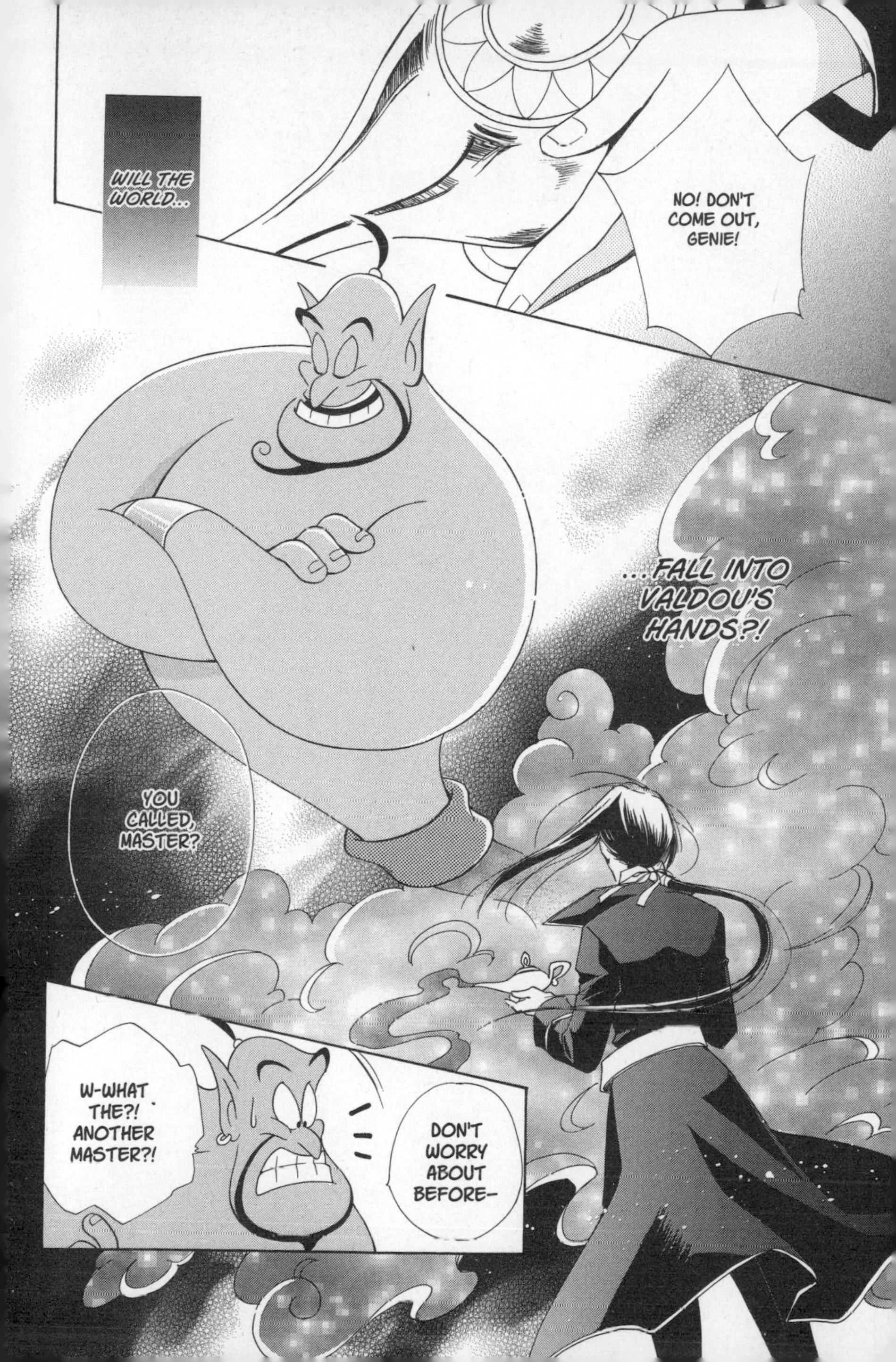
NO! DON'T COME OUT, GENIE!
WILL THE WORLD...
...FALL INTO VALDOU'S HANDS?!
YOU CALLED, MASTER?
DON'T WORRY ABOUT BEFORE–
W-WHAT THE?! ANOTHER MASTER?!

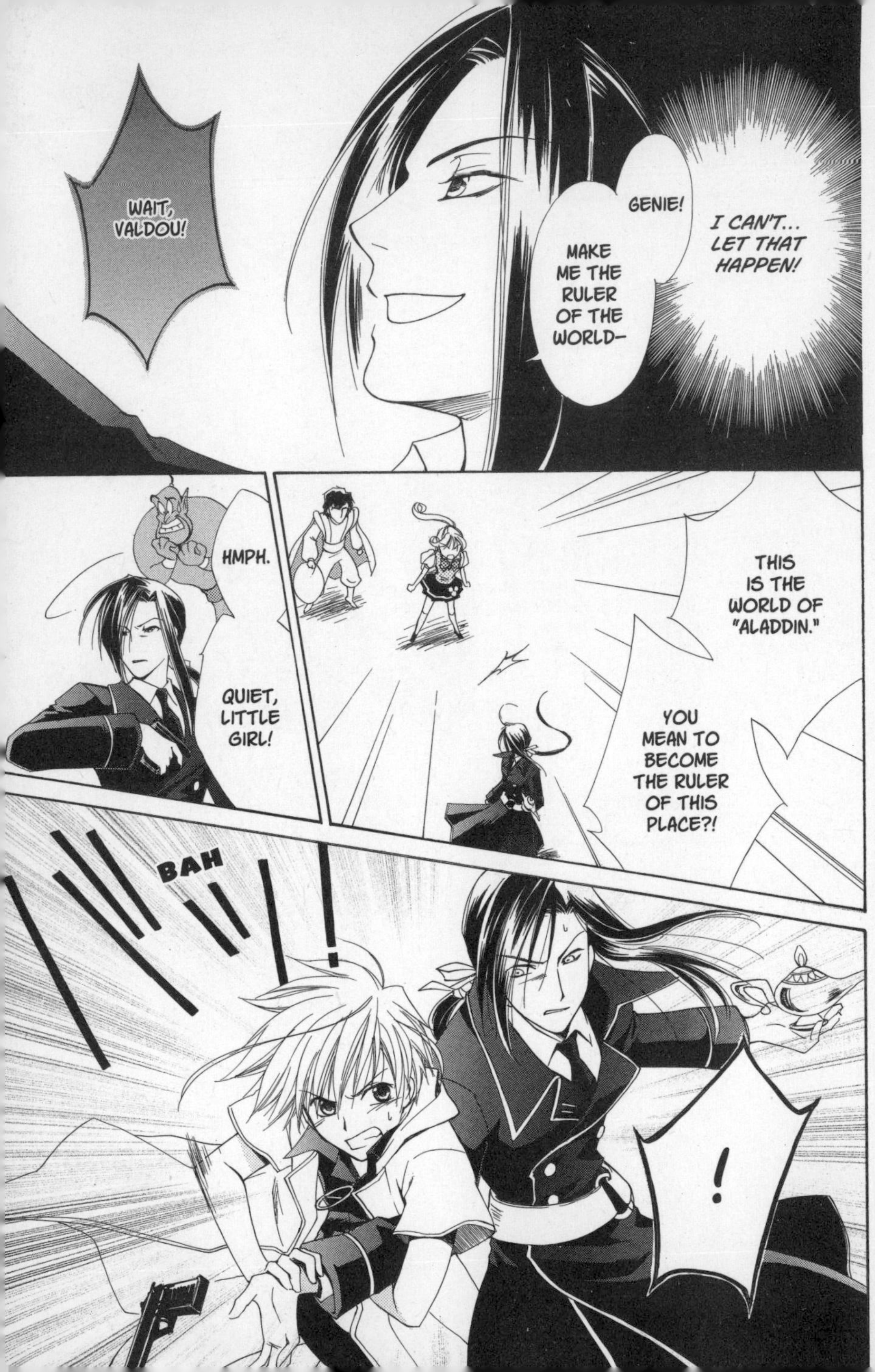
I CAN'T... LET THAT HAPPEN!
GENIE!
MAKE ME THE RULER OF THE WORLD–
WAIT, VALDOU!
THIS IS THE WORLD OF "ALADDIN."
YOU MEAN TO BECOME THE RULER OF THIS PLACE?!
HMPH.
QUIET, LITTLE GIRL!
!
BAH
!

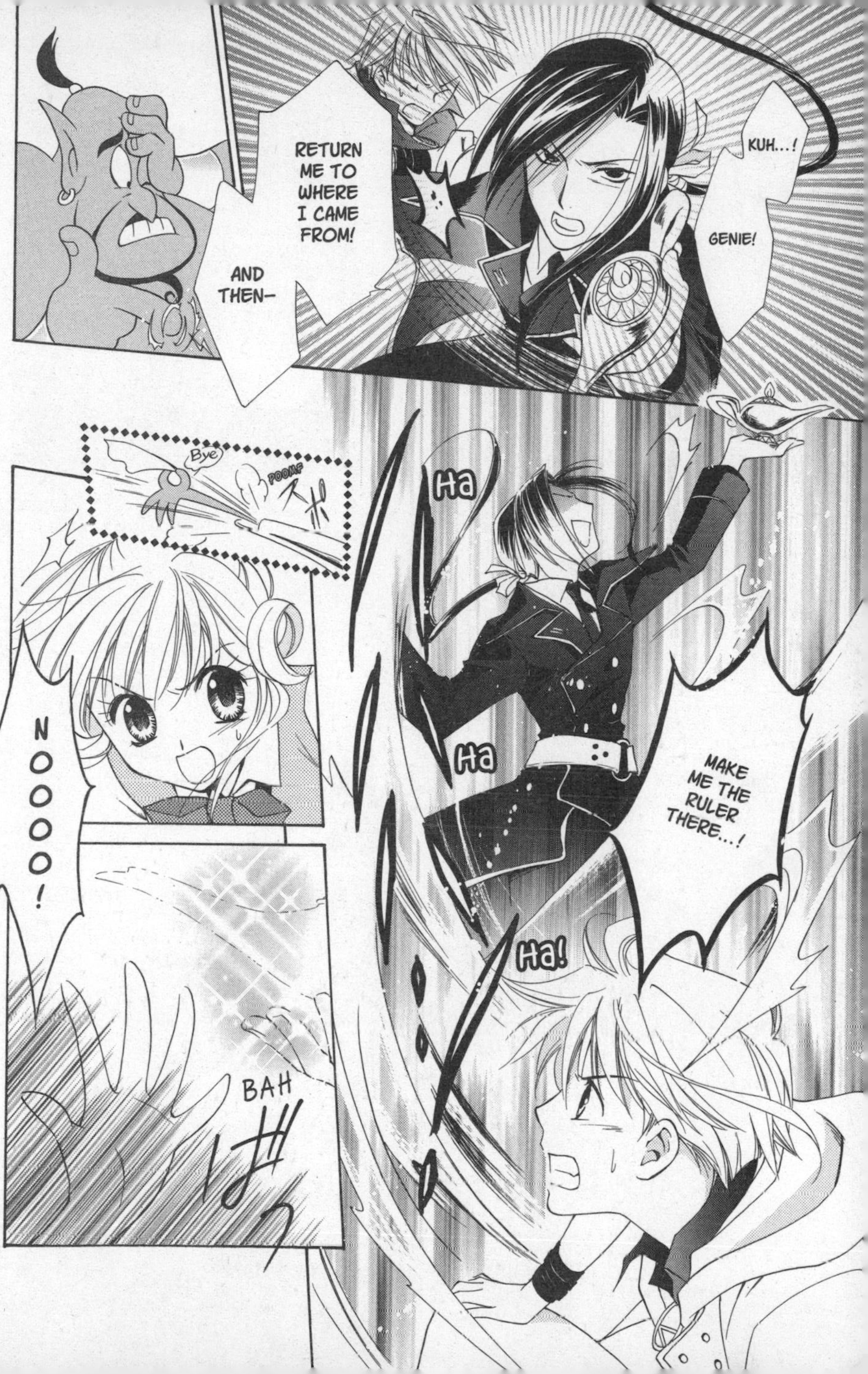
KUH...!
GENIE!
RETURN ME TO WHERE I CAME FROM!
AND THEN-
Ha
Ha
MAKE ME THE RULER THERE...!
Ha!
Bye
POOMF
スポ
NOOOOO!
BAH

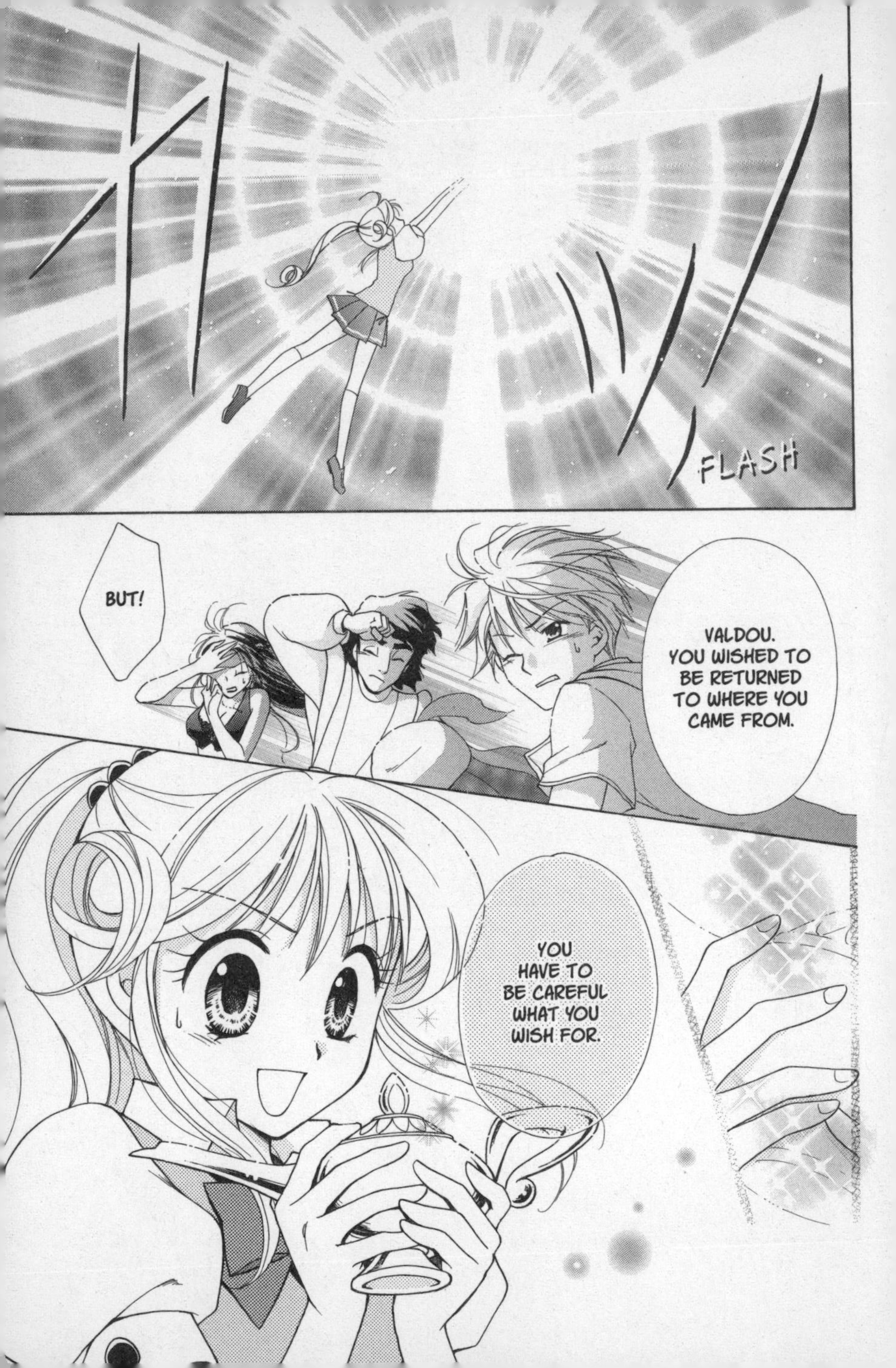
FLASH
VALDOU. YOU WISHED TO BE RETURNED TO WHERE YOU CAME FROM.
BUT!
YOU HAVE TO BE CAREFUL WHAT YOU WISH FOR.

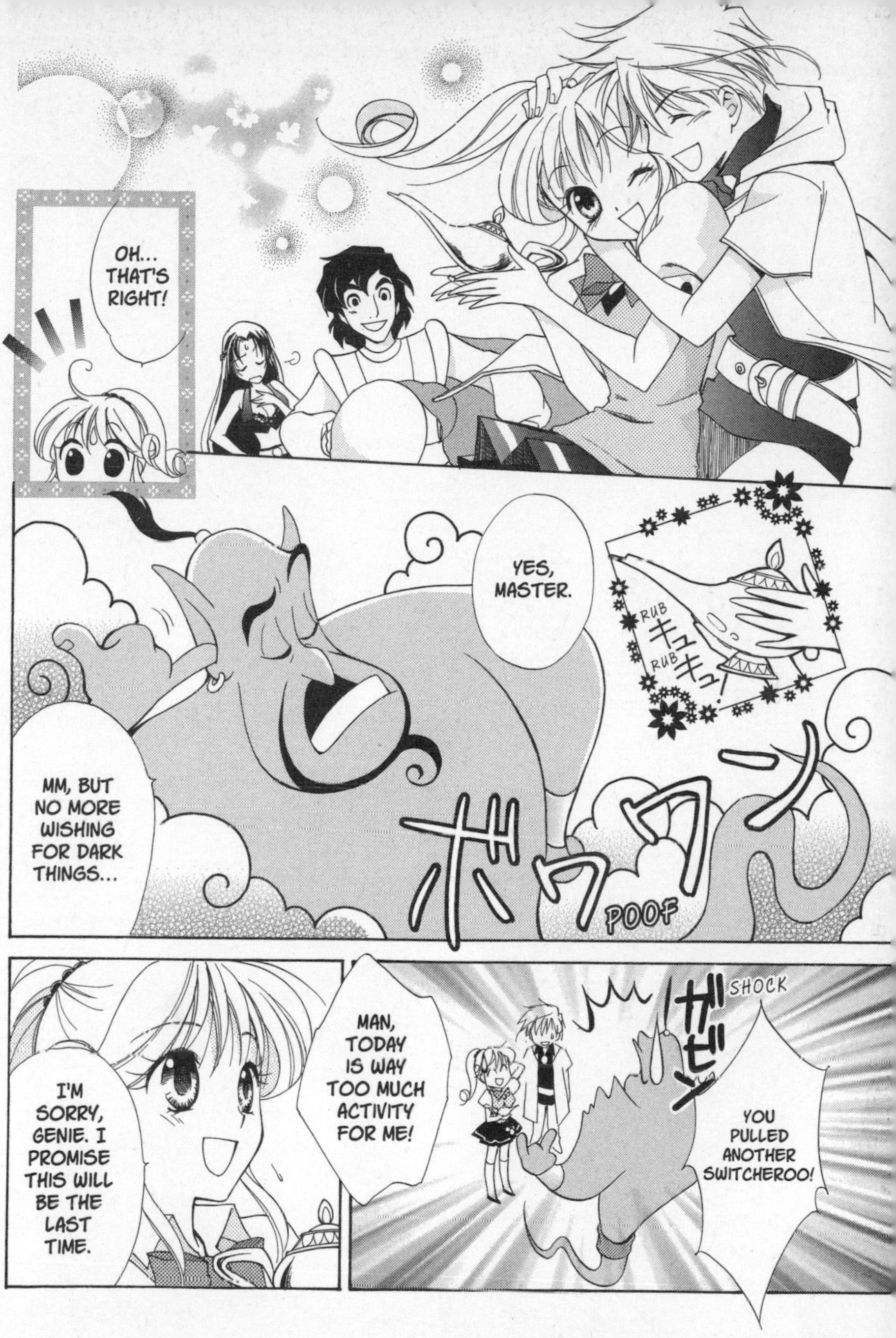
OH... THAT'S RIGHT!
RUB キュ RUB キュ!
YES, MASTER.
ボワーン POOF
MM, BUT NO MORE WISHING FOR DARK THINGS...
SHOCK ガビン
YOU PULLED ANOTHER SWITCHEROO!
MAN, TODAY IS WAY TOO MUCH ACTIVITY FOR ME!
I'M SORRY, GENIE. I PROMISE THIS WILL BE THE LAST TIME.

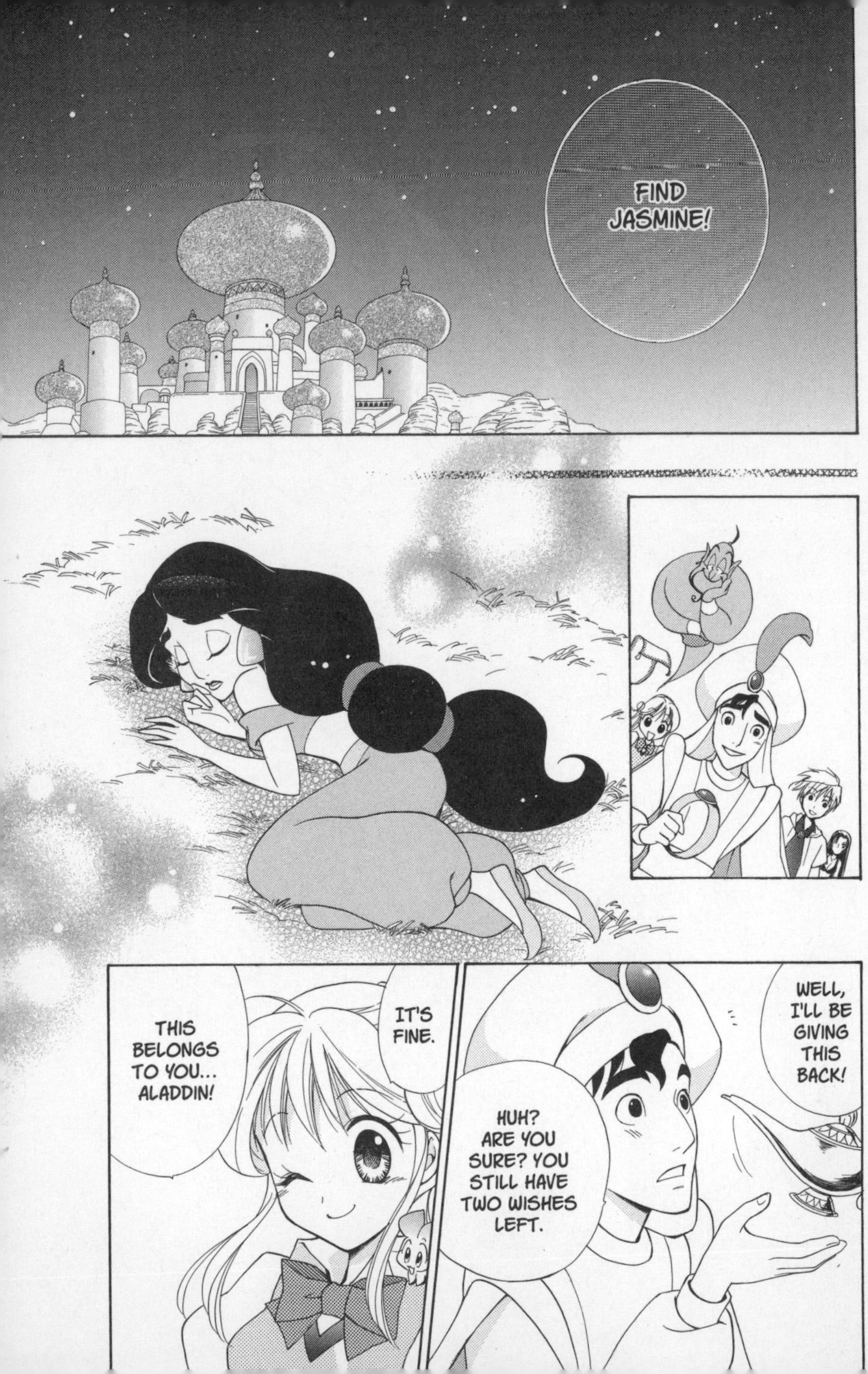
FIND JASMINE!
WELL, I'LL BE GIVING THIS BACK!
HUH? ARE YOU SURE? YOU STILL HAVE TWO WISHES LEFT.
IT'S FINE.
THIS BELONGS TO YOU... ALADDIN!

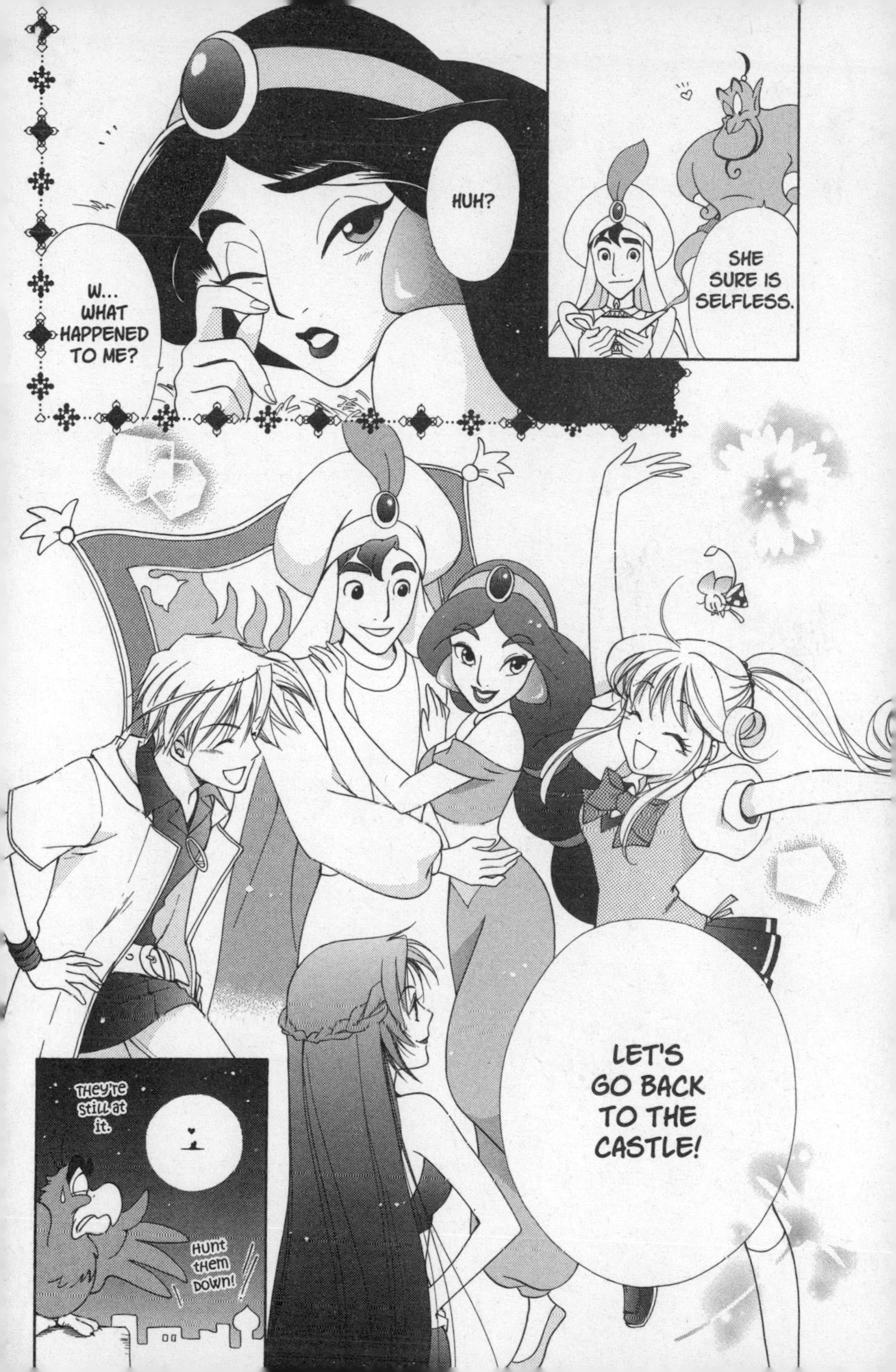
SHE SURE IS SELFLESS.
HUH?
W... WHAT HAPPENED TO ME?
LET'S GO BACK TO THE CASTLE!
They're still at it.
Hunt them down!

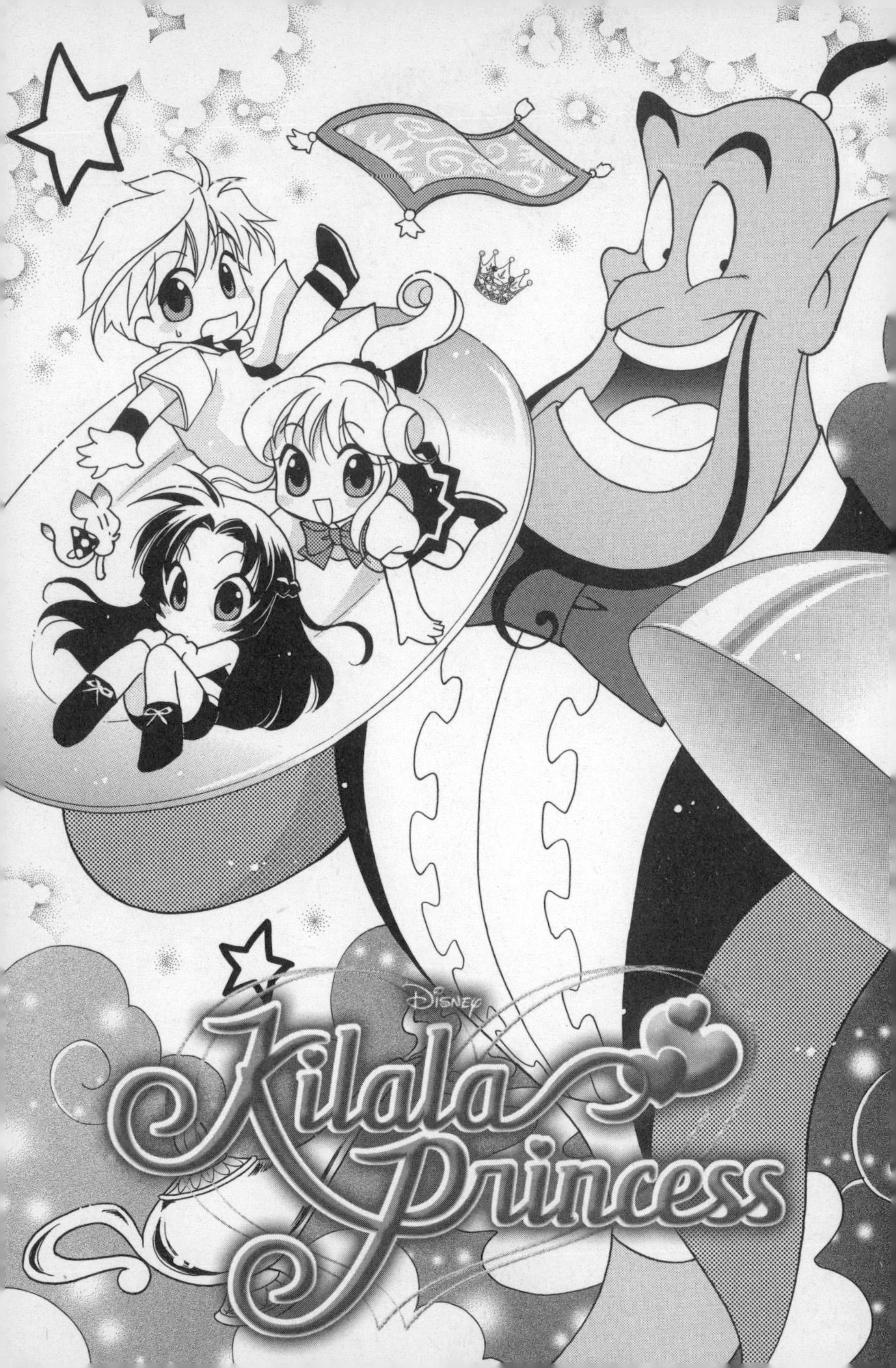
Disney
Kilala Princess

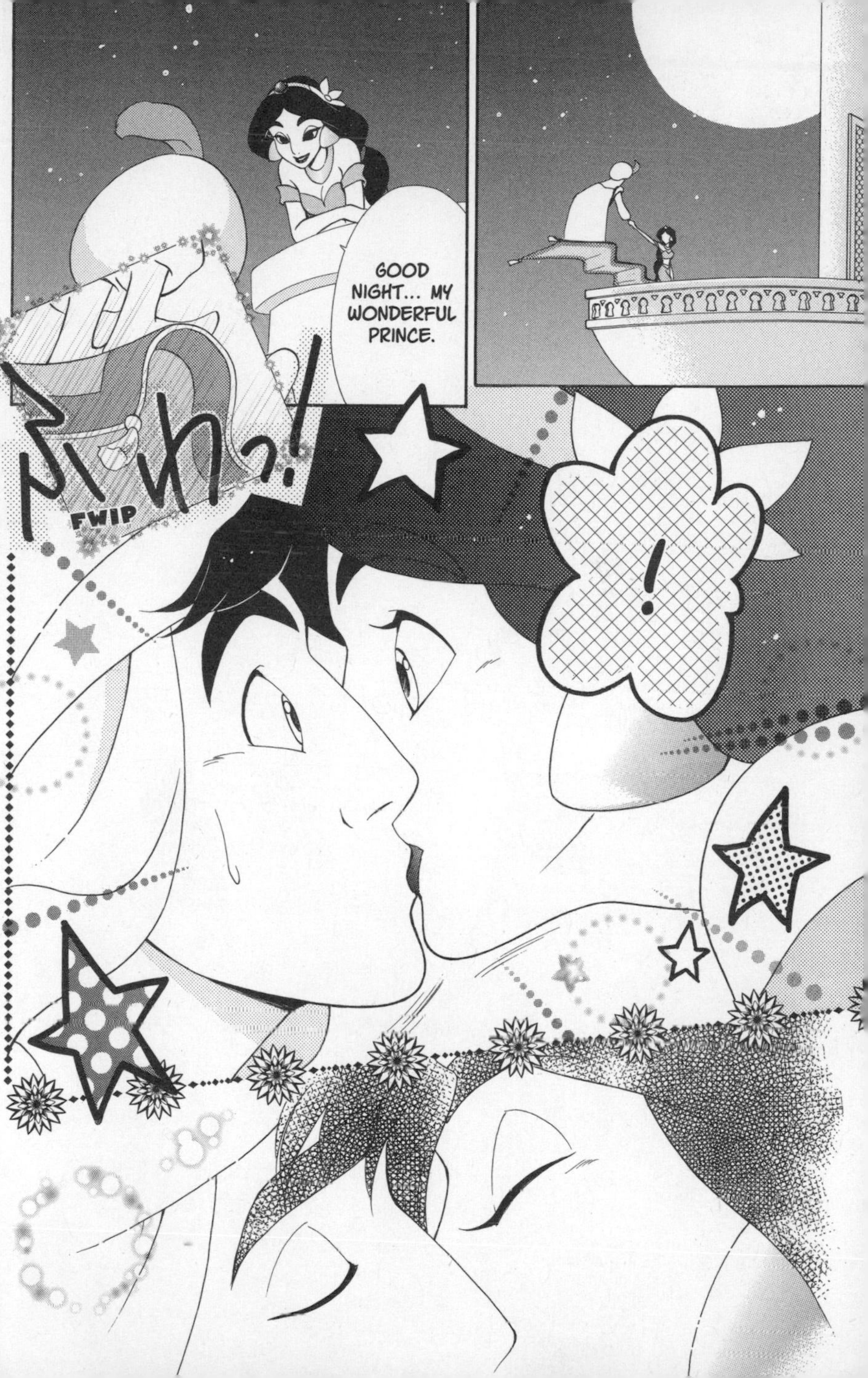
GOOD NIGHT... MY WONDERFUL PRINCE.
ふわっ!
FWIP
!

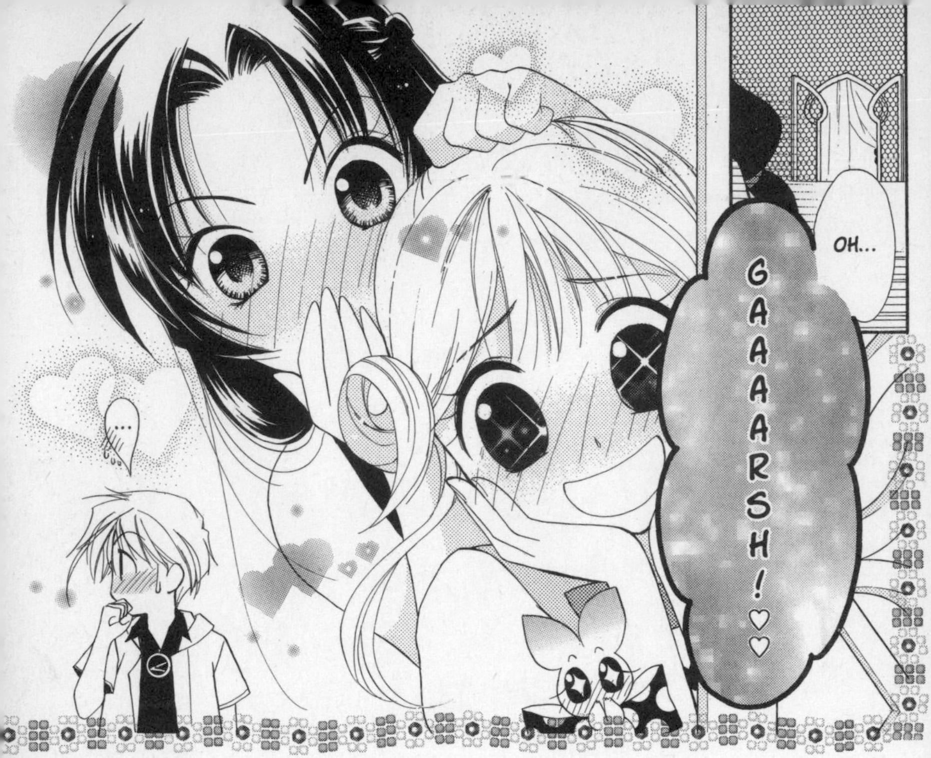
OH...
GAAAARSH!♥♥
...

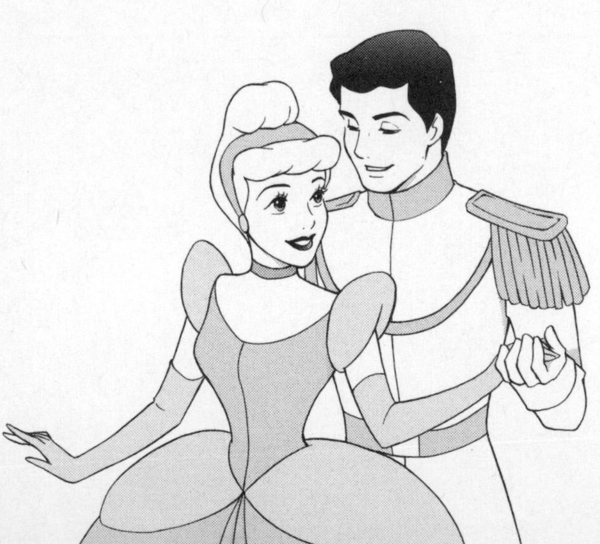

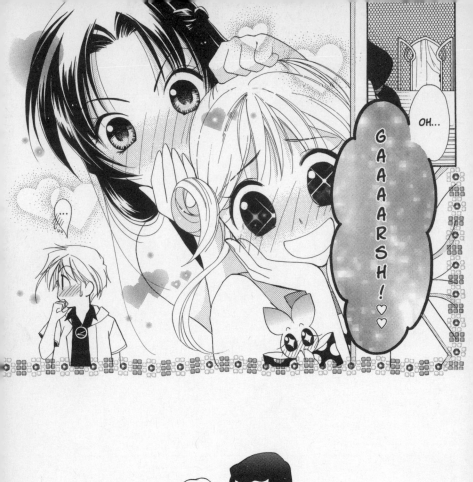

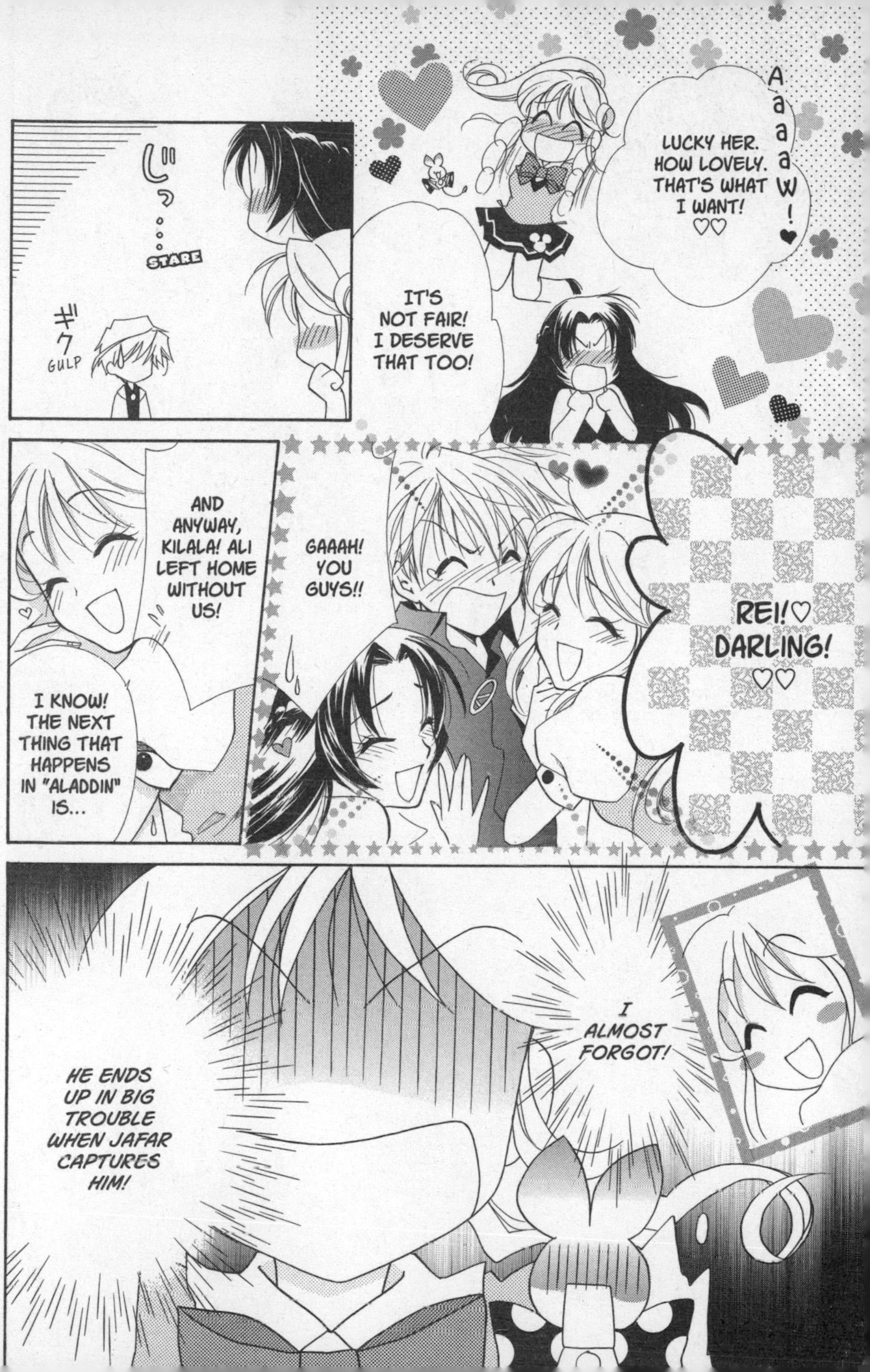
Aaaaw!
LUCKY HER. HOW LOVELY. THAT'S WHAT I WANT! ♡♡
IT'S NOT FAIR! I DESERVE THAT TOO!
じっ。。。。
STARE
ギク
GULP
REI!♡ DARLING! ♡♡
GAAAH! YOU GUYS!!
AND ANYWAY, KILALA! ALI LEFT HOME WITHOUT US!
I KNOW! THE NEXT THING THAT HAPPENS IN "ALADDIN" IS...
I ALMOST FORGOT!
HE ENDS UP IN BIG TROUBLE WHEN JAFAR CAPTURES HIM!

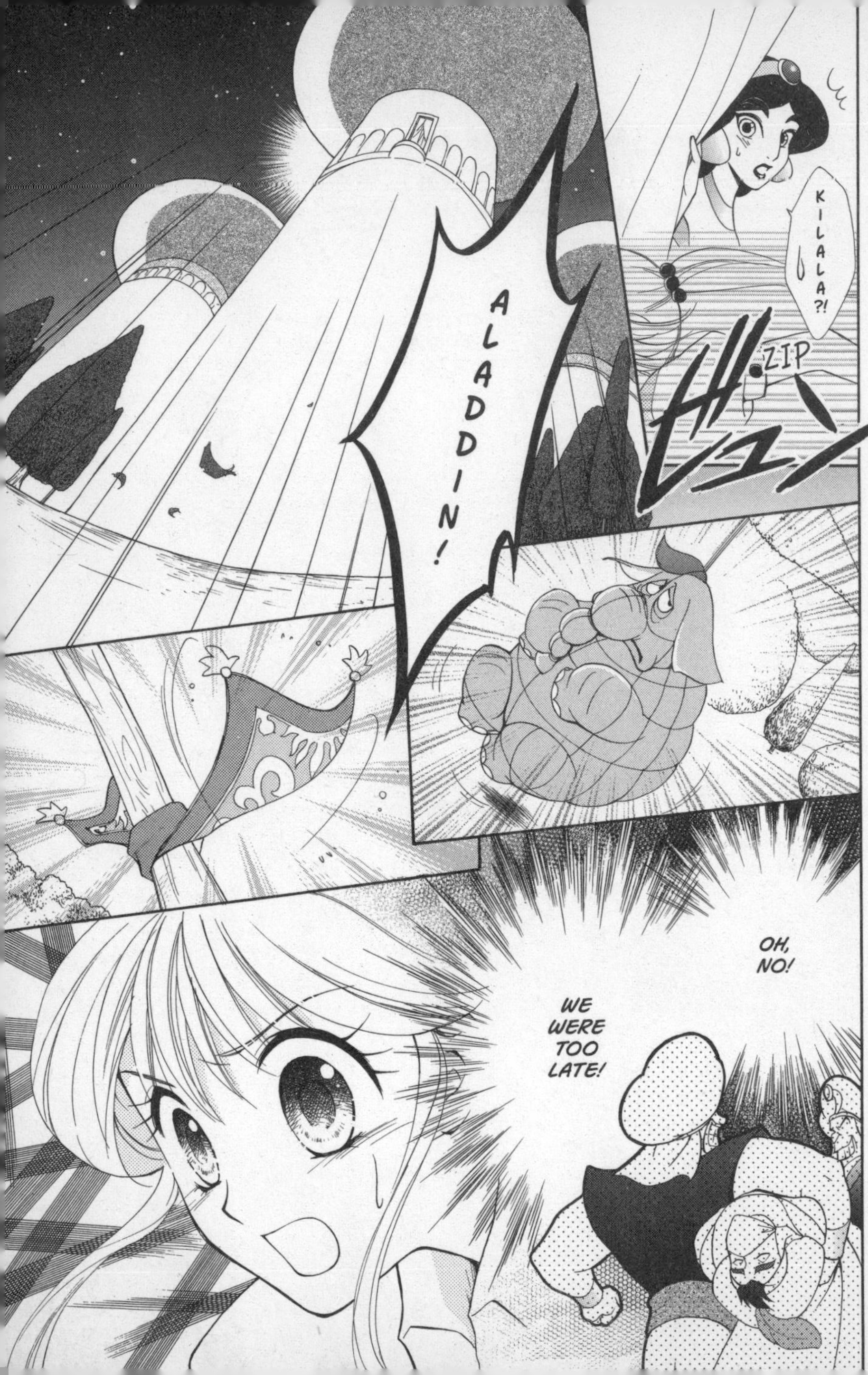

KILALA?!
ZIP
ALADDIN!
OH, NO!
WE WERE TOO LATE!

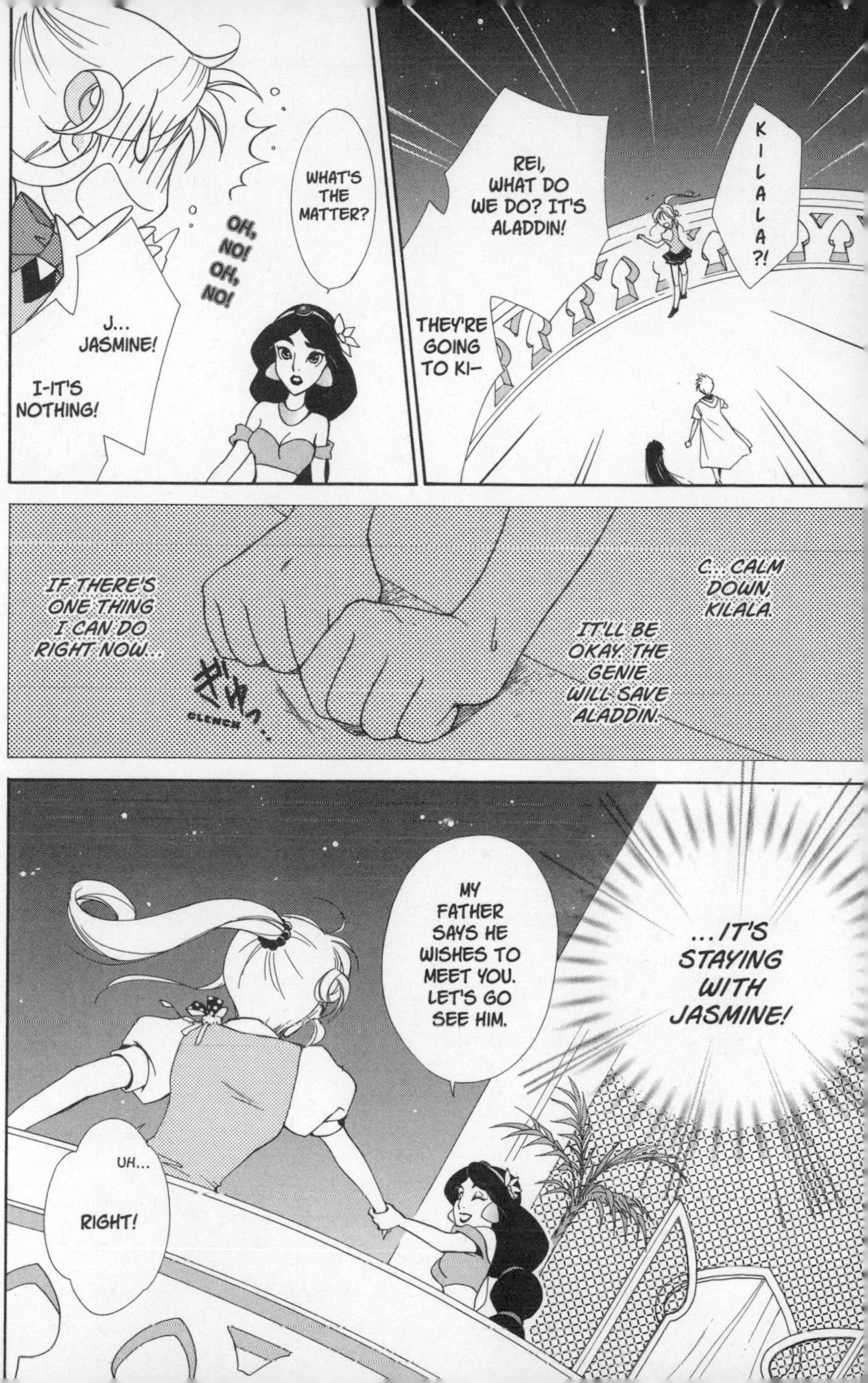
KILALA?!
REI, WHAT DO WE DO? IT'S ALADDIN!
THEY'RE GOING TO KI–
WHAT'S THE MATTER?
OH, NO! OH, NO!
J... JASMINE!
I-IT'S NOTHING!
C... CALM DOWN, KILALA.
IT'LL BE OKAY. THE GENIE WILL SAVE ALADDIN.
IF THERE'S ONE THING I CAN DO RIGHT NOW...
CLENCH
...IT'S STAYING WITH JASMINE!
MY FATHER SAYS HE WISHES TO MEET YOU. LET'S GO SEE HIM.
UH...
RIGHT!

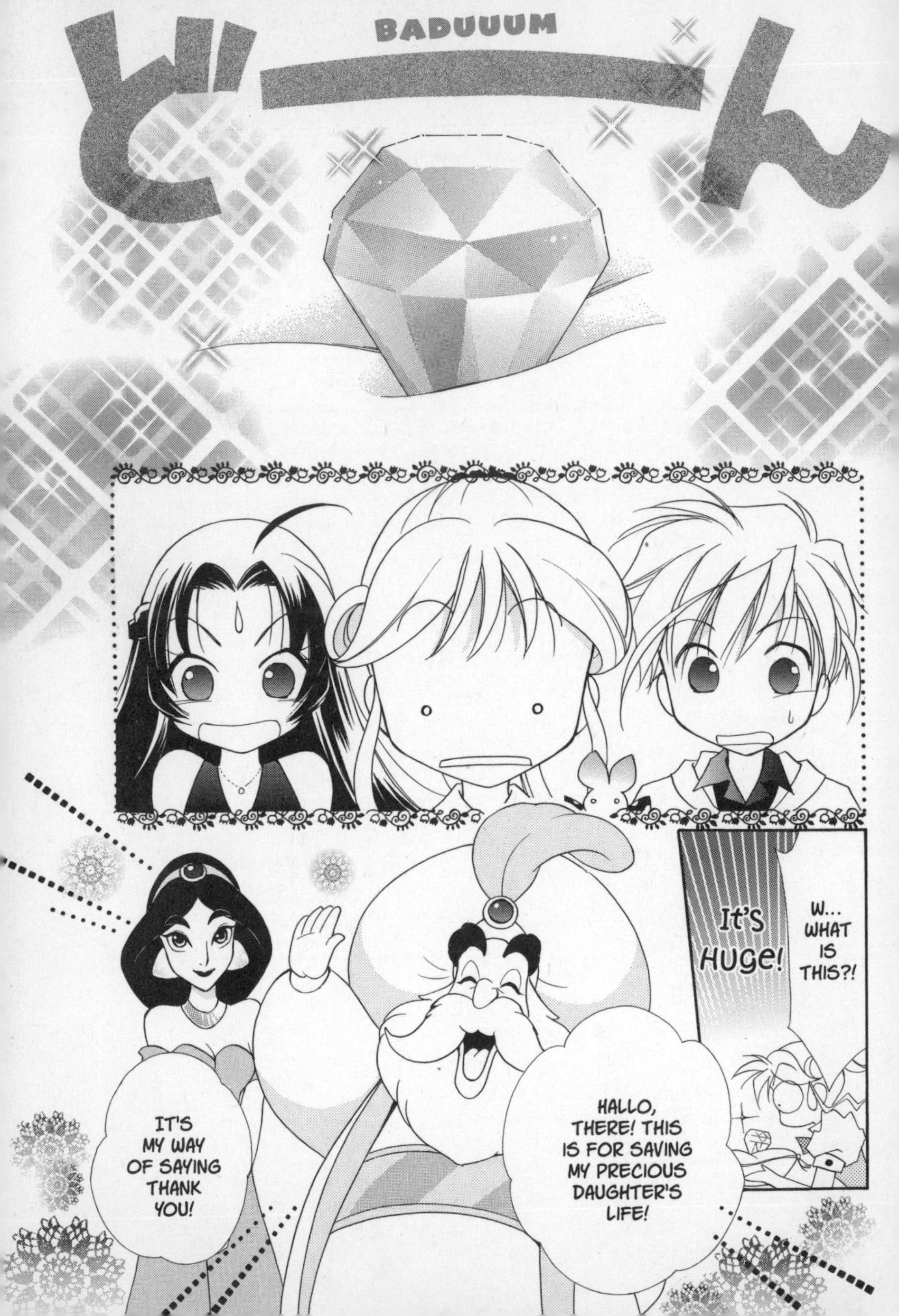
BADUUUM
どーん
W... WHAT IS THIS?!
It's Huge!
HALLO, THERE! THIS IS FOR SAVING MY PRECIOUS DAUGHTER'S LIFE!
IT'S MY WAY OF SAYING THANK YOU!

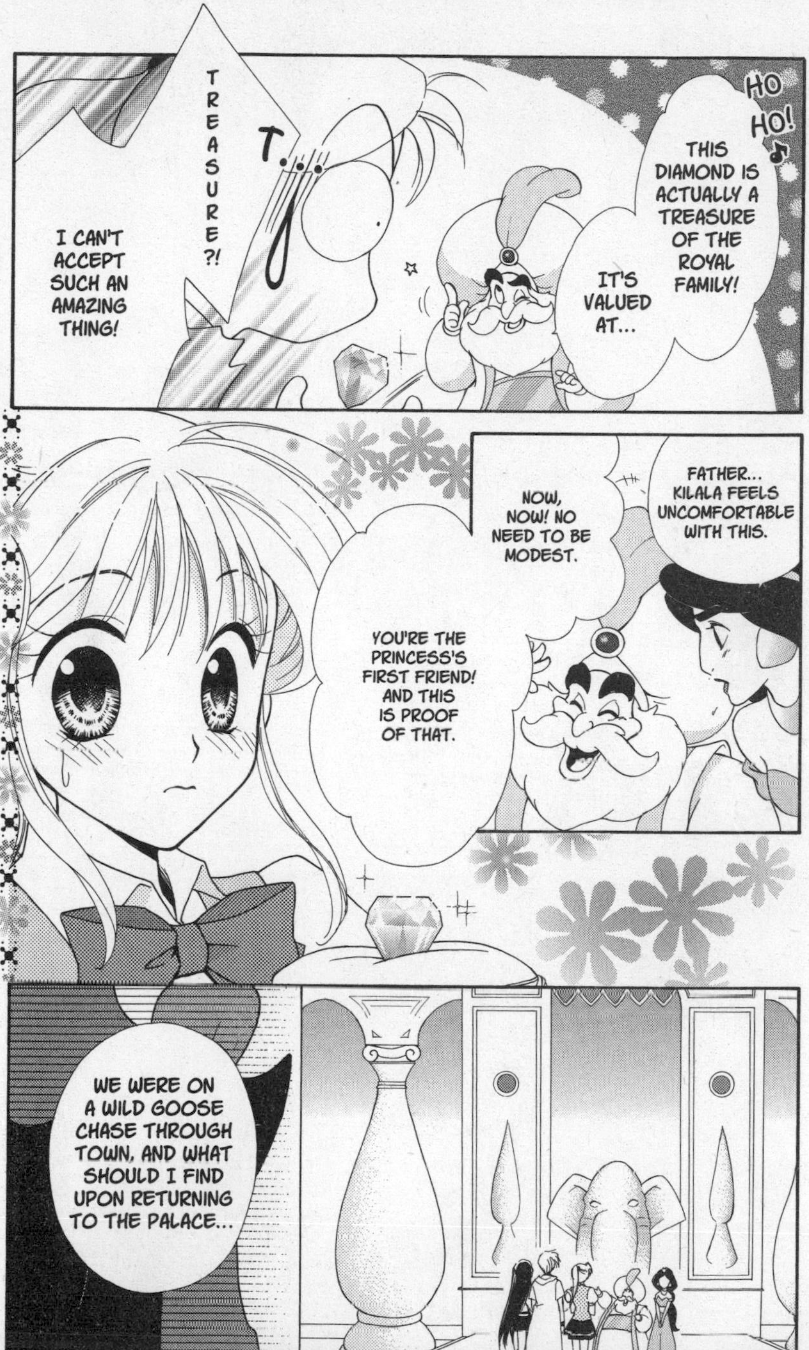
HO HO! ♪
THIS DIAMOND IS ACTUALLY A TREASURE OF THE ROYAL FAMILY!
IT'S VALUED AT...
T...
TREASURE?!
I CAN'T ACCEPT SUCH AN AMAZING THING!
FATHER... KILALA FEELS UNCOMFORTABLE WITH THIS.
NOW, NOW! NO NEED TO BE MODEST.
YOU'RE THE PRINCESS'S FIRST FRIEND! AND THIS IS PROOF OF THAT.
WE WERE ON A WILD GOOSE CHASE THROUGH TOWN, AND WHAT SHOULD I FIND UPON RETURNING TO THE PALACE...

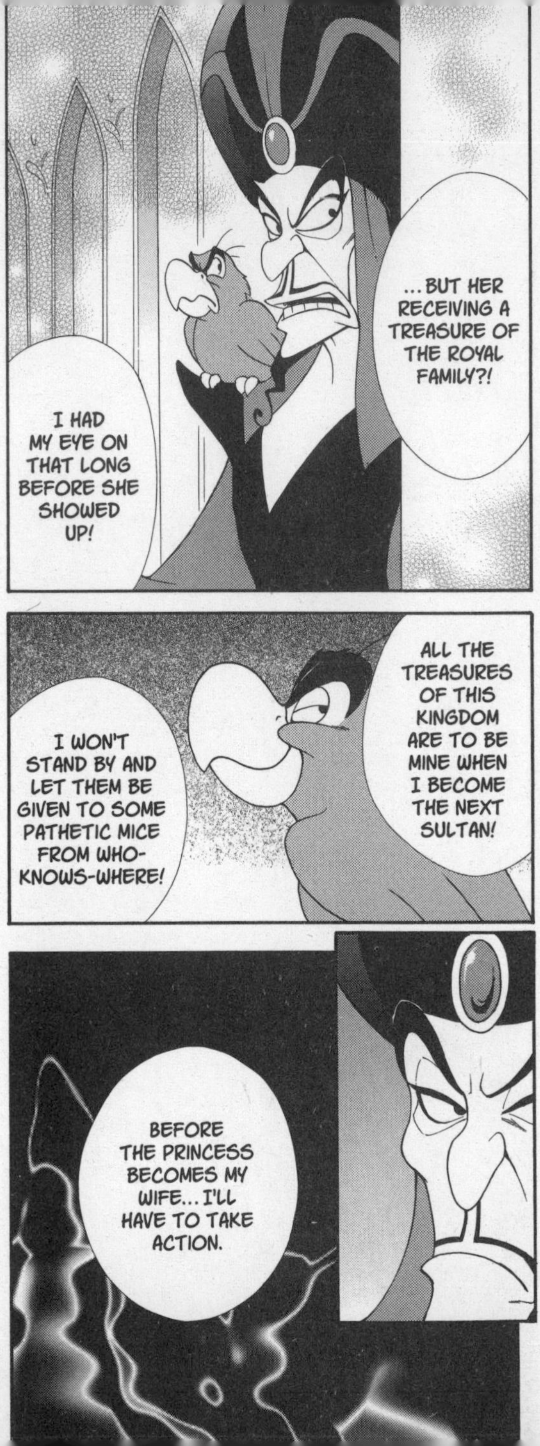
...BUT HER RECEIVING A TREASURE OF THE ROYAL FAMILY?!
I HAD MY EYE ON THAT LONG BEFORE SHE SHOWED UP!
ALL THE TREASURES OF THIS KINGDOM ARE TO BE MINE WHEN I BECOME THE NEXT SULTAN!
I WON'T STAND BY AND LET THEM BE GIVEN TO SOME PATHETIC MICE FROM WHO-KNOWS-WHERE!
BEFORE THE PRINCESS BECOMES MY WIFE... I'LL HAVE TO TAKE ACTION.
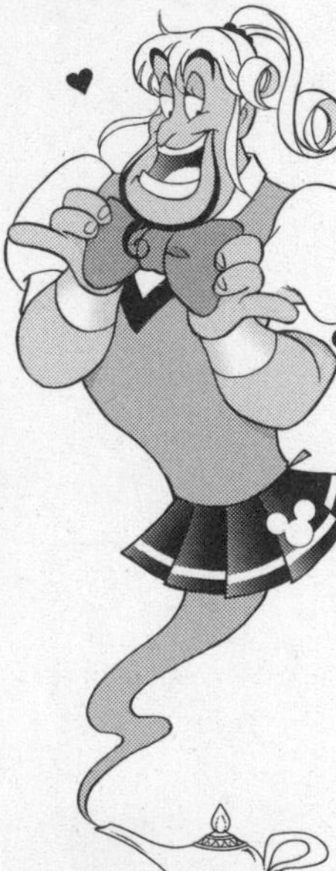

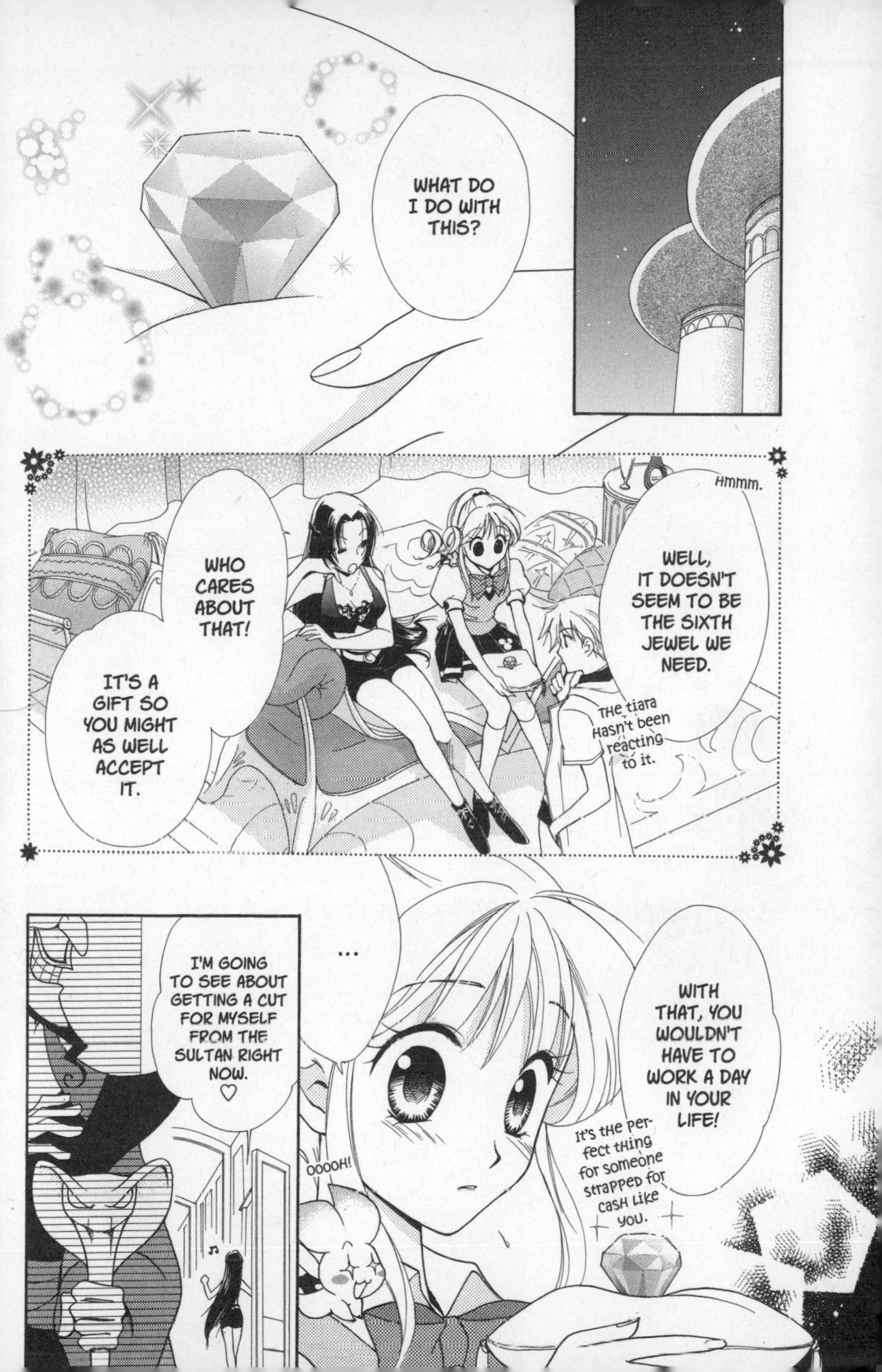
WHAT DO I DO WITH THIS?
Hmmm.
WELL, IT DOESN'T SEEM TO BE THE SIXTH JEWEL WE NEED.
THE tiara Hasn't been reacting to it.
WHO CARES ABOUT THAT!
IT'S A GIFT SO YOU MIGHT AS WELL ACCEPT IT.
WITH THAT, YOU WOULDN'T HAVE TO WORK A DAY IN YOUR LIFE!
It's tHe per-fect tHing for someone strapped for casH like you.
OOOOH!
...
I'M GOING TO SEE ABOUT GETTING A CUT FOR MYSELF FROM THE SULTAN RIGHT NOW. ♡

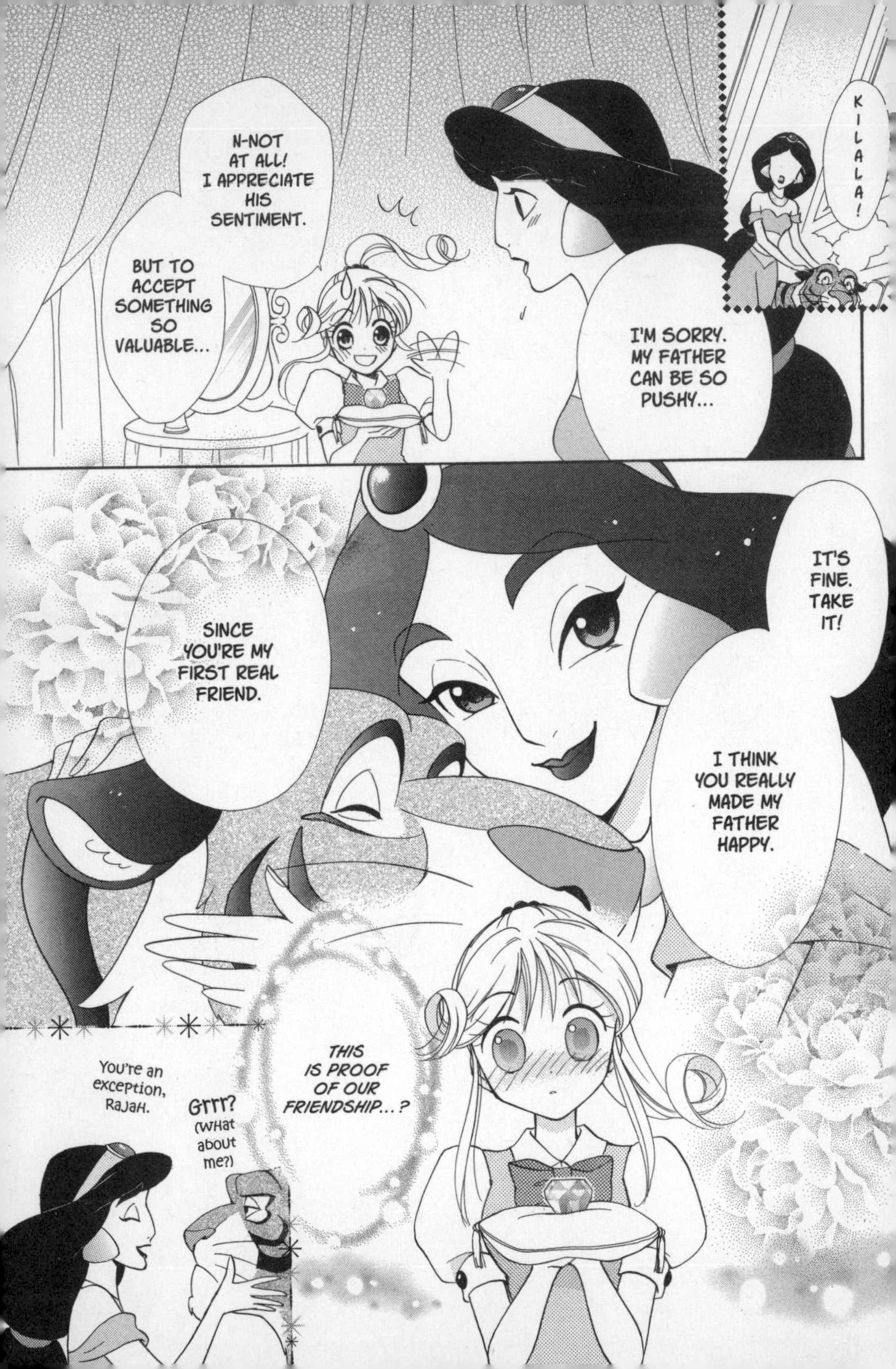
KILALA!
I'M SORRY. MY FATHER CAN BE SO PUSHY...
N-NOT AT ALL! I APPRECIATE HIS SENTIMENT.
BUT TO ACCEPT SOMETHING SO VALUABLE...
IT'S FINE. TAKE IT!
I THINK YOU REALLY MADE MY FATHER HAPPY.
SINCE YOU'RE MY FIRST REAL FRIEND.
THIS IS PROOF OF OUR FRIENDSHIP...?
Grrr? (What about me?)
You're an exception, Rajah.

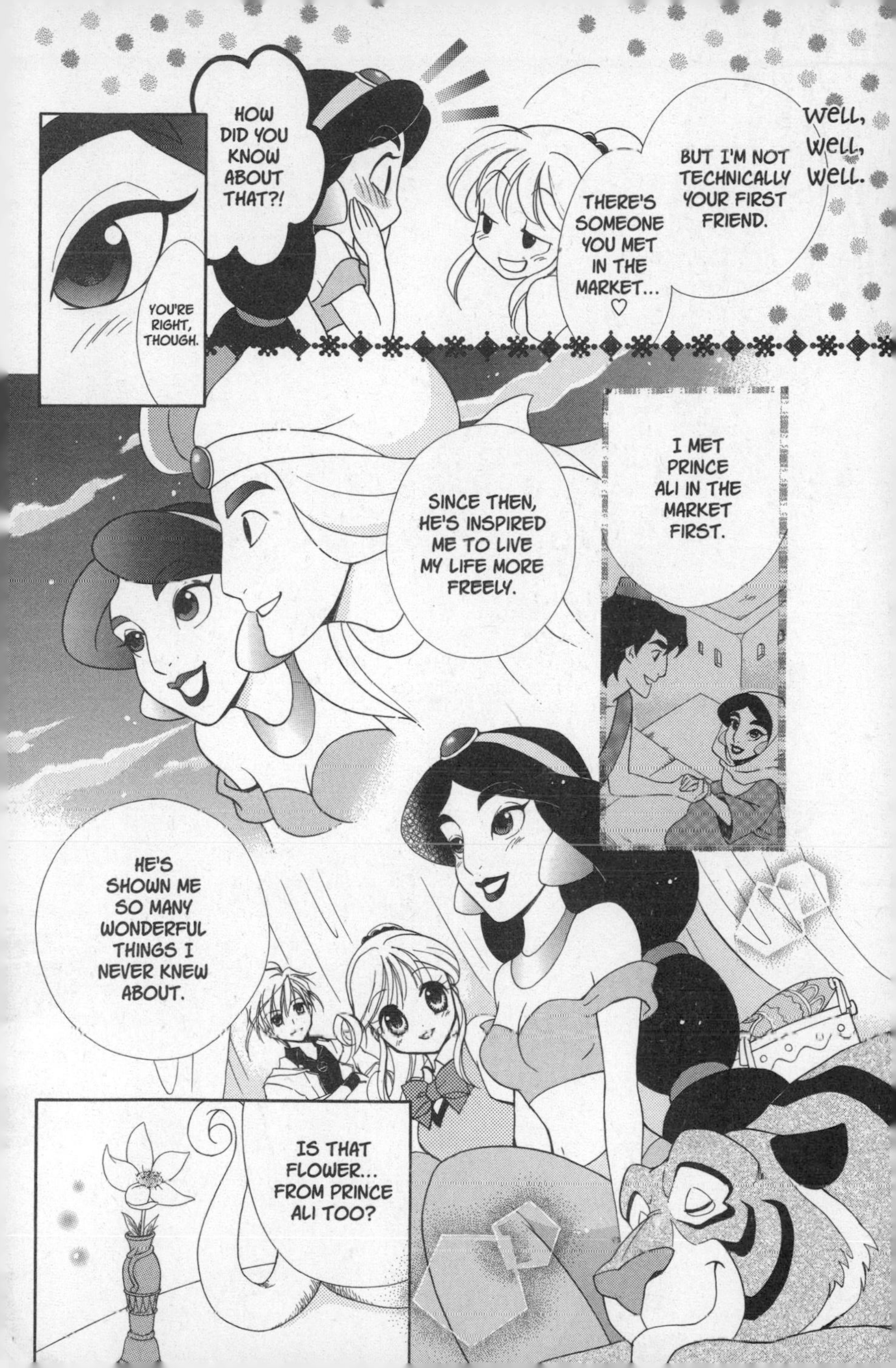
WELL, WELL, WELL.
BUT I'M NOT TECHNICALLY YOUR FIRST FRIEND.
THERE'S SOMEONE YOU MET IN THE MARKET... ♡
HOW DID YOU KNOW ABOUT THAT?!
YOU'RE RIGHT, THOUGH.
I MET PRINCE ALI IN THE MARKET FIRST.
SINCE THEN, HE'S INSPIRED ME TO LIVE MY LIFE MORE FREELY.
HE'S SHOWN ME SO MANY WONDERFUL THINGS I NEVER KNEW ABOUT.
IS THAT FLOWER... FROM PRINCE ALI TOO?

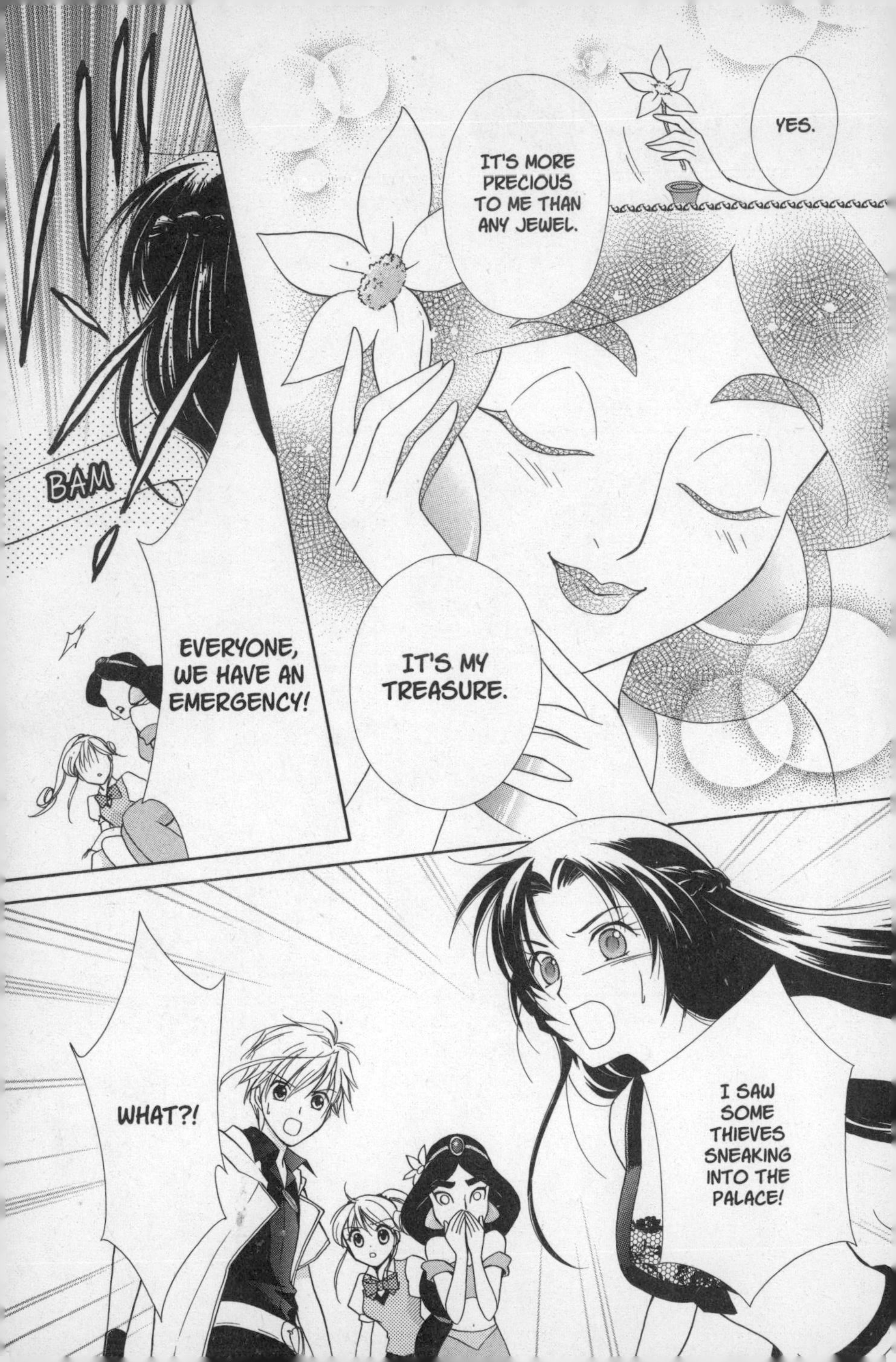
YES.
IT'S MORE PRECIOUS TO ME THAN ANY JEWEL.
IT'S MY TREASURE.
BAM
EVERYONE, WE HAVE AN EMERGENCY!
I SAW SOME THIEVES SNEAKING INTO THE PALACE!
WHAT?!

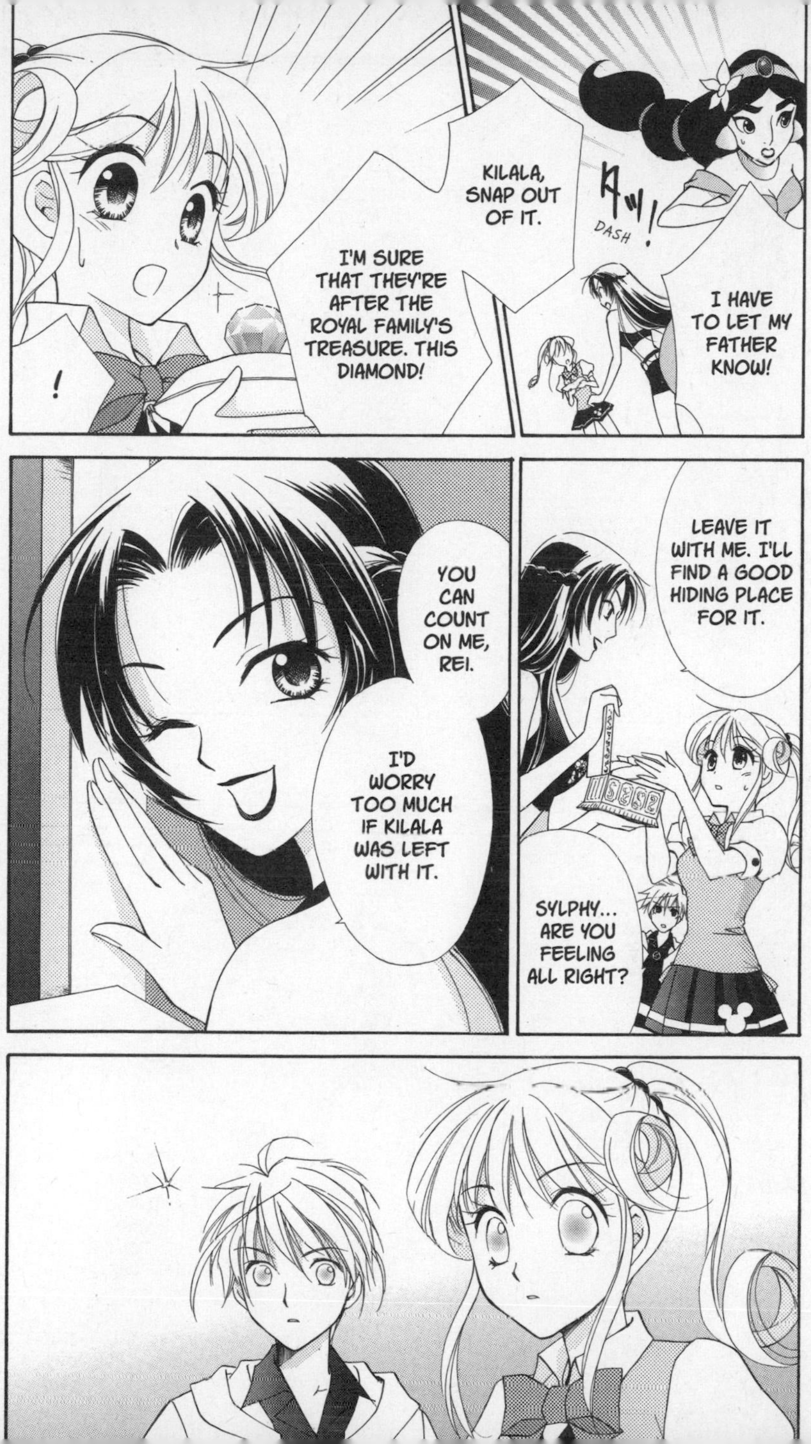
KILALA, SNAP OUT OF IT.
I'M SURE THAT THEY'RE AFTER THE ROYAL FAMILY'S TREASURE. THIS DIAMOND!
ダッ!
DASH
I HAVE TO LET MY FATHER KNOW!
!
LEAVE IT WITH ME. I'LL FIND A GOOD HIDING PLACE FOR IT.
SYLPHY... ARE YOU FEELING ALL RIGHT?
YOU CAN COUNT ON ME, REI.
I'D WORRY TOO MUCH IF KILALA WAS LEFT WITH IT.

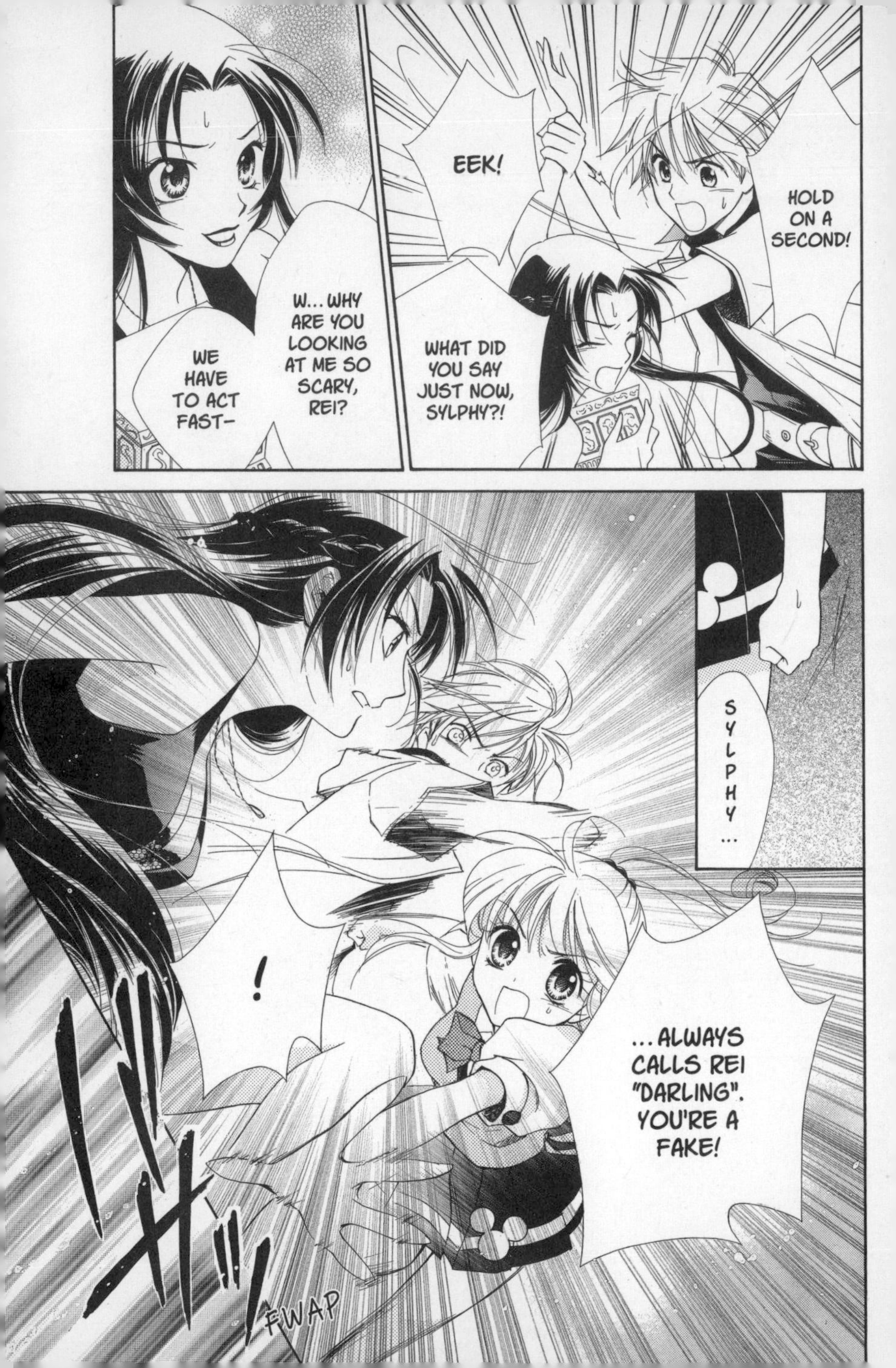
HOLD ON A SECOND!
EEK!
WHAT DID YOU SAY JUST NOW, SYLPHY?!
W... WHY ARE YOU LOOKING AT ME SO SCARY, REI?
WE HAVE TO ACT FAST-
SYLPHY...
...ALWAYS CALLS REI "DARLING". YOU'RE A FAKE!
!
FWAP

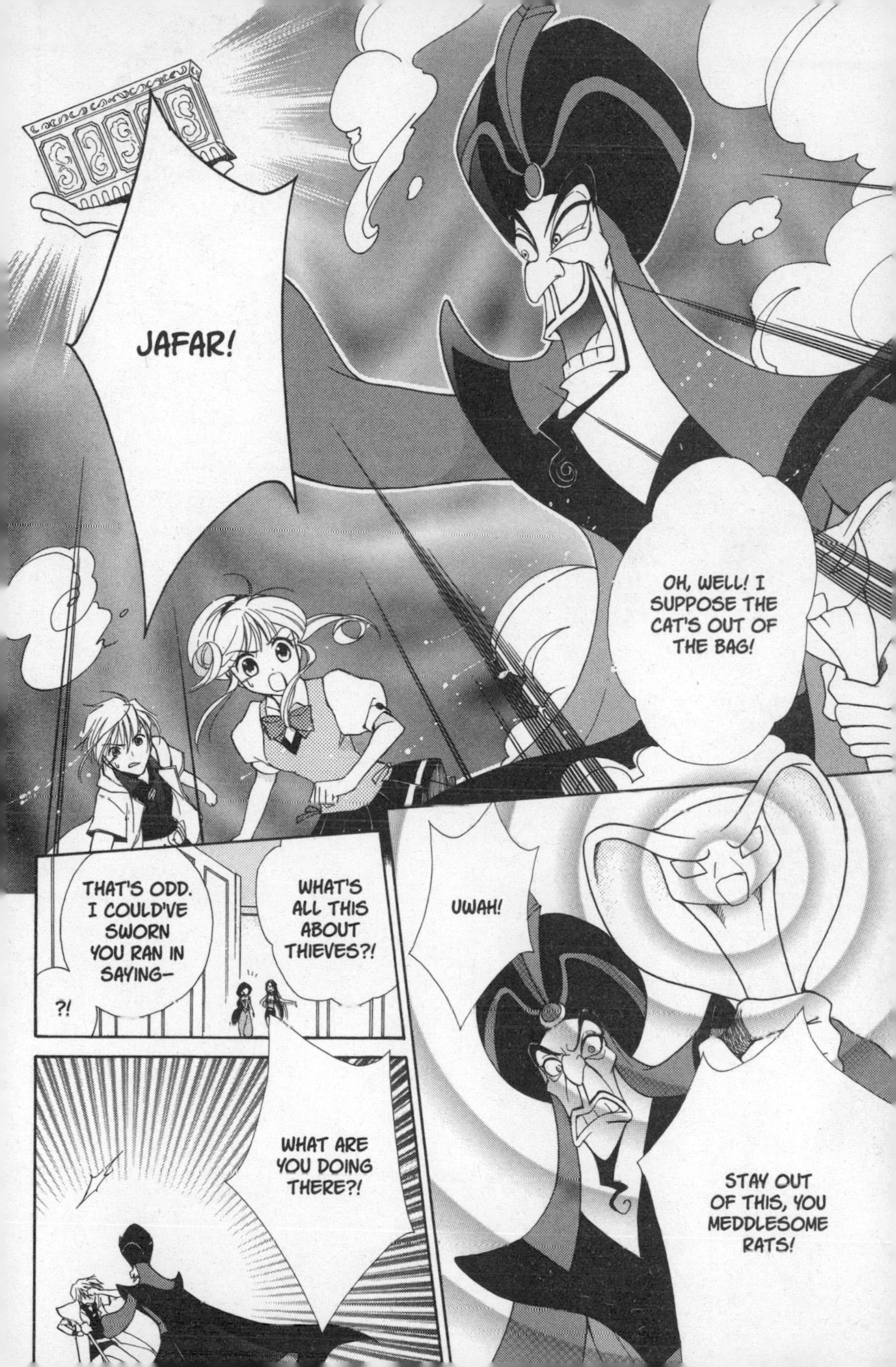
JAFAR!
OH, WELL! I SUPPOSE THE CAT'S OUT OF THE BAG!
UWAH!
STAY OUT OF THIS, YOU MEDDLESOME RATS!
WHAT'S ALL THIS ABOUT THIEVES?!
THAT'S ODD. I COULD'VE SWORN YOU RAN IN SAYING—
?!
WHAT ARE YOU DOING THERE?!

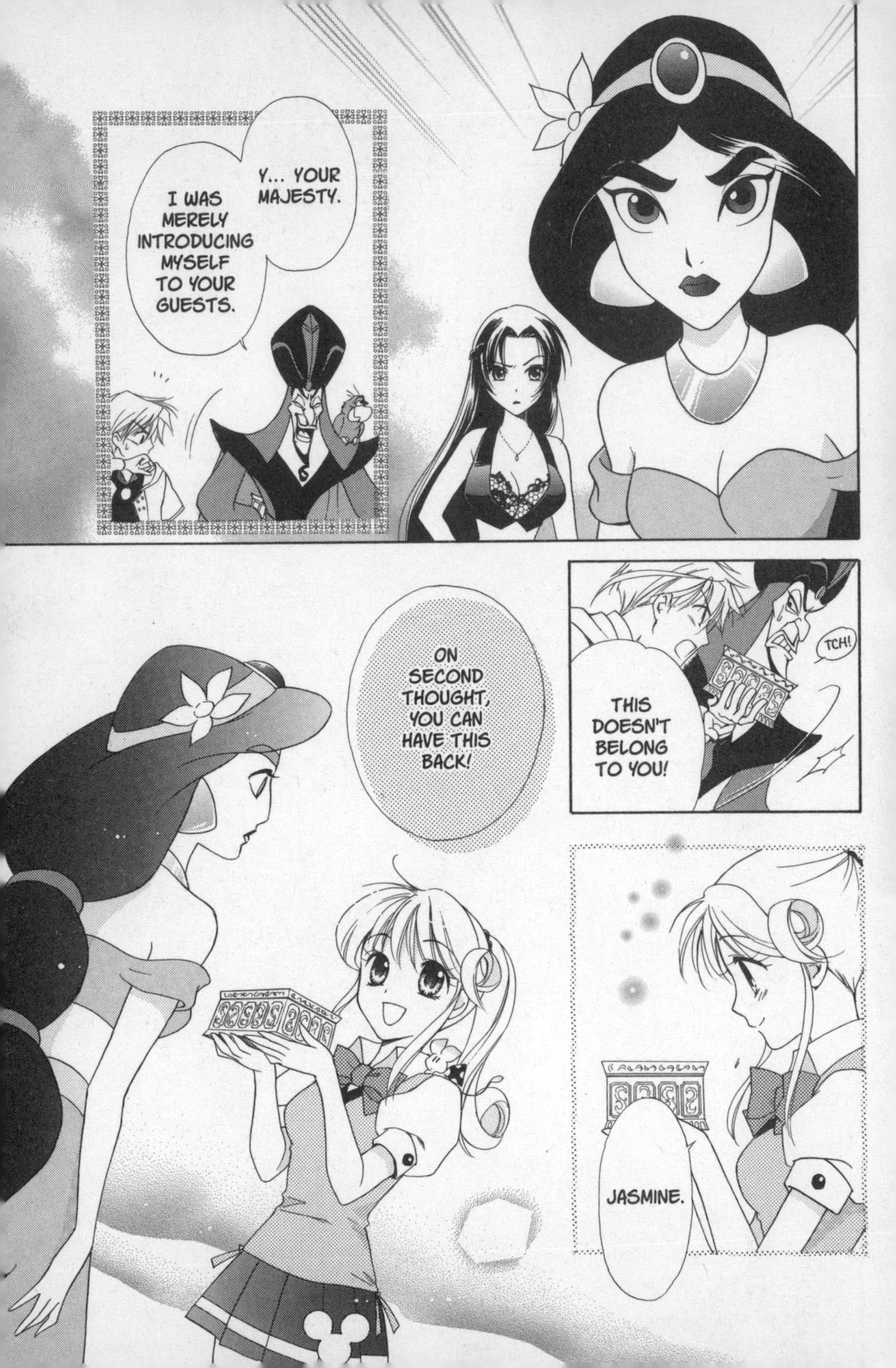
Y... YOUR MAJESTY.
I WAS MERELY INTRODUCING MYSELF TO YOUR GUESTS.
THIS DOESN'T BELONG TO YOU!
TCH!
JASMINE.
ON SECOND THOUGHT, YOU CAN HAVE THIS BACK!

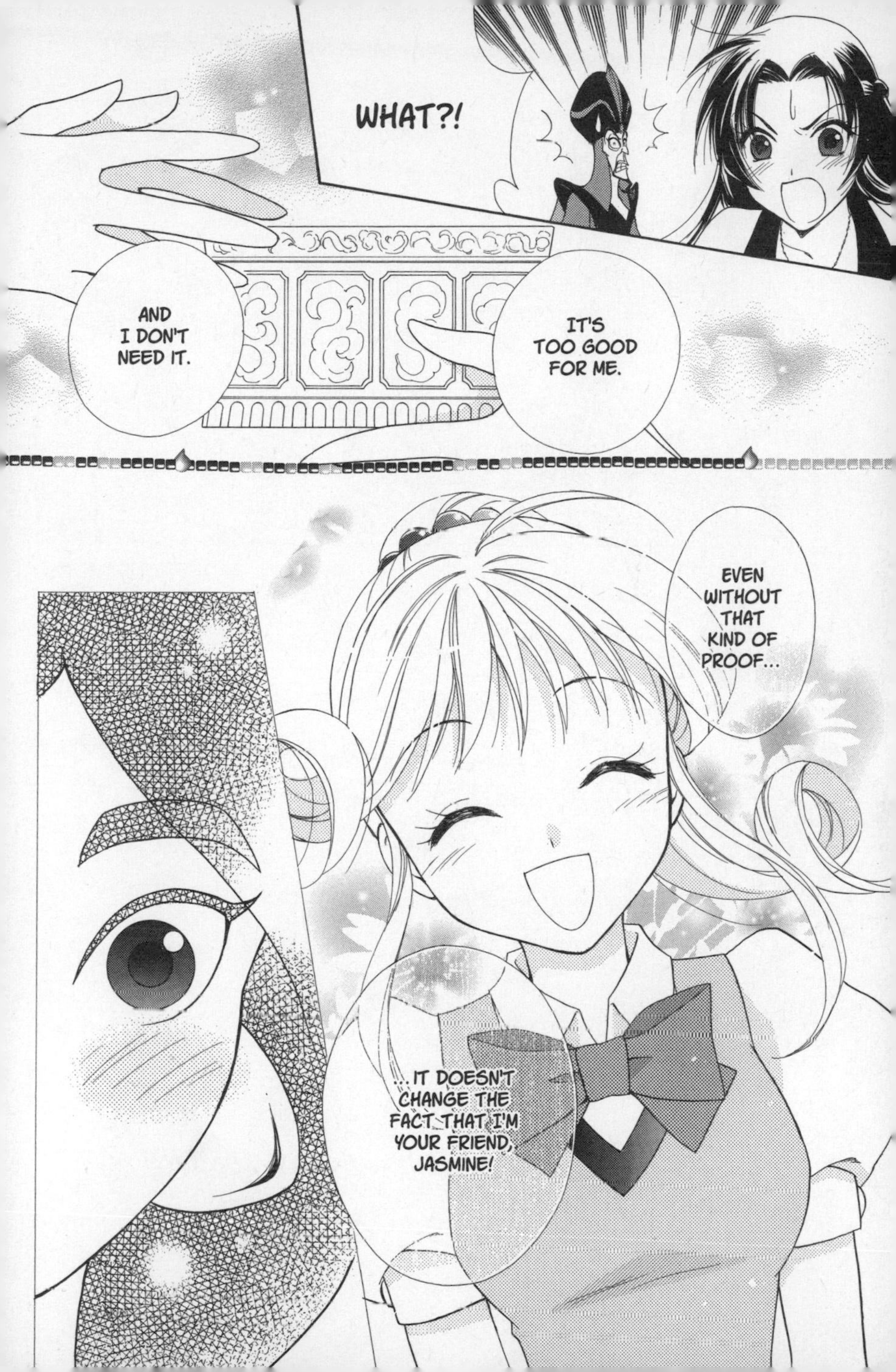
WHAT?!
IT'S TOO GOOD FOR ME.
AND I DON'T NEED IT.
EVEN WITHOUT THAT KIND OF PROOF...
...IT DOESN'T CHANGE THE FACT THAT I'M YOUR FRIEND, JASMINE!

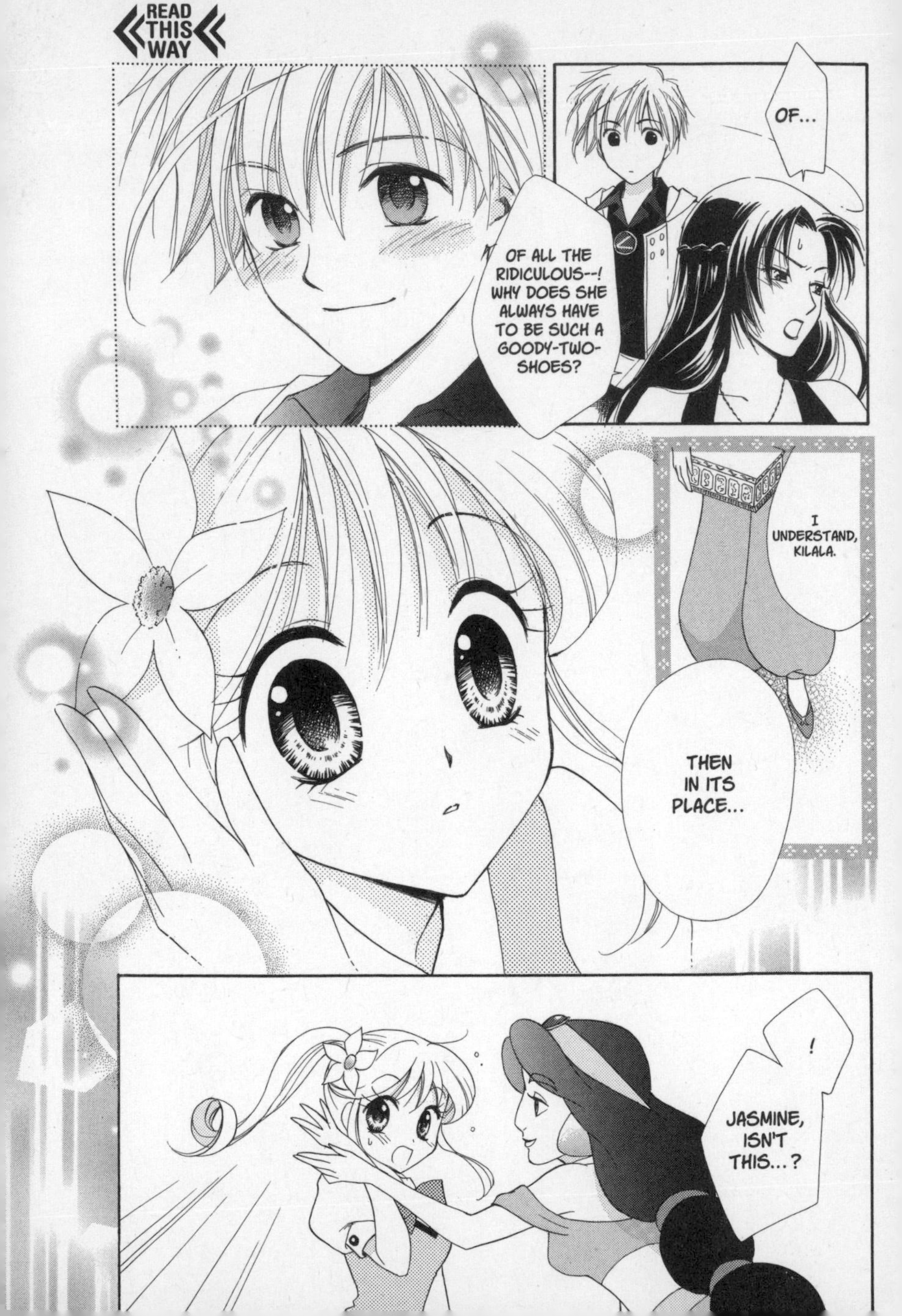
READ THIS WAY
OF...
OF ALL THE RIDICULOUS--! WHY DOES SHE ALWAYS HAVE TO BE SUCH A GOODY-TWO-SHOES?
I UNDERSTAND, KILALA.
THEN IN ITS PLACE...
!
JASMINE, ISN'T THIS...?

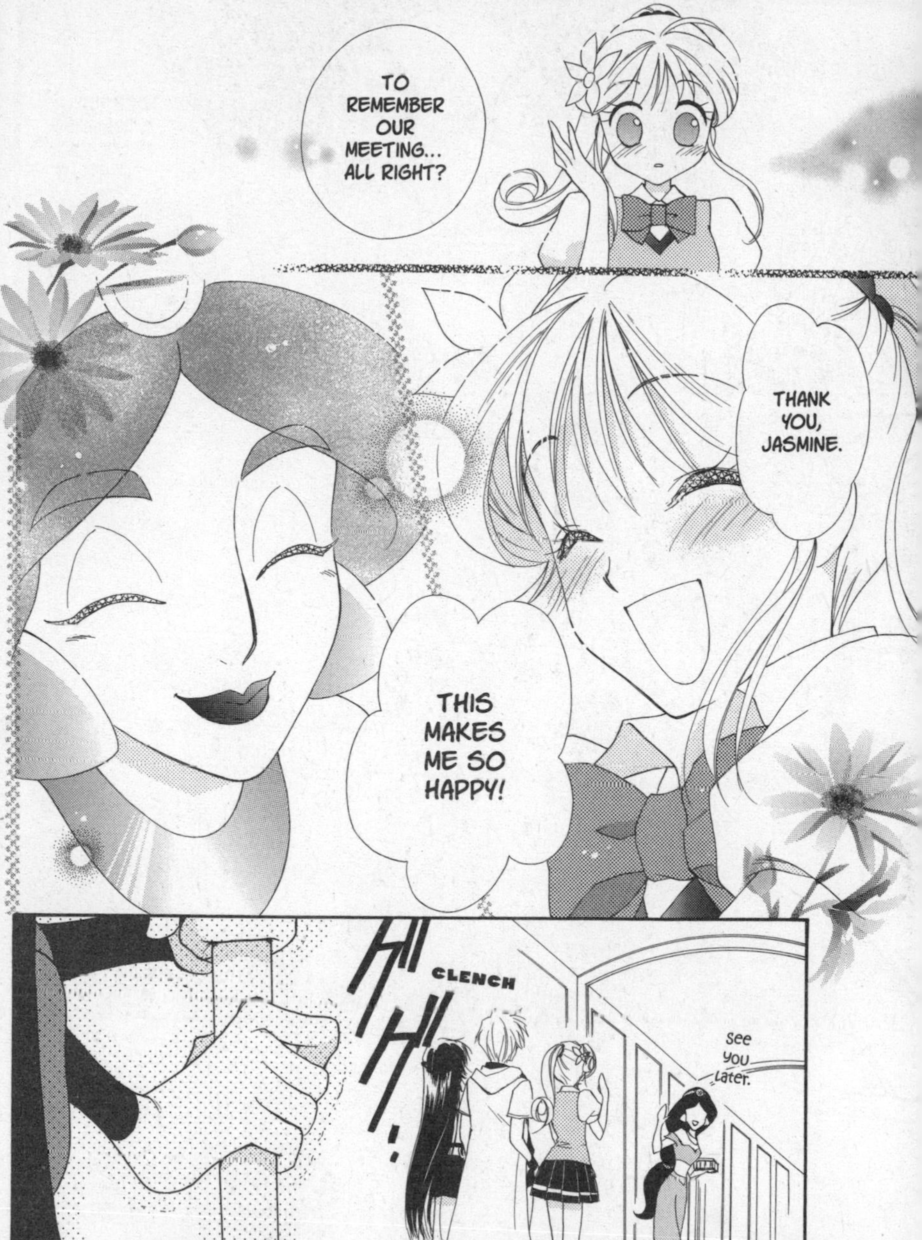
TO REMEMBER OUR MEETING... ALL RIGHT?
THANK YOU, JASMINE.
THIS MAKES ME SO HAPPY!
See you later.
HII
CLENCH
HII
!

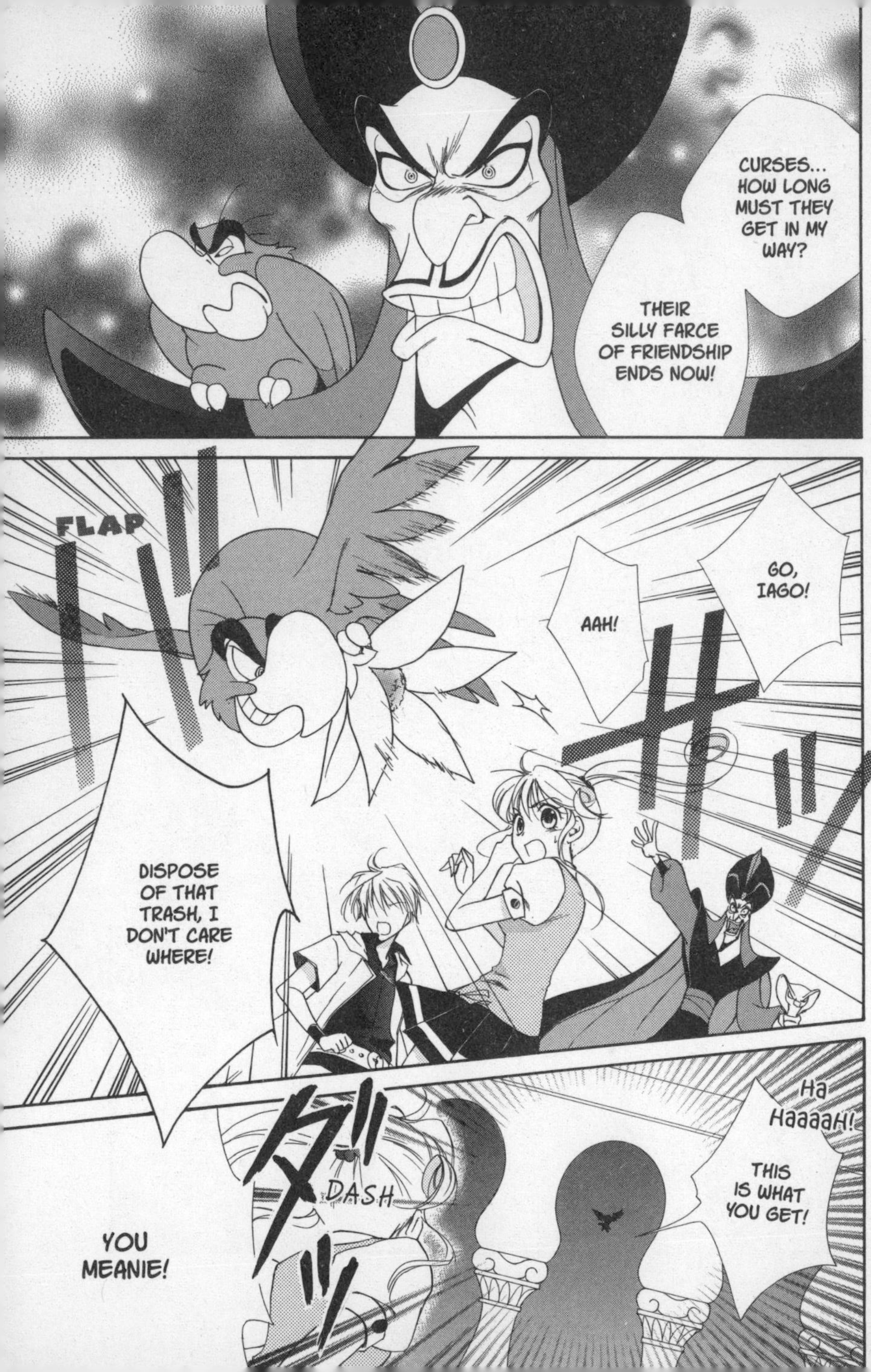
CURSES... HOW LONG MUST THEY GET IN MY WAY?
THEIR SILLY FARCE OF FRIENDSHIP ENDS NOW!
GO, IAGO!
AAH!
FLAP
DISPOSE OF THAT TRASH, I DON'T CARE WHERE!
Ha Haaaaah!
THIS IS WHAT YOU GET!
DASH
YOU MEANIE!

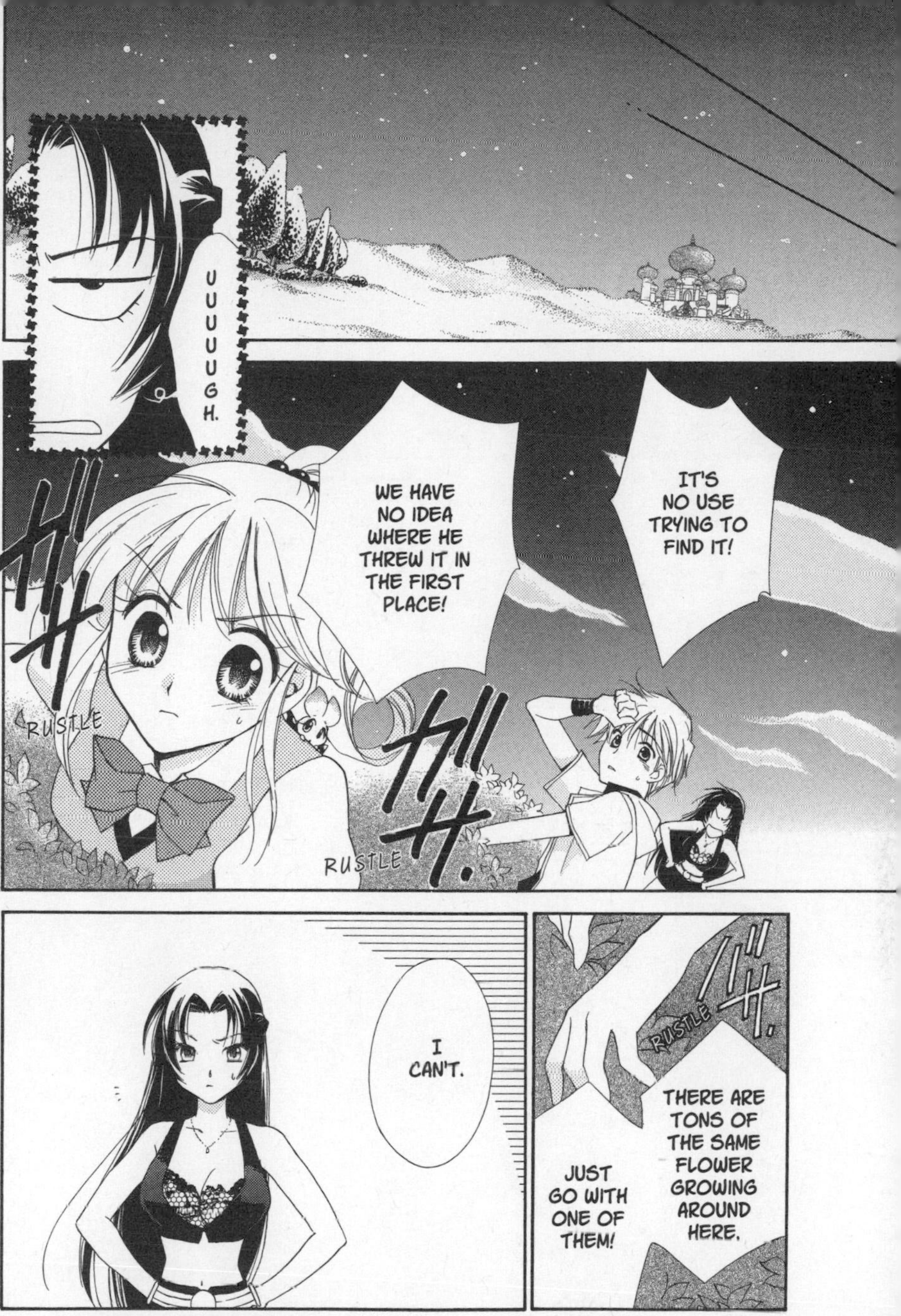
UUUUUGH.
IT'S NO USE TRYING TO FIND IT!
WE HAVE NO IDEA WHERE HE THREW IT IN THE FIRST PLACE!
RUSTLE
RUSTLE
RUSTLE
THERE ARE TONS OF THE SAME FLOWER GROWING AROUND HERE.
JUST GO WITH ONE OF THEM!
I CAN'T.

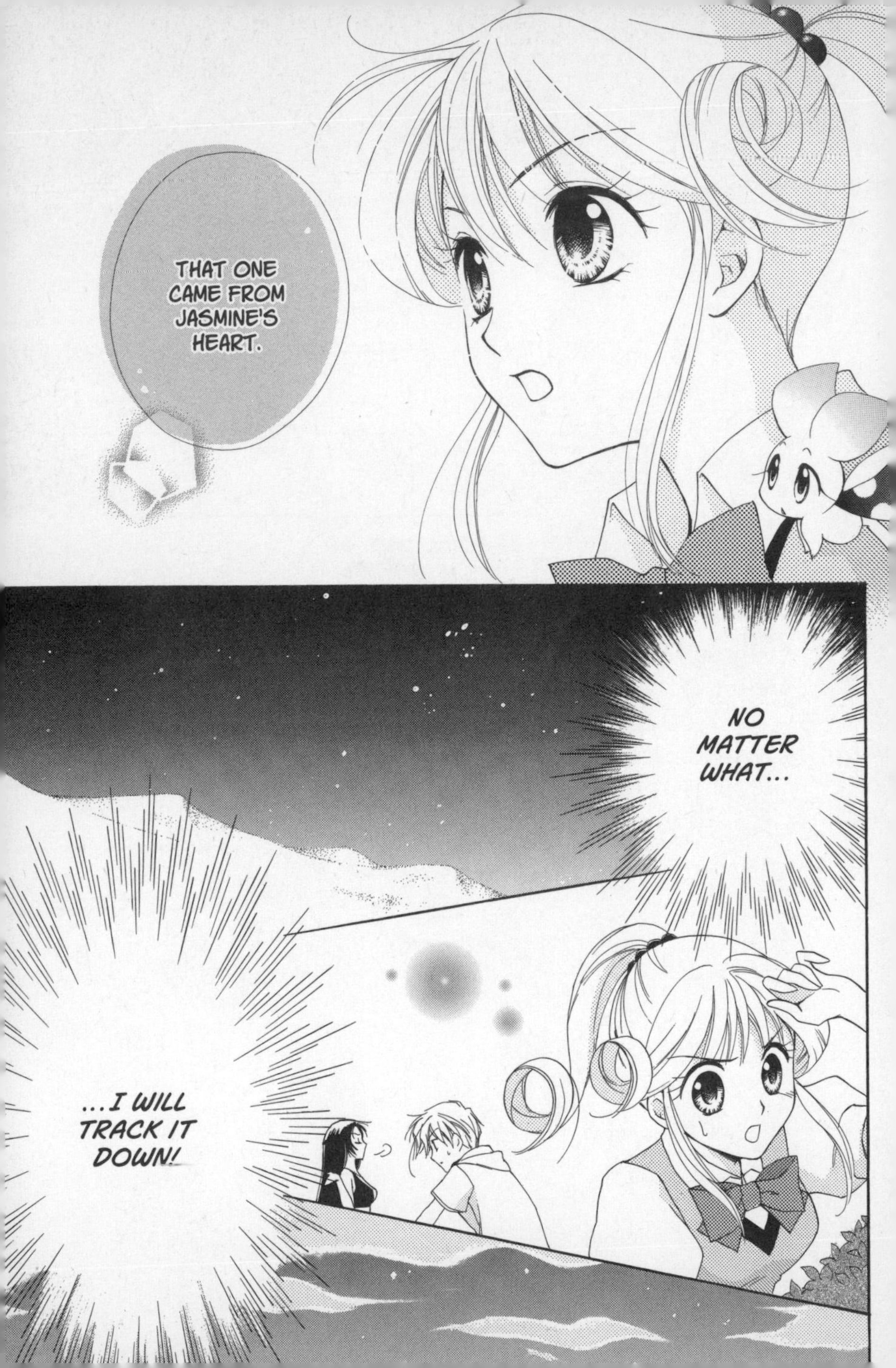
THAT ONE CAME FROM JASMINE'S HEART.
NO MATTER WHAT...
...I WILL TRACK IT DOWN!

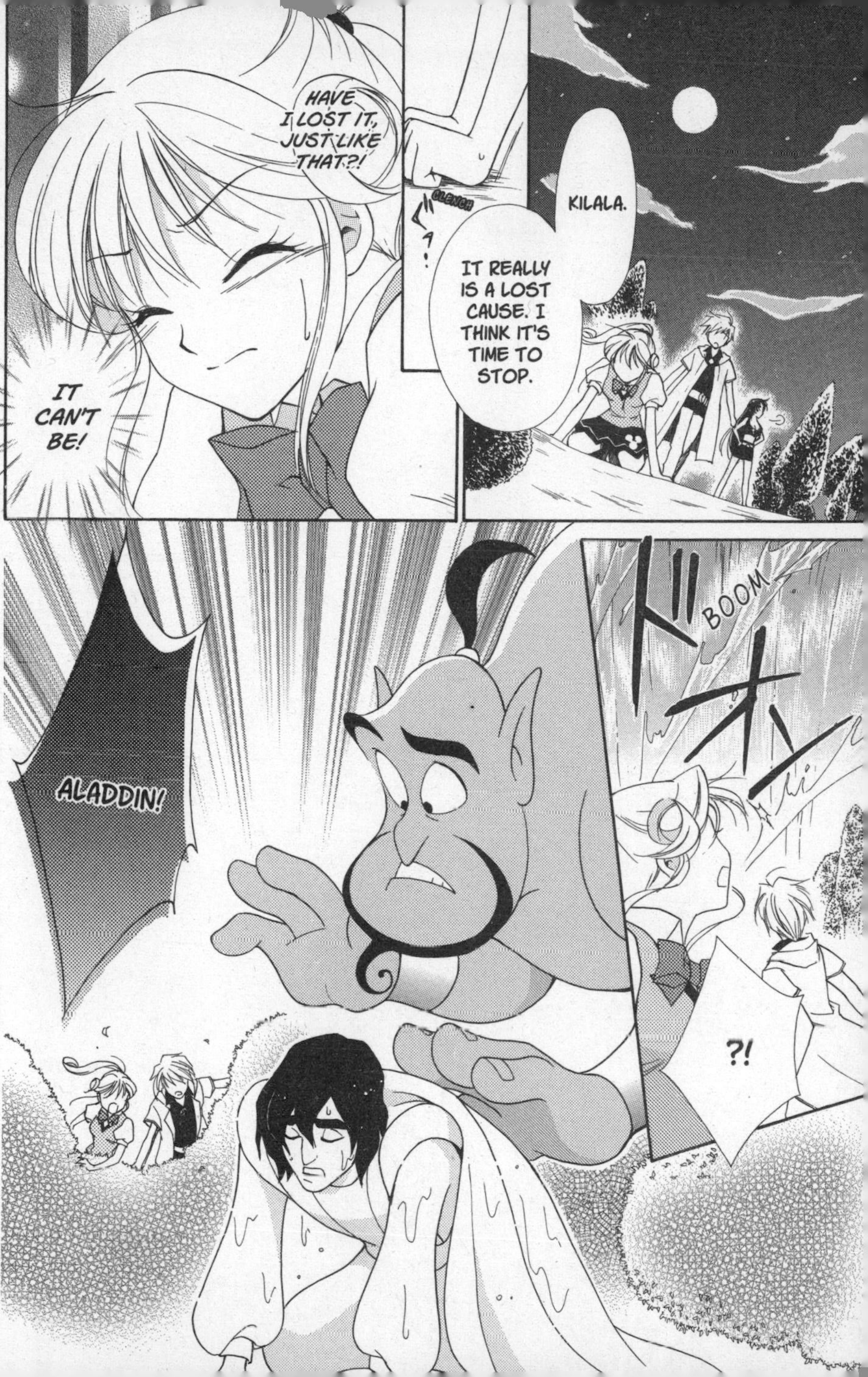
KILALA.
IT REALLY IS A LOST CAUSE. I THINK IT'S TIME TO STOP.
CLENCH
HAVE I LOST IT, JUST LIKE THAT?!
IT CAN'T BE!
BOOM
?!
ALADDIN!

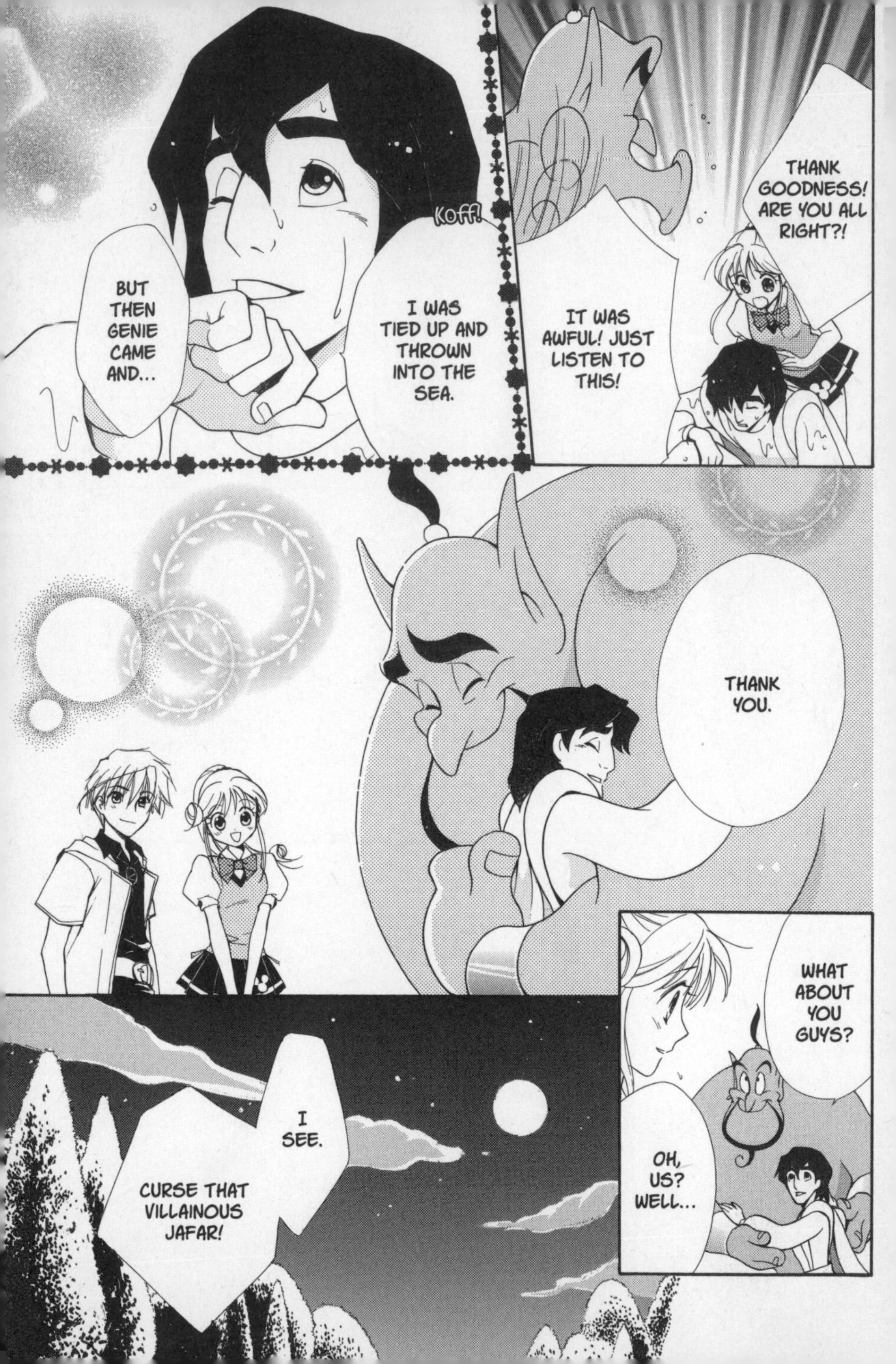
THANK GOODNESS! ARE YOU ALL RIGHT?!
IT WAS AWFUL! JUST LISTEN TO THIS!
KOFF!
I WAS TIED UP AND THROWN INTO THE SEA.
BUT THEN GENIE CAME AND...
THANK YOU.
WHAT ABOUT YOU GUYS?
OH, US? WELL...
I SEE.
CURSE THAT VILLAINOUS JAFAR!

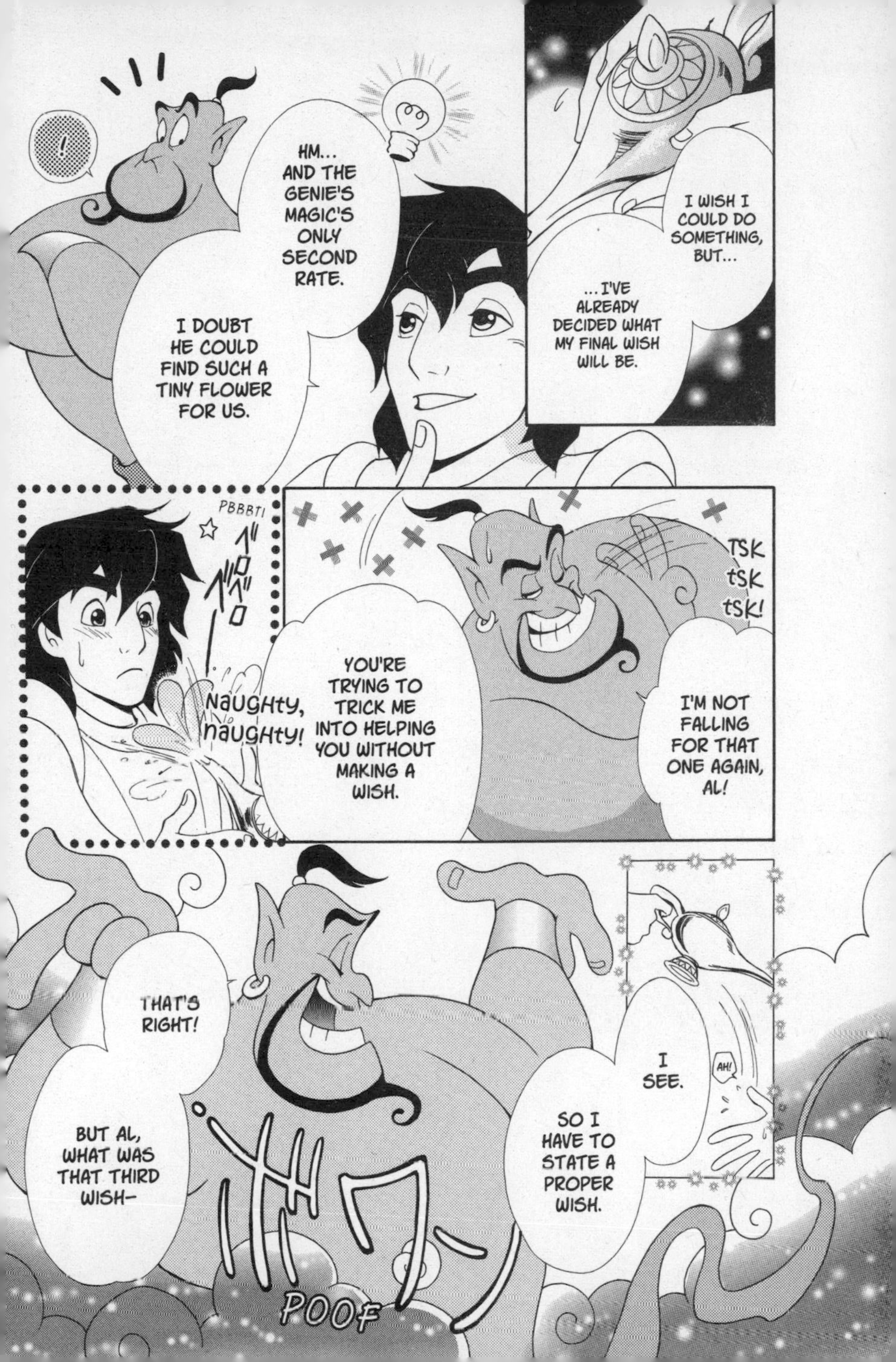
I WISH I COULD DO SOMETHING, BUT...
...I'VE ALREADY DECIDED WHAT MY FINAL WISH WILL BE.
!
HM... AND THE GENIE'S MAGIC'S ONLY SECOND RATE.
I DOUBT HE COULD FIND SUCH A TINY FLOWER FOR US.
TSK tSK tSK!
I'M NOT FALLING FOR THAT ONE AGAIN, AL!
YOU'RE TRYING TO TRICK ME INTO HELPING YOU WITHOUT MAKING A WISH.
PBBBT!
naughty, naughty!
AH!
I SEE.
SO I HAVE TO STATE A PROPER WISH.
THAT'S RIGHT!
BUT AL, WHAT WAS THAT THIRD WISH-
POOF

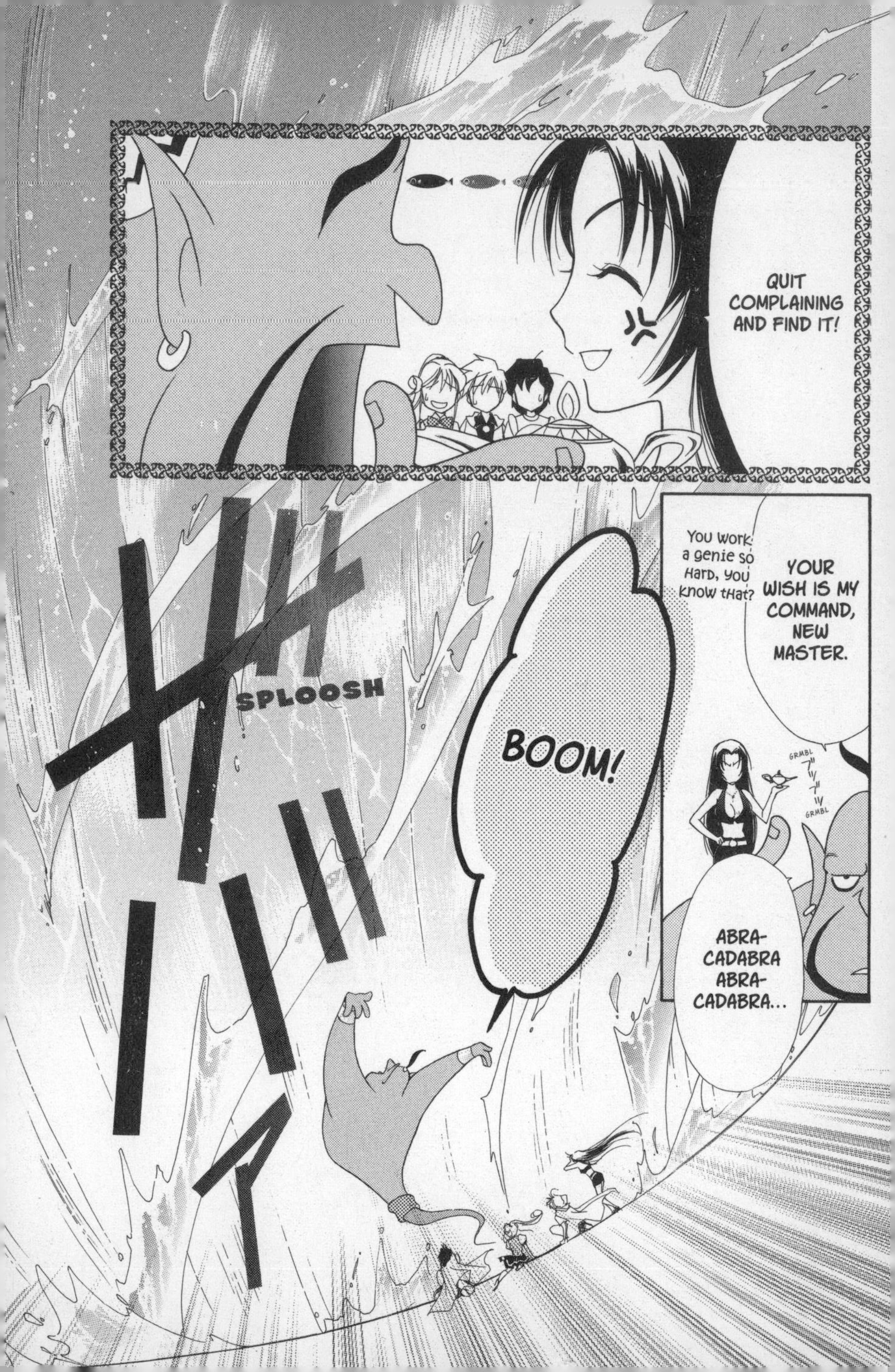
QUIT COMPLAINING AND FIND IT!
YOUR WISH IS MY COMMAND, NEW MASTER.
You work a genie so Hard, you know tHat?
GRMBL
GRMBL
ABRA-CADABRA ABRA-CADABRA...
BOOM!
SPLOOSH

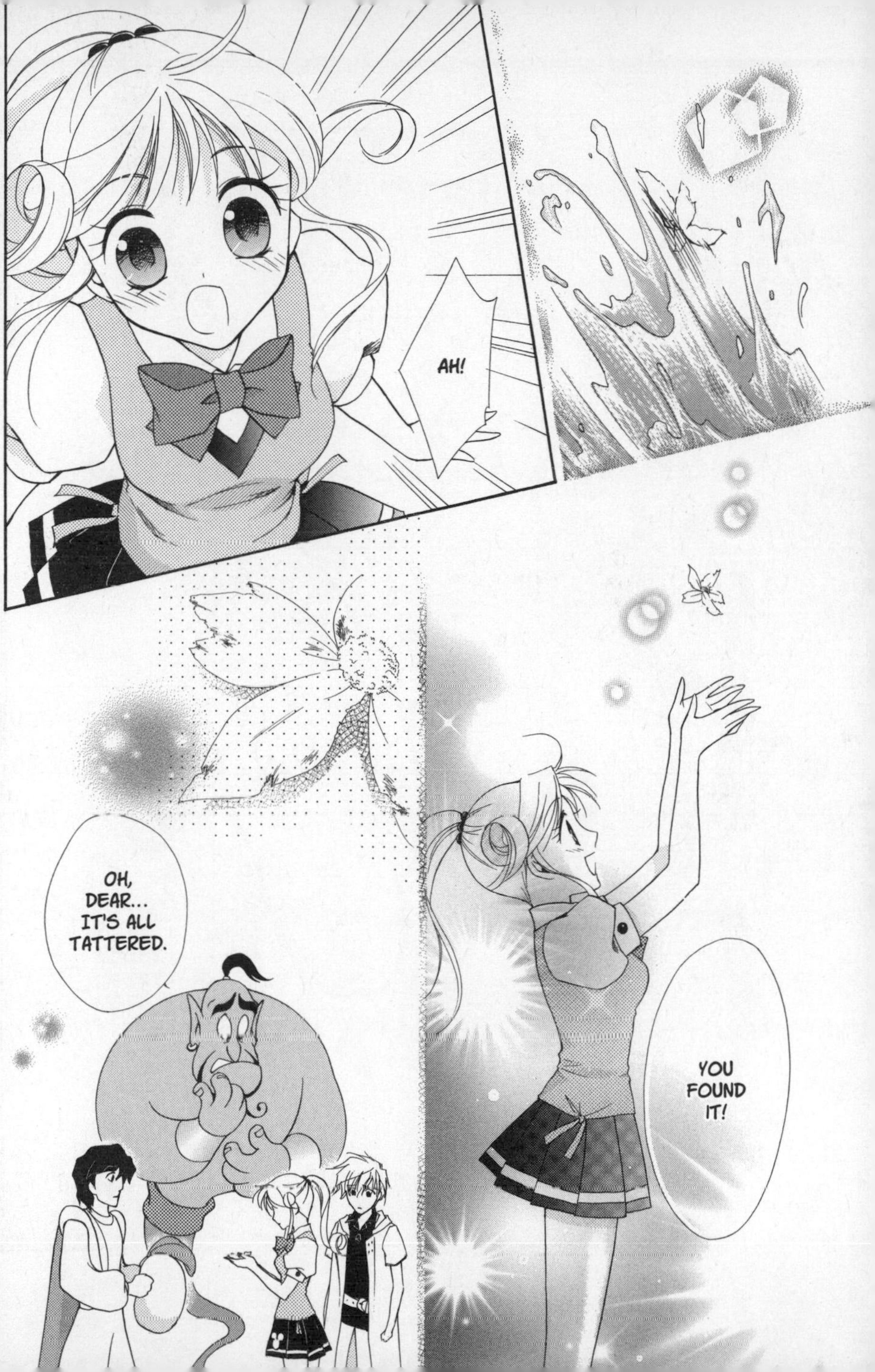
AH!
YOU FOUND IT!
OH, DEAR... IT'S ALL TATTERED.

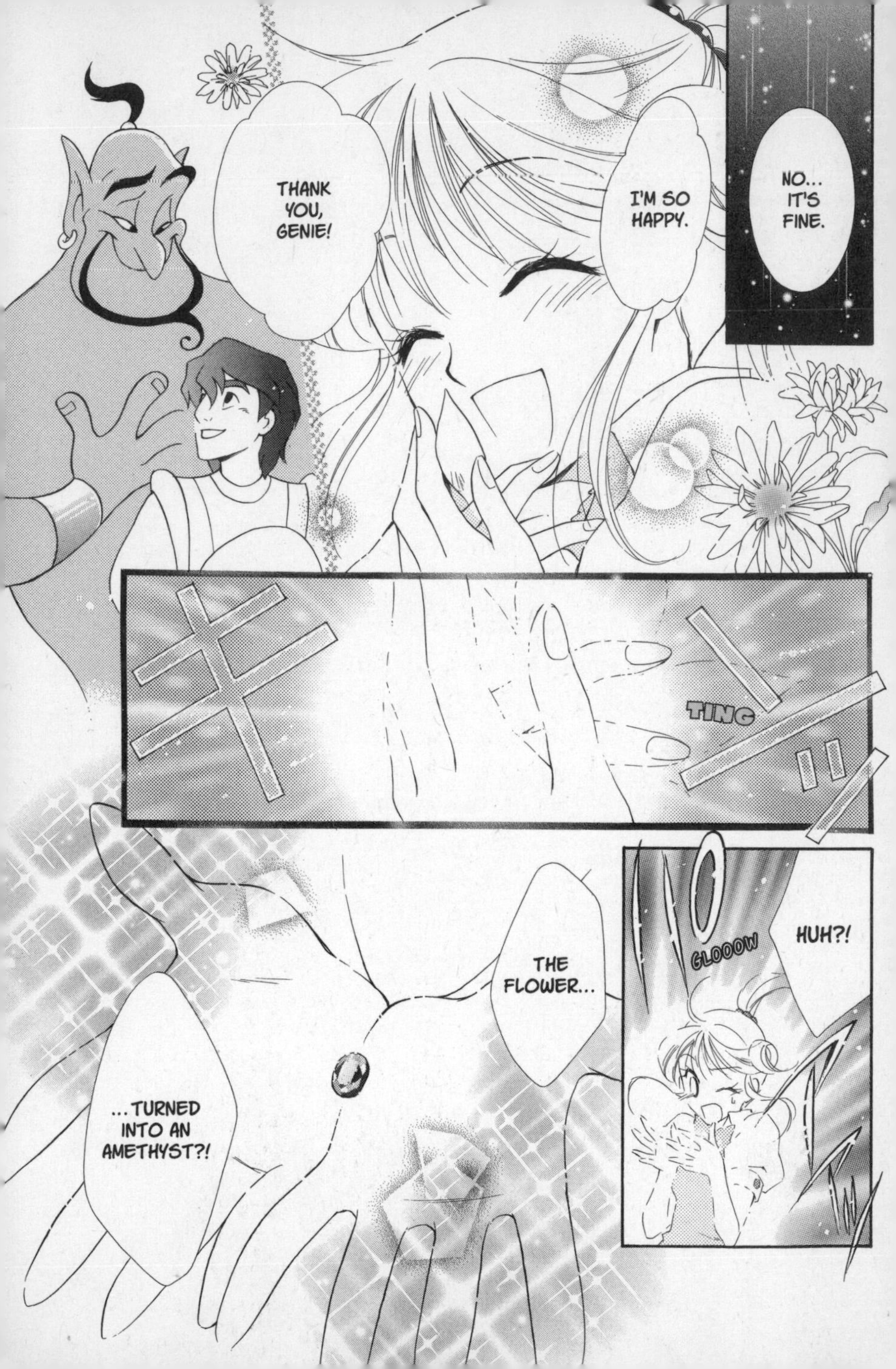
NO... IT'S FINE.
I'M SO HAPPY.
THANK YOU, GENIE!
TING
HUH?!
GLOOOW
THE FLOWER...
...TURNED INTO AN AMETHYST?!

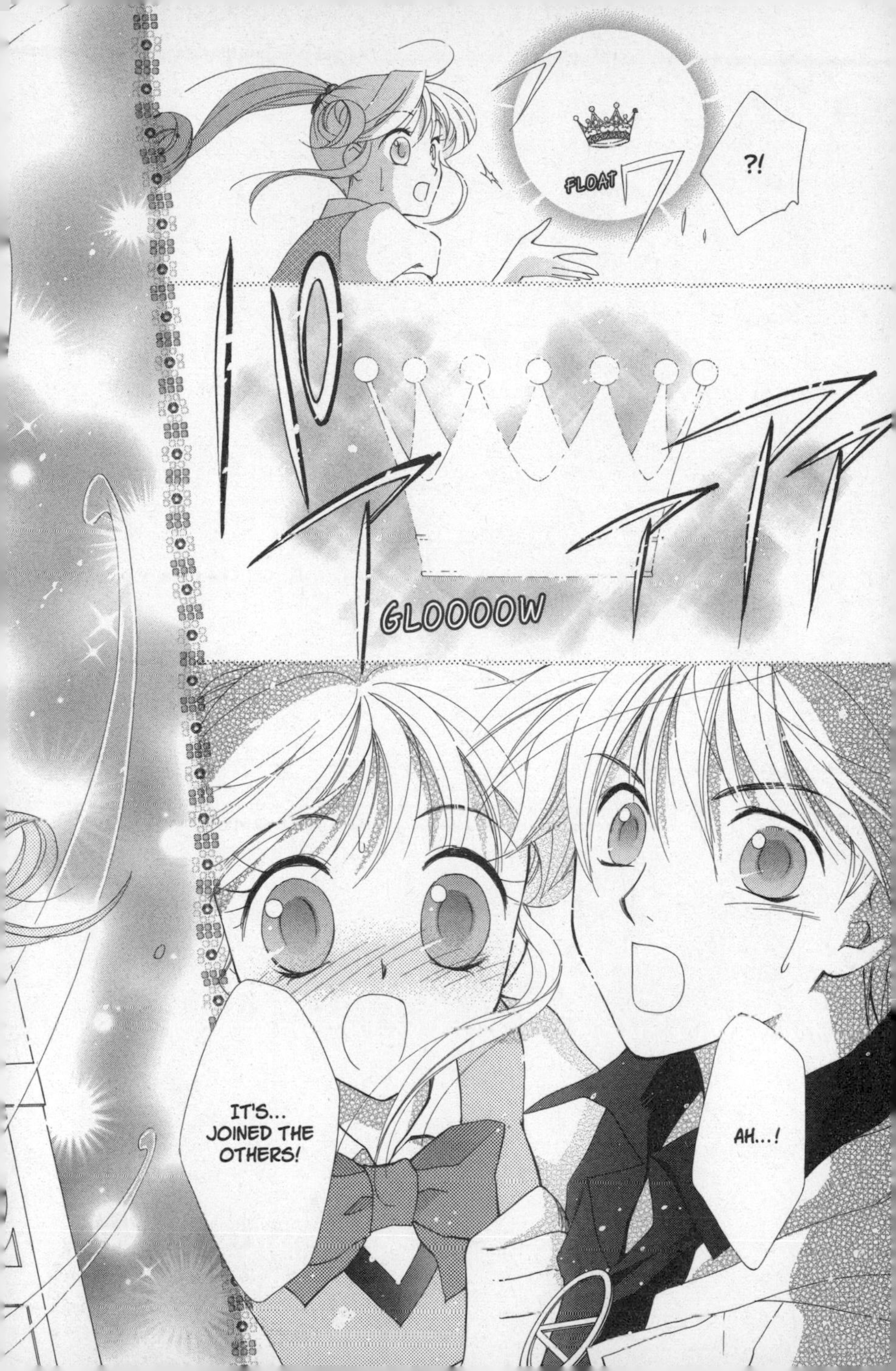
?!
FLOAT
GLOOOOW
AH...!
IT'S... JOINED THE OTHERS!

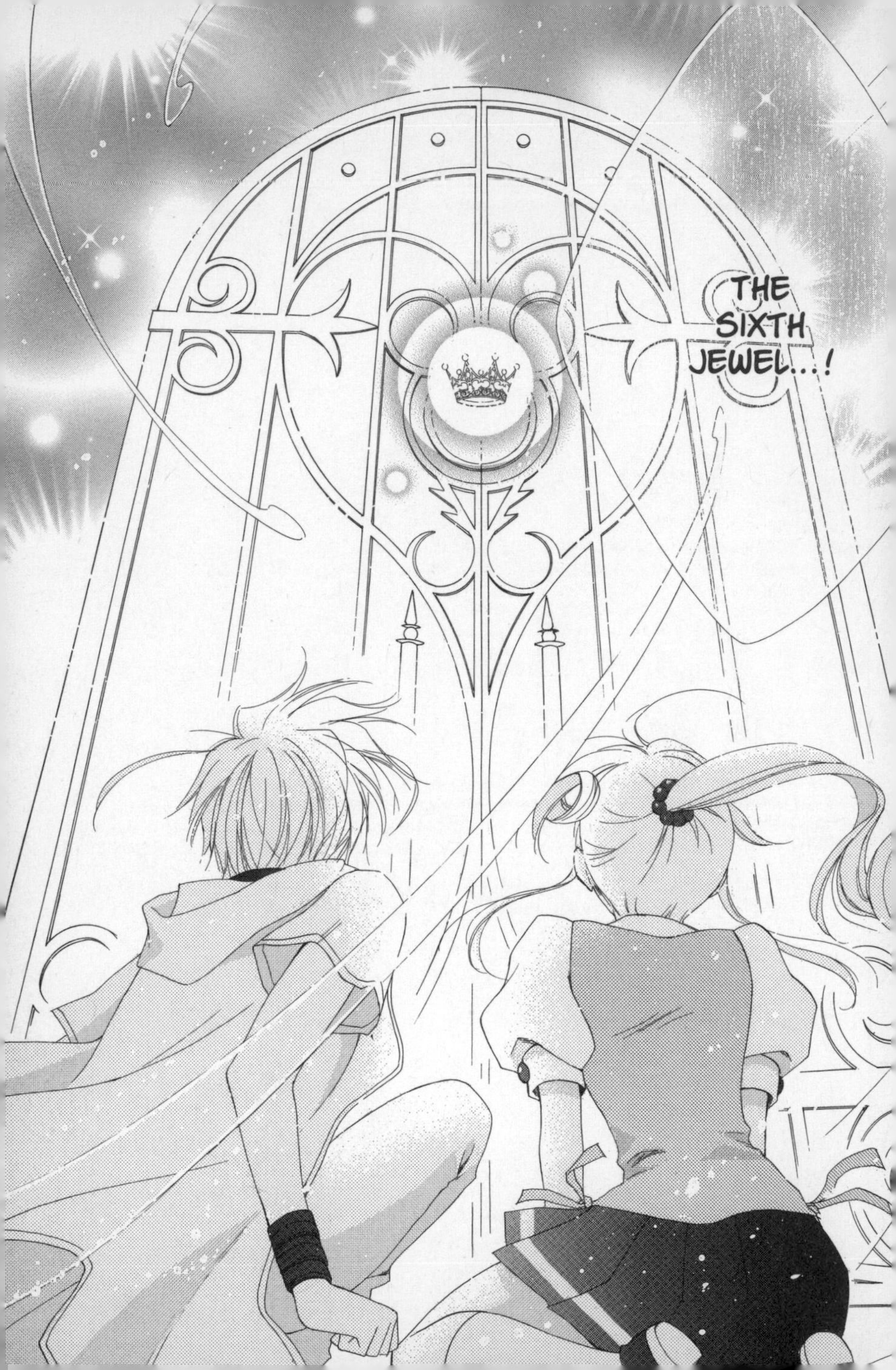
THE SIXTH JEWEL...!

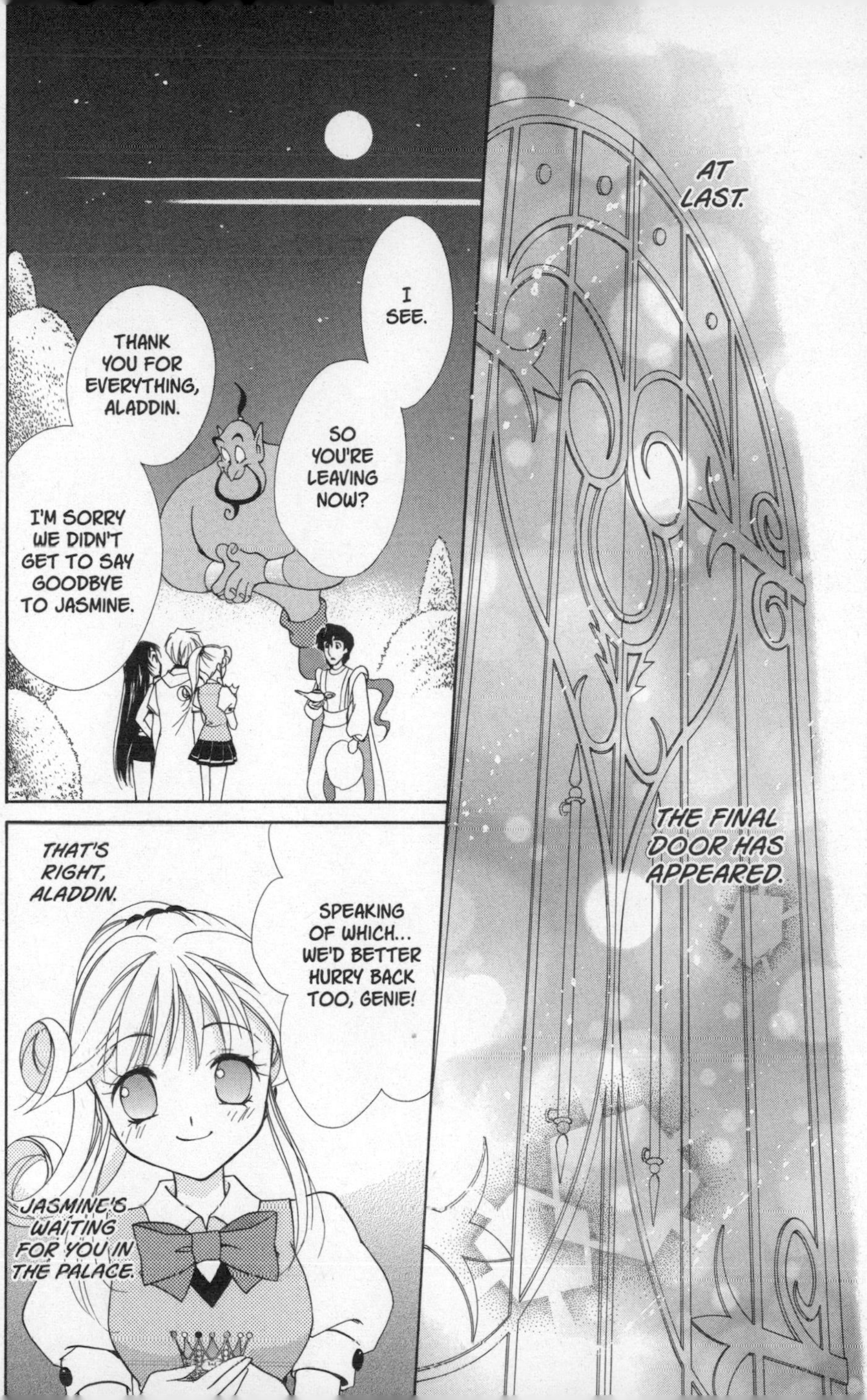
AT LAST.
THE FINAL DOOR HAS APPEARED.
I SEE.
SO YOU'RE LEAVING NOW?
THANK YOU FOR EVERYTHING, ALADDIN.
I'M SORRY WE DIDN'T GET TO SAY GOODBYE TO JASMINE.
SPEAKING OF WHICH... WE'D BETTER HURRY BACK TOO, GENIE!
THAT'S RIGHT, ALADDIN.
JASMINE'S WAITING FOR YOU IN THE PALACE.

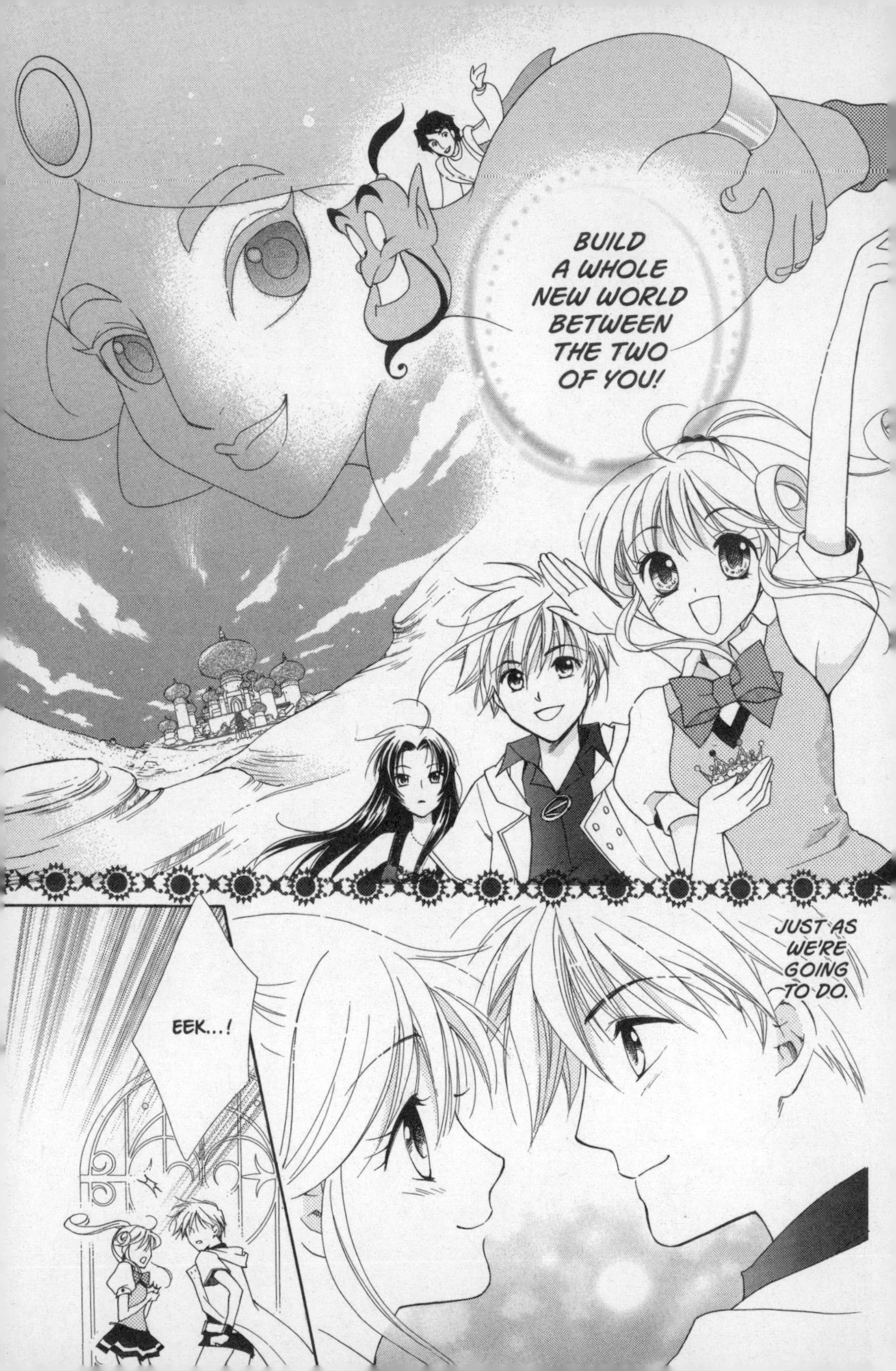
BUILD A WHOLE NEW WORLD BETWEEN THE TWO OF YOU!
JUST AS WE'RE GOING TO DO.
EEK...!

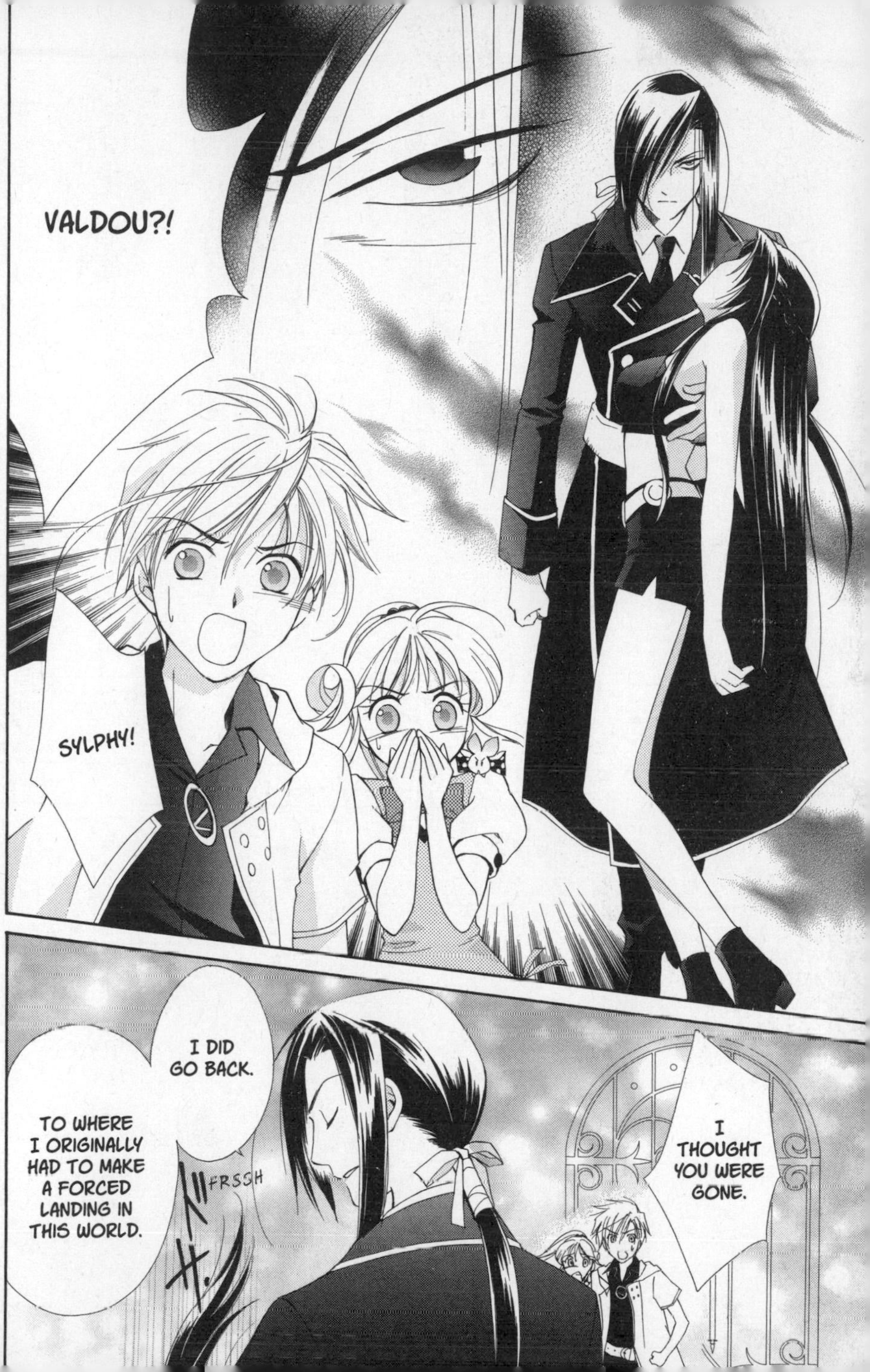
VALDOU?!
SYLPHY!
I THOUGHT YOU WERE GONE.
I DID GO BACK.
TO WHERE I ORIGINALLY HAD TO MAKE A FORCED LANDING IN THIS WORLD.
FRSSH

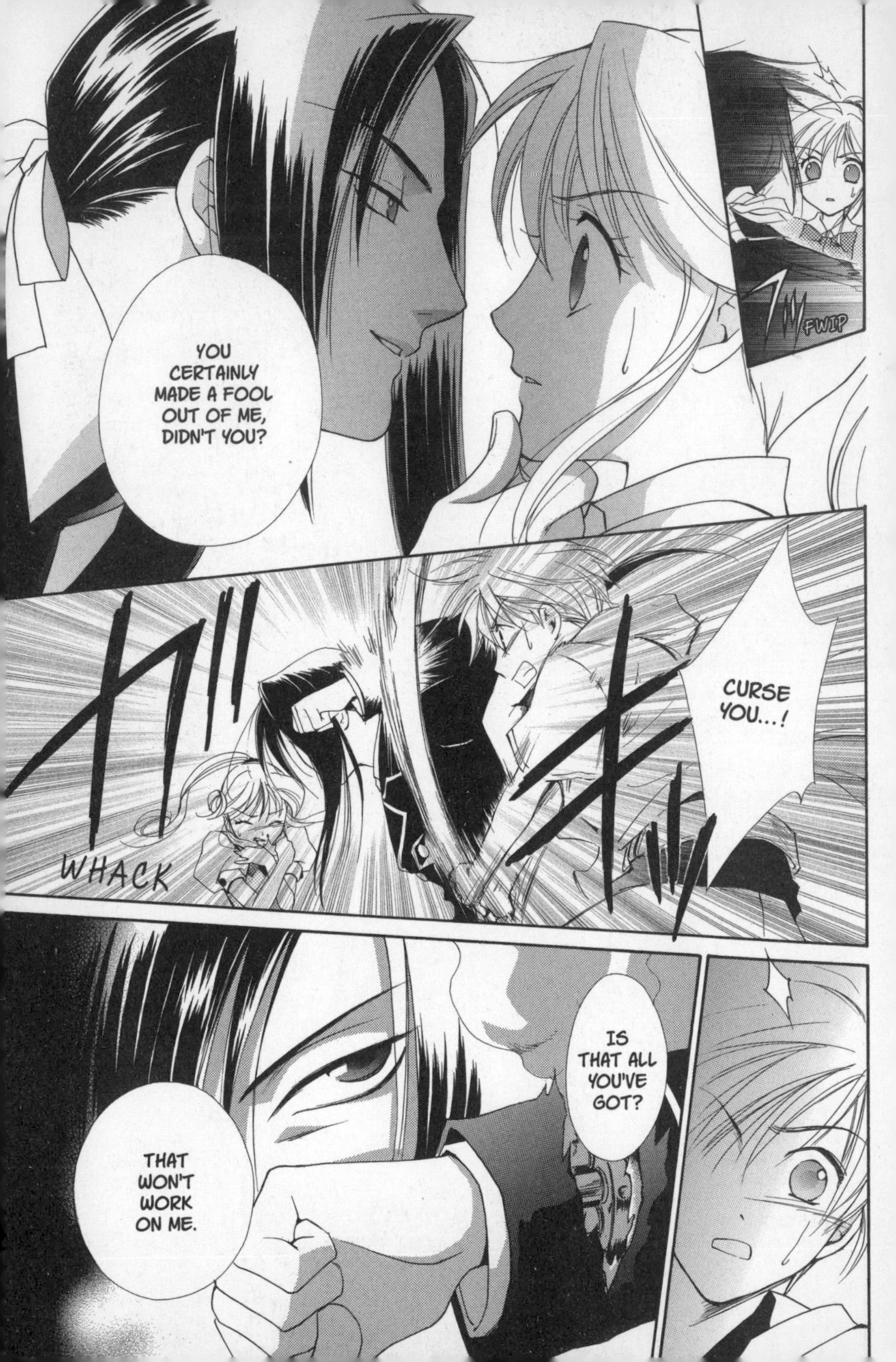
FWIP
YOU CERTAINLY MADE A FOOL OUT OF ME, DIDN'T YOU?
CURSE YOU...!
WHACK
IS THAT ALL YOU'VE GOT?
THAT WON'T WORK ON ME.

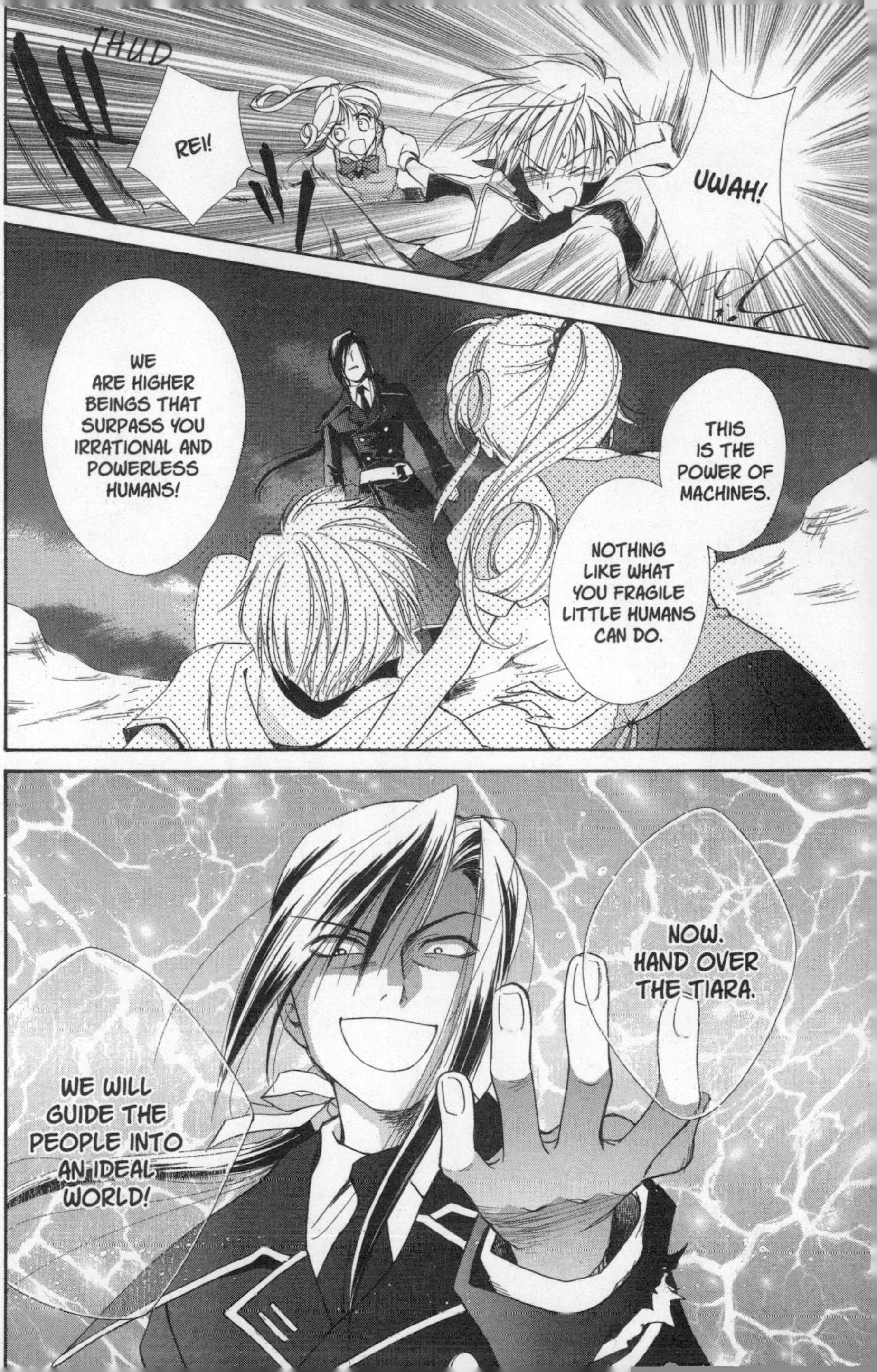
UWAH!
THUD
REI!
THIS IS THE POWER OF MACHINES.
NOTHING LIKE WHAT YOU FRAGILE LITTLE HUMANS CAN DO.
WE ARE HIGHER BEINGS THAT SURPASS YOU IRRATIONAL AND POWERLESS HUMANS!
NOW. HAND OVER THE TIARA.
WE WILL GUIDE THE PEOPLE INTO AN IDEAL WORLD!

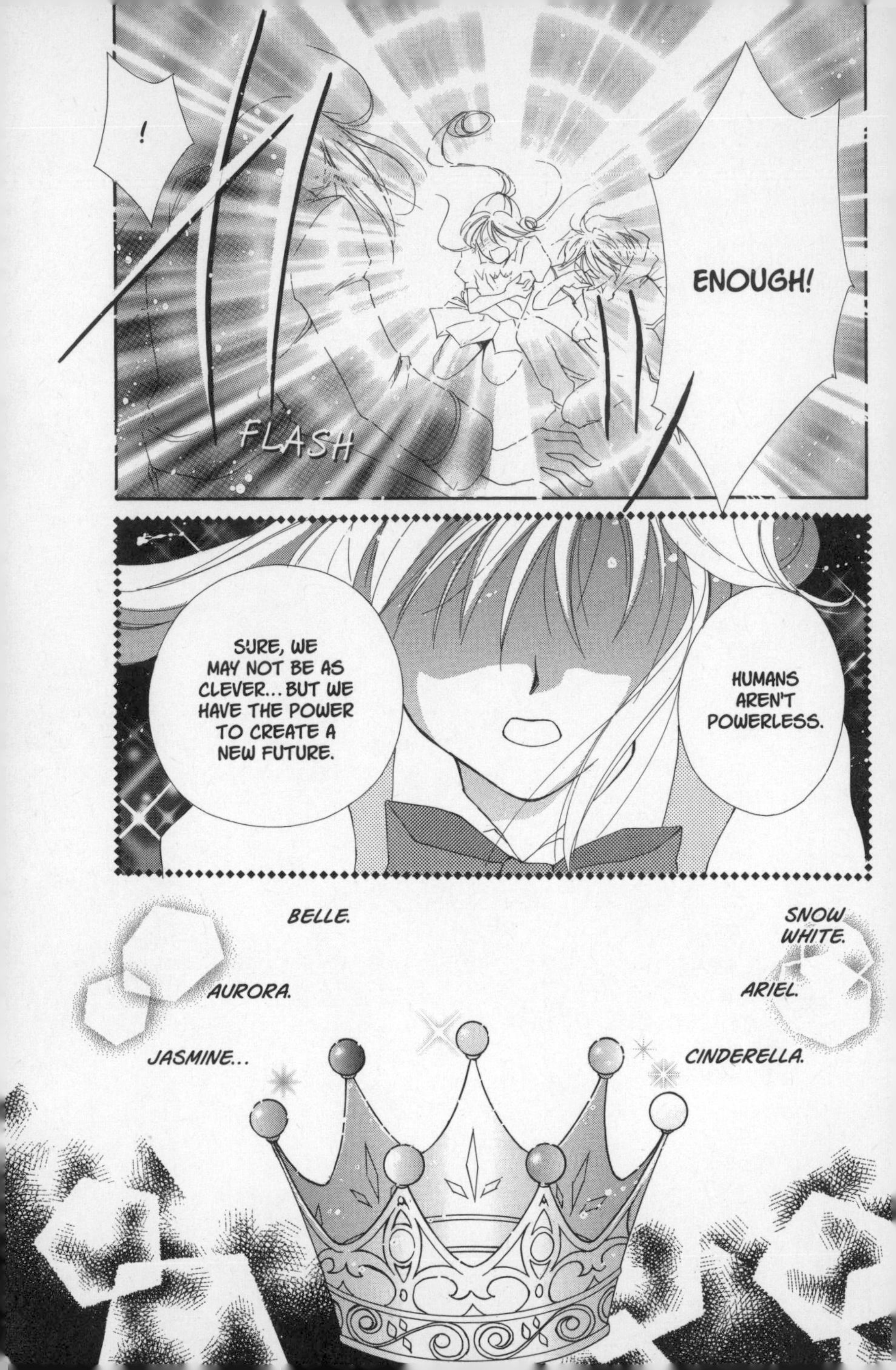
ENOUGH!
!
FLASH
HUMANS AREN'T POWERLESS.
SURE, WE MAY NOT BE AS CLEVER... BUT WE HAVE THE POWER TO CREATE A NEW FUTURE.
SNOW WHITE.
BELLE.
ARIEL.
AURORA.
CINDERELLA.
JASMINE...

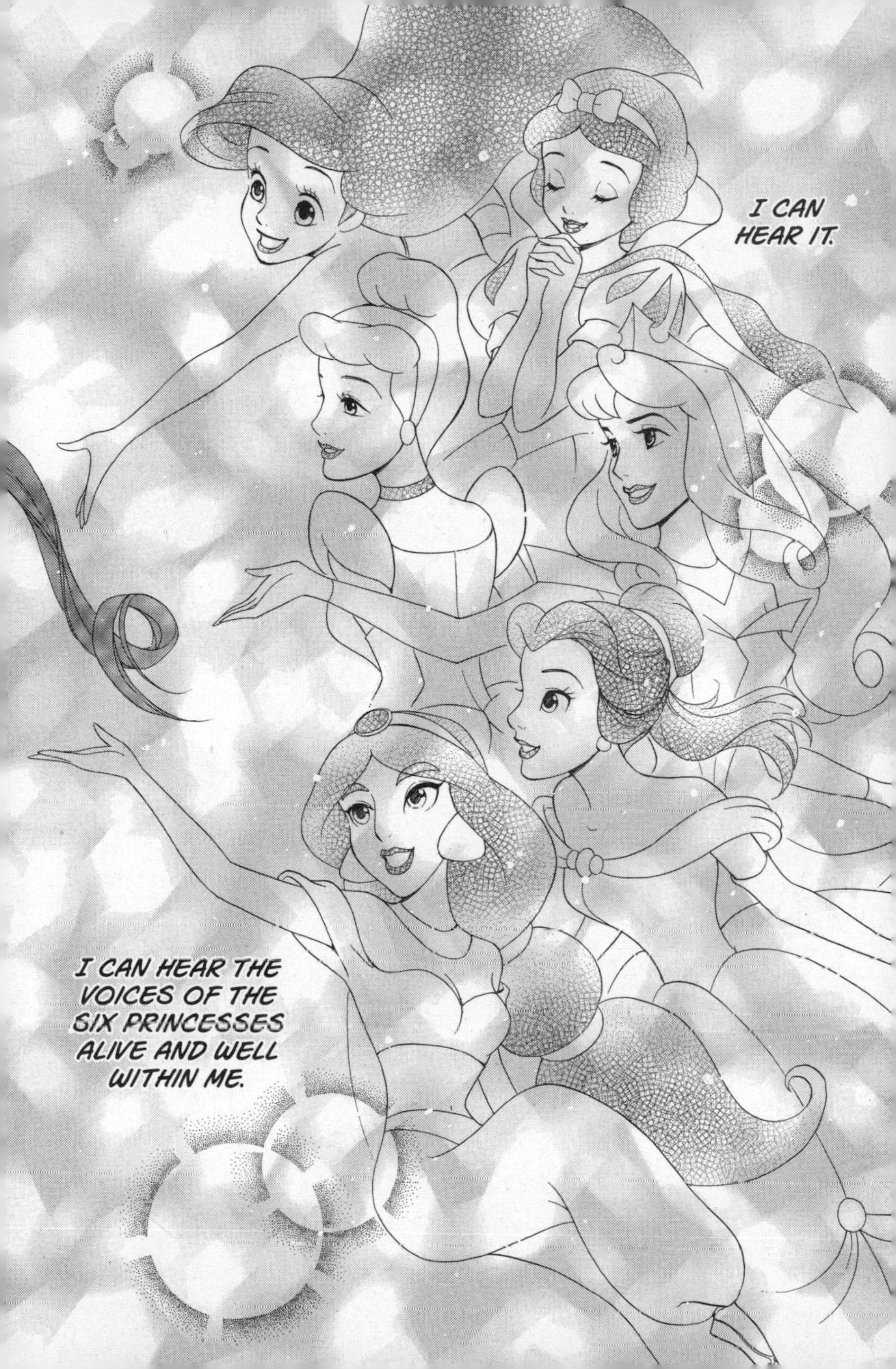
I CAN HEAR IT.
I CAN HEAR THE VOICES OF THE SIX PRINCESSES ALIVE AND WELL WITHIN ME.

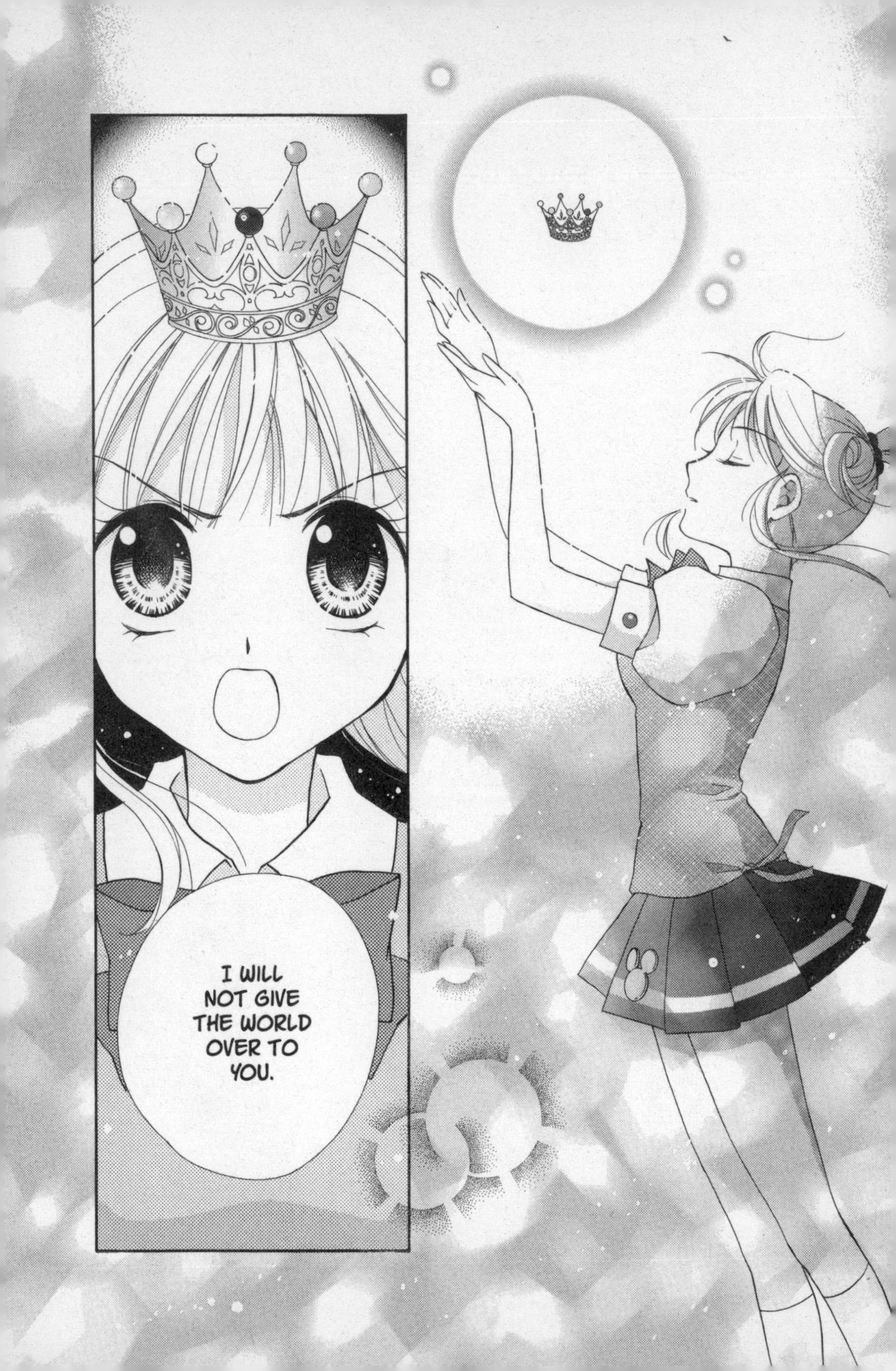
I WILL NOT GIVE THE WORLD OVER TO YOU.

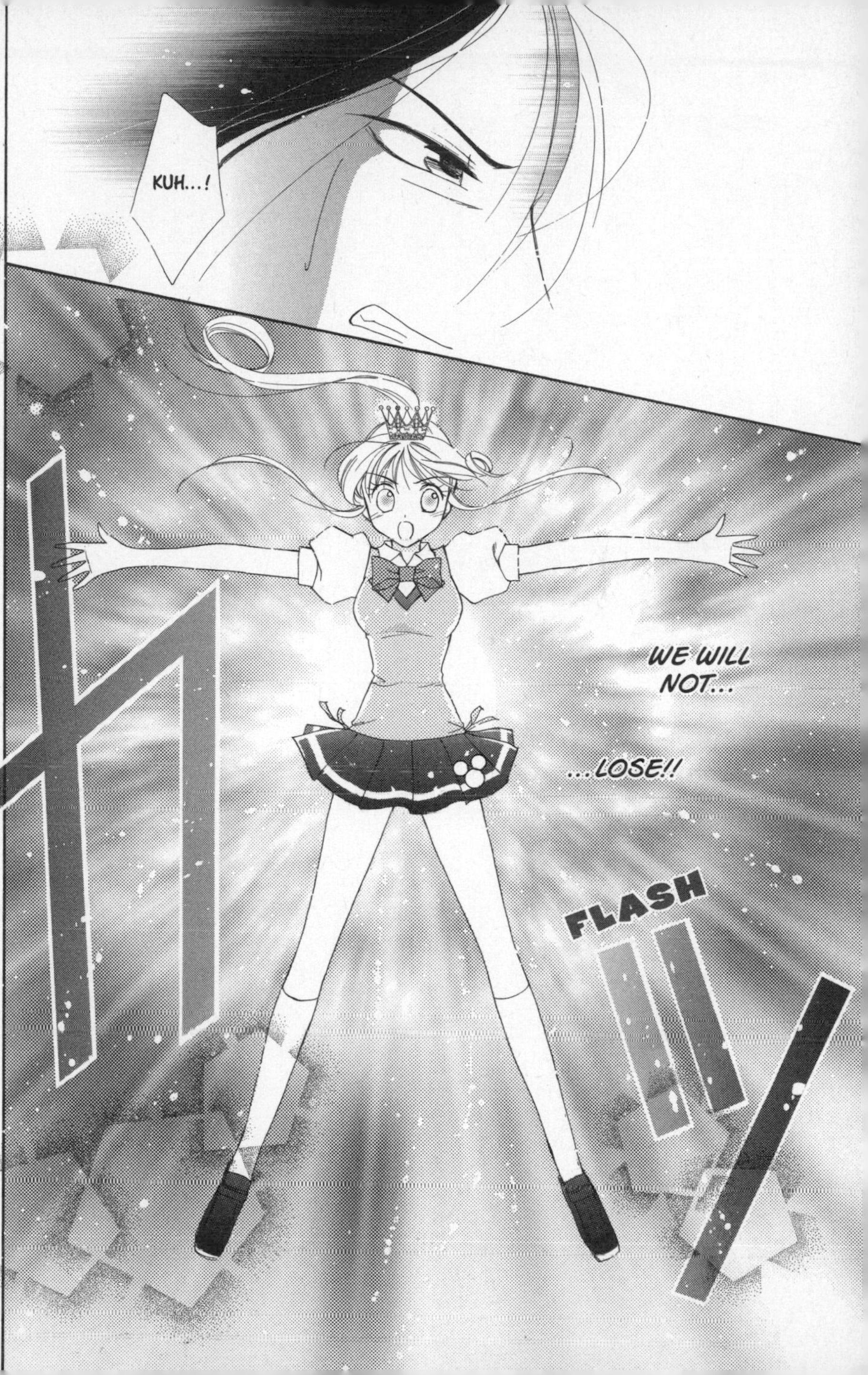
KUH...!
WE WILL NOT...
...LOSE!!
FLASH

HELLO! THIS IS RIKA TANAKA, THE AUTHOR OF THIS STORY. "KILALA PRINCESS" IS NOW AT THE FINAL VOLUME. THE TIME I SPENT WITH KILALA, REI, AND ALL THE PRINCESSES MADE MY HEART DANCE AND WAS FULL OF MOMENTS THAT FELT LIKE SOMETHING OUT OF A DREAM.

THERE WAS THE KIND-HEARTED SNOW WHITE; TOMBOYISH FREE SPIRIT ARIEL; ENDLESSLY POSITIVE AND OPTIMISTIC CINDERELLA; ELEGANT BEAUTY AURORA; INTELLIGENT AND INDEPENDENT BELLE; AND ARDENTLY WISHING TO SEE THE OUTSIDE WORLD JASMINE. EACH OF THESE GIRLS WAS UNIQUE IN HER OWN WAY, WHICH MADE WRITING THIS STORY A WHOLE LOT OF FUN. ☆ THINKING BACK ON IT NOW, I FEEL LIKE I WAS TRAVELING TO THE WORLDS OF THE PRINCESSES RIGHT ALONGSIDE KILALA THIS WHOLE TIME...

KILALA WILL GET THE SEVENTH JEWEL AND BECOME THE SEVENTH PRINCESS SOON ENOUGH. THIS IS "THE END" FOR OUR STORY, BUT ONLY THE START TO HER LIFE AS A PRINCESS. I'M SURE SHE'LL LEAD THE UNCONVENTIONAL AND HIGHLY INDEPENDENT PRINCESS LIFE THAT IS JUST IN LINE WITH HOW SHE DOES THINGS. (IT MIGHT BE EVEN A LITTLE FRIGHTENING AT TIMES!) GOOD LUCK TO THE NEW PRINCESS KILALA!!

BY THE WAY, IT'S BEEN DECIDED THAT "KILALA PRINCESS" WILL BE ADAPTED INTO A NOVEL! IT MIGHT TELL THE STORY OF KILALA AND REI IN A SLIGHTLY DIFFERENT FLAVOR FROM WHAT WE SAW IN THE COMIC. PLEASE LOOK FORWARD TO IT. ☆

ON ONE FINAL NOTE, I'D LIKE TO GIVE MY MOST HEARTFELT THANKS TO NAO KODAKA-SENSEI, KAYO ISOMURA-SAMA FROM THE EDITORIAL DEPARTMENT, AND EVERYONE ELSE INVOLVED IN THE TIRELESS EFFORT IT TOOK TO PUT TOGETHER "KILALA PRINCESS". THANK YOU VERY VERY MUCH.

RIKA TANAKA

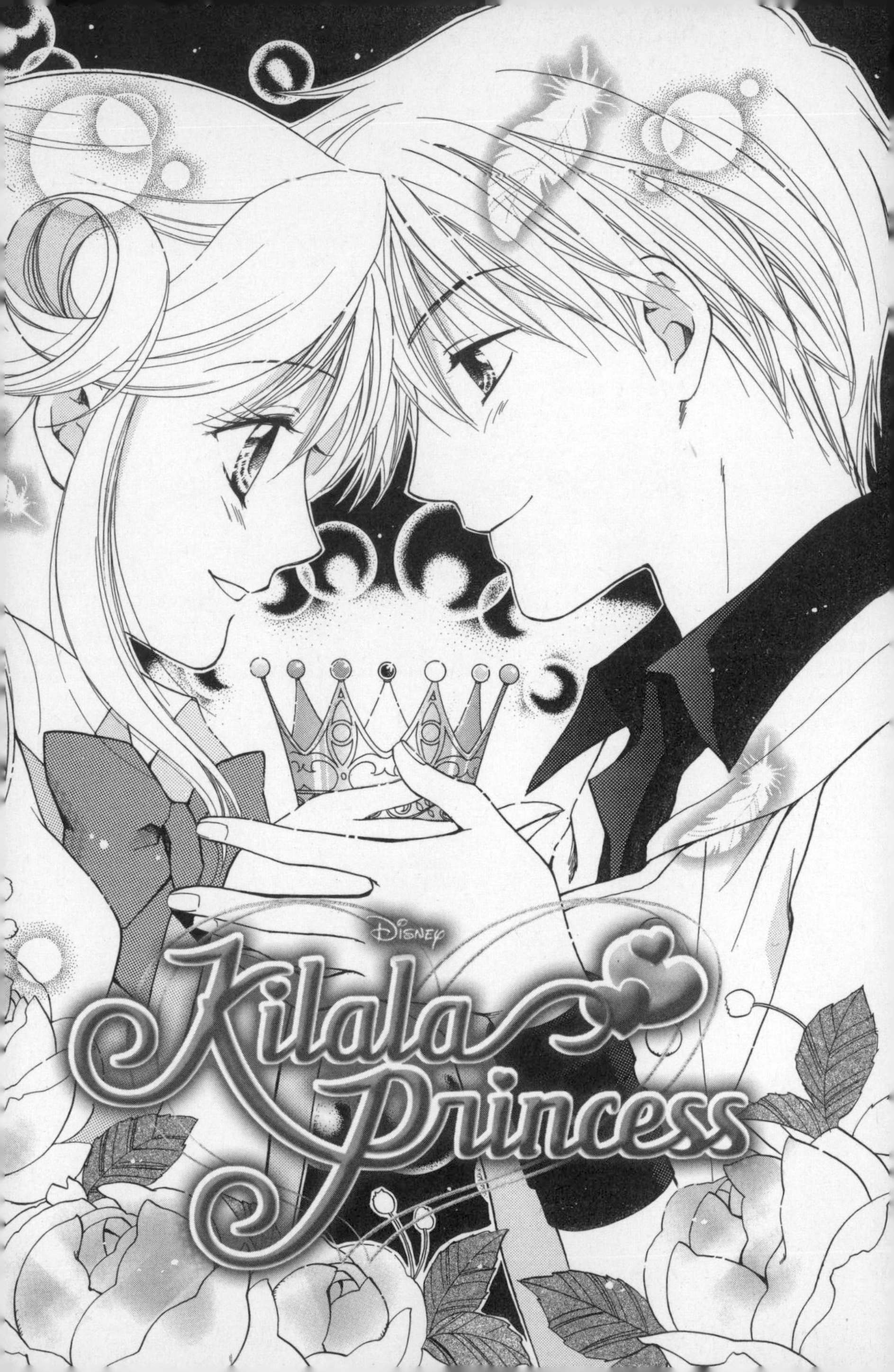
Disney
Kilala Princess

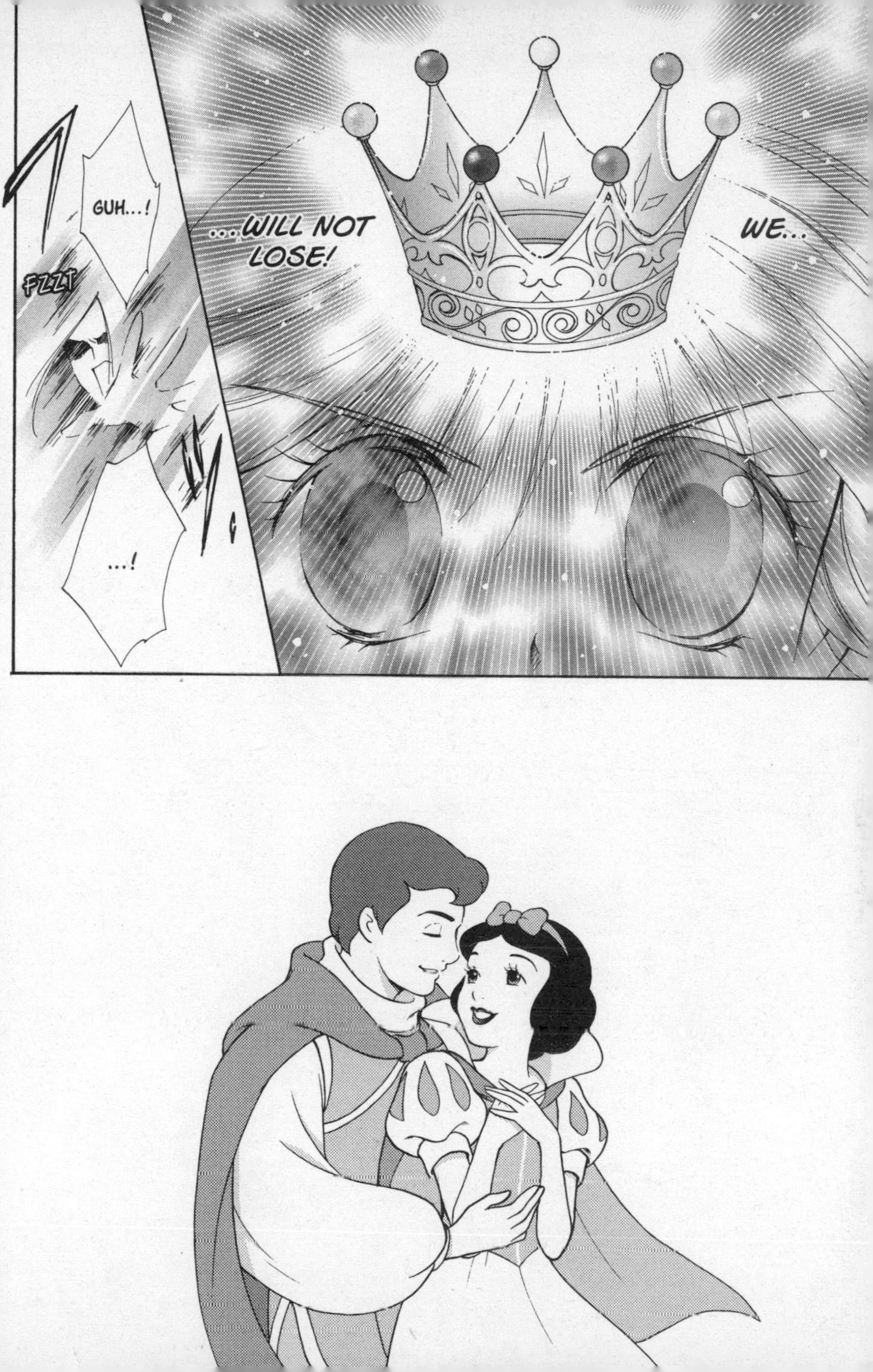
WE...
...WILL NOT LOSE!
GUH...!
FZZT
...!

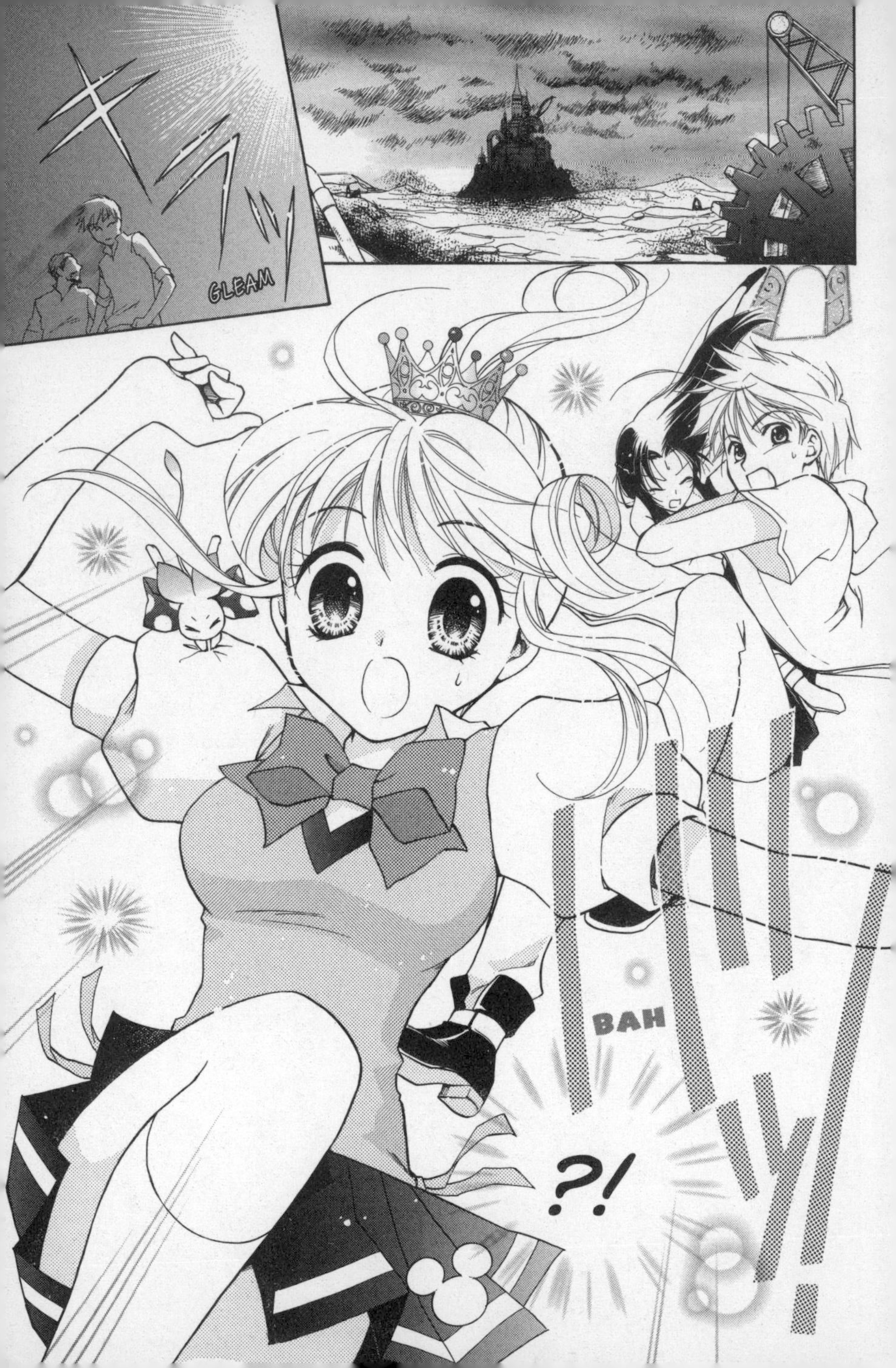
キラッ
GLEAM
BAH
?!

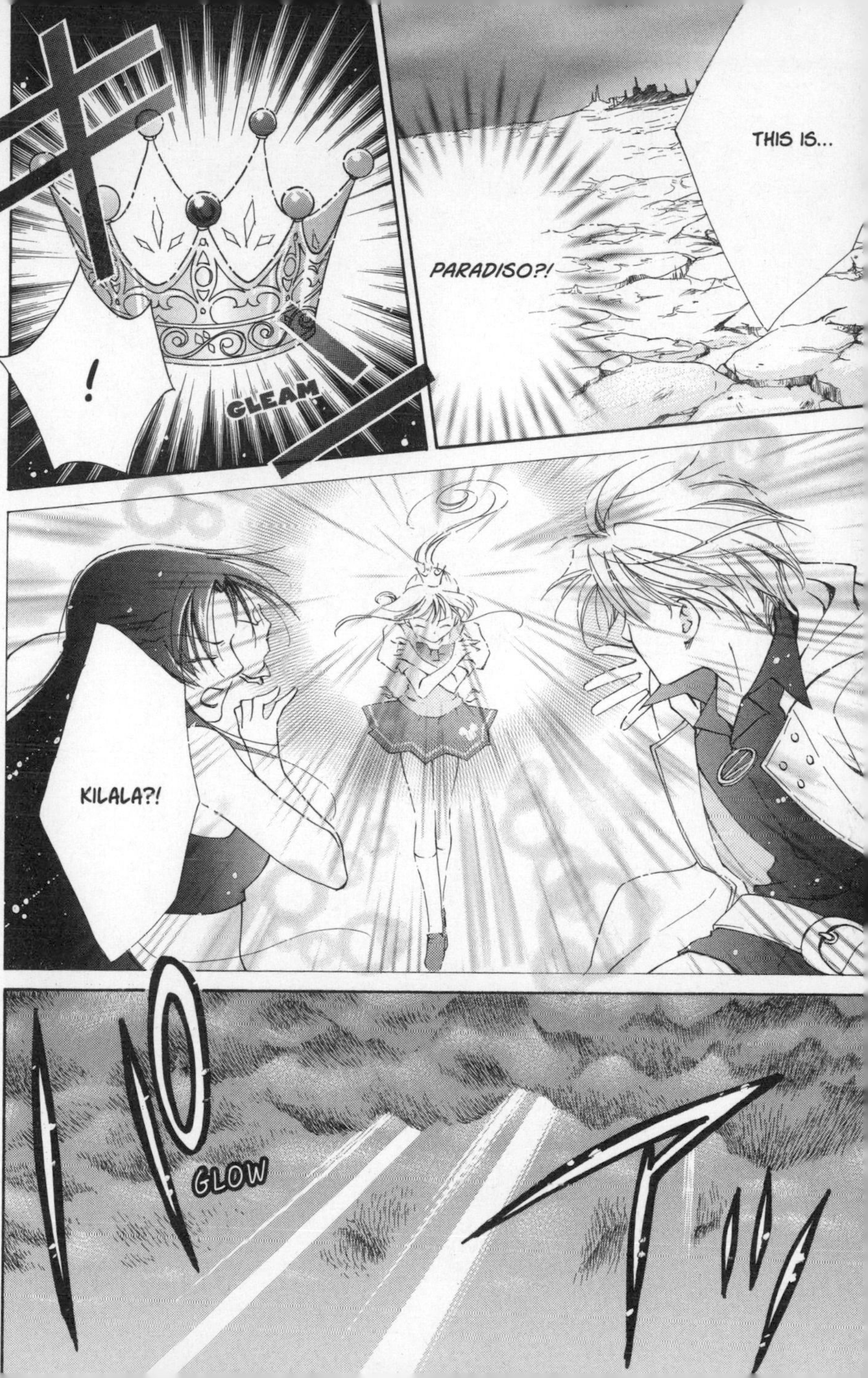
THIS IS...
PARADISO?!
!
GLEAM
KILALA?!
GLOW

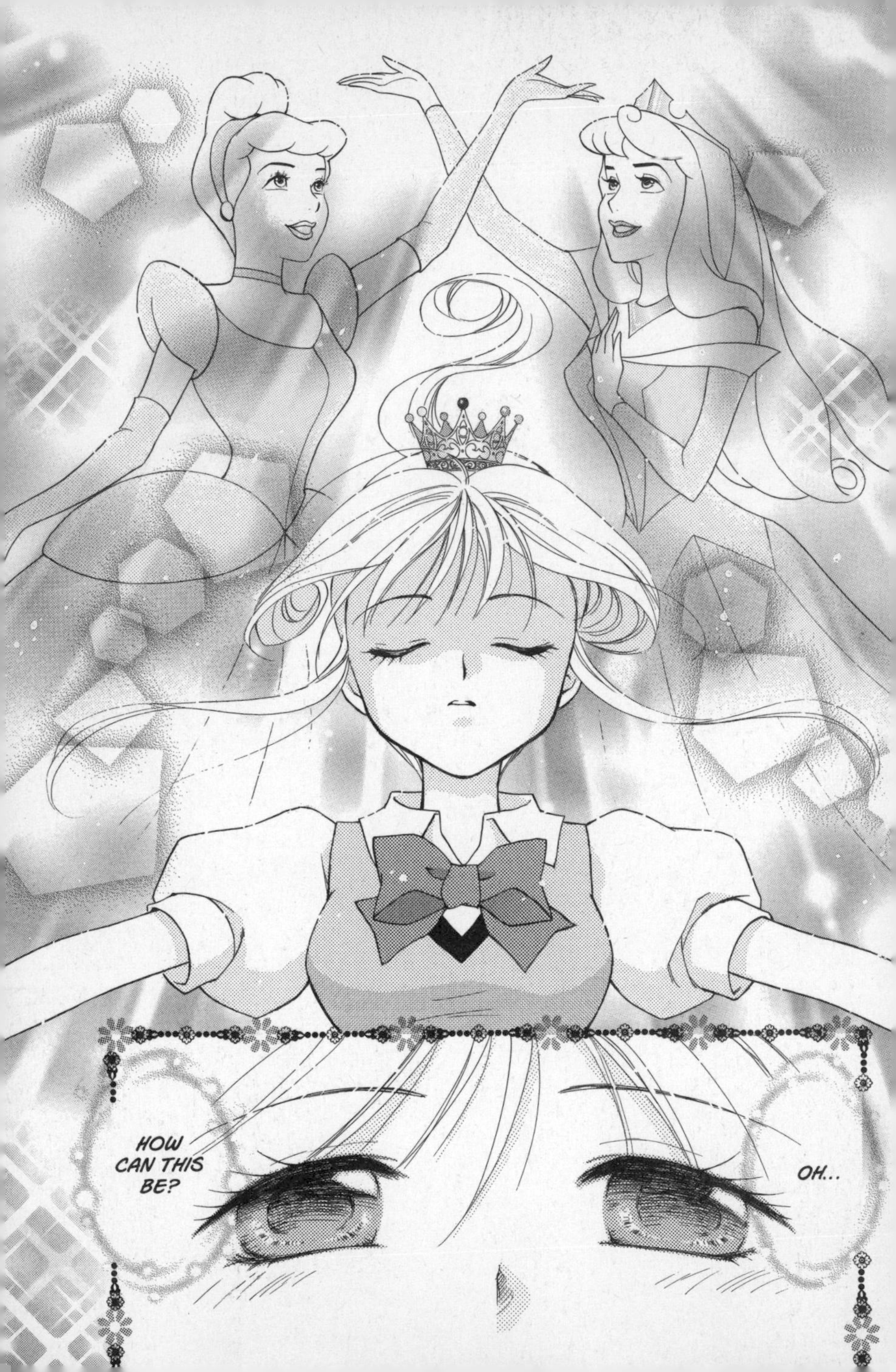
OH...
HOW CAN THIS BE?

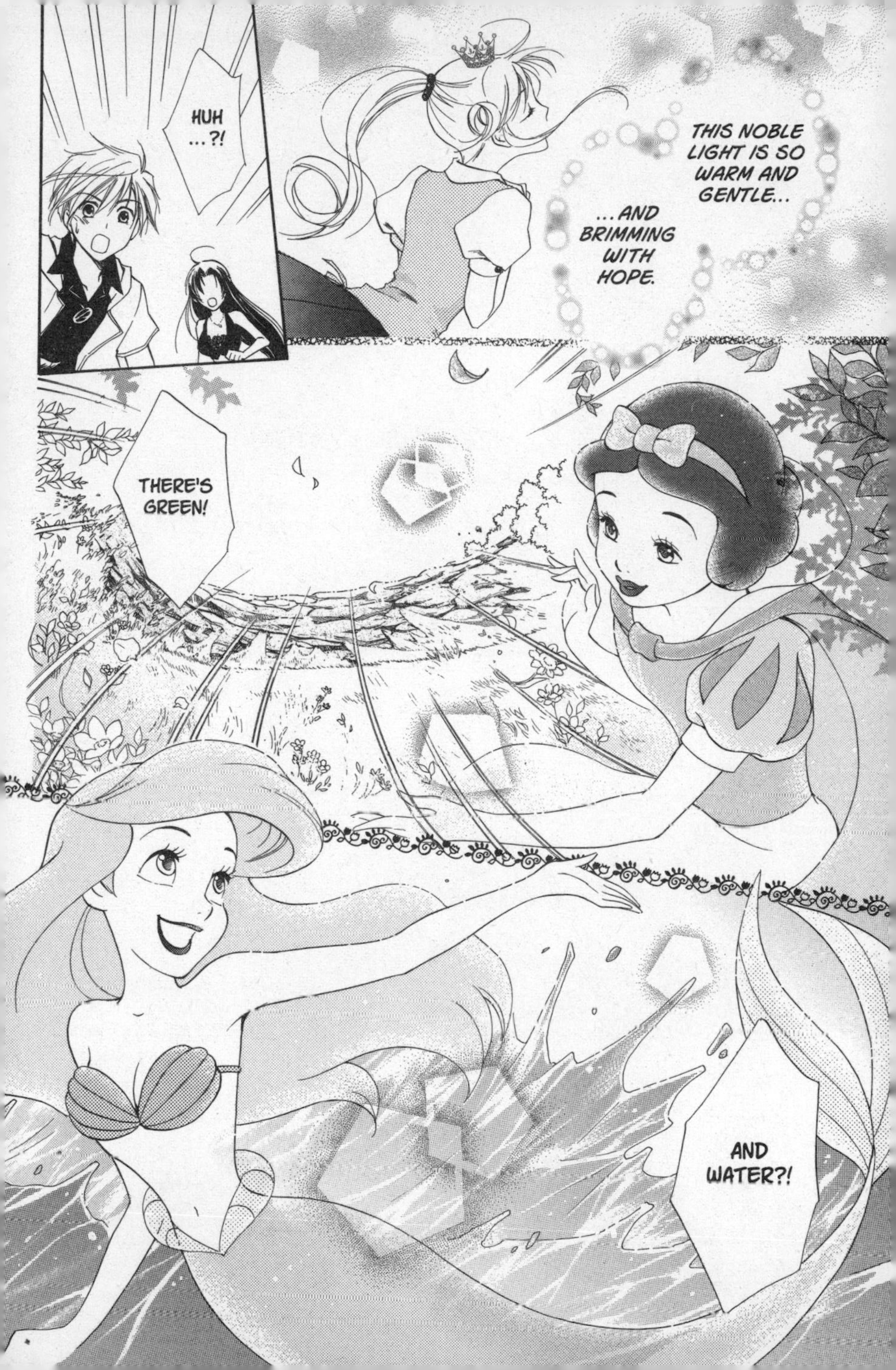
THIS NOBLE LIGHT IS SO WARM AND GENTLE...
...AND BRIMMING WITH HOPE.
HUH ...?!
THERE'S GREEN!
AND WATER?!

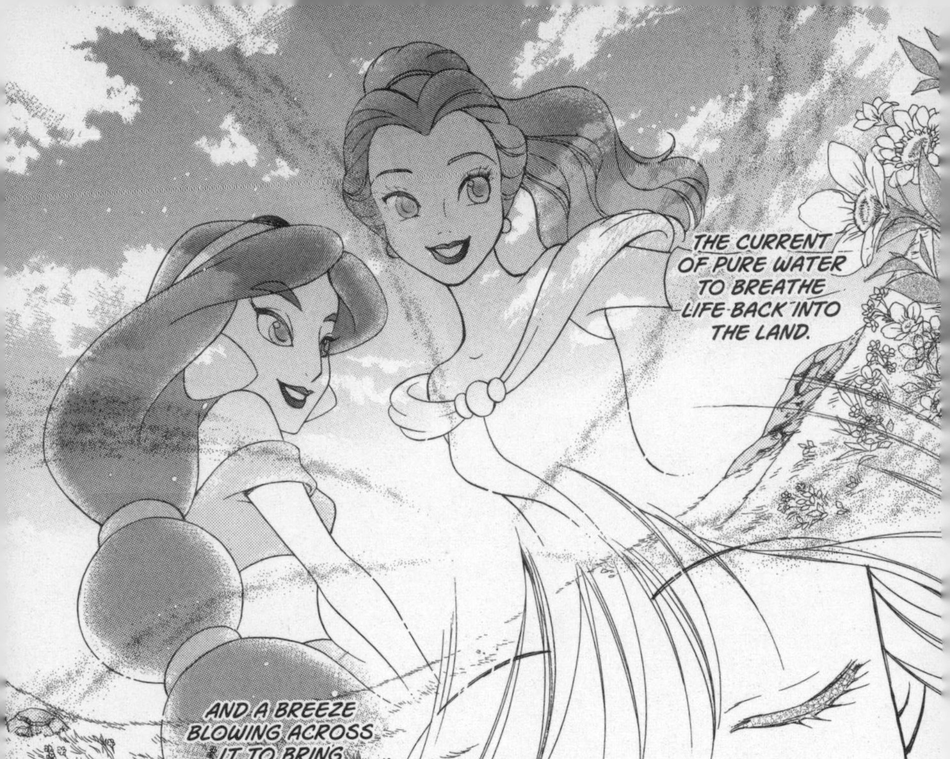
THE CURRENT OF PURE WATER TO BREATHE LIFE BACK INTO THE LAND.
AND A BREEZE BLOWING ACROSS IT TO BRING NEW LIFE.
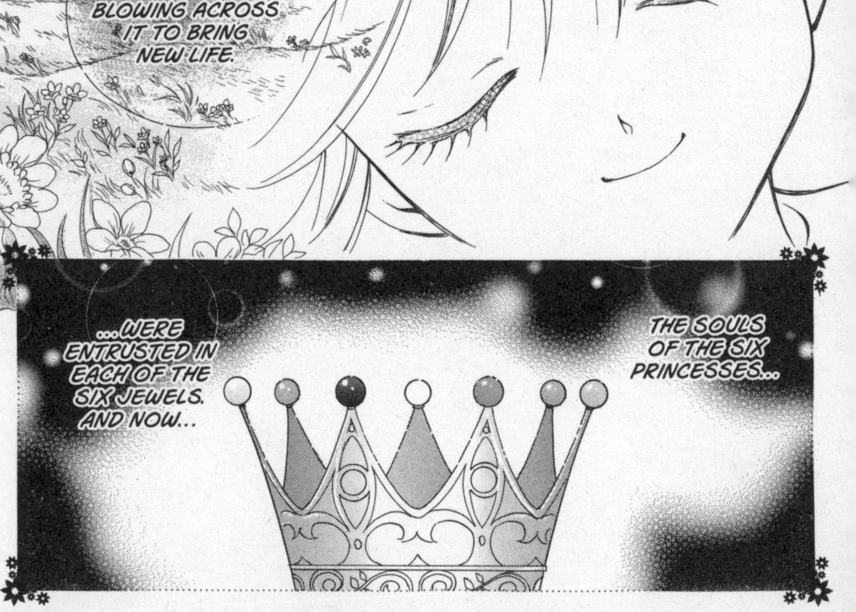
THE SOULS OF THE SIX PRINCESSES...
...WERE ENTRUSTED IN EACH OF THE SIX JEWELS. AND NOW...

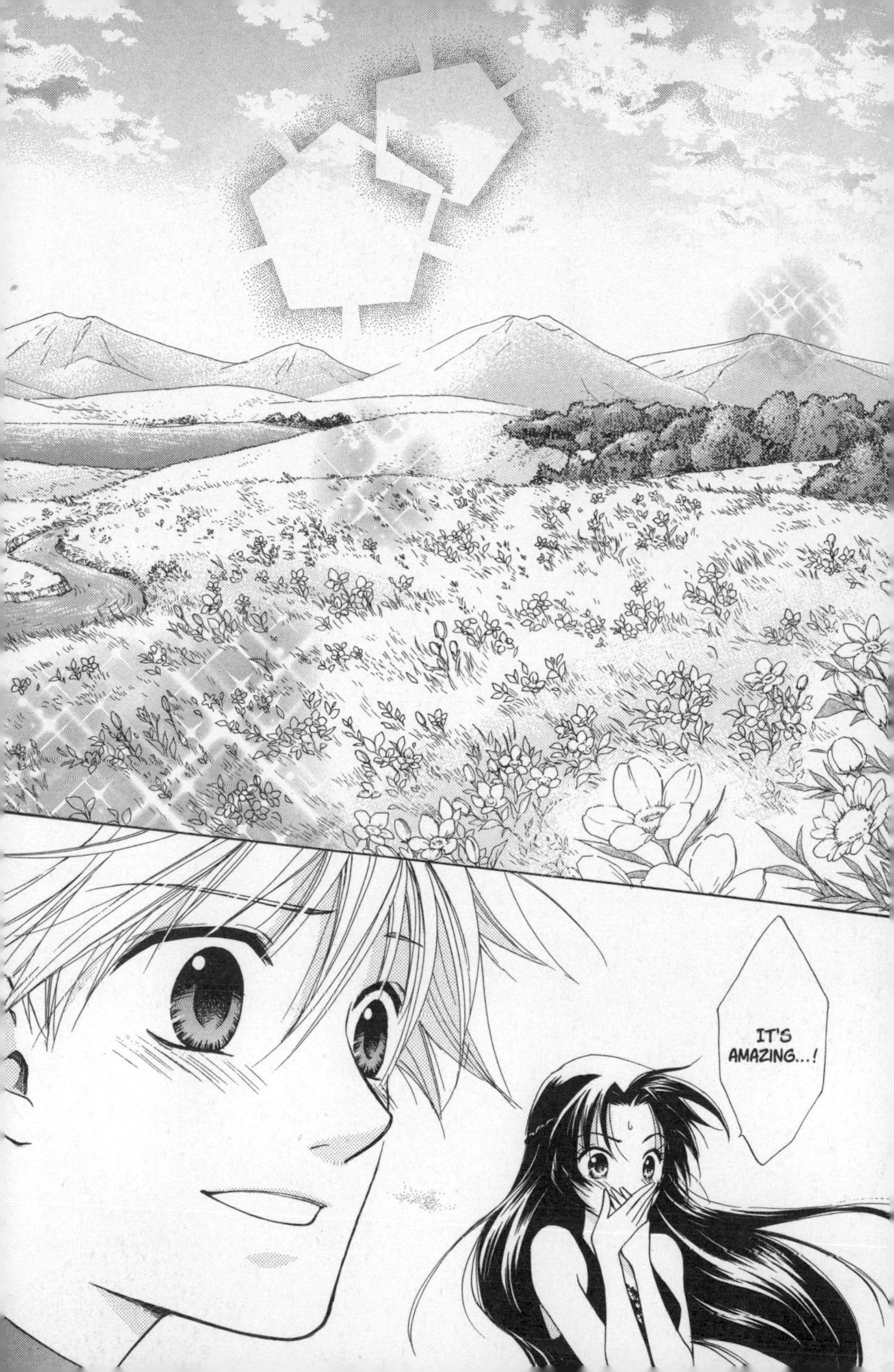
IT'S AMAZING...!

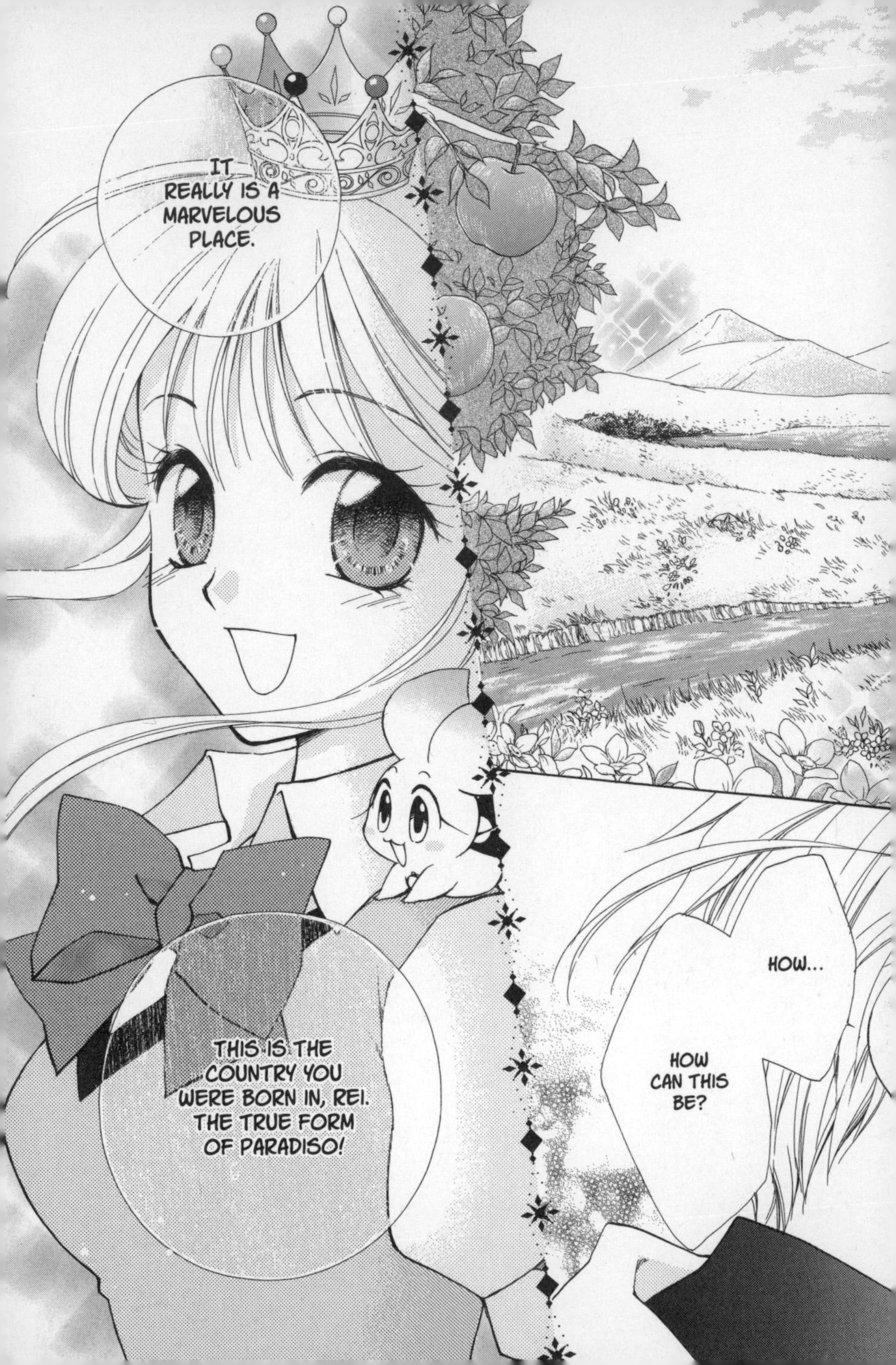
HOW...
HOW CAN THIS BE?
IT REALLY IS A MARVELOUS PLACE.
THIS IS THE COUNTRY YOU WERE BORN IN, REI. THE TRUE FORM OF PARADISO!

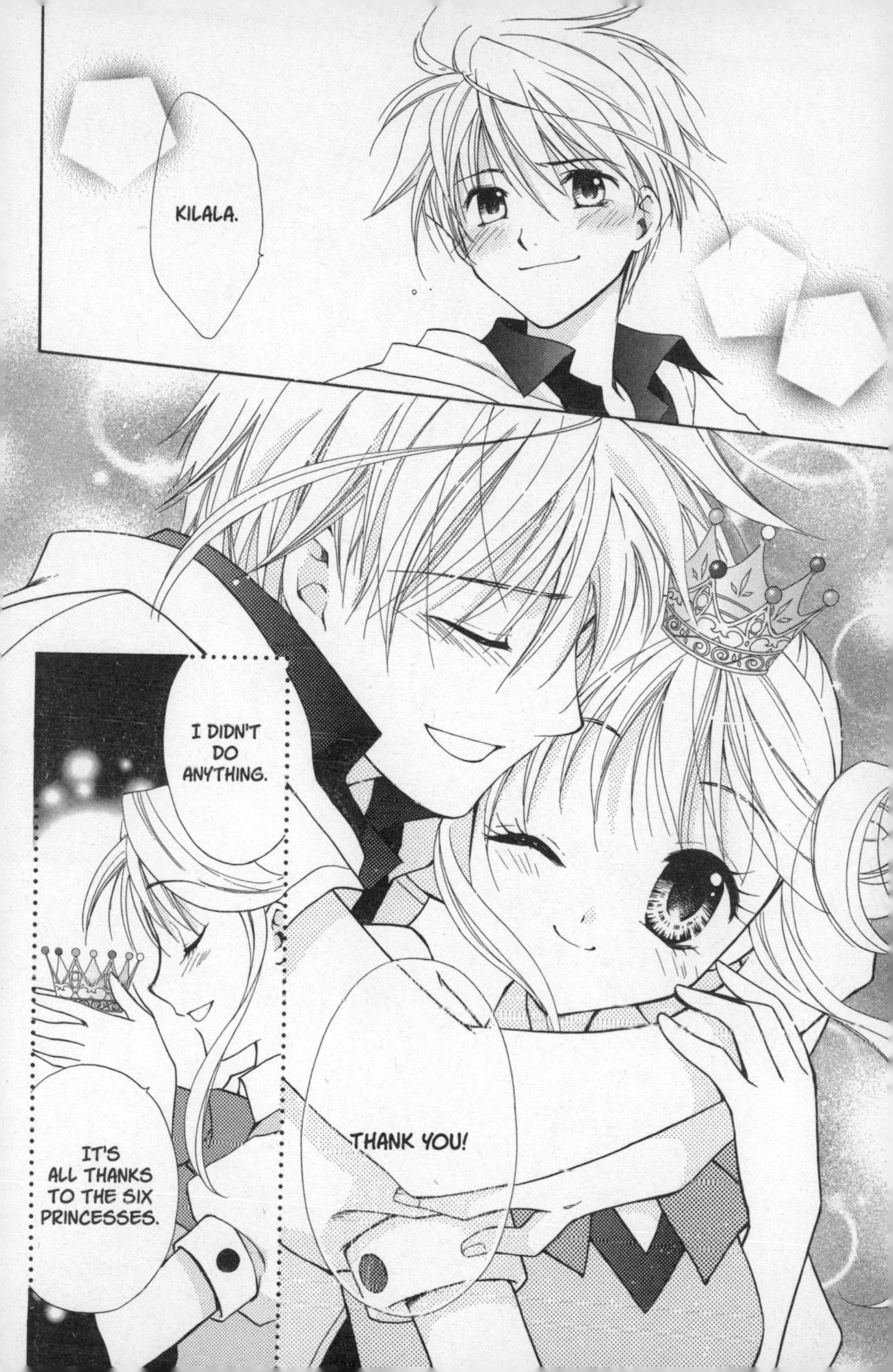
KILALA.
I DIDN'T DO ANYTHING.
THANK YOU!
IT'S ALL THANKS TO THE SIX PRINCESSES.

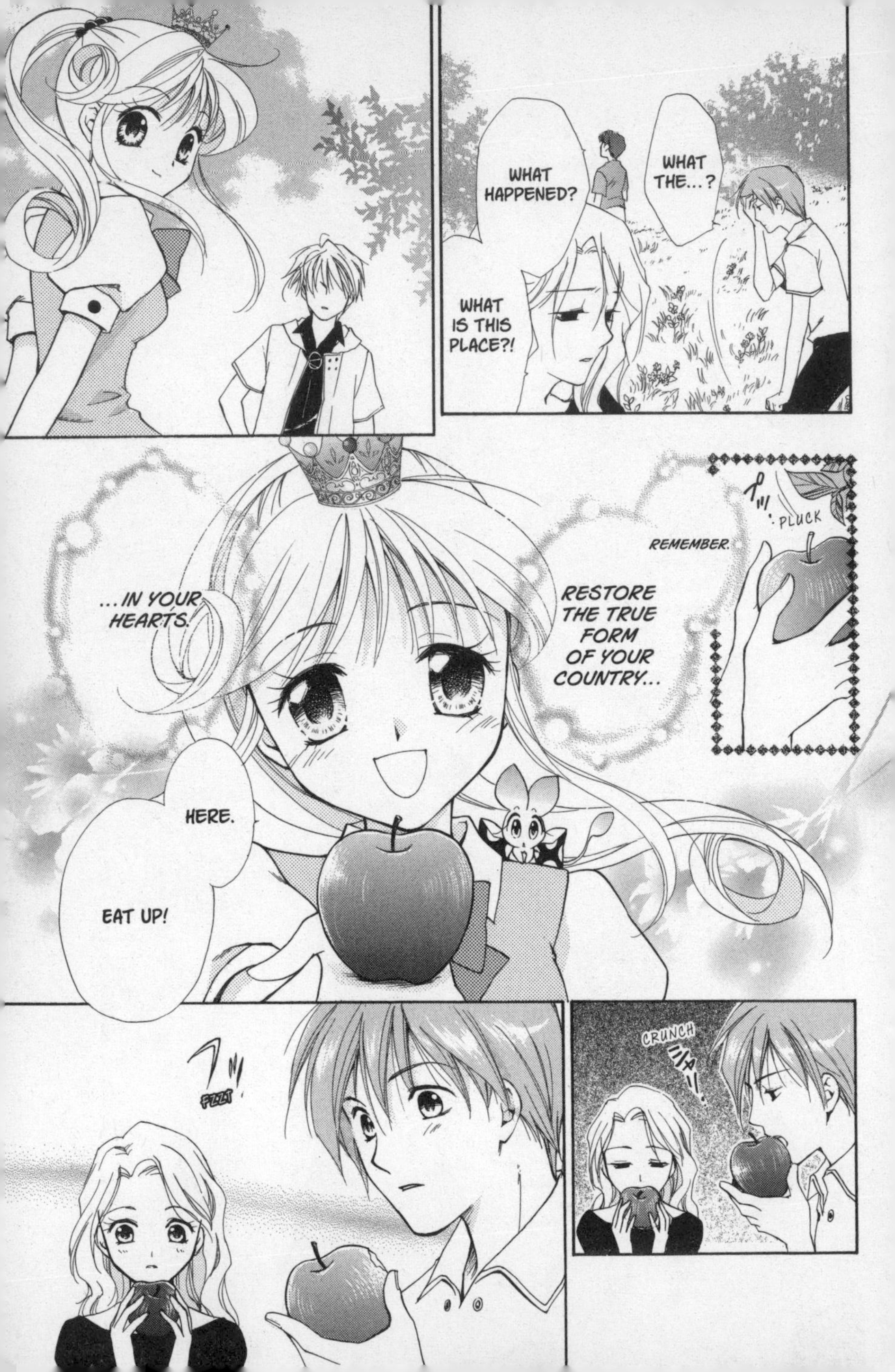
WHAT THE...?
WHAT HAPPENED?
WHAT IS THIS PLACE?!
PLUCK
REMEMBER.
RESTORE THE TRUE FORM OF YOUR COUNTRY...
...IN YOUR HEARTS.
HERE.
EAT UP!
CRUNCH
FZZT

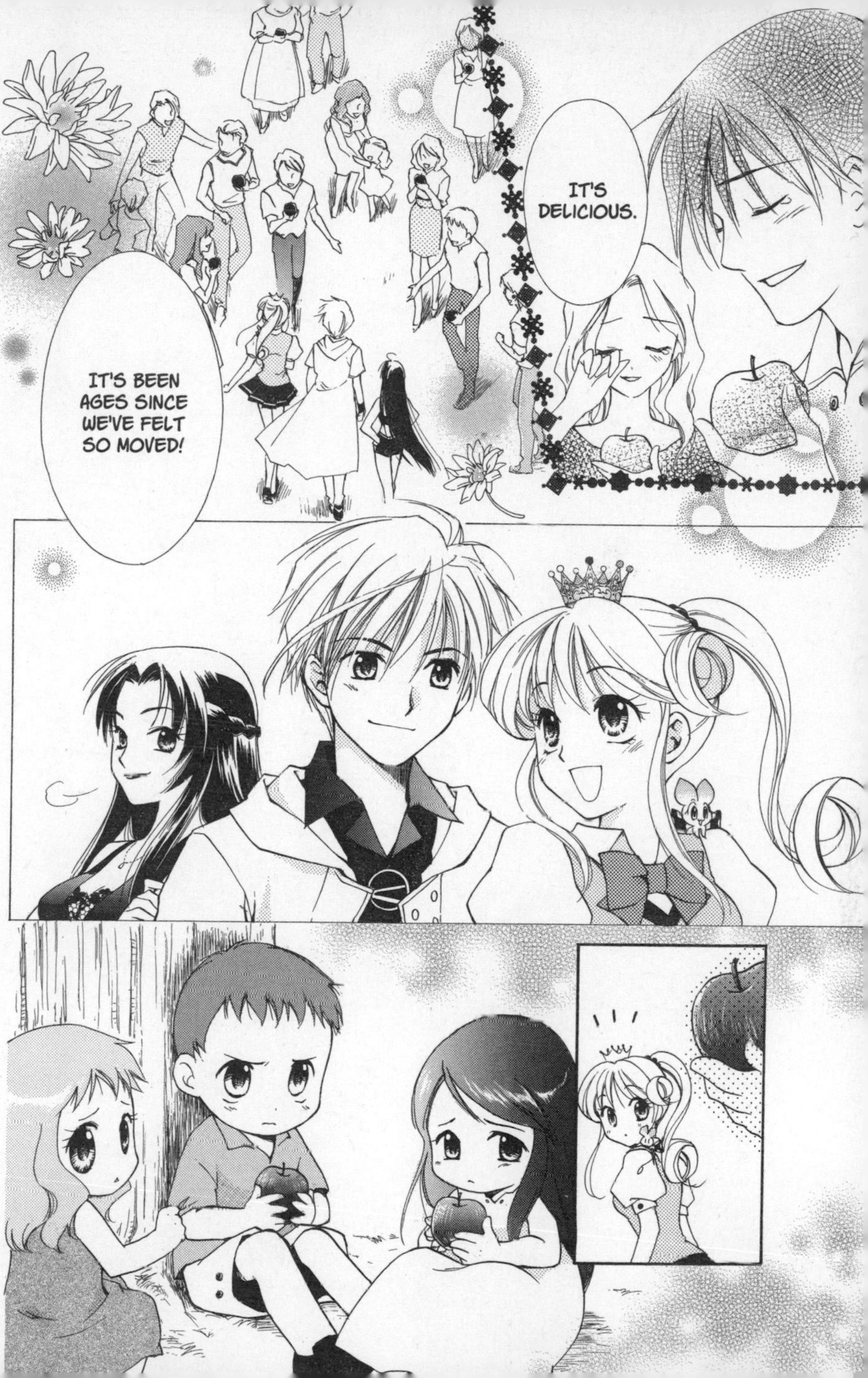
IT'S DELICIOUS.
IT'S BEEN AGES SINCE WE'VE FELT SO MOVED!

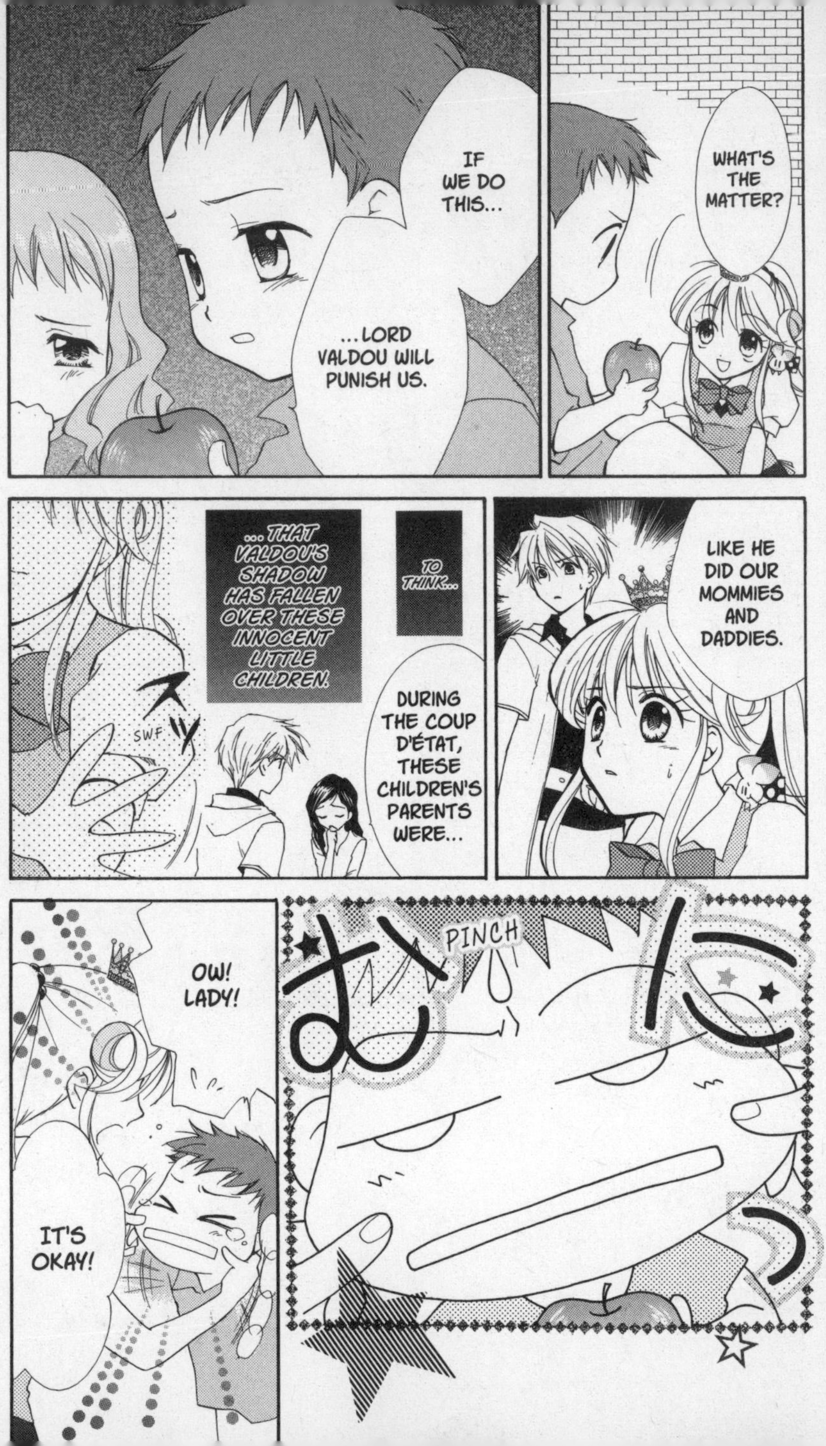
WHAT'S THE MATTER?
IF WE DO THIS...
...LORD VALDOU WILL PUNISH US.
LIKE HE DID OUR MOMMIES AND DADDIES.
DURING THE COUP D'ÉTAT, THESE CHILDREN'S PARENTS WERE...
TO THINK...
...THAT VALDOU'S SHADOW HAS FALLEN OVER THESE INNOCENT LITTLE CHILDREN.
SWF
PINCH
むにっ
OW! LADY!
IT'S OKAY!

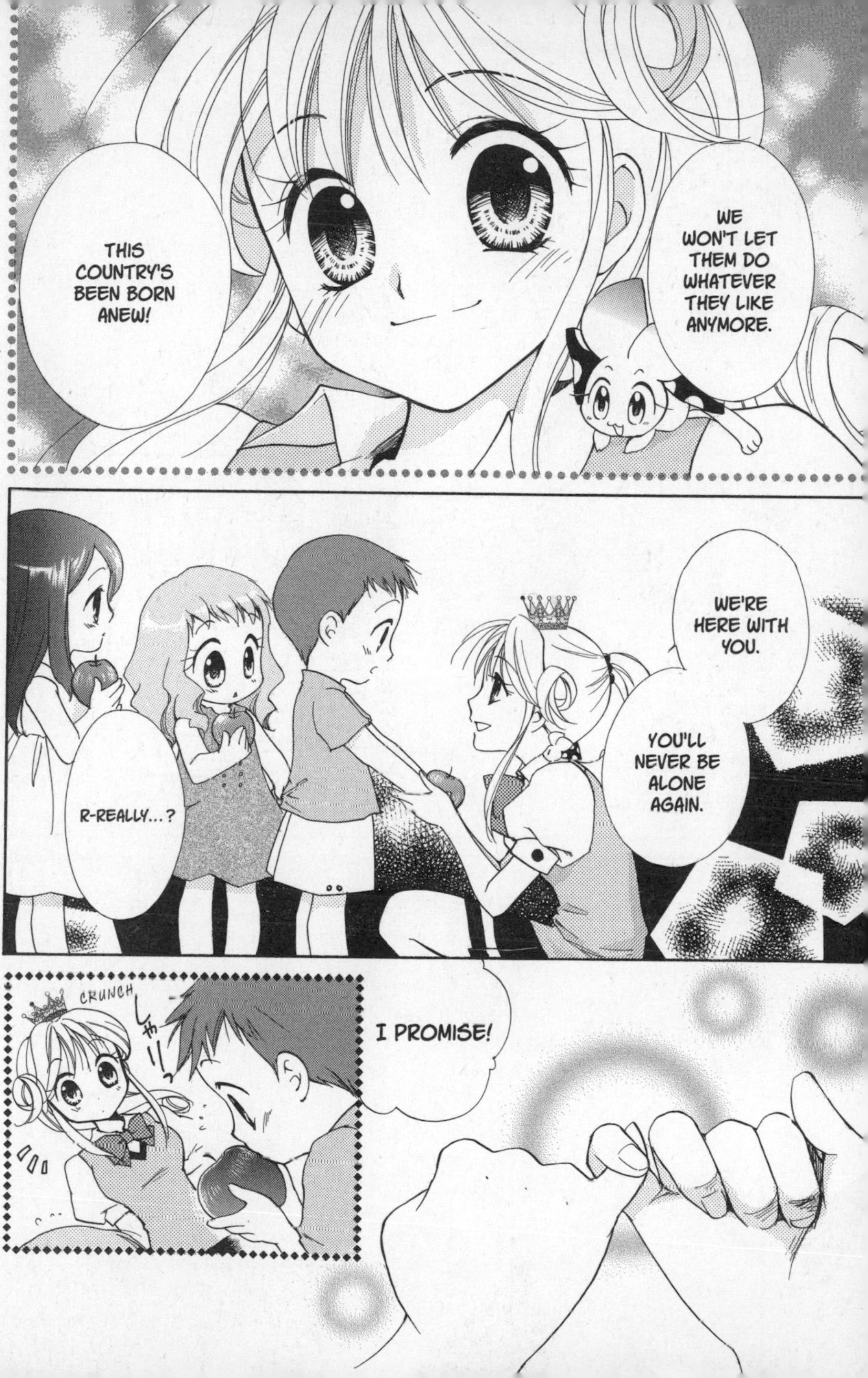
WE WON'T LET THEM DO WHATEVER THEY LIKE ANYMORE.
THIS COUNTRY'S BEEN BORN ANEW!
WE'RE HERE WITH YOU.
YOU'LL NEVER BE ALONE AGAIN.
R-REALLY...?
I PROMISE!
CRUNCH

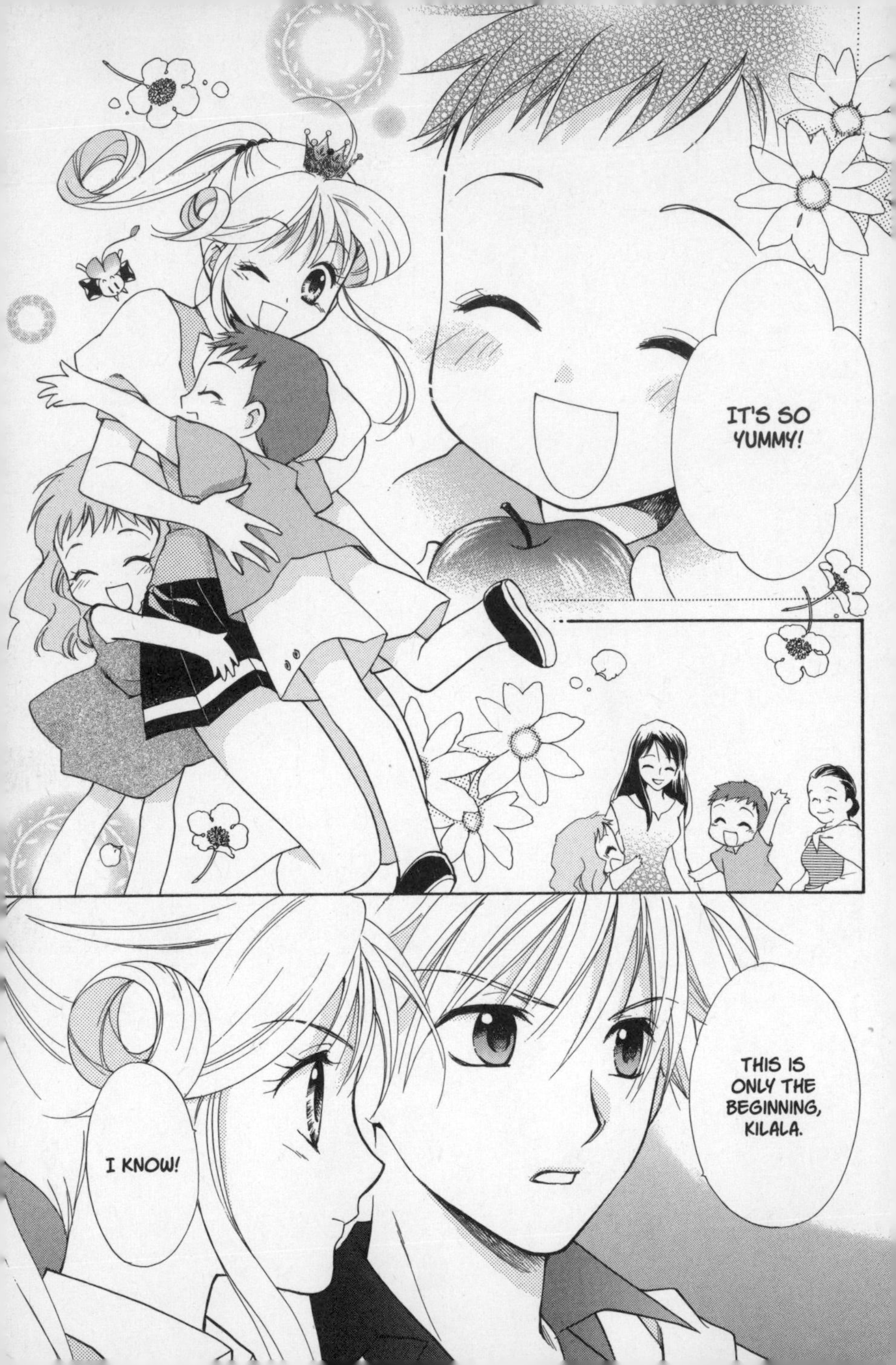
IT'S SO YUMMY!
THIS IS ONLY THE BEGINNING, KILALA.
I KNOW!

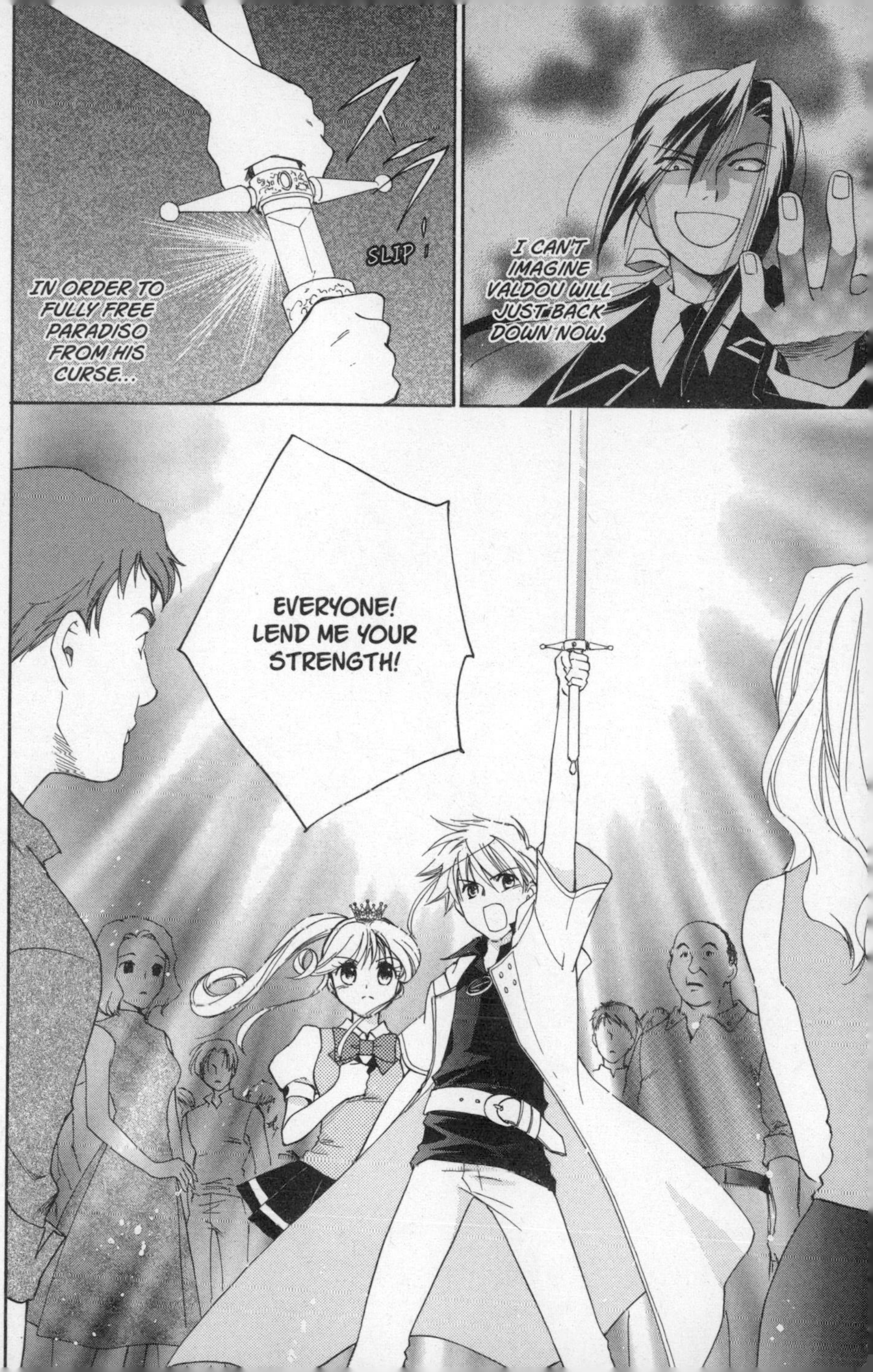
I CAN'T IMAGINE VALDOU WILL JUST BACK DOWN NOW.
SLIP
IN ORDER TO FULLY FREE PARADISO FROM HIS CURSE...
EVERYONE! LEND ME YOUR STRENGTH!

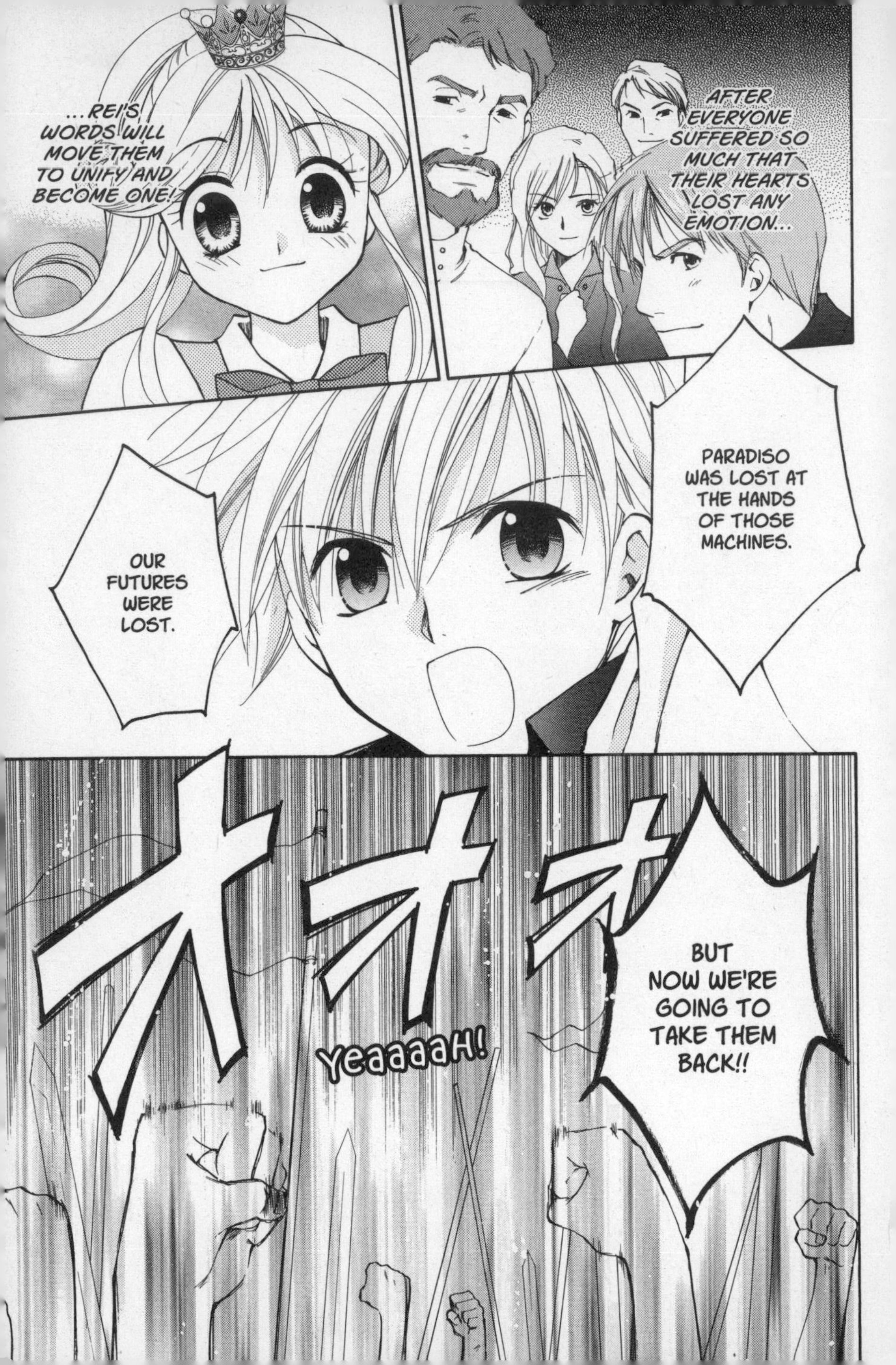
AFTER EVERYONE SUFFERED SO MUCH THAT THEIR HEARTS LOST ANY EMOTION...
...REI'S WORDS WILL MOVE THEM TO UNIFY AND BECOME ONE!
PARADISO WAS LOST AT THE HANDS OF THOSE MACHINES.
OUR FUTURES WERE LOST.
BUT NOW WE'RE GOING TO TAKE THEM BACK!!
オオオ
YEAAAAH!

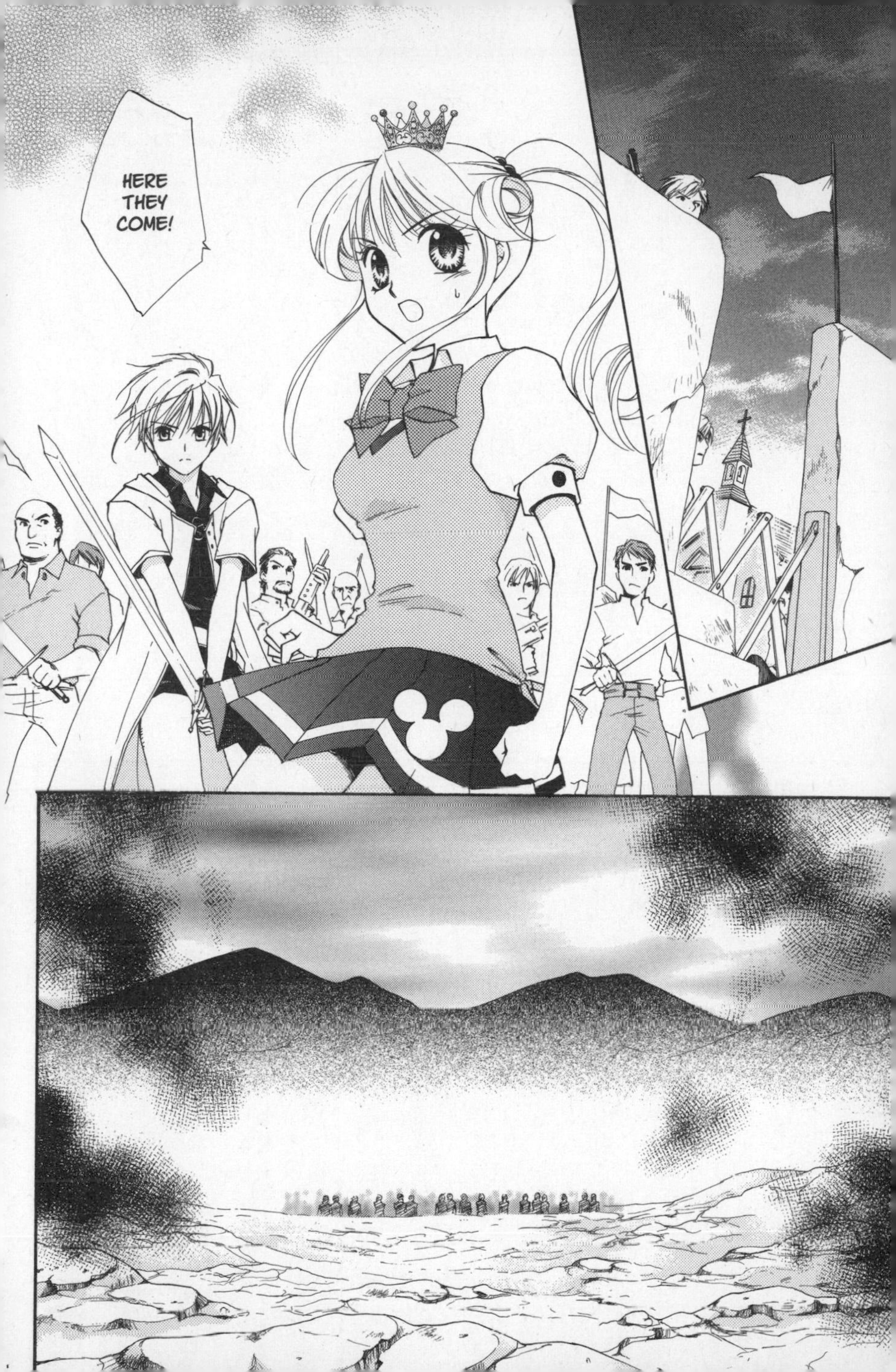
HERE THEY COME!

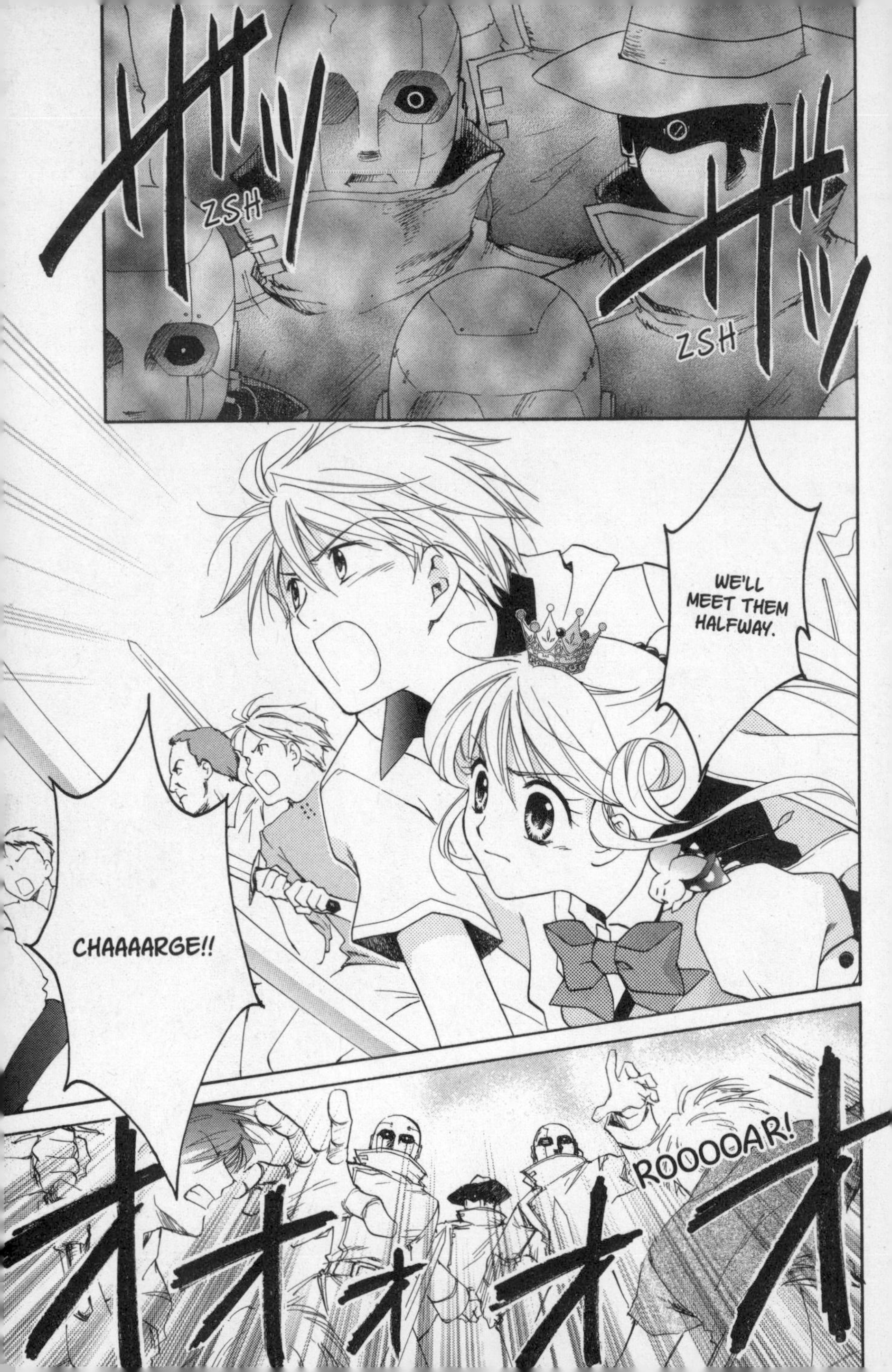
ZSH
ZSH
WE'LL MEET THEM HALFWAY.
CHAAAARGE!!
ROOOOAR!

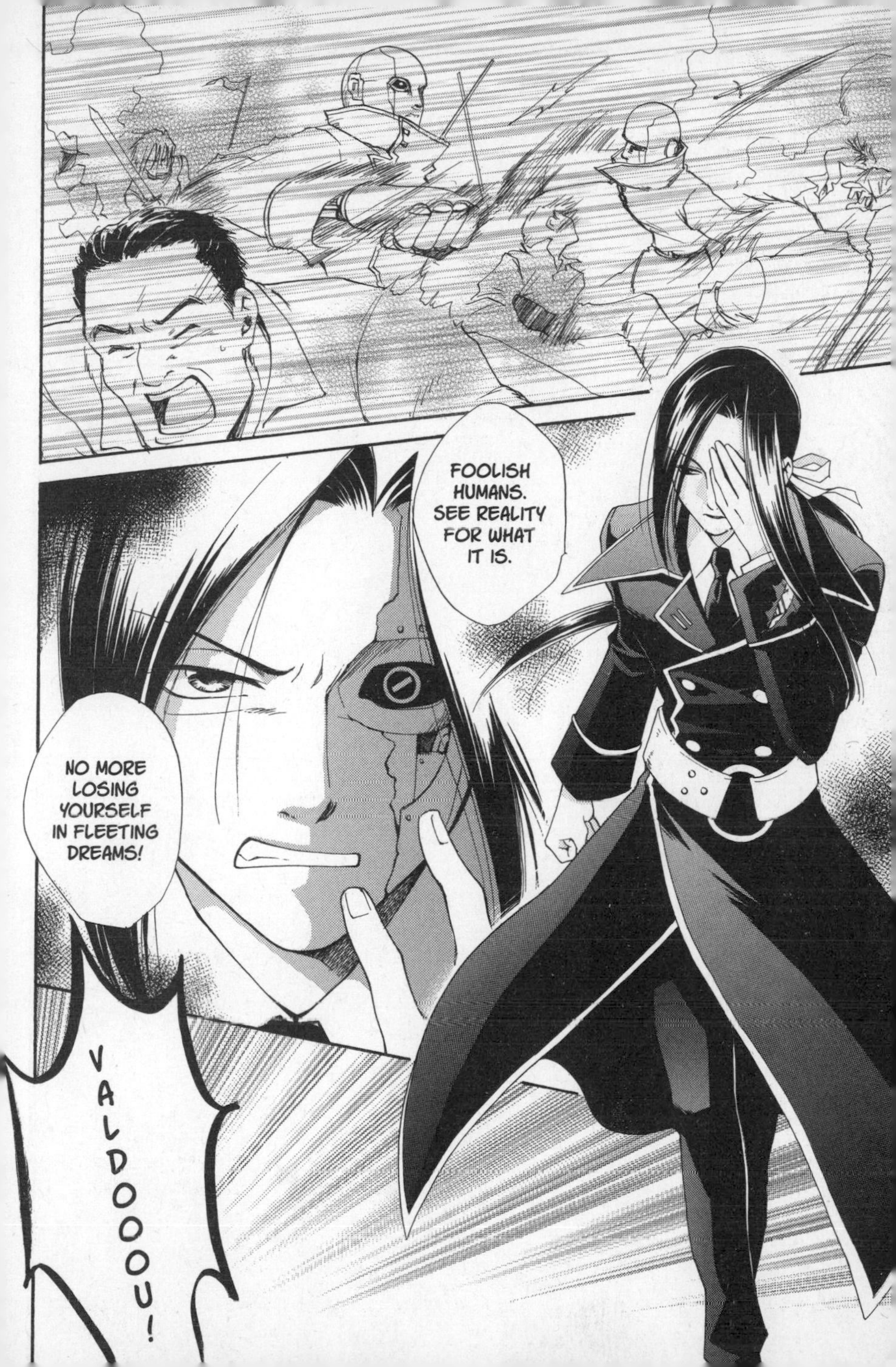
FOOLISH HUMANS. SEE REALITY FOR WHAT IT IS.
NO MORE LOSING YOURSELF IN FLEETING DREAMS!
VALDOOOU!

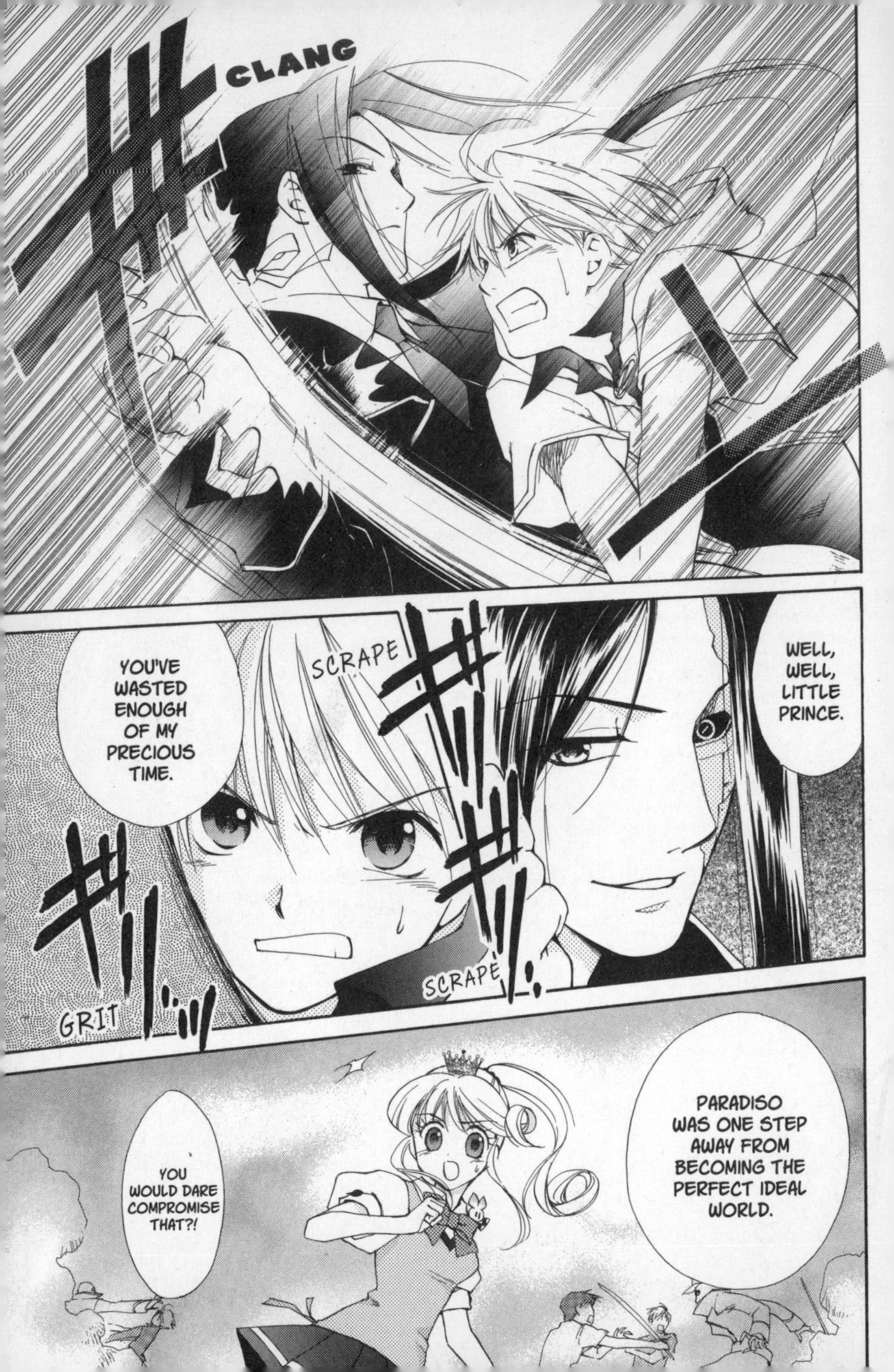
CLANG
WELL, WELL, LITTLE PRINCE.
SCRAPE
YOU'VE WASTED ENOUGH OF MY PRECIOUS TIME.
SCRAPE
GRIT
PARADISO WAS ONE STEP AWAY FROM BECOMING THE PERFECT IDEAL WORLD.
YOU WOULD DARE COMPROMISE THAT?!

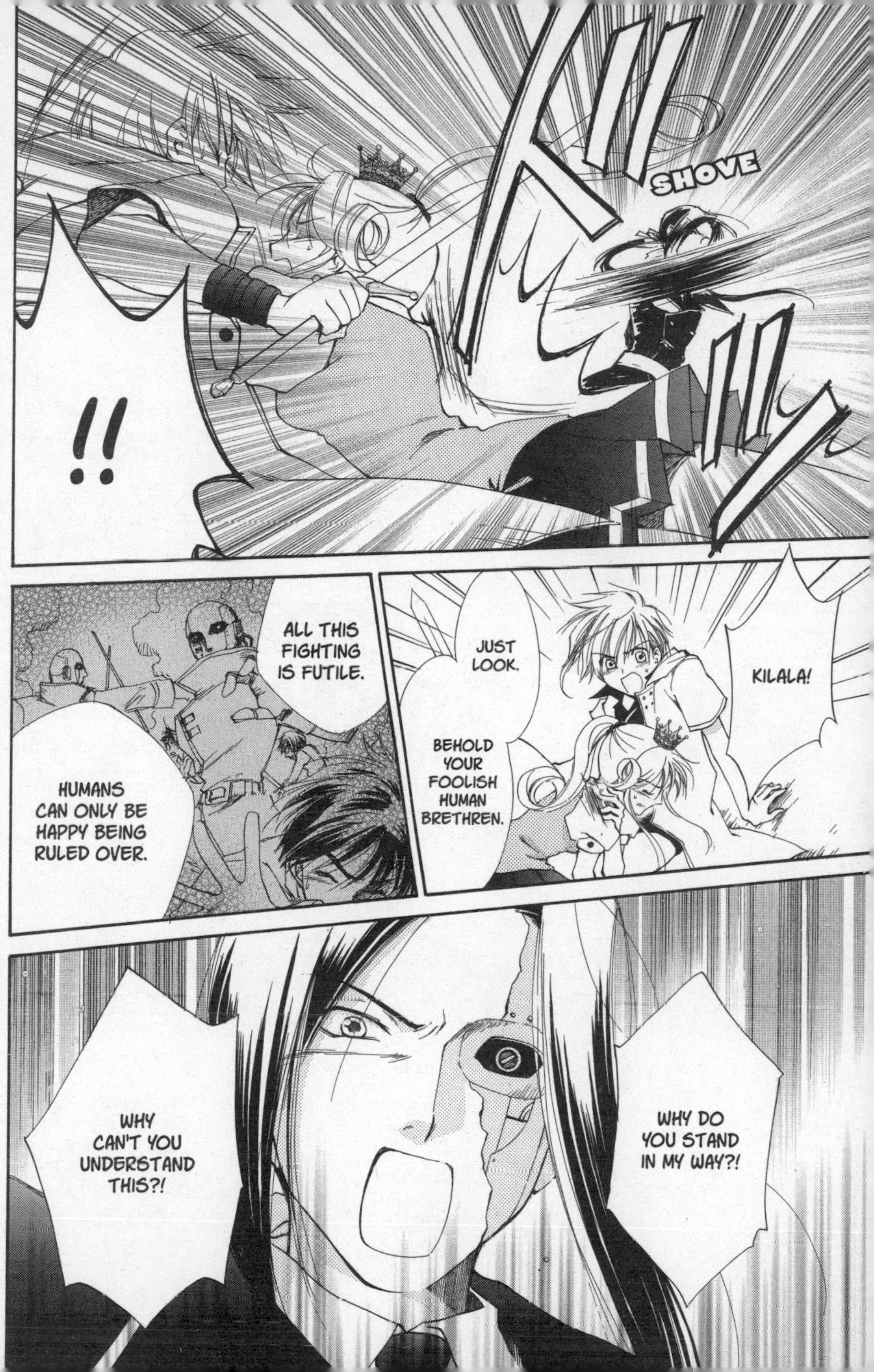
SHOVE
!!
KILALA!
JUST LOOK.
BEHOLD YOUR FOOLISH HUMAN BRETHREN.
ALL THIS FIGHTING IS FUTILE.
HUMANS CAN ONLY BE HAPPY BEING RULED OVER.
WHY DO YOU STAND IN MY WAY?!
WHY CAN'T YOU UNDERSTAND THIS?!

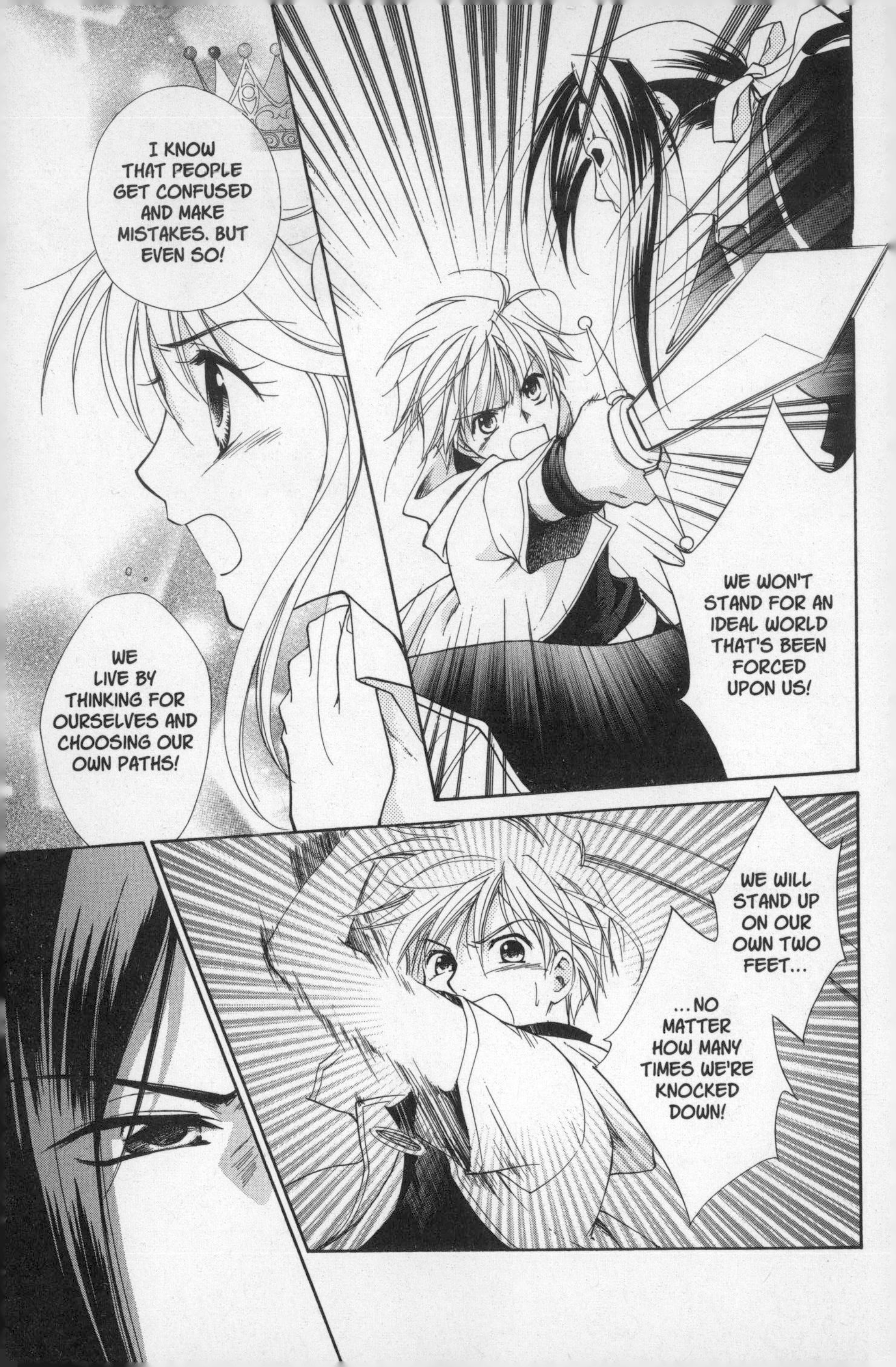
WE WON'T STAND FOR AN IDEAL WORLD THAT'S BEEN FORCED UPON US!
I KNOW THAT PEOPLE GET CONFUSED AND MAKE MISTAKES. BUT EVEN SO!
WE LIVE BY THINKING FOR OURSELVES AND CHOOSING OUR OWN PATHS!
WE WILL STAND UP ON OUR OWN TWO FEET...
...NO MATTER HOW MANY TIMES WE'RE KNOCKED DOWN!

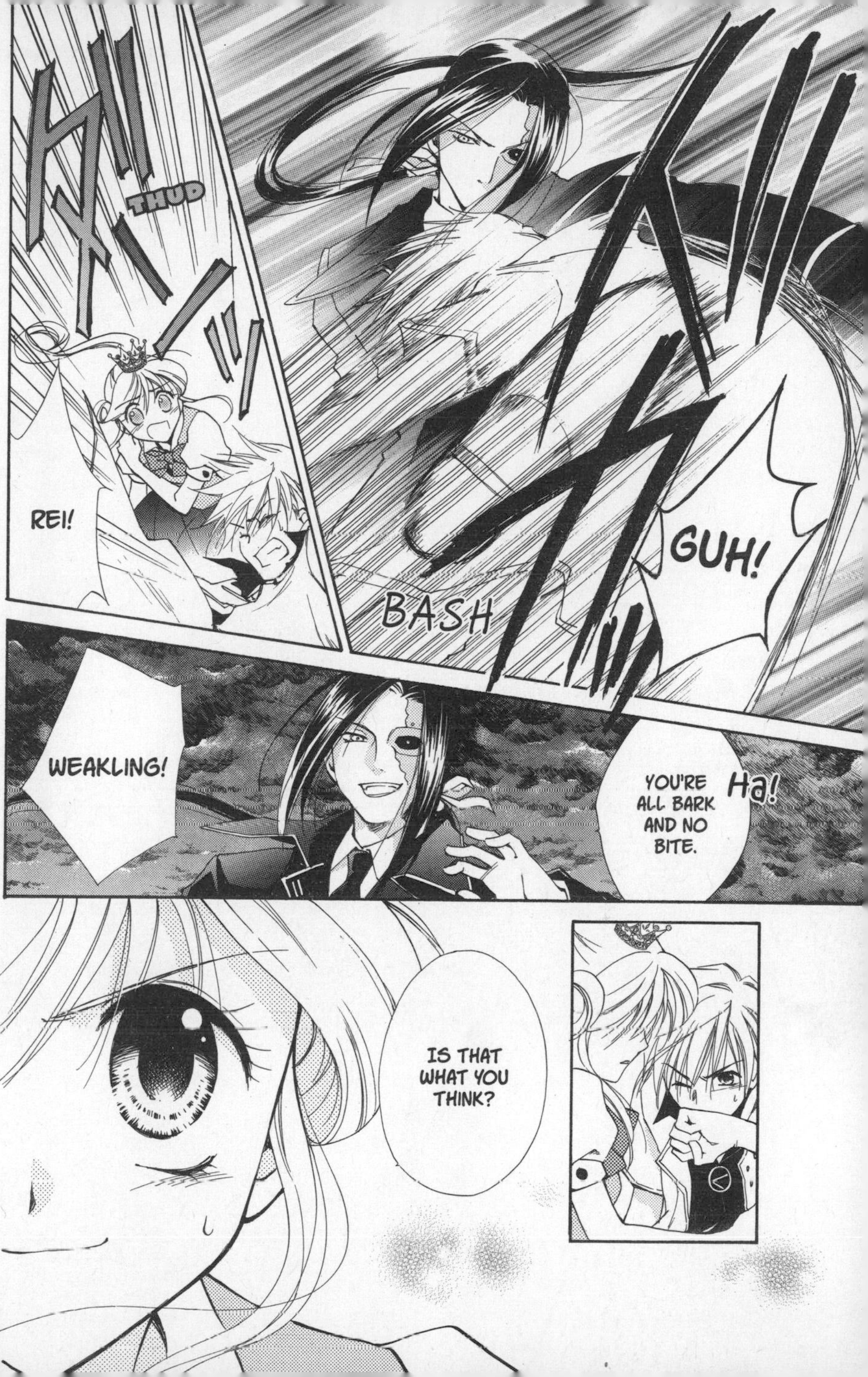
GUH!
BASH
THUD
REI!
Ha!
YOU'RE ALL BARK AND NO BITE.
WEAKLING!
IS THAT WHAT YOU THINK?

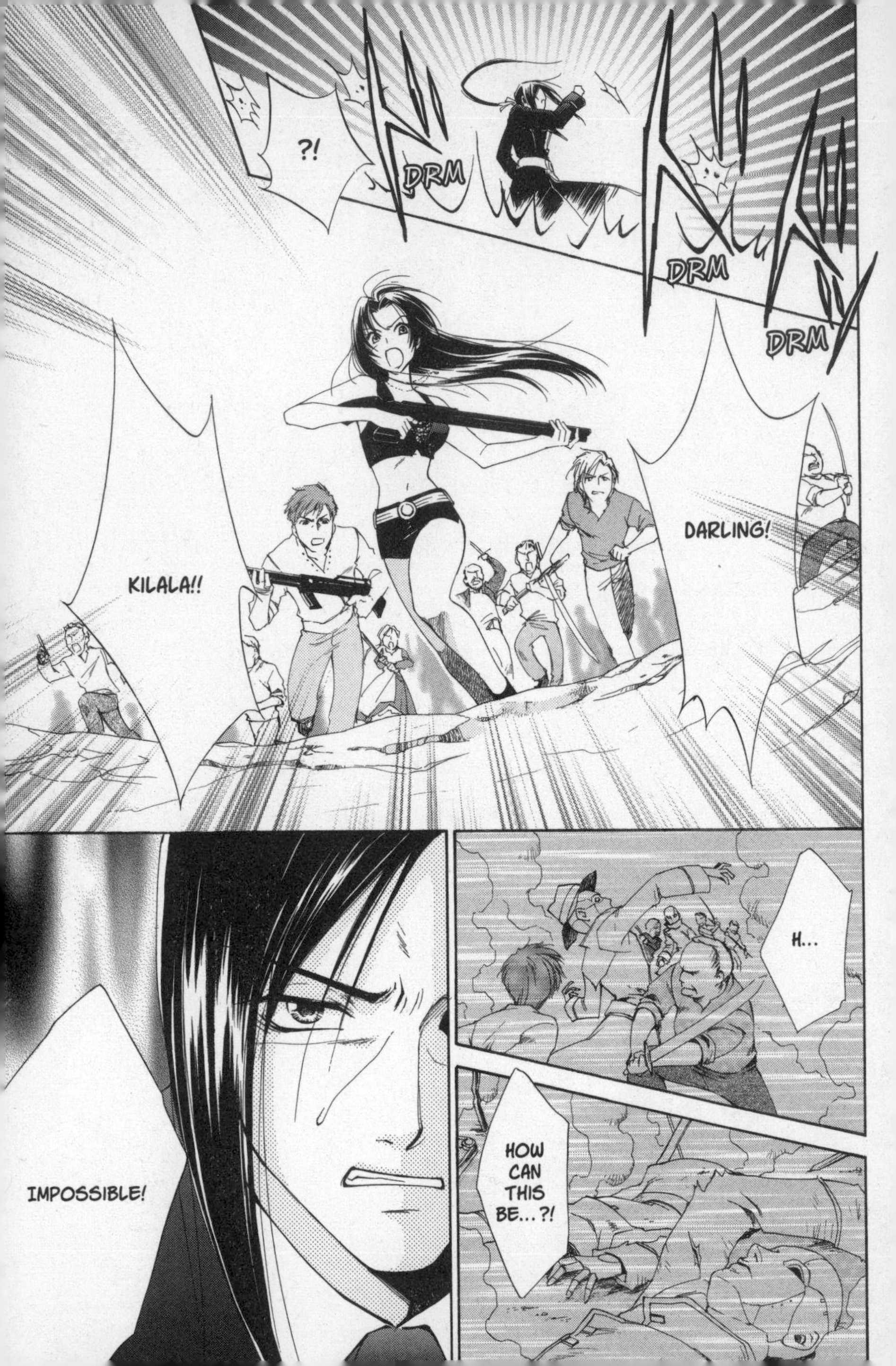
DRM
DRM
?!
DRM
DARLING!
KILALA!!
H...
HOW CAN THIS BE...?!
IMPOSSIBLE!

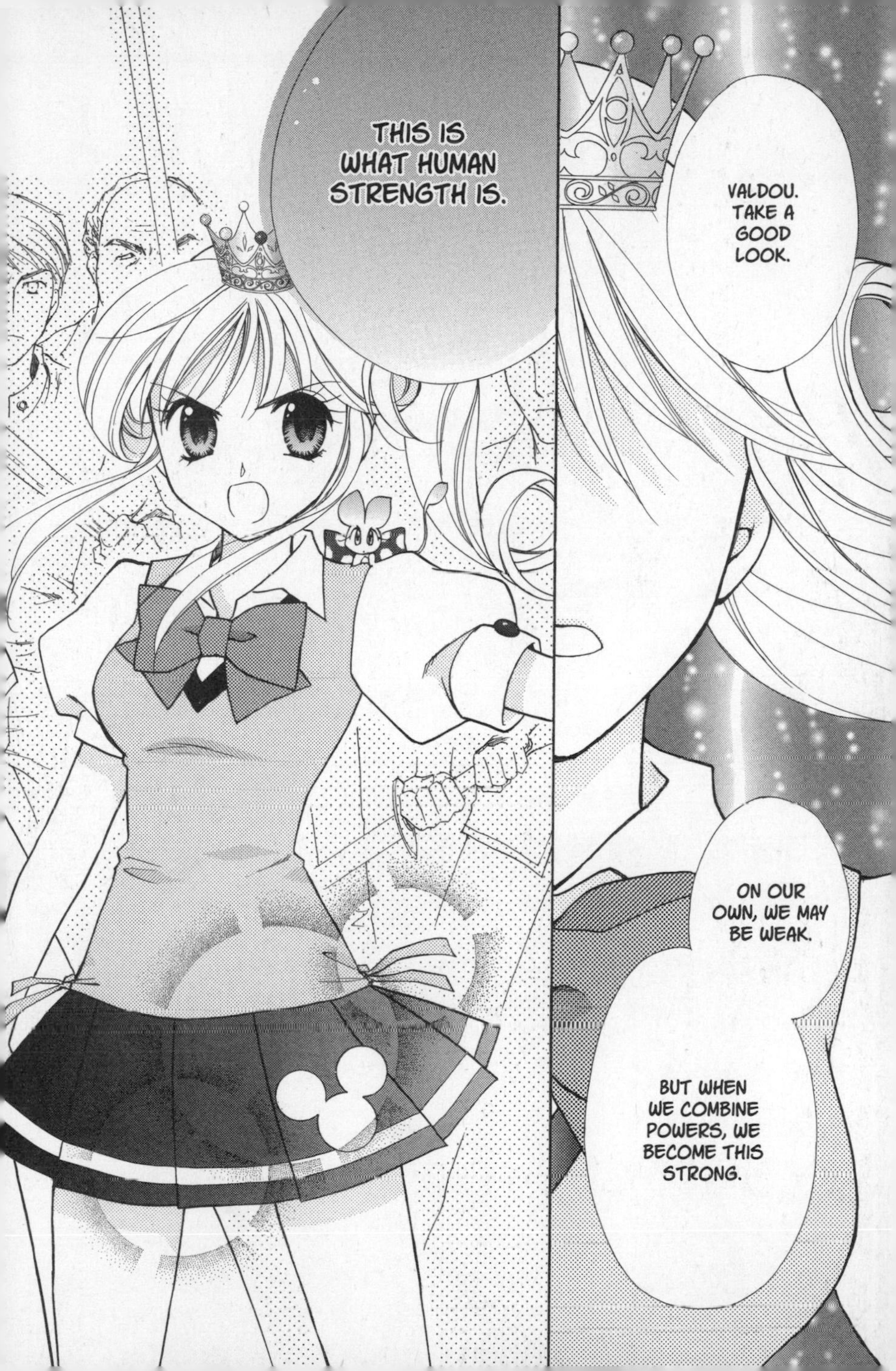
VALDOU. TAKE A GOOD LOOK.
ON OUR OWN, WE MAY BE WEAK.
BUT WHEN WE COMBINE POWERS, WE BECOME THIS STRONG.
THIS IS WHAT HUMAN STRENGTH IS.

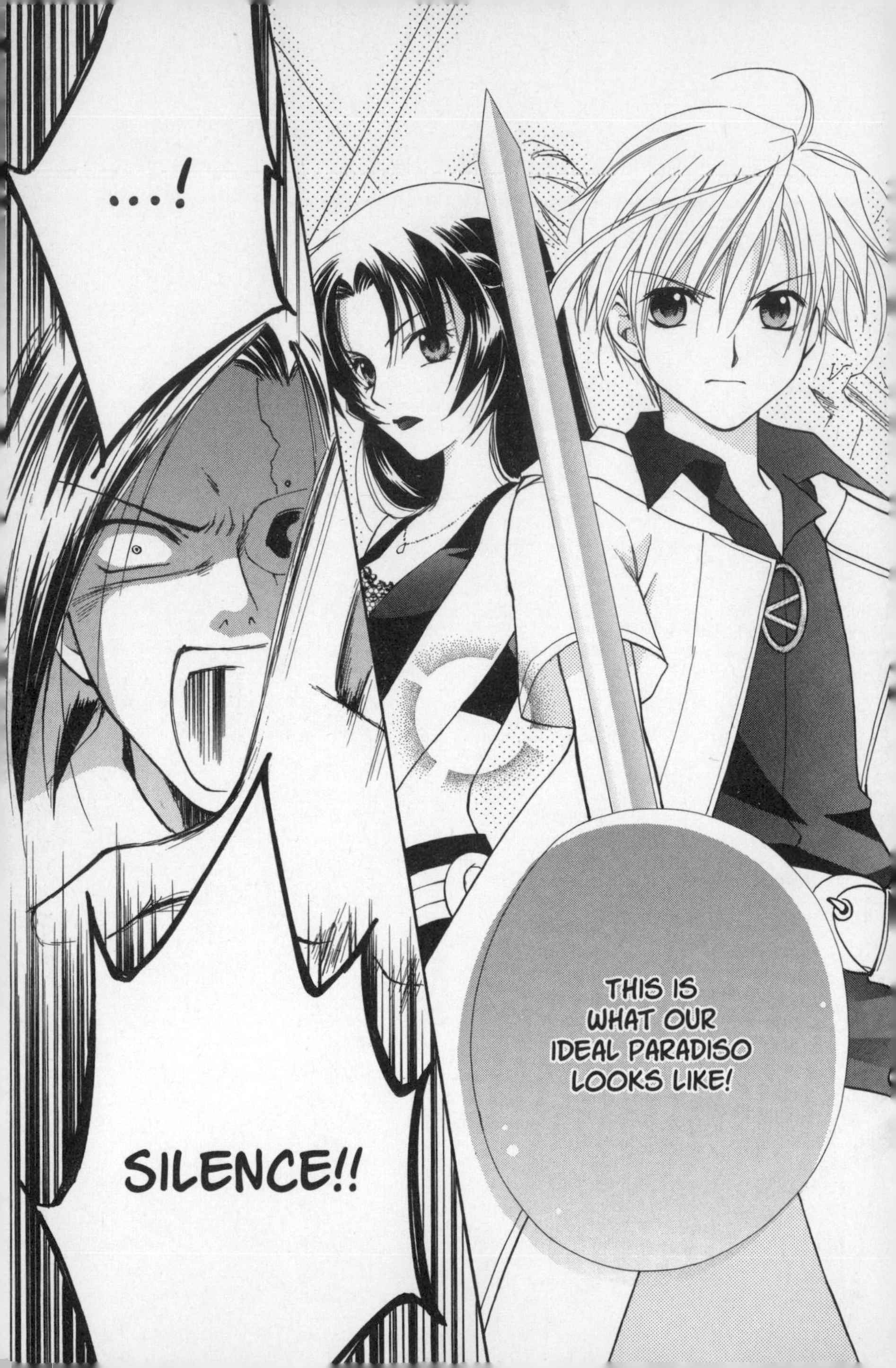
THIS IS WHAT OUR IDEAL PARADISO LOOKS LIKE!
...!
SILENCE!!

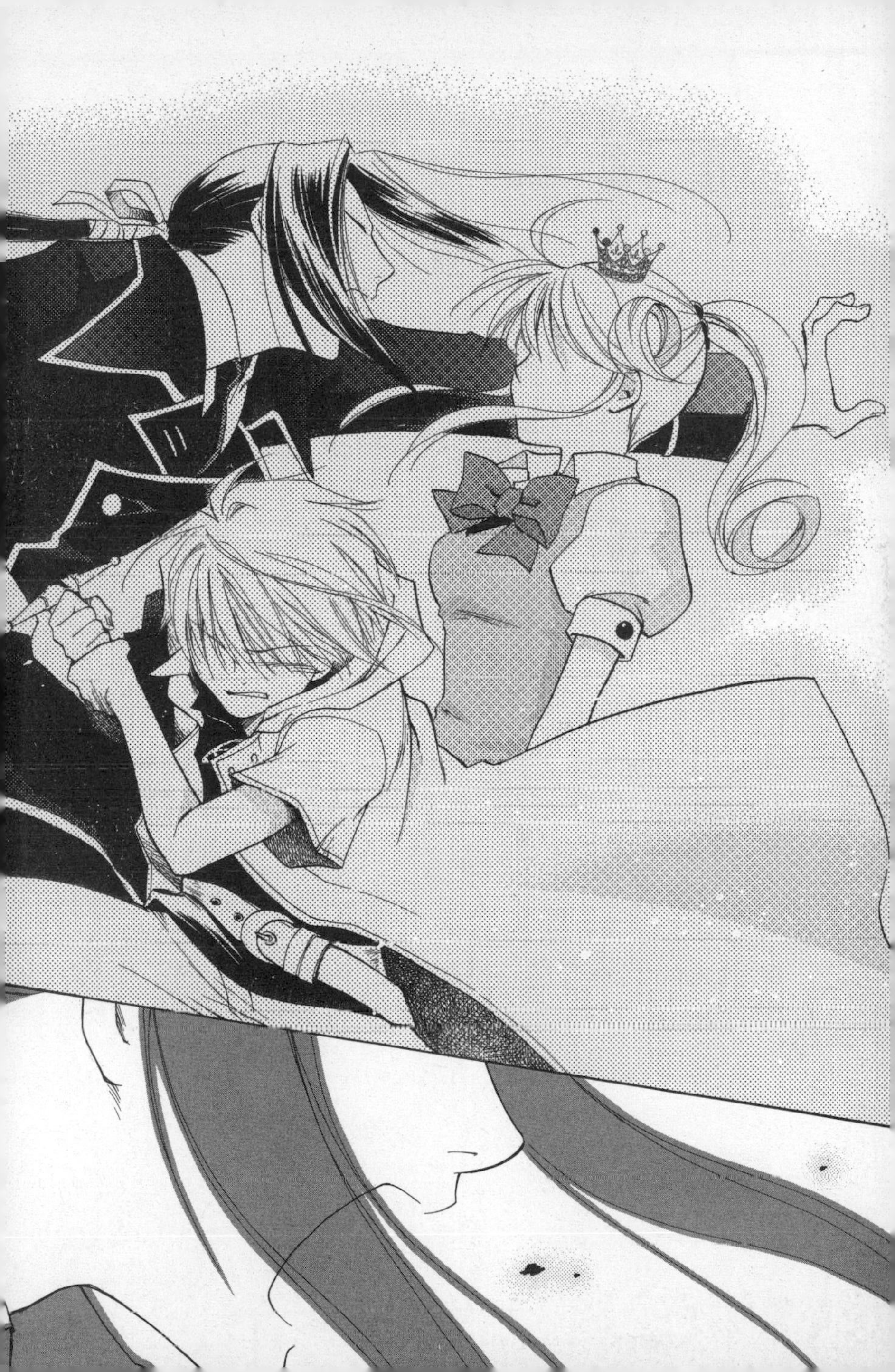

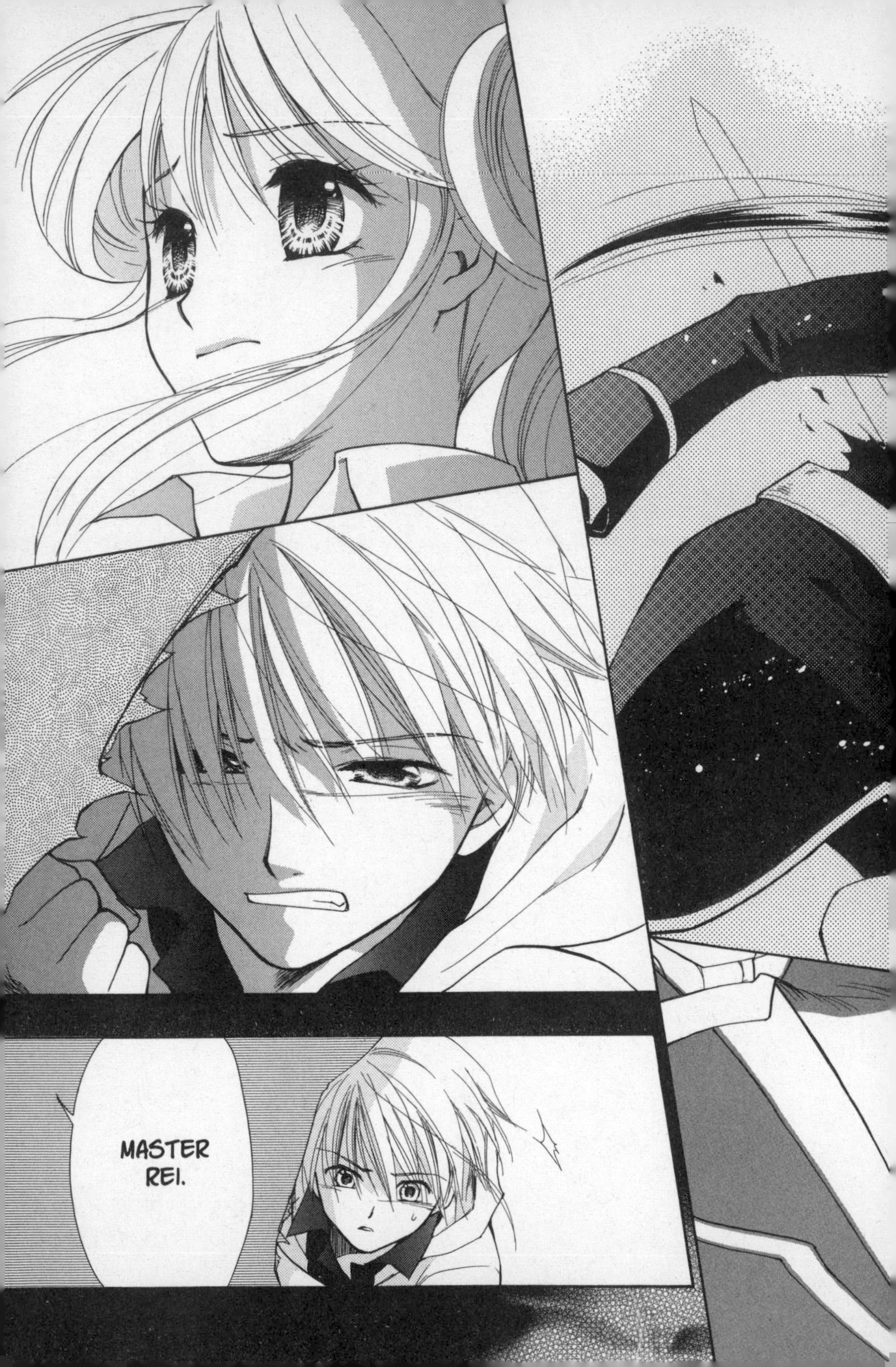
MASTER REI.

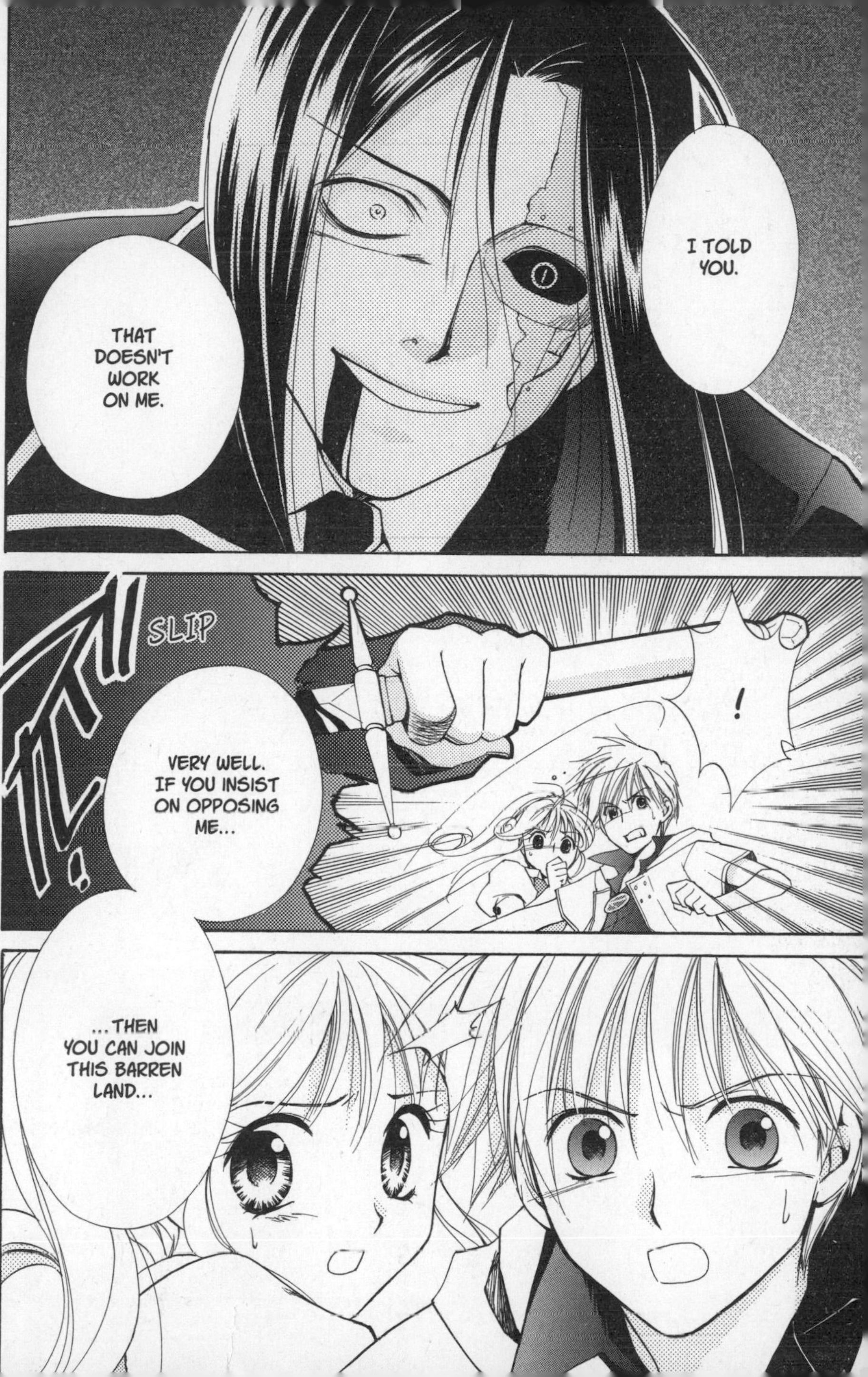
I TOLD YOU.
THAT DOESN'T WORK ON ME.
SLIP
!
VERY WELL. IF YOU INSIST ON OPPOSING ME...
...THEN YOU CAN JOIN THIS BARREN LAND...

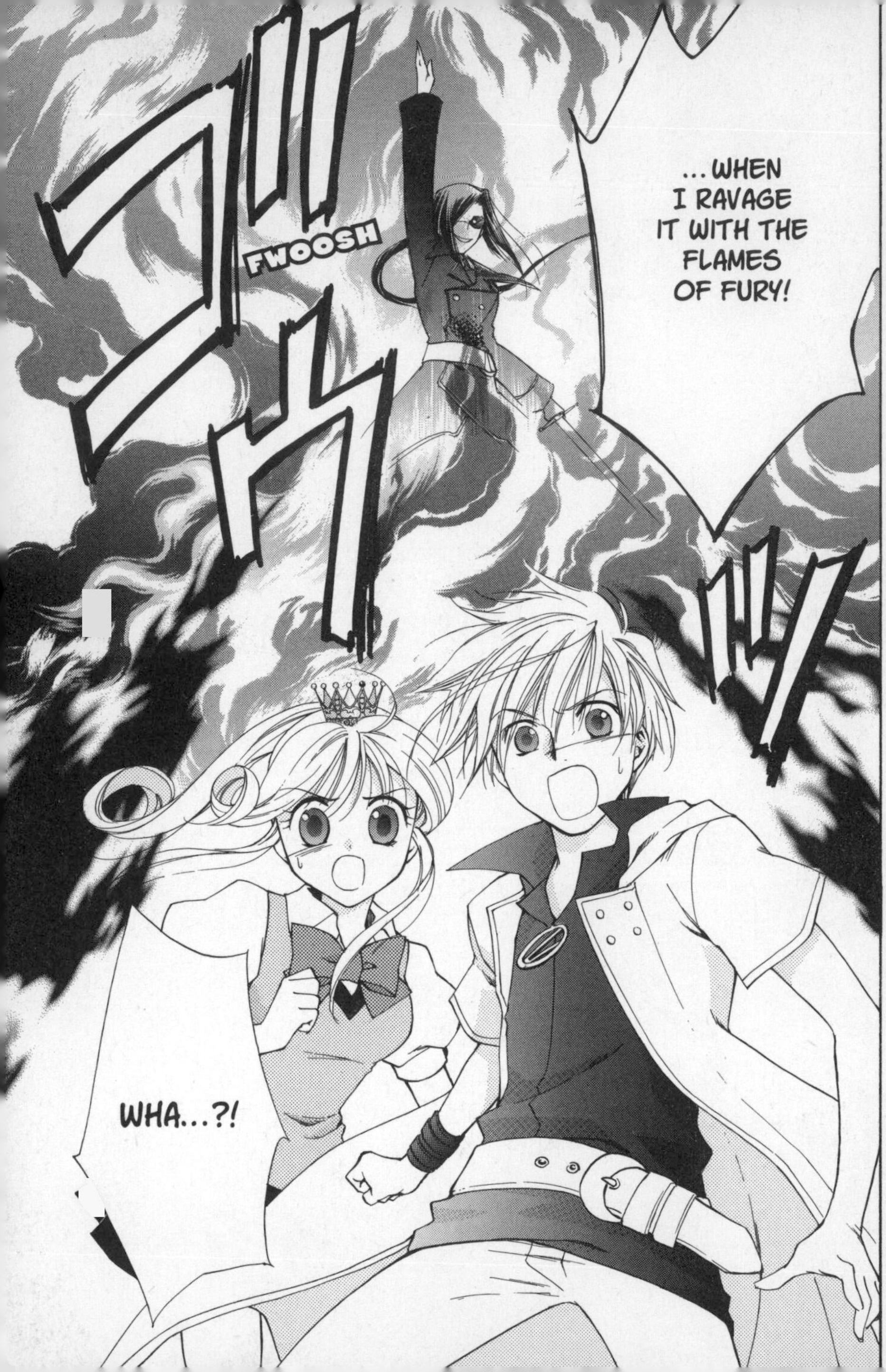
...WHEN
I RAVAGE
IT WITH THE
FLAMES
OF FURY!
FWOOSH
WHA...?!

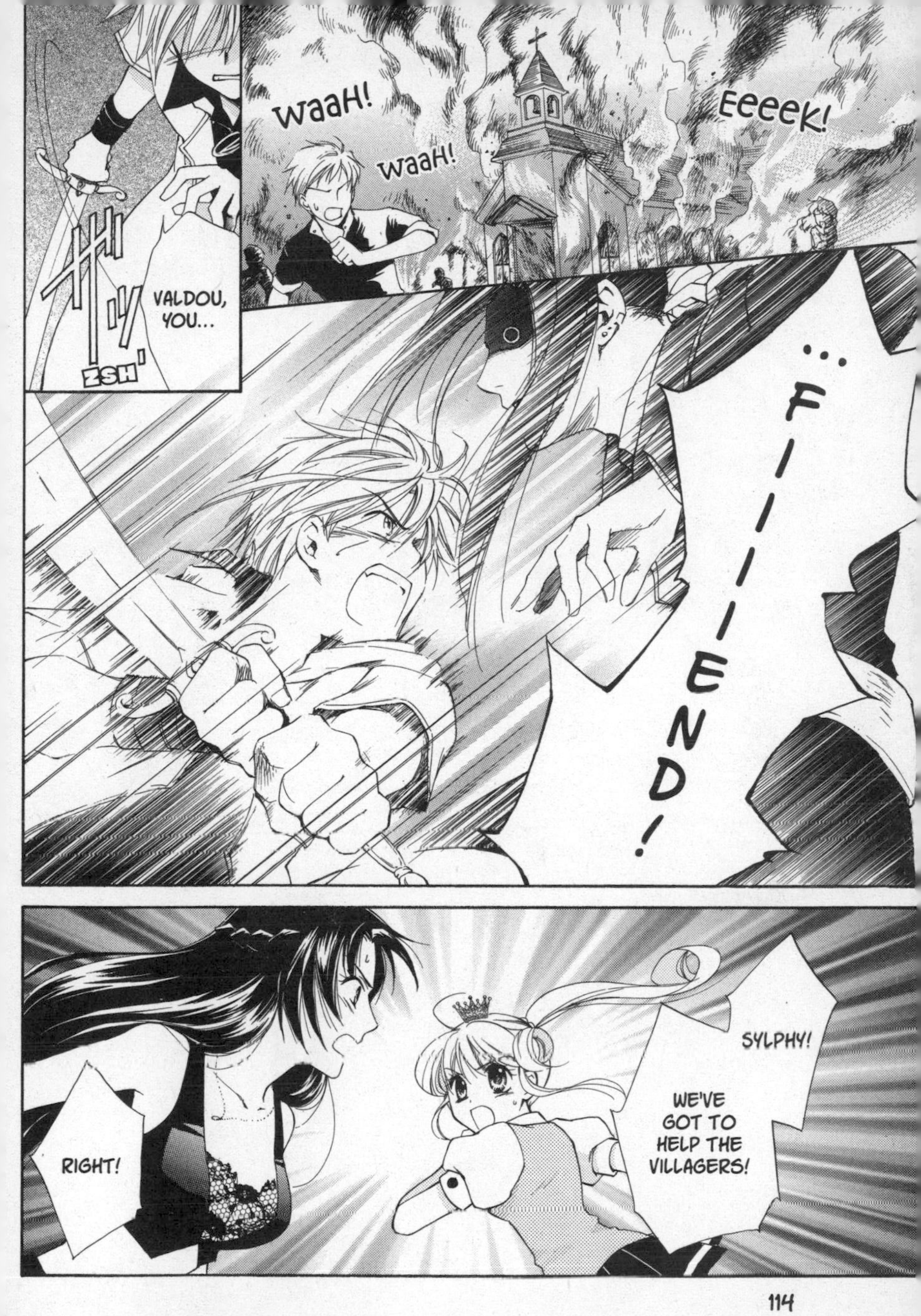
EEEEK!
WAAH!
WAAH!
VALDOU, YOU...
ZSH
...FIIIEND!
SYLPHY!
WE'VE GOT TO HELP THE VILLAGERS!
RIGHT!

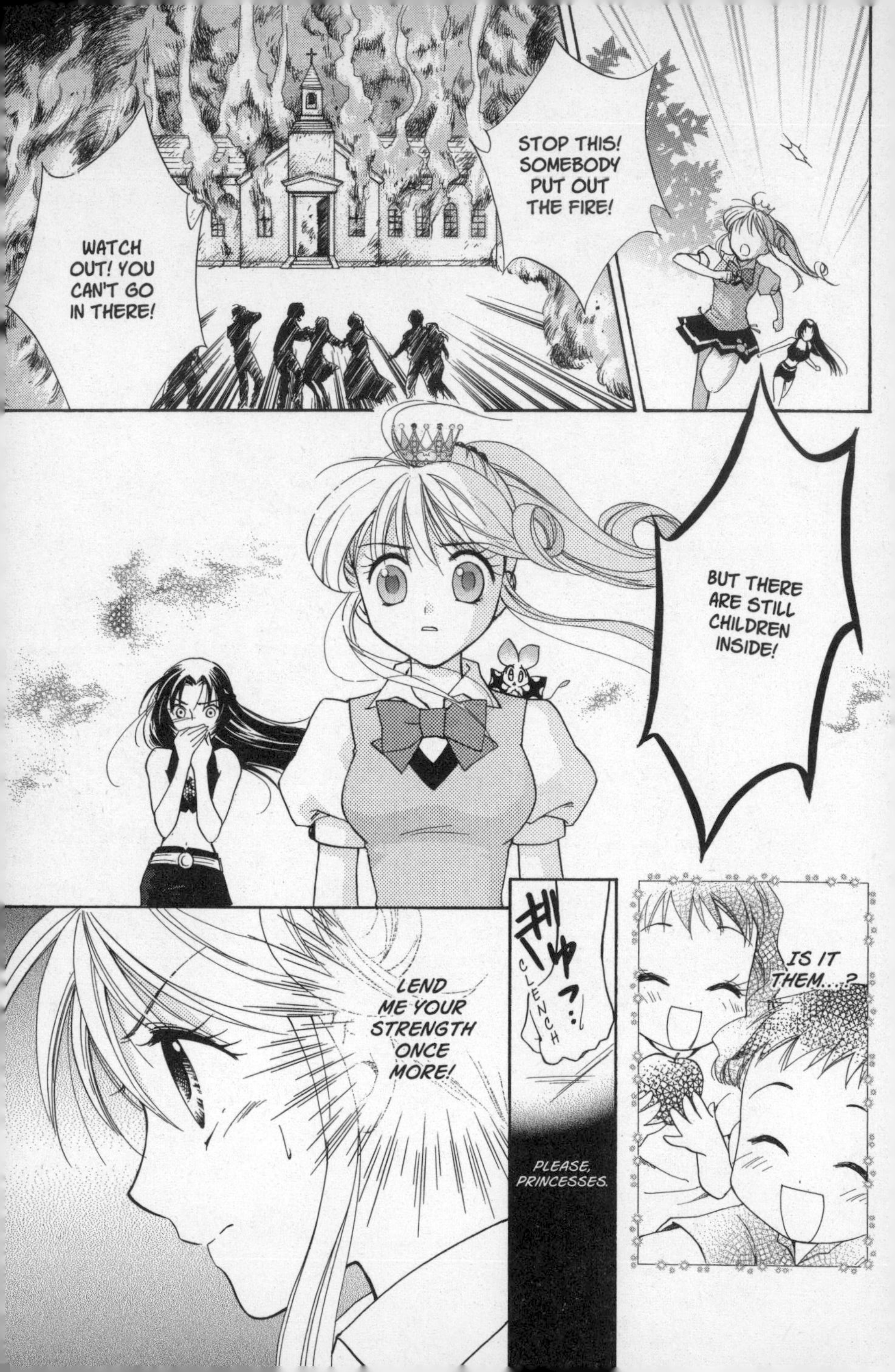
STOP THIS! SOMEBODY PUT OUT THE FIRE!
WATCH OUT! YOU CAN'T GO IN THERE!
BUT THERE ARE STILL CHILDREN INSIDE!
IS IT THEM...?
ぎゅっ
CLENCH
PLEASE, PRINCESSES.
LEND ME YOUR STRENGTH ONCE MORE!

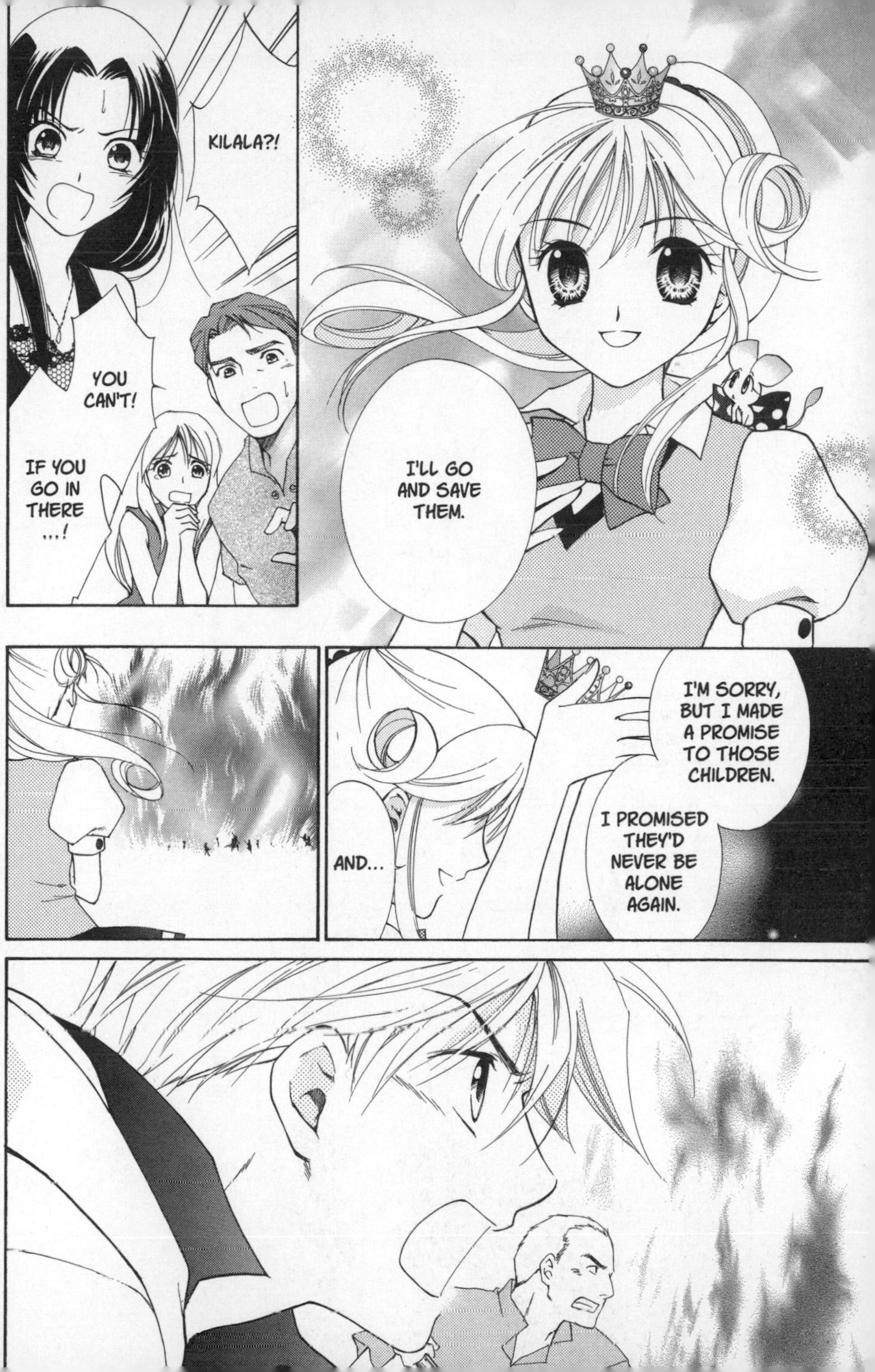
I'LL GO AND SAVE THEM.
KILALA?!
YOU CAN'T!
IF YOU GO IN THERE ...!
I'M SORRY, BUT I MADE A PROMISE TO THOSE CHILDREN.
I PROMISED THEY'D NEVER BE ALONE AGAIN.
AND...

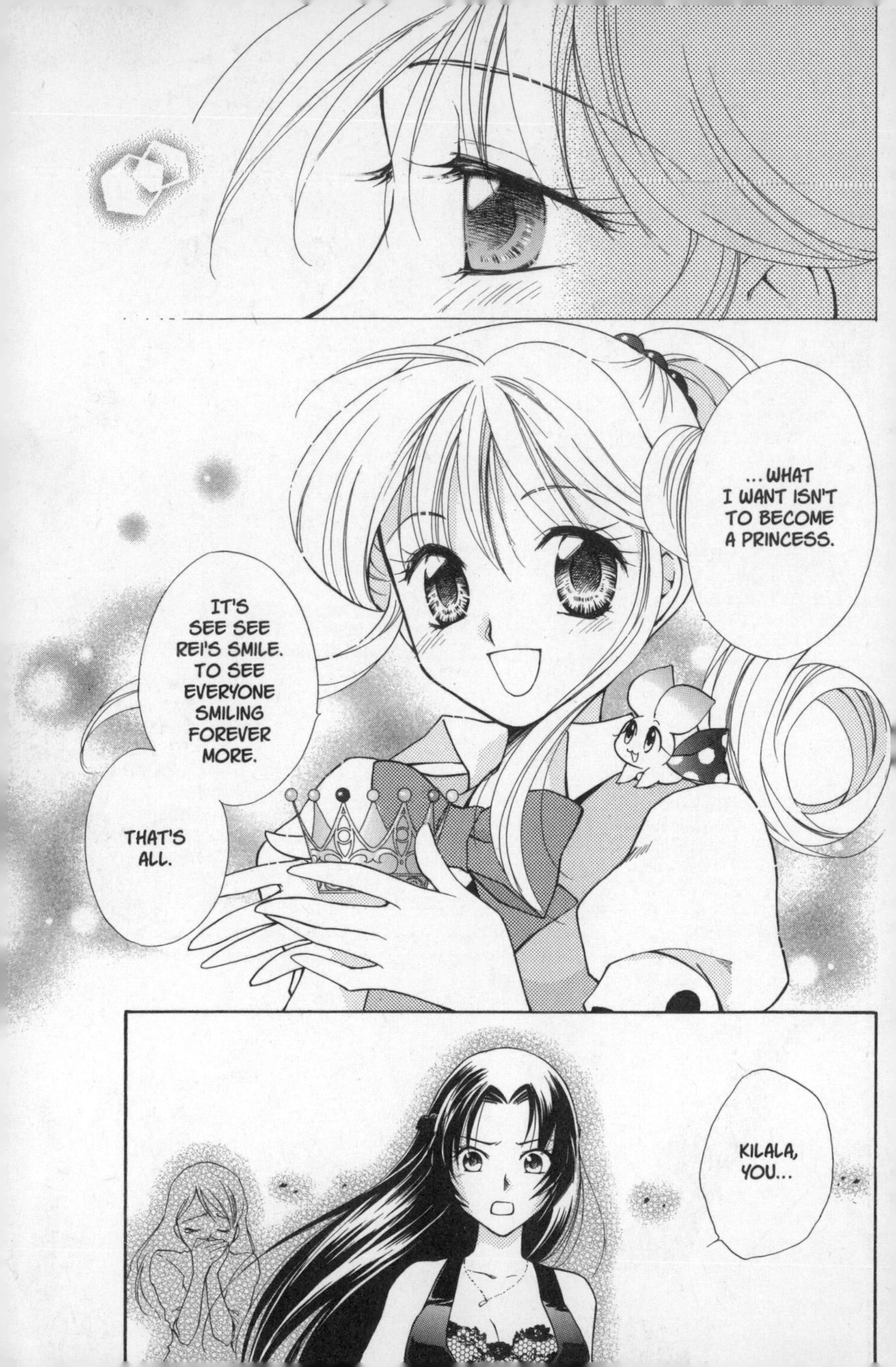
...WHAT I WANT ISN'T TO BECOME A PRINCESS.
IT'S SEE SEE REI'S SMILE. TO SEE EVERYONE SMILING FOREVER MORE.
THAT'S ALL.
KILALA, YOU...

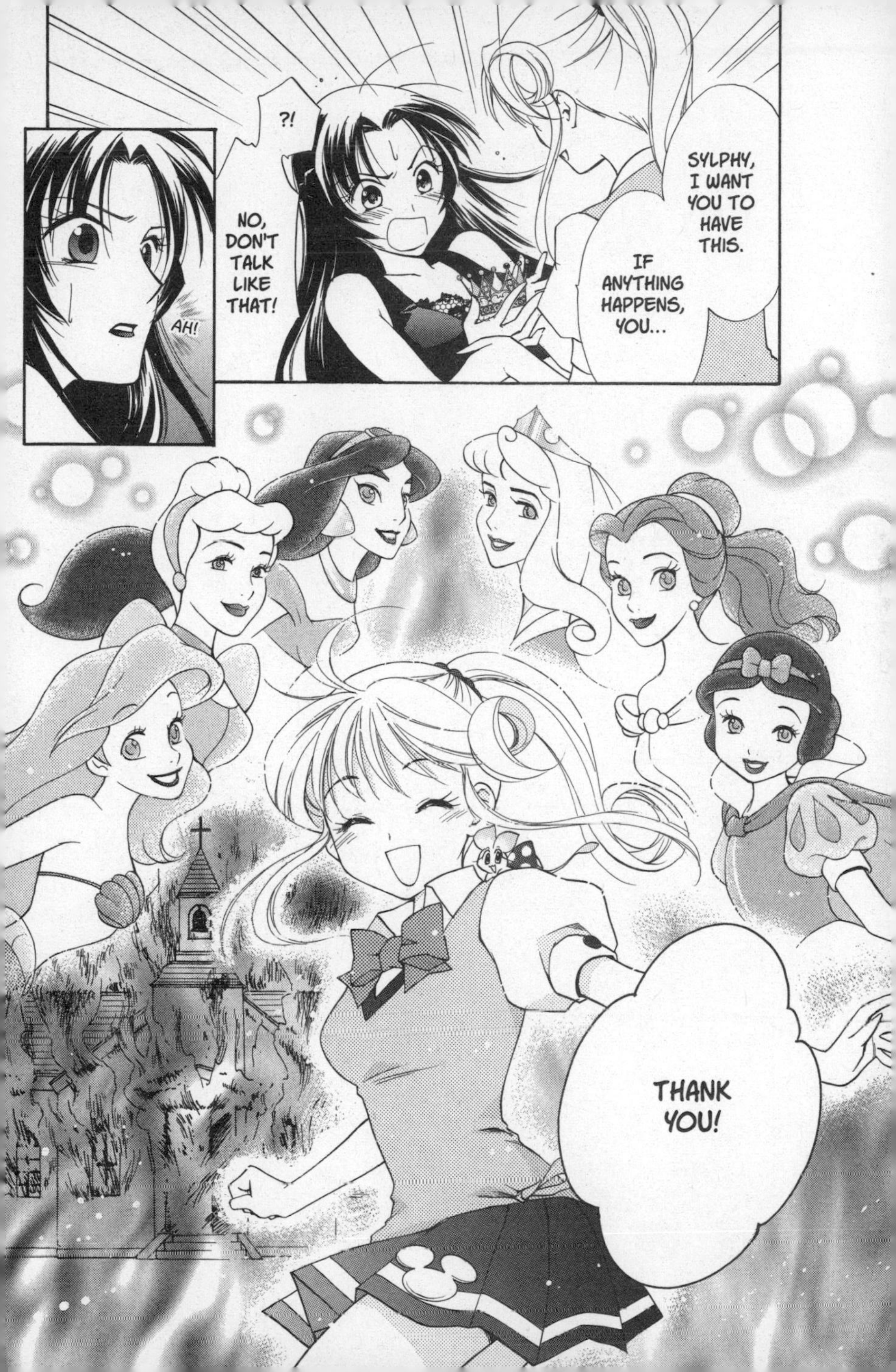
SYLPHY, I WANT YOU TO HAVE THIS.
IF ANYTHING HAPPENS, YOU...
?!
NO, DON'T TALK LIKE THAT!
AH!
THANK YOU!

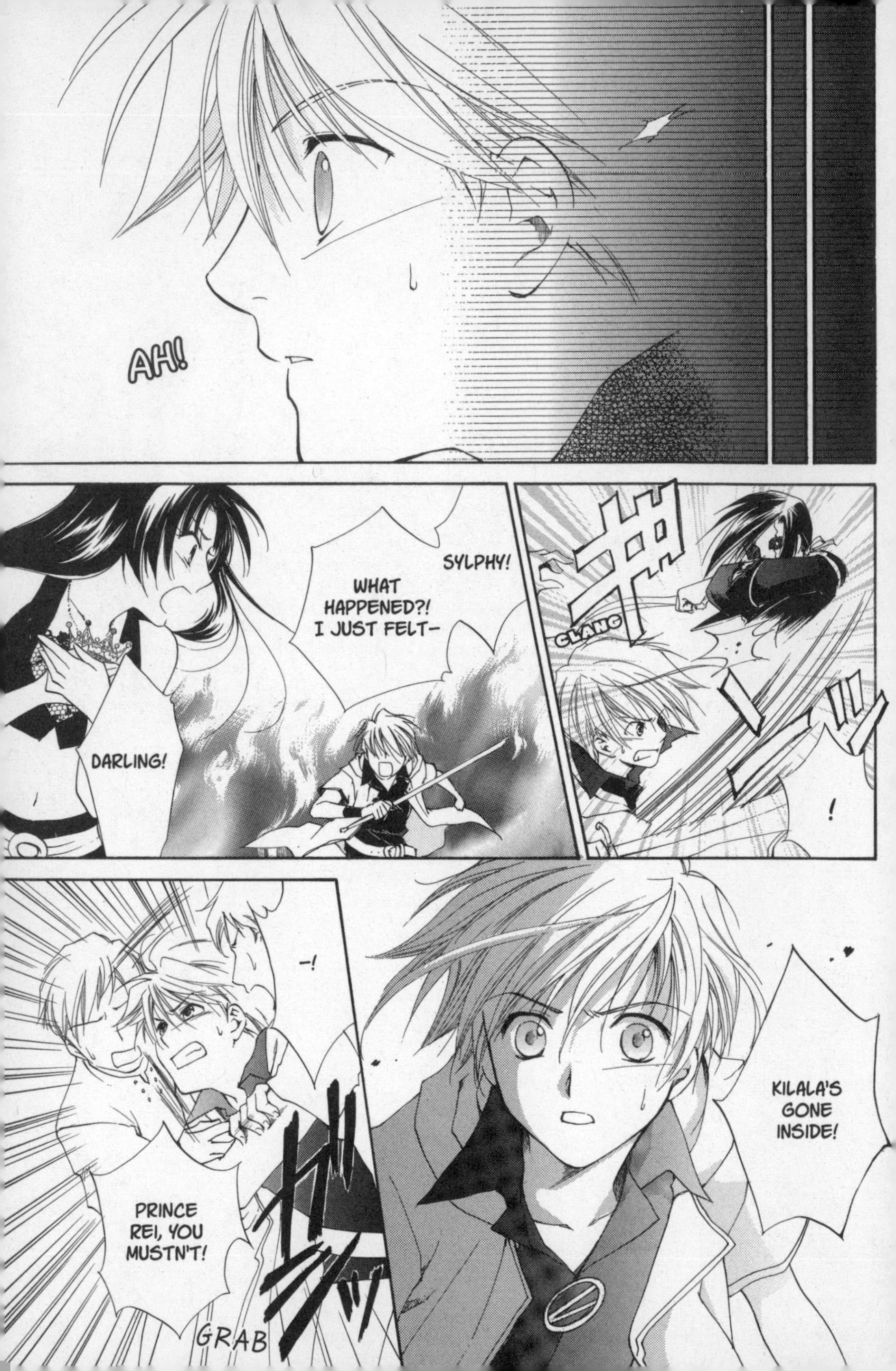
AH!
CLANG
!
SYLPHY!
WHAT HAPPENED?! I JUST FELT-
DARLING!
KILALA'S GONE INSIDE!
-!
PRINCE REI, YOU MUSTN'T!
GRAB

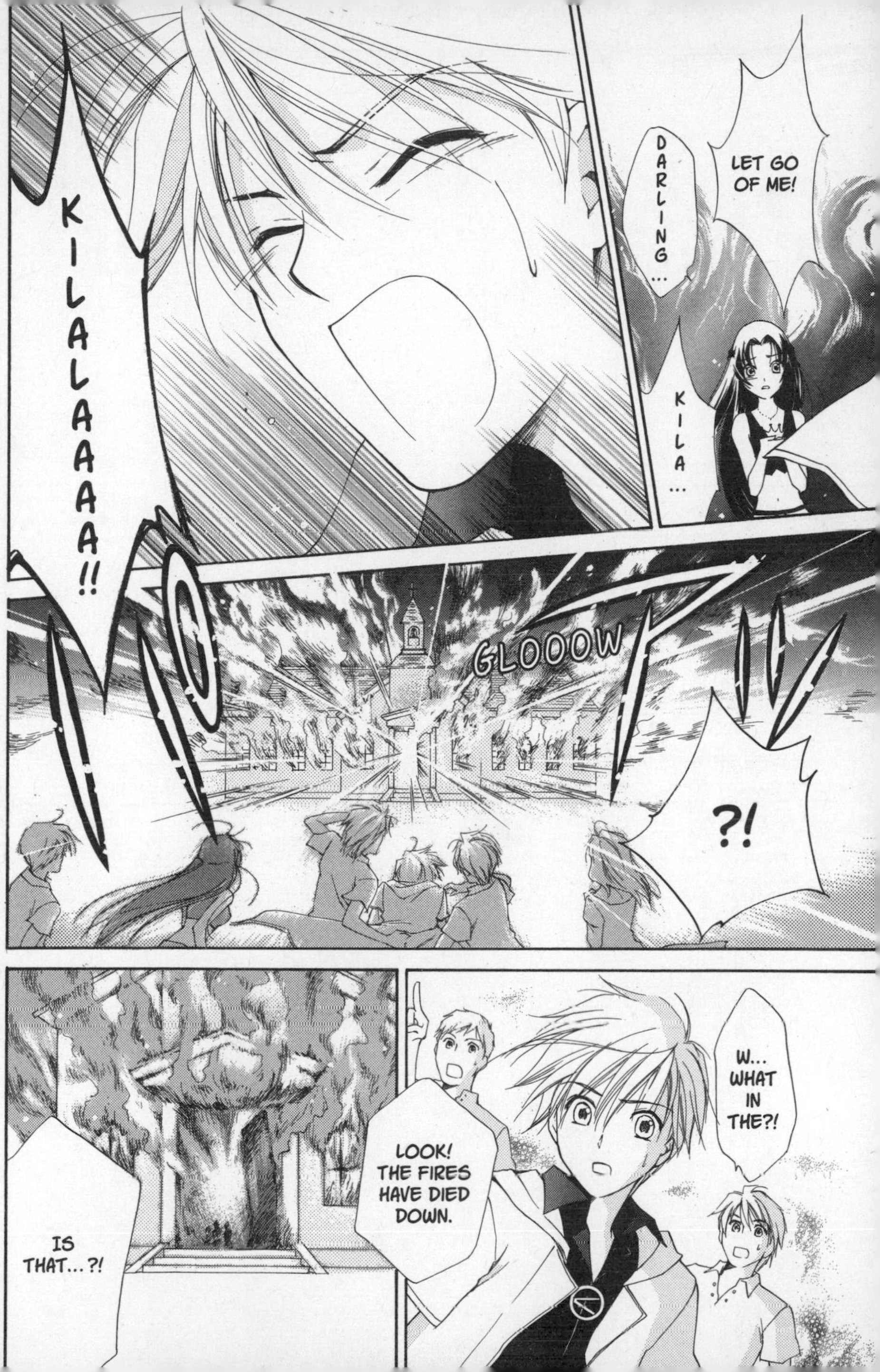
LET GO OF ME!
DARLING...
KILA...
KILALAAAAA!!
GLOOOW
?!
W... WHAT IN THE?!
LOOK! THE FIRES HAVE DIED DOWN.
IS THAT...?!

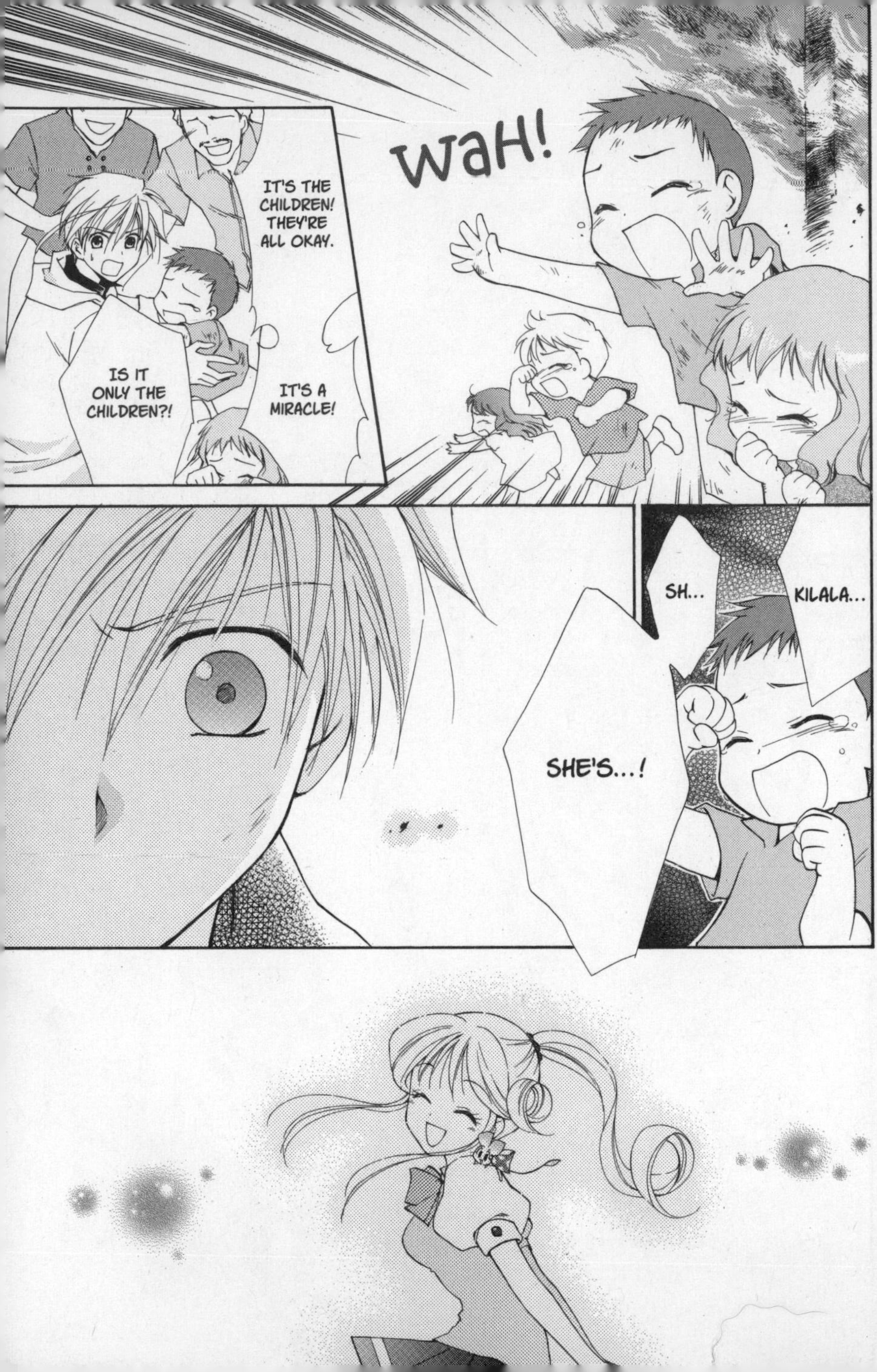
WAH!
IT'S THE CHILDREN! THEY'RE ALL OKAY.
IT'S A MIRACLE!
IS IT ONLY THE CHILDREN?!
KILALA...
SH...
SHE'S...!

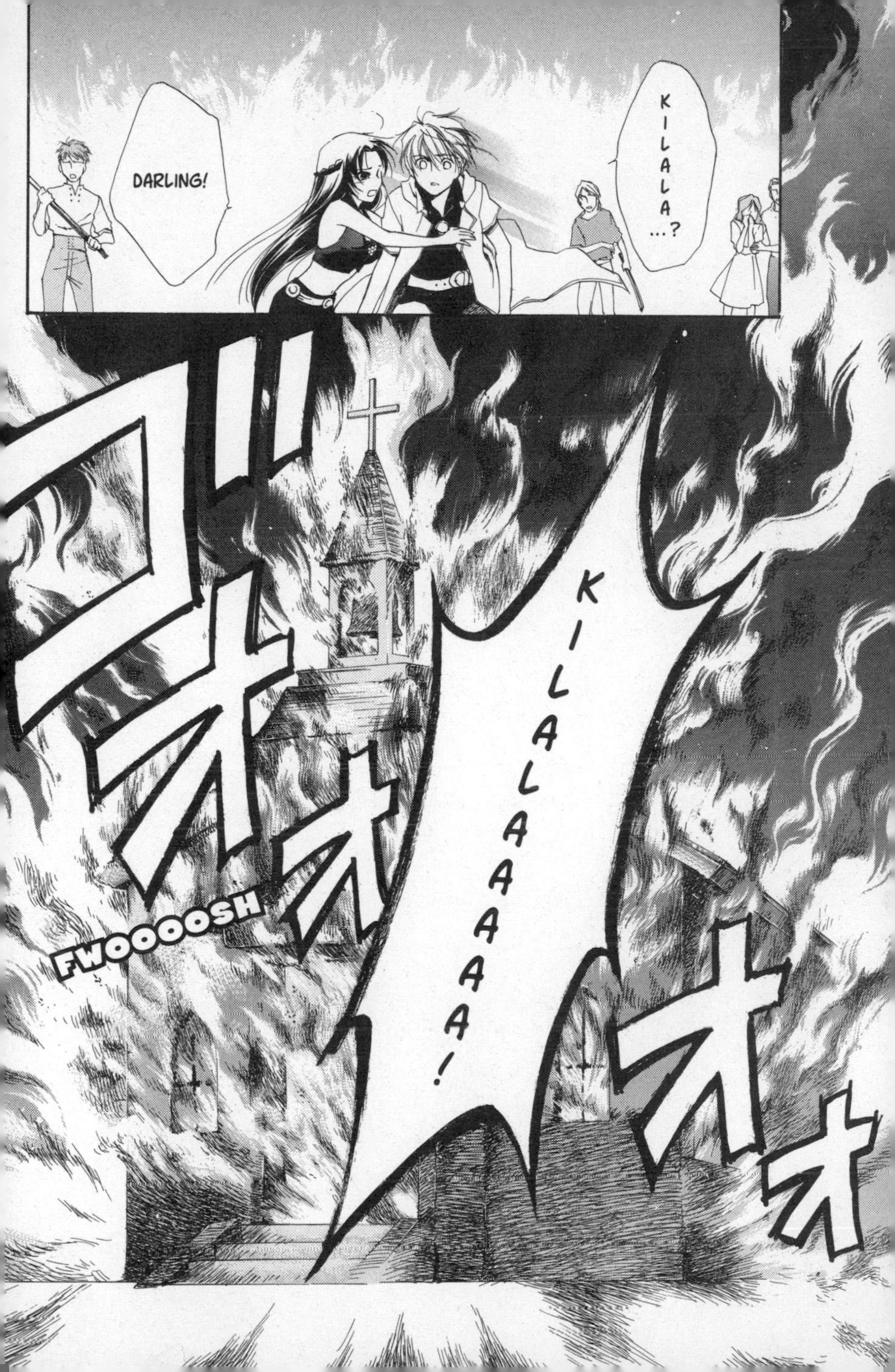
KILALA...?
DARLING!
KILALAAAAA!
FWOOOOOSH

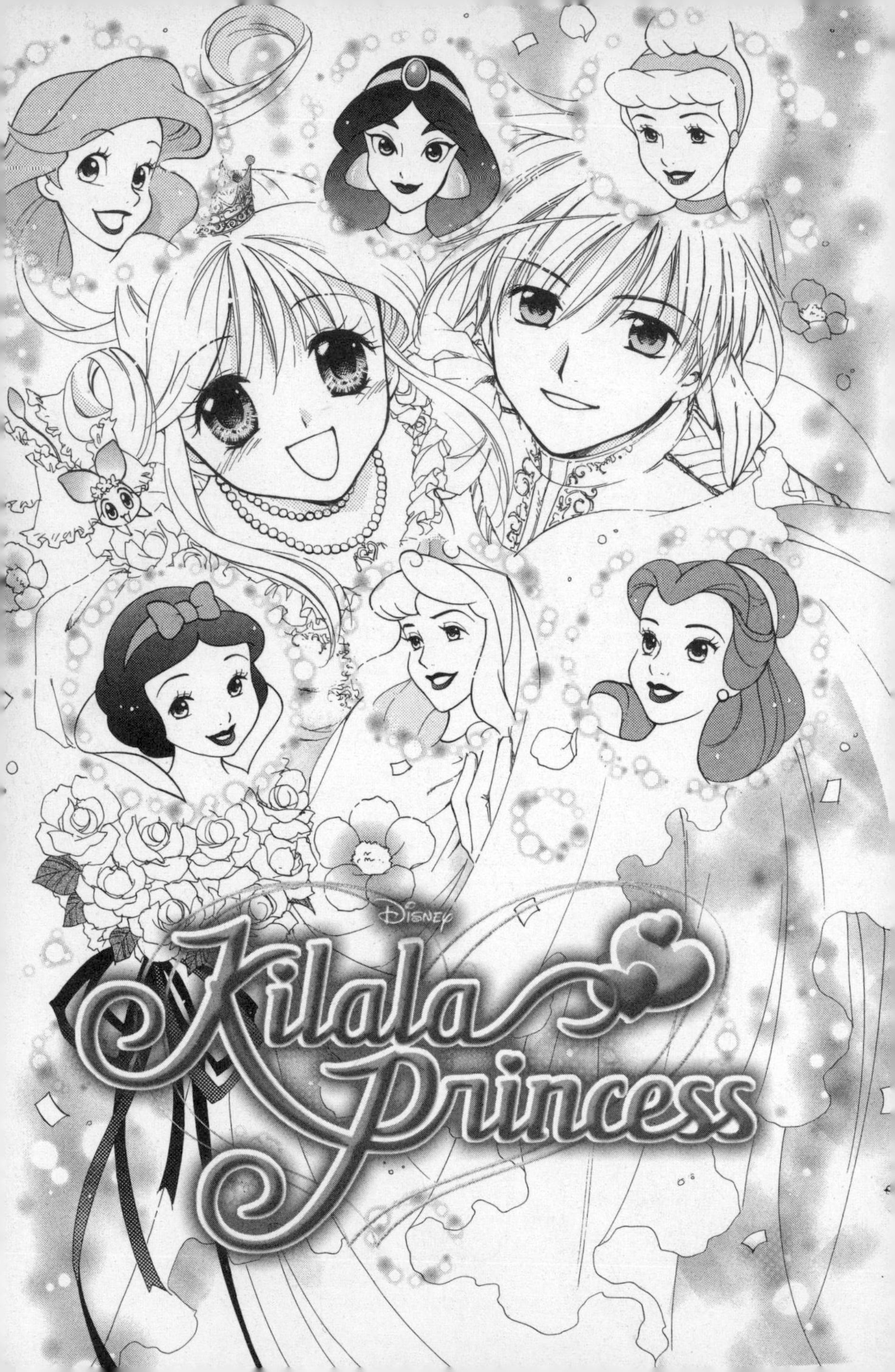

Disney
Kilala Princess

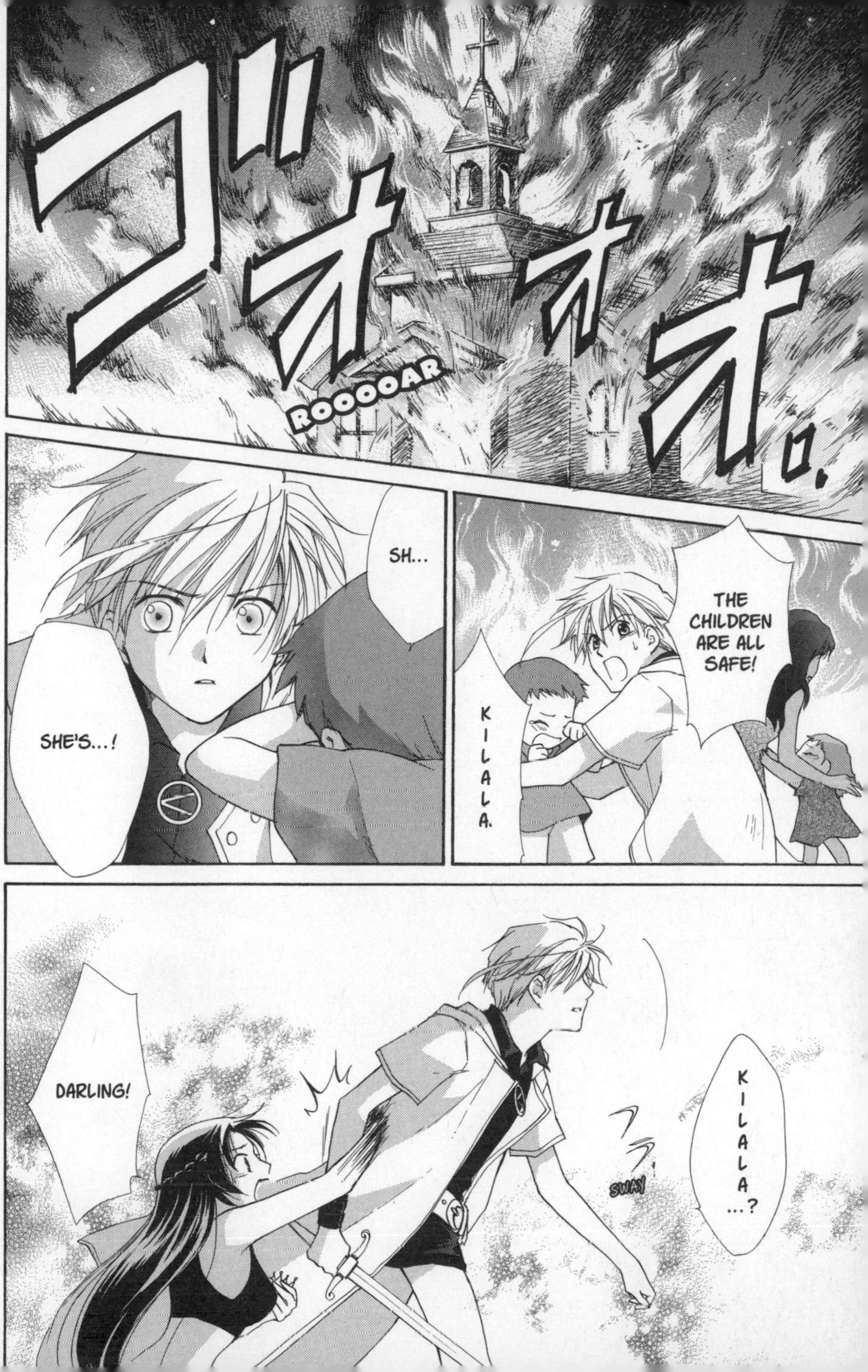
ゴオオオ。
ROOOOAR
THE CHILDREN ARE ALL SAFE!
KILALA.
SH...
SHE'S...!
KILALA...?
フラ
SWAY
DARLING!

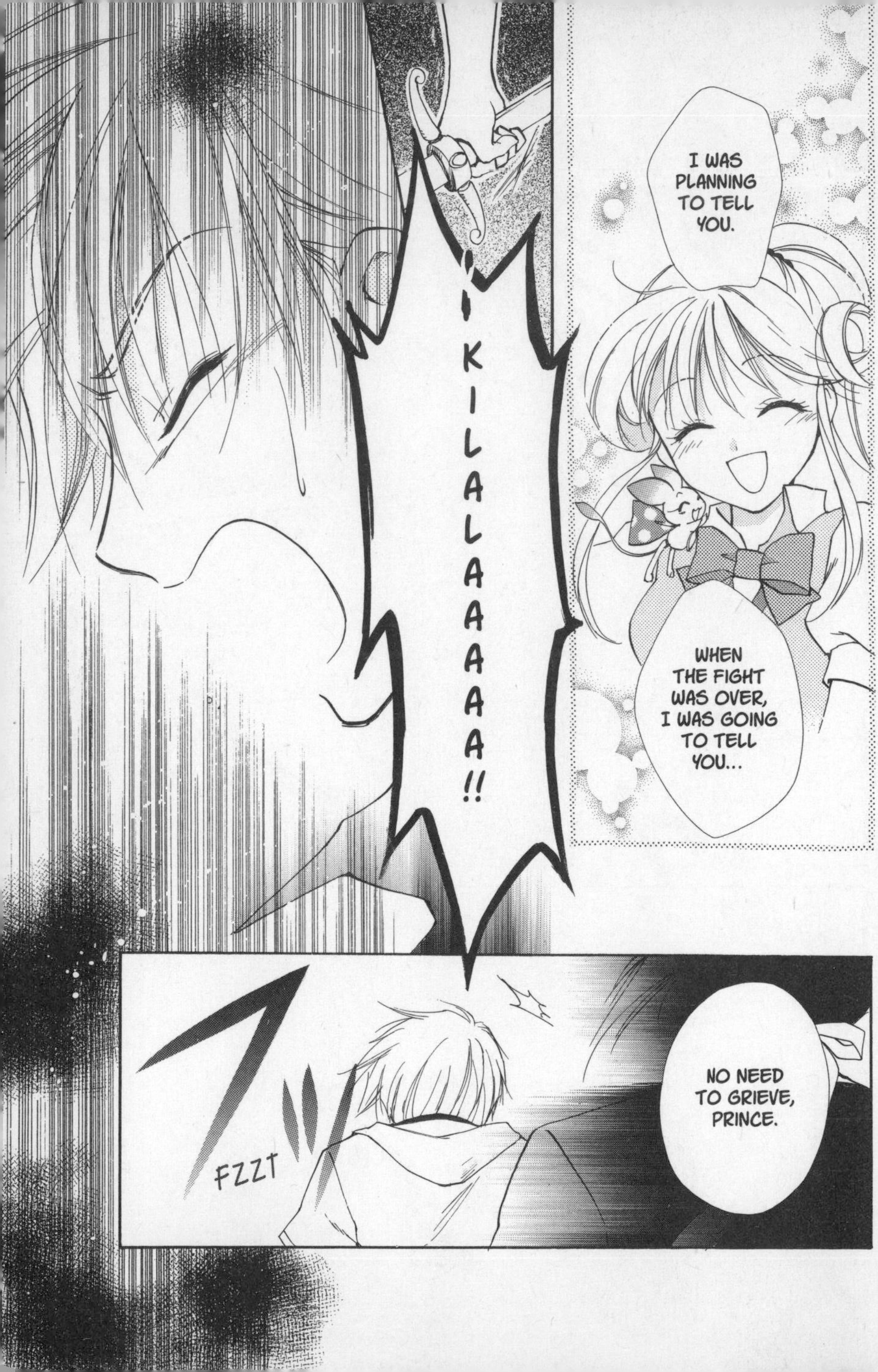
I WAS PLANNING TO TELL YOU.
WHEN THE FIGHT WAS OVER, I WAS GOING TO TELL YOU...
KILALAAAAA!!
NO NEED TO GRIEVE, PRINCE.
FZZT

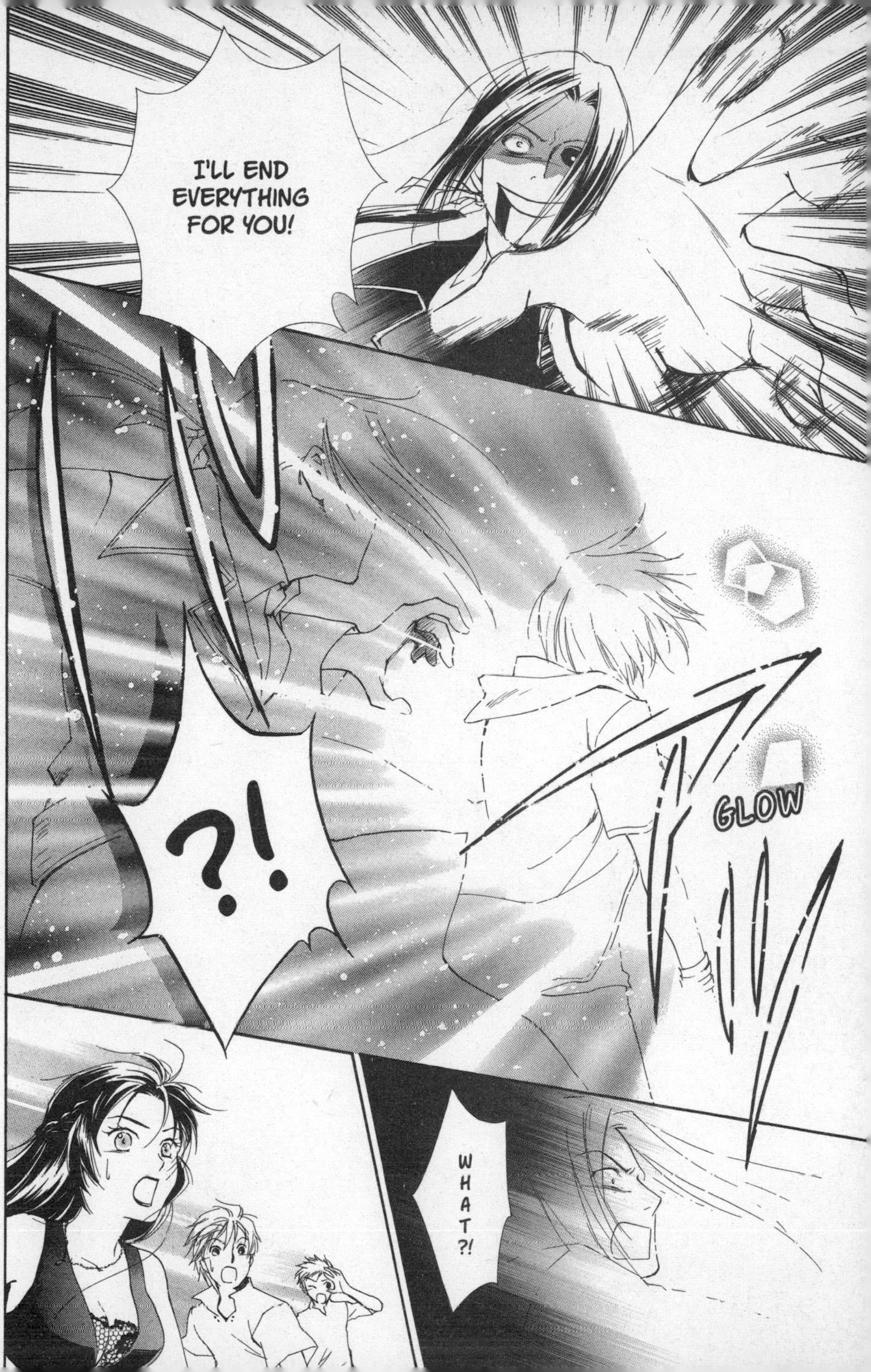
I'LL END EVERYTHING FOR YOU!
?!
GLOW
WHAT?!

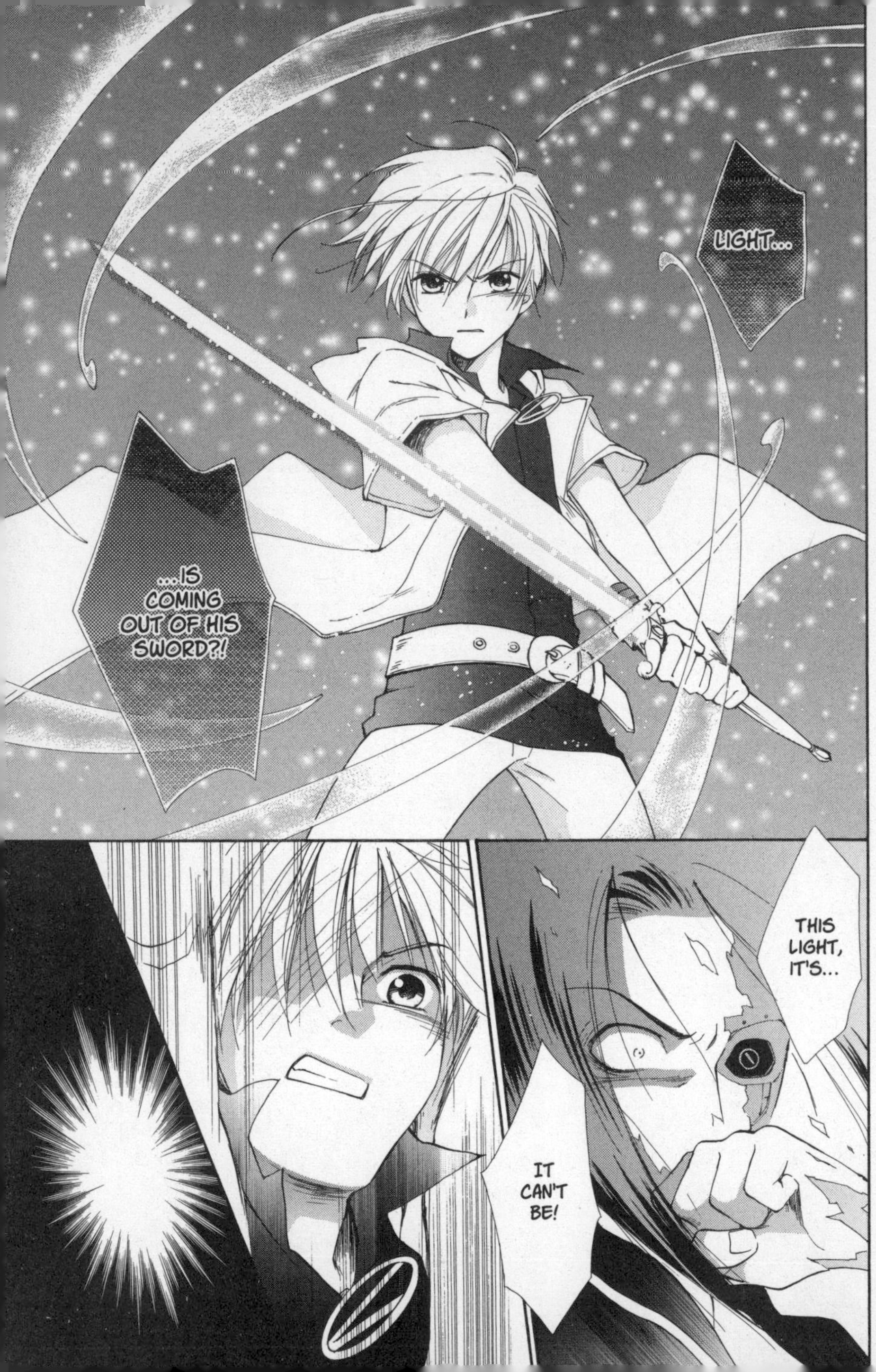
LIGHT...
...IS COMING OUT OF HIS SWORD?!
THIS LIGHT, IT'S...
IT CAN'T BE!

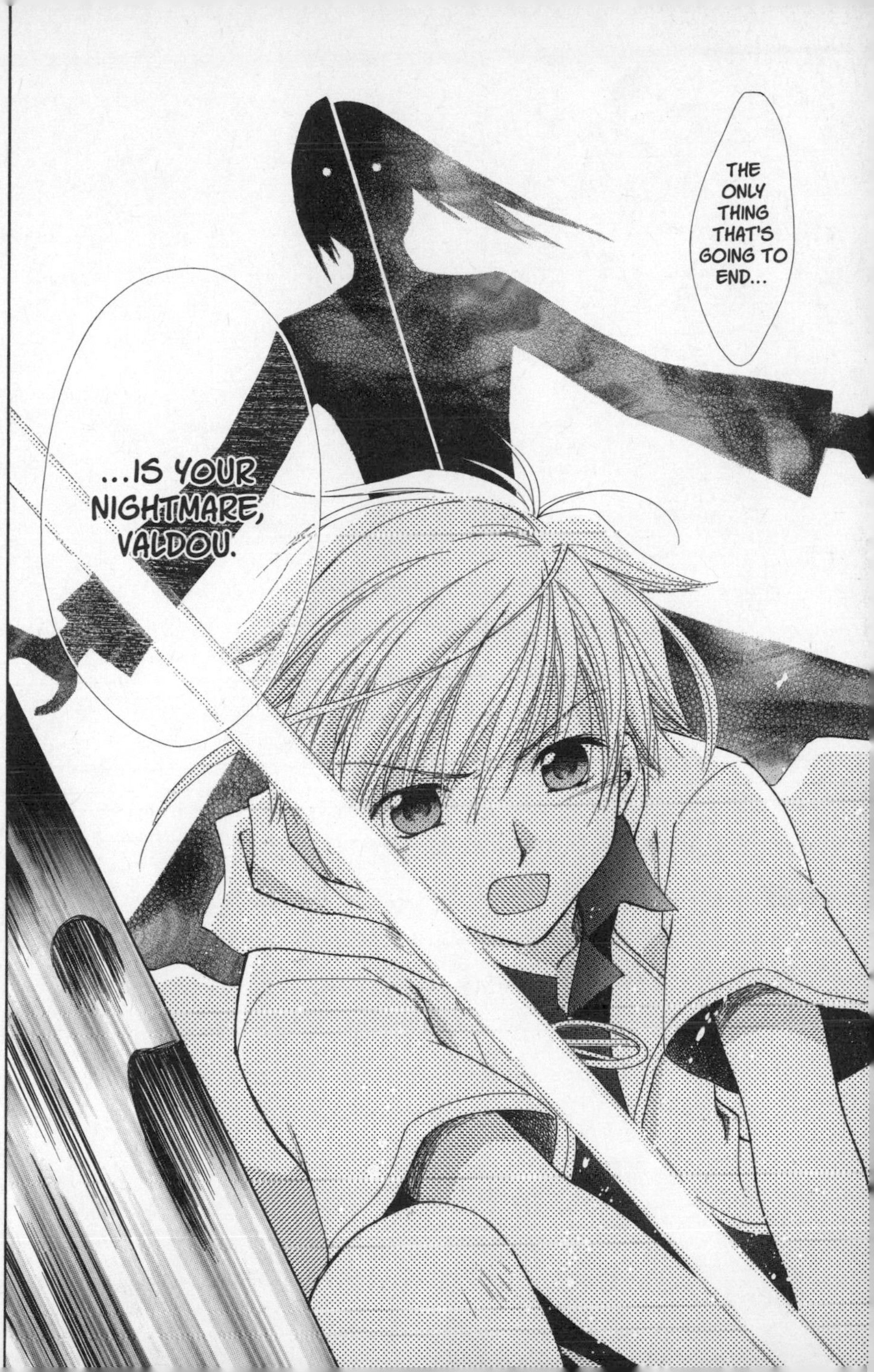
THE ONLY THING THAT'S GOING TO END...
...IS YOUR NIGHTMARE, VALDOU.

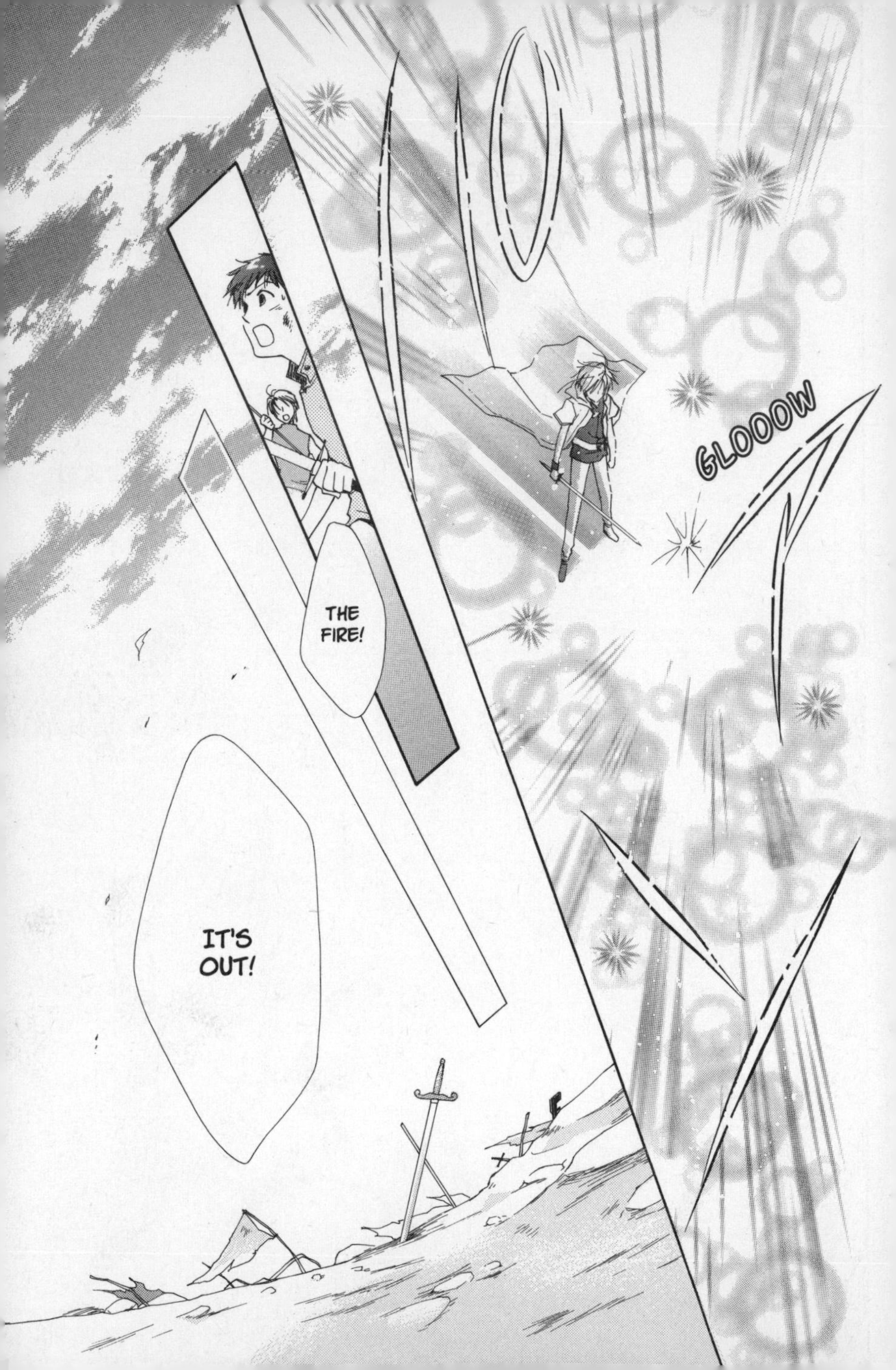
GLOOOW
THE FIRE!
IT'S OUT!

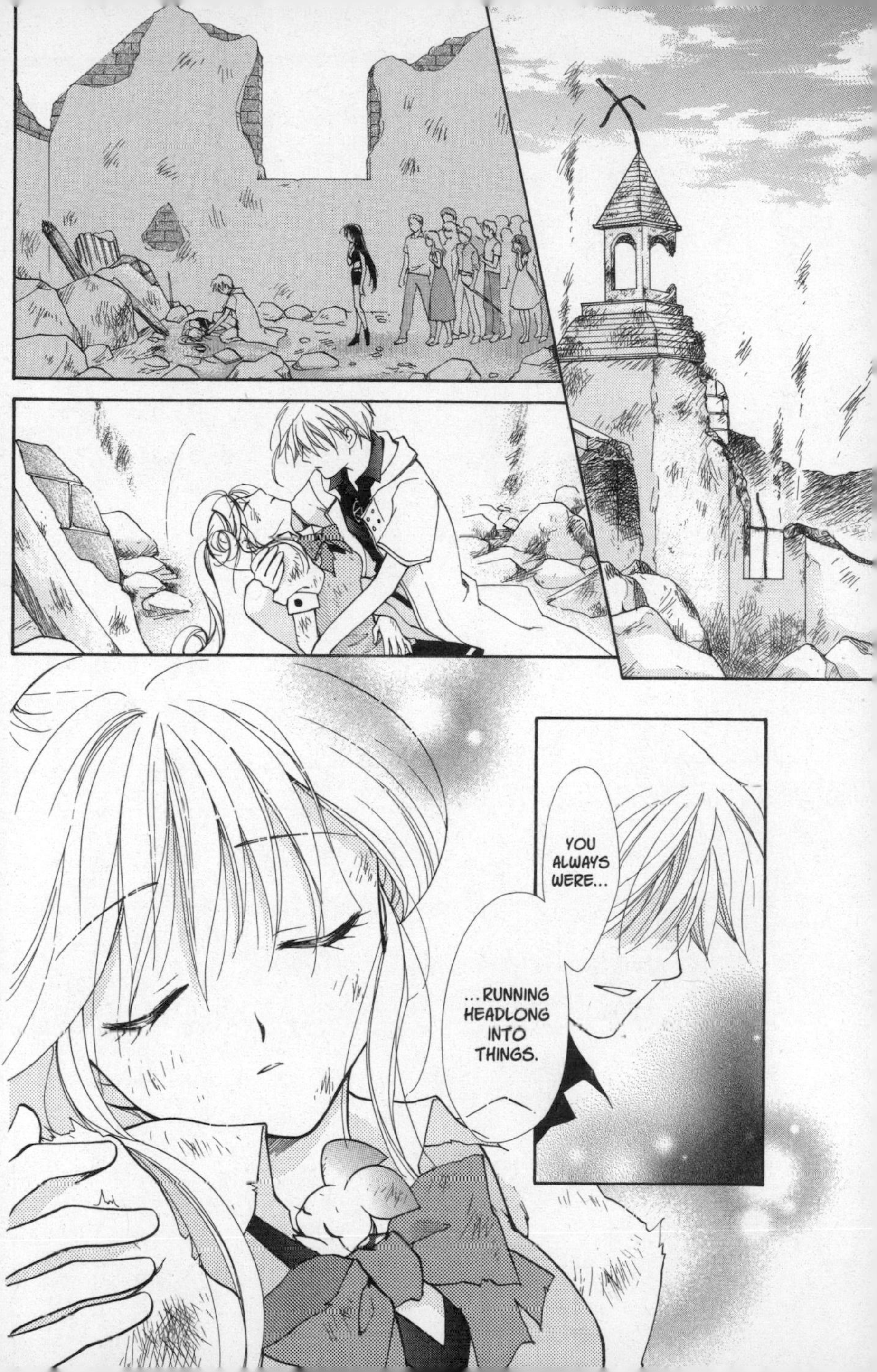
YOU ALWAYS WERE...
...RUNNING HEADLONG INTO THINGS.

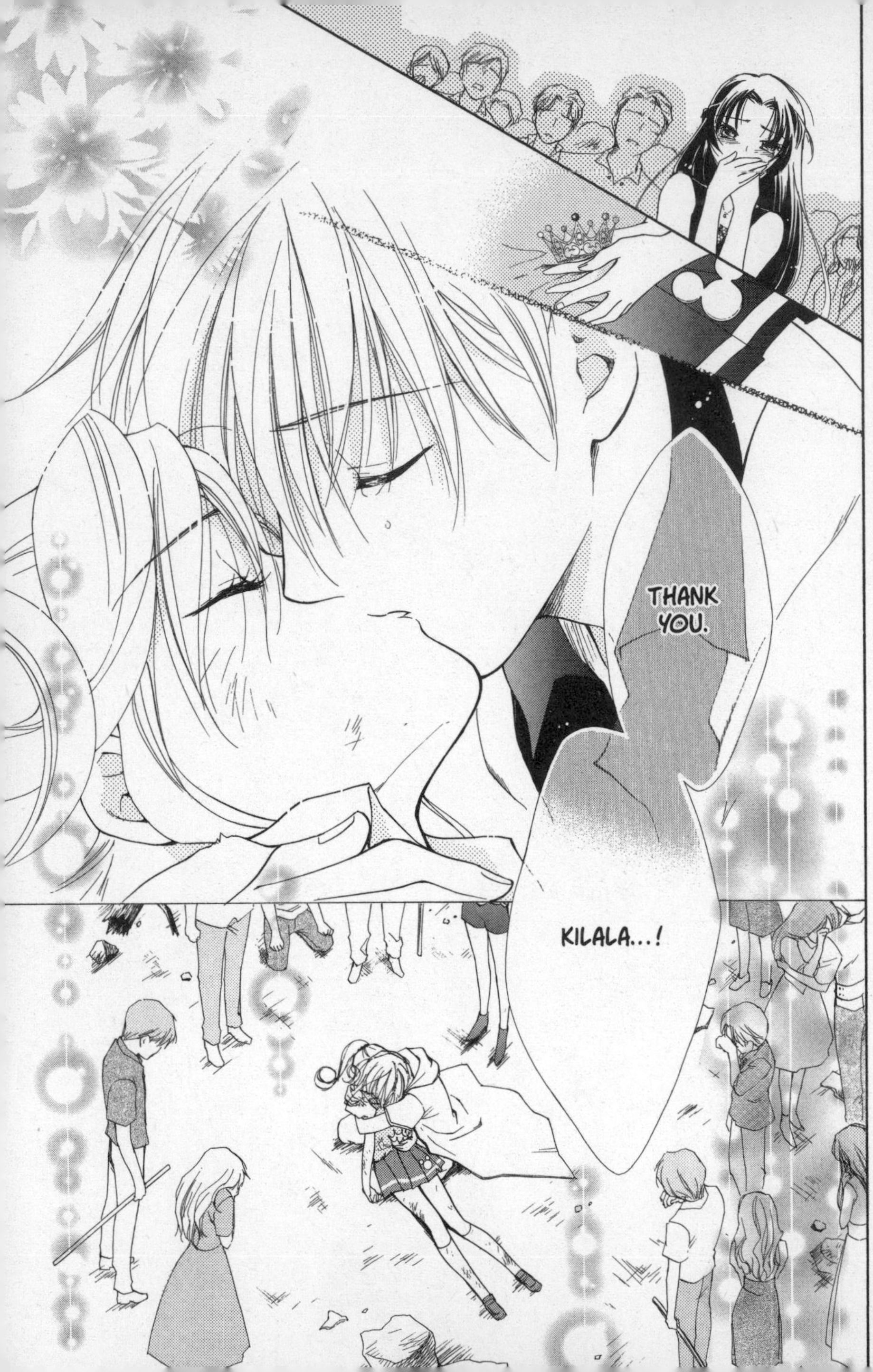
THANK YOU.
KILALA...!

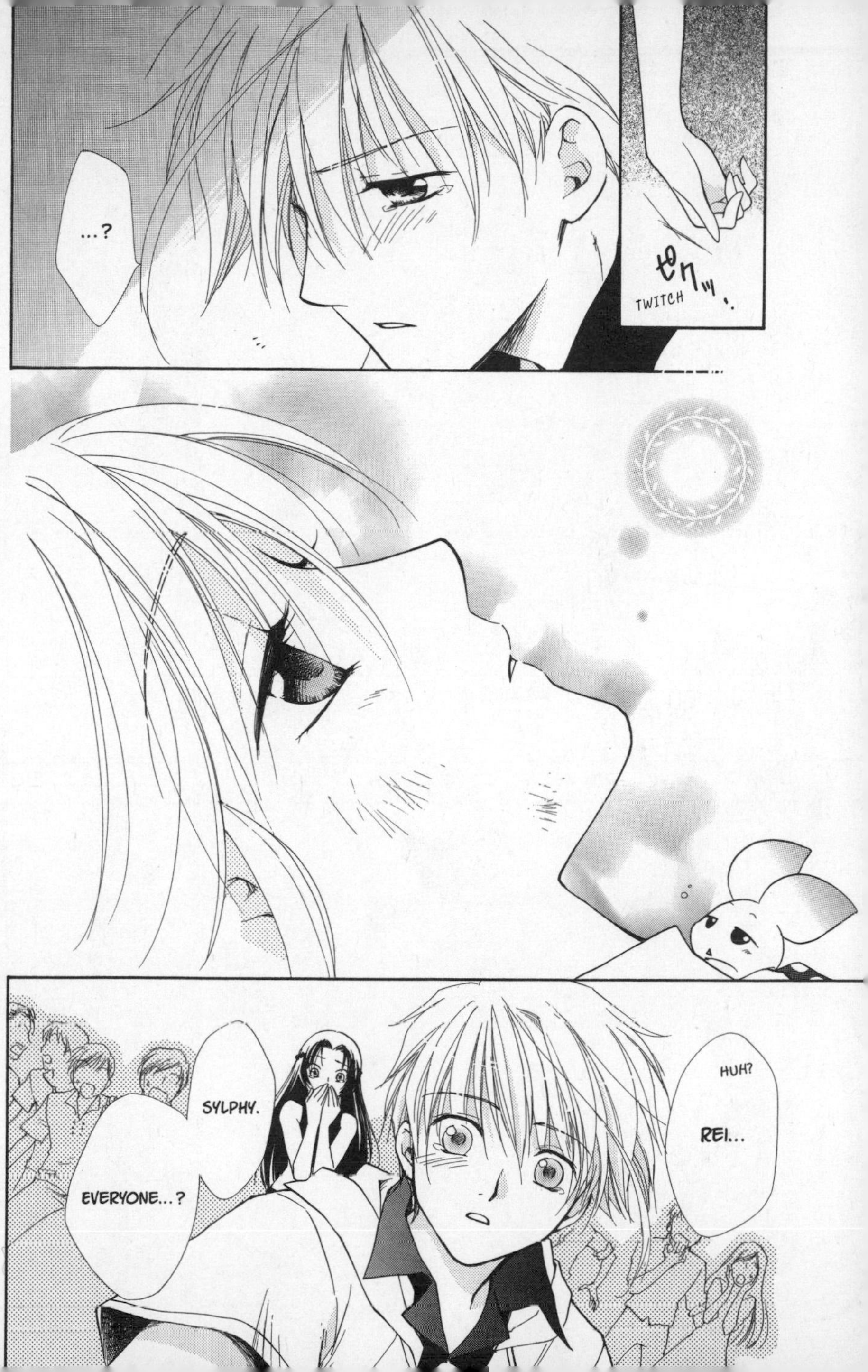
TWITCH
...?
HUH?
REI...
SYLPHY.
EVERYONE...?

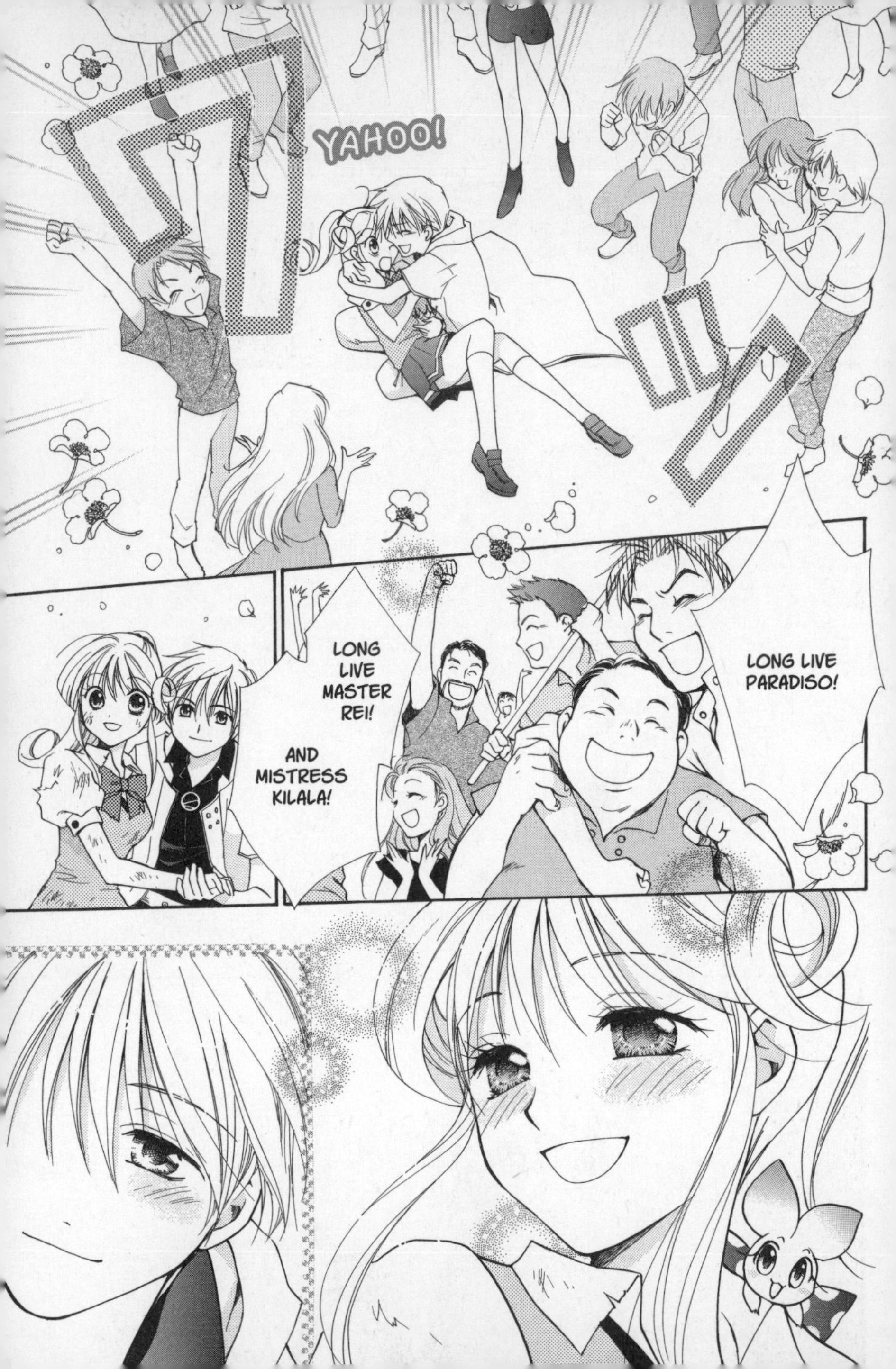
YAHOO!
LONG LIVE PARADISO!
LONG LIVE MASTER REI!
AND MISTRESS KILALA!

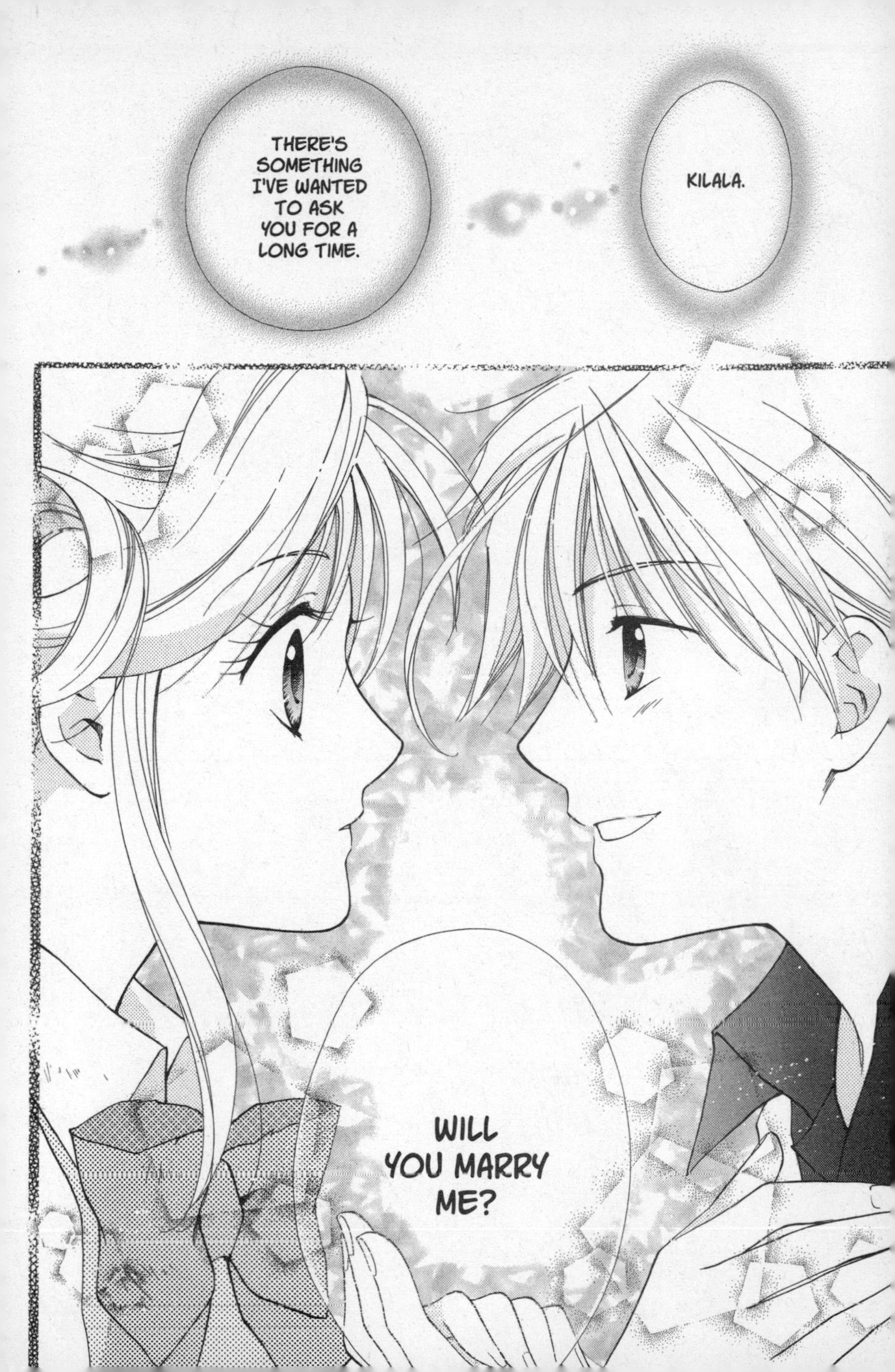
KILALA.
THERE'S SOMETHING I'VE WANTED TO ASK YOU FOR A LONG TIME.
WILL YOU MARRY ME?

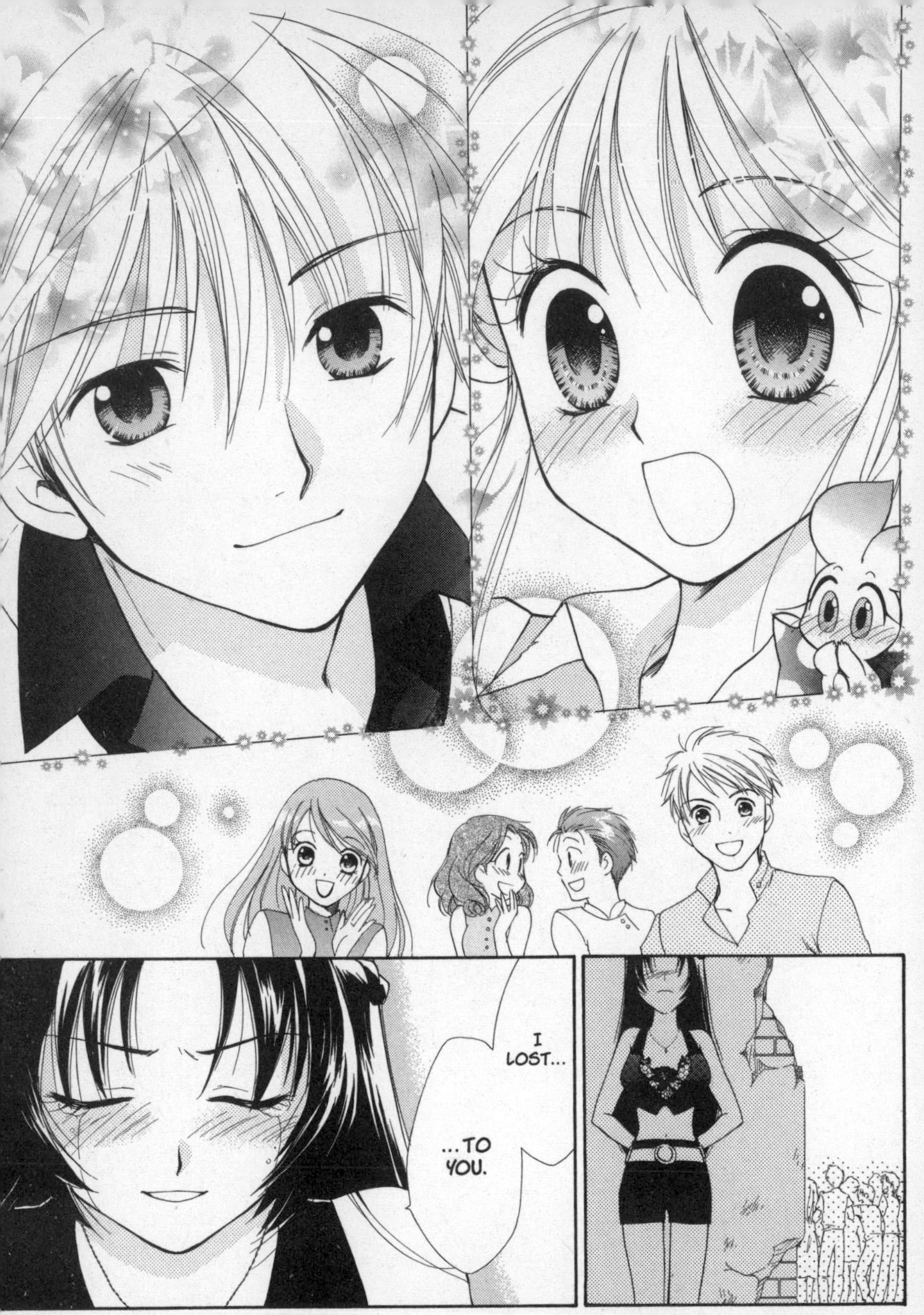
I LOST...
...TO YOU.

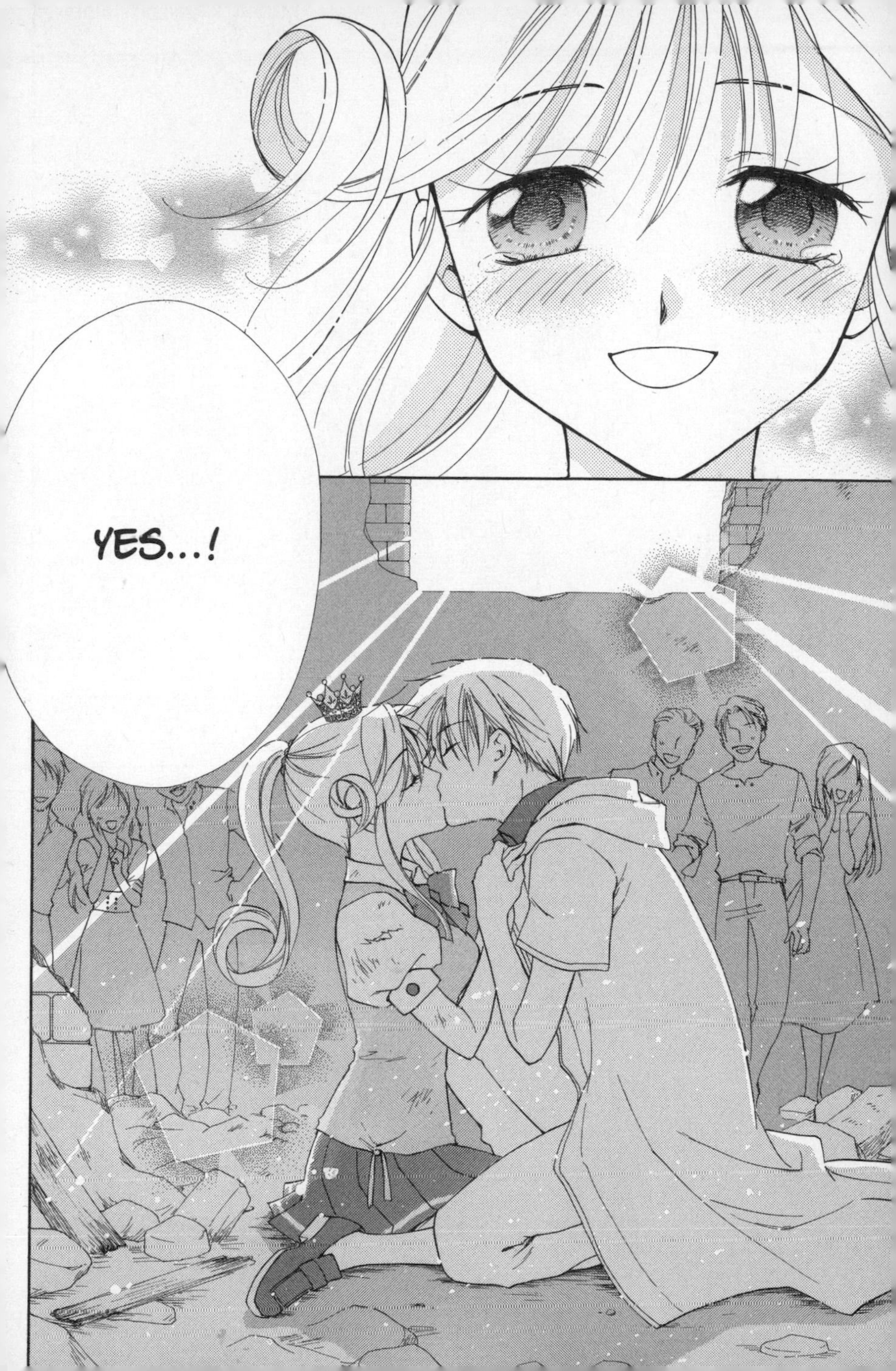
YES...!

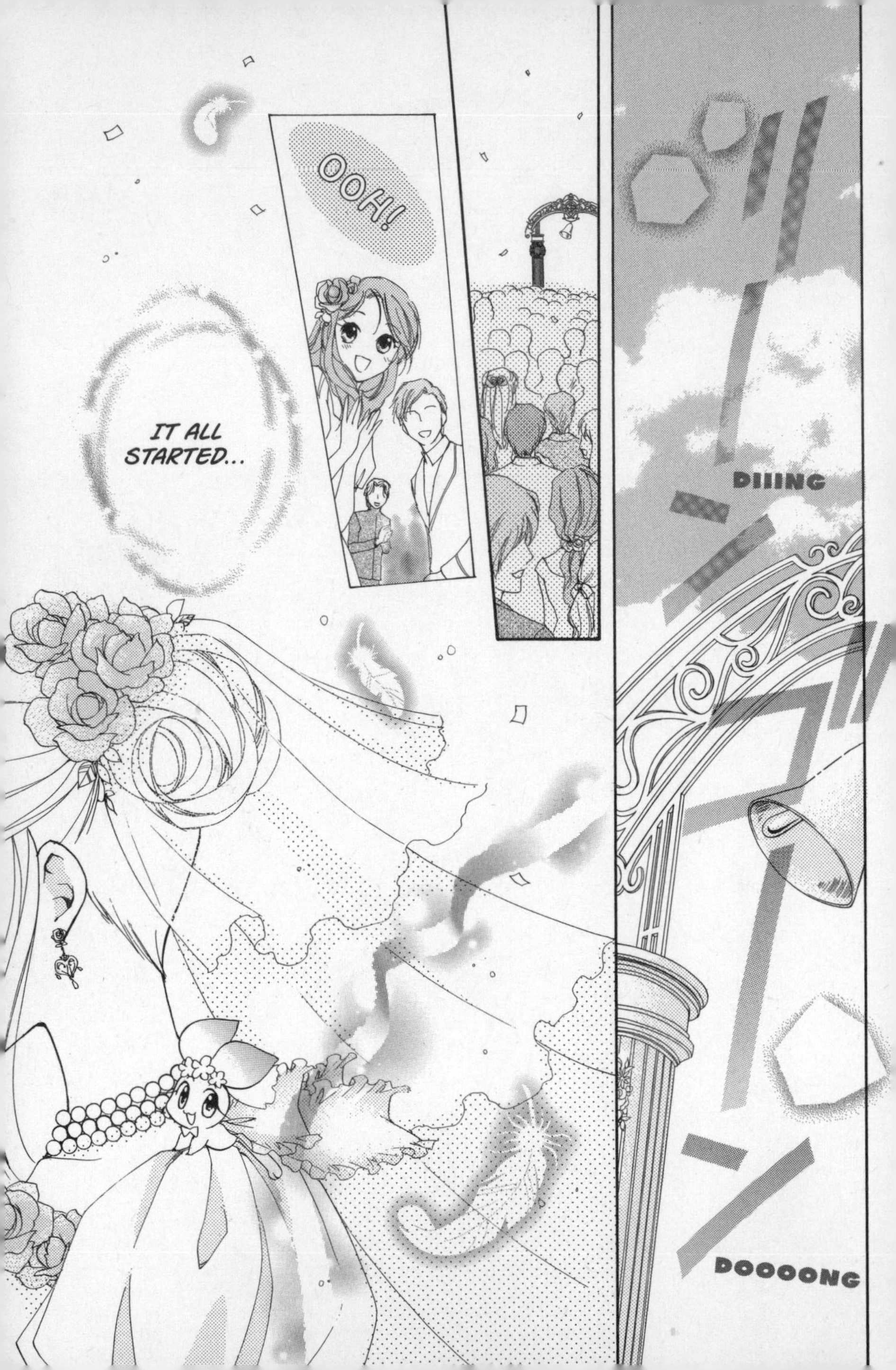
DIIING
DOOOONG
OOH!
IT ALL STARTED...

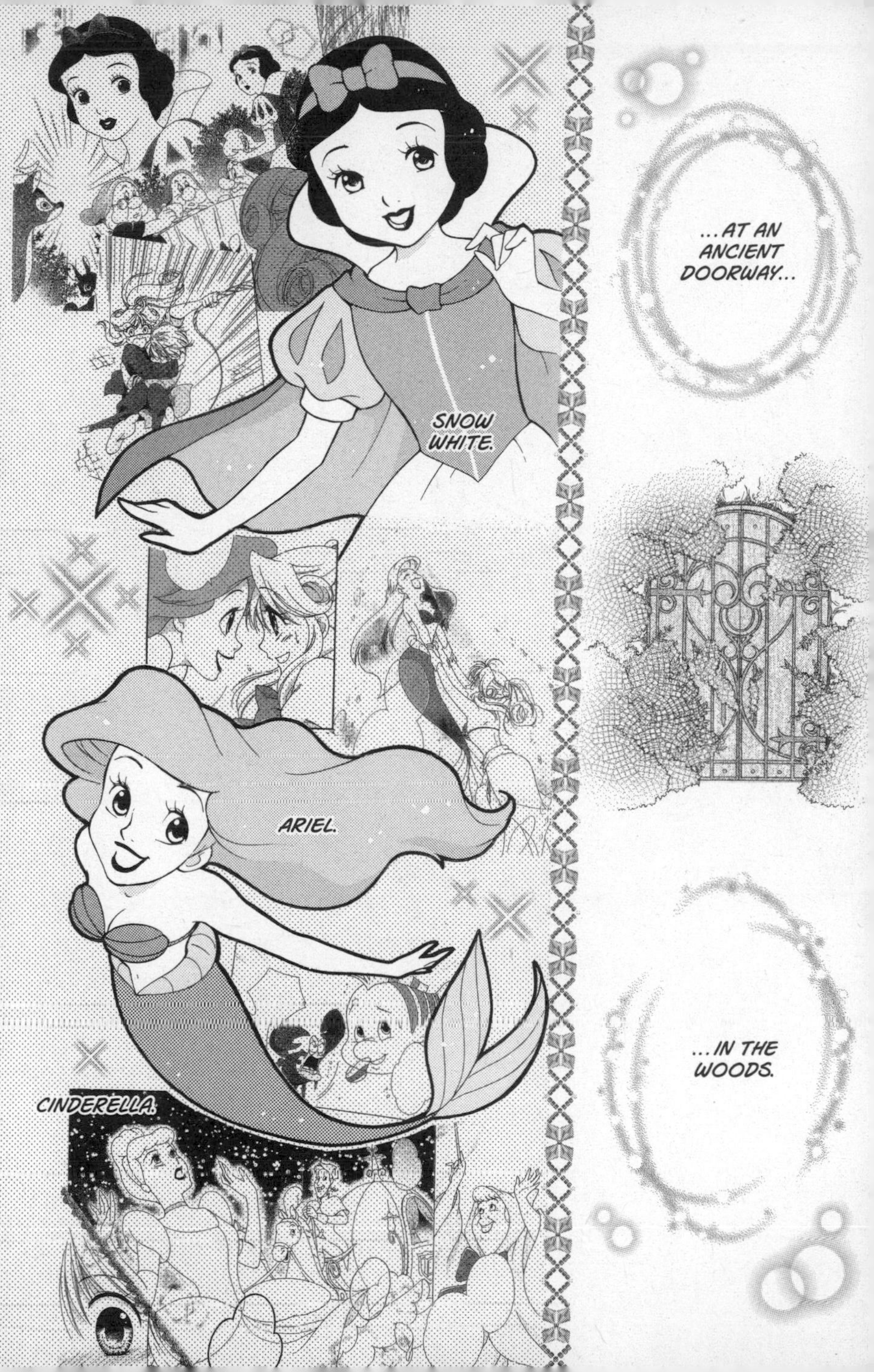
...AT AN ANCIENT DOORWAY...
...IN THE WOODS.
SNOW WHITE.
ARIEL.
CINDERELLA.

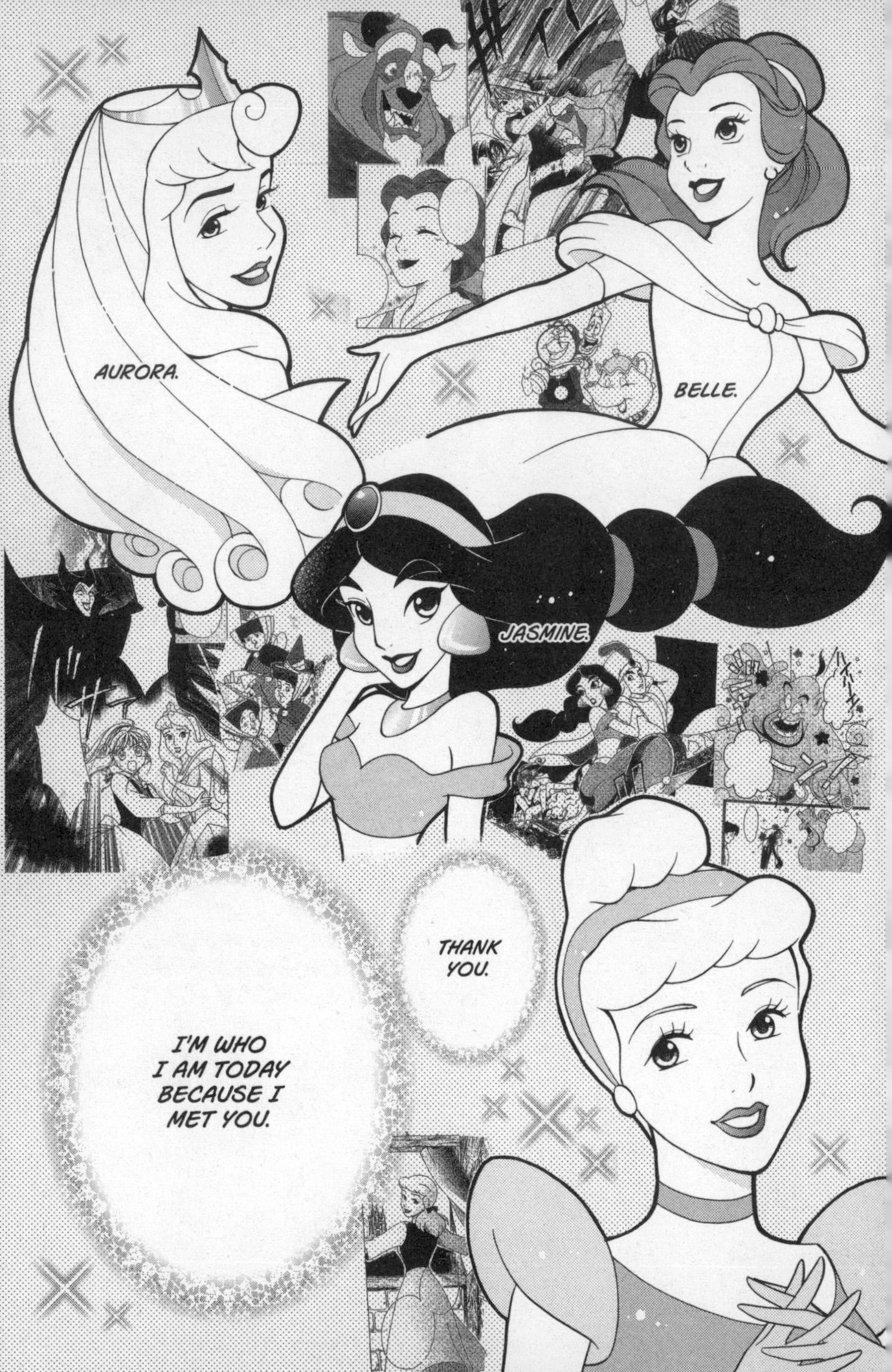
BELLE.
AURORA.
JASMINE.
THANK YOU.
I'M WHO I AM TODAY BECAUSE I MET YOU.

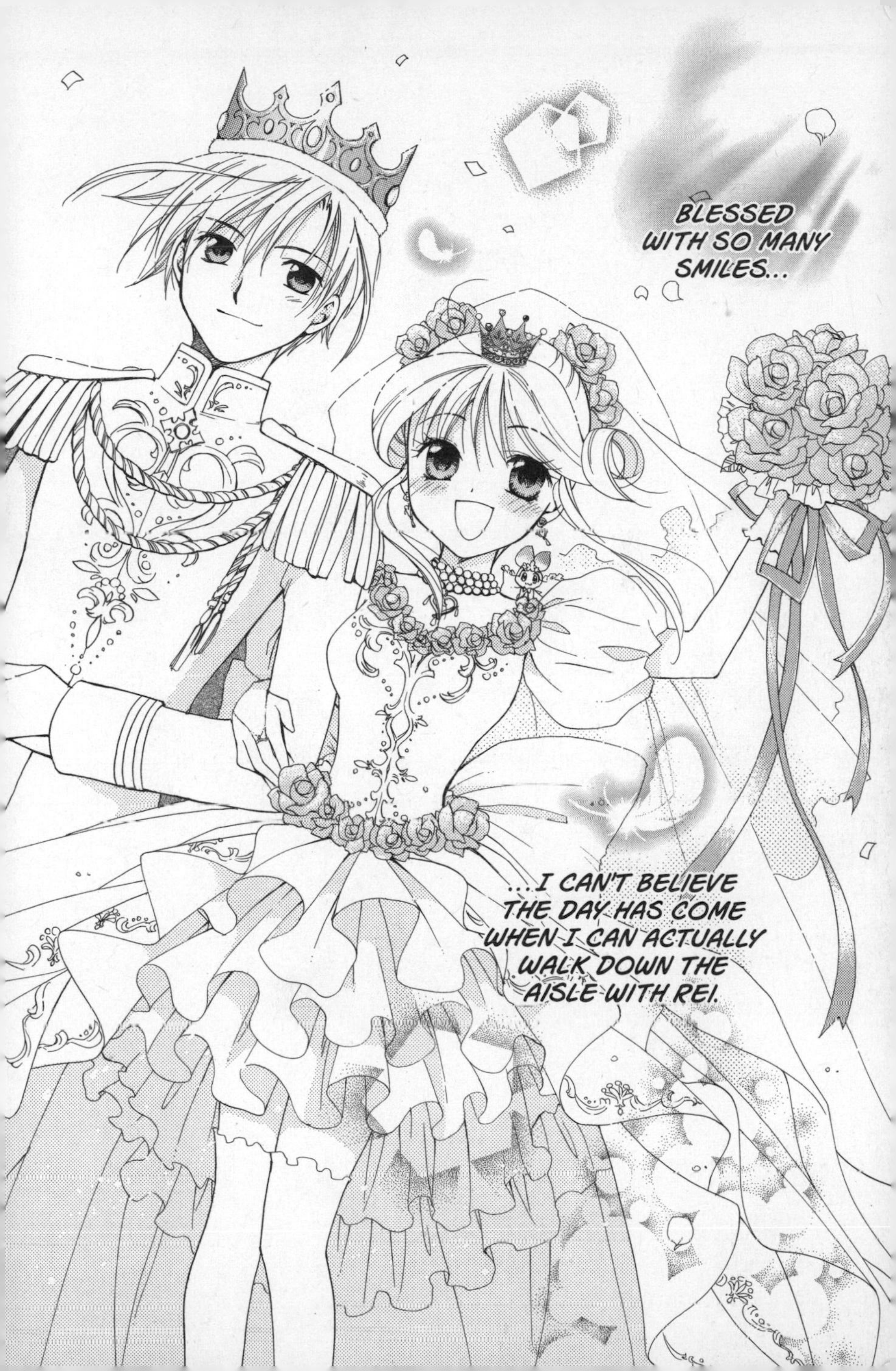
BLESSED WITH SO MANY SMILES...
...I CAN'T BELIEVE THE DAY HAS COME WHEN I CAN ACTUALLY WALK DOWN THE AISLE WITH REI.

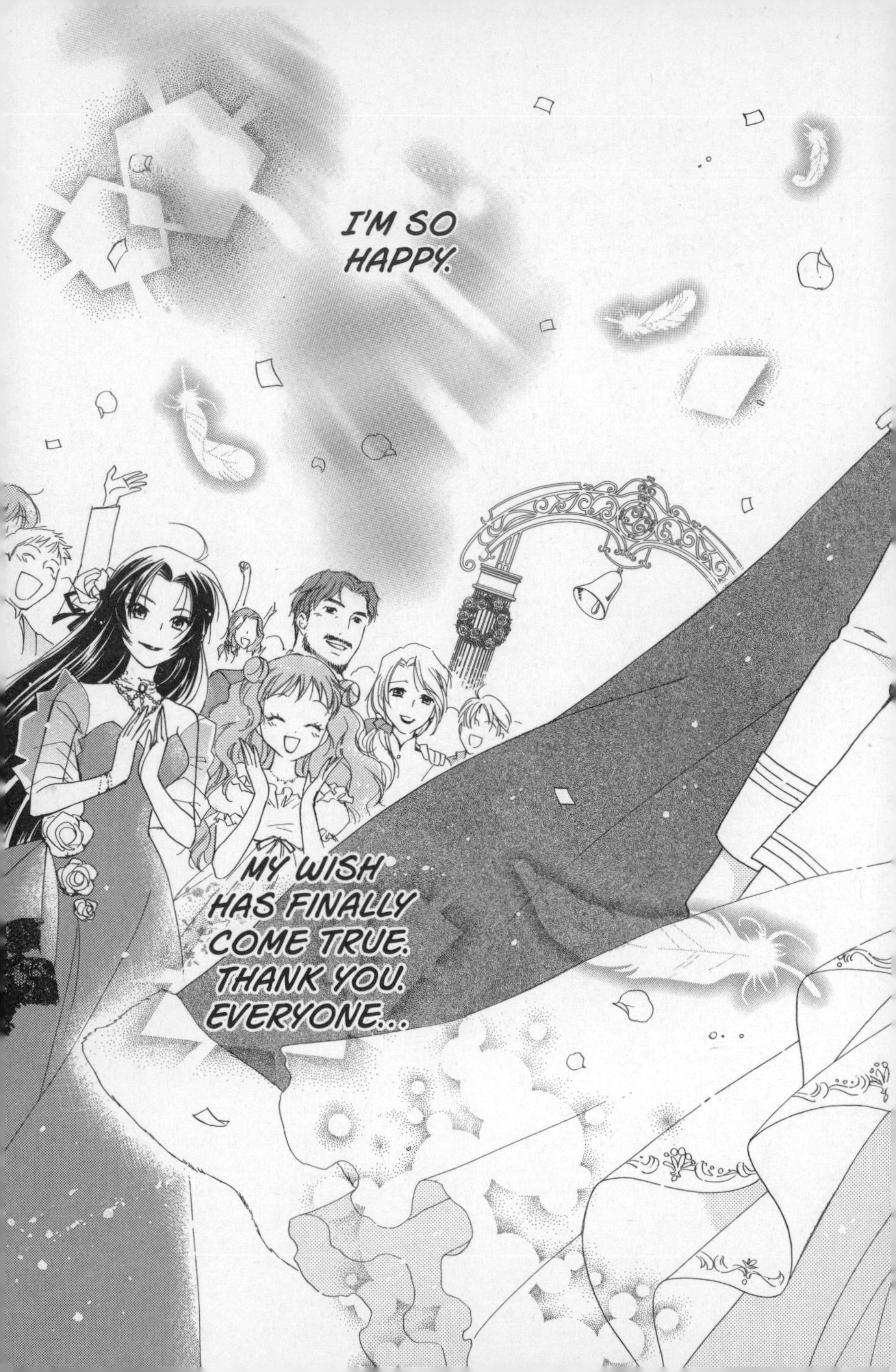
I'M SO HAPPY.
MY WISH HAS FINALLY COME TRUE. THANK YOU. EVERYONE...

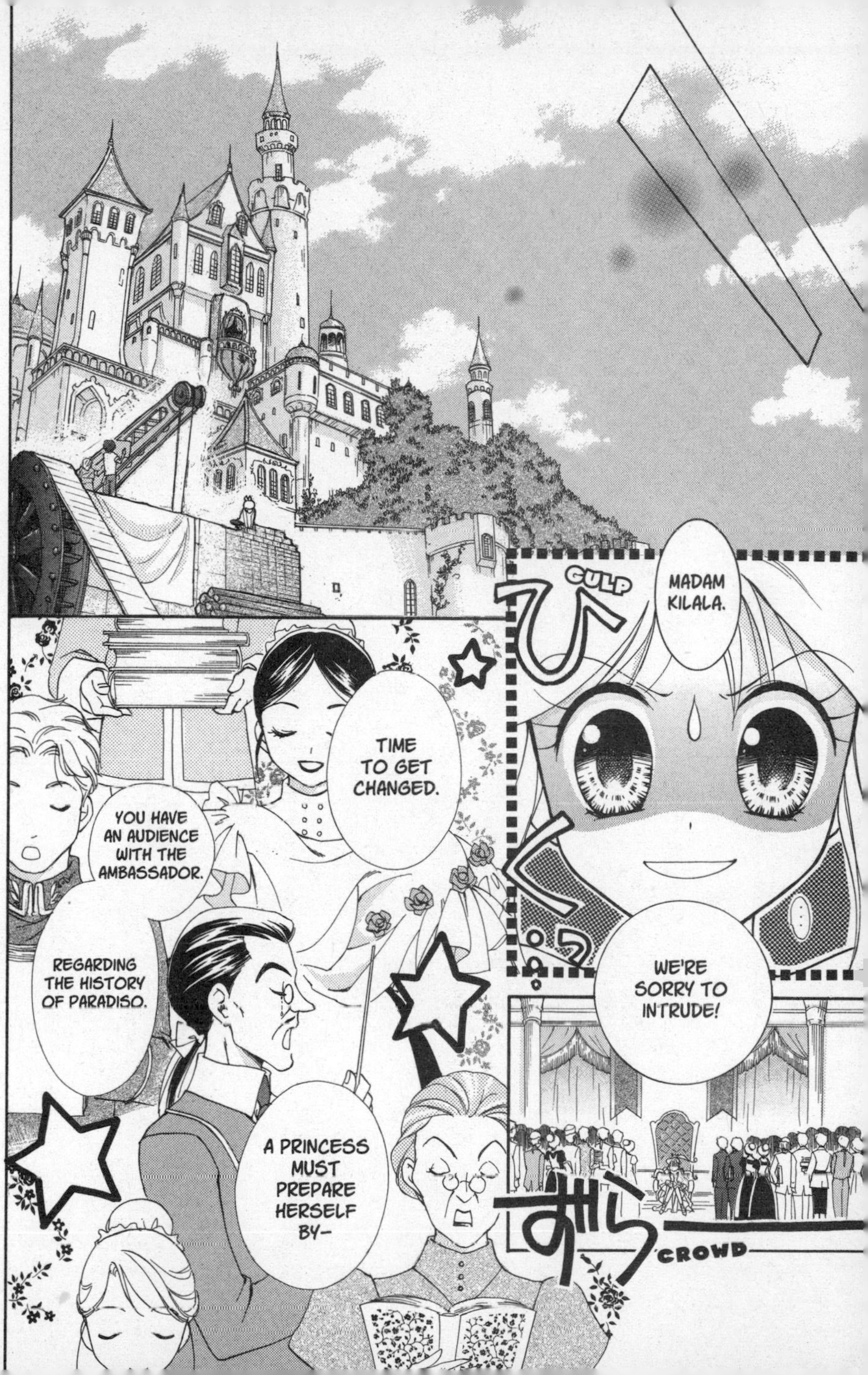
GULP
MADAM KILALA.
WE'RE SORRY TO INTRUDE!
CROWD
TIME TO GET CHANGED.
YOU HAVE AN AUDIENCE WITH THE AMBASSADOR.
REGARDING THE HISTORY OF PARADISO.
A PRINCESS MUST PREPARE HERSELF BY–

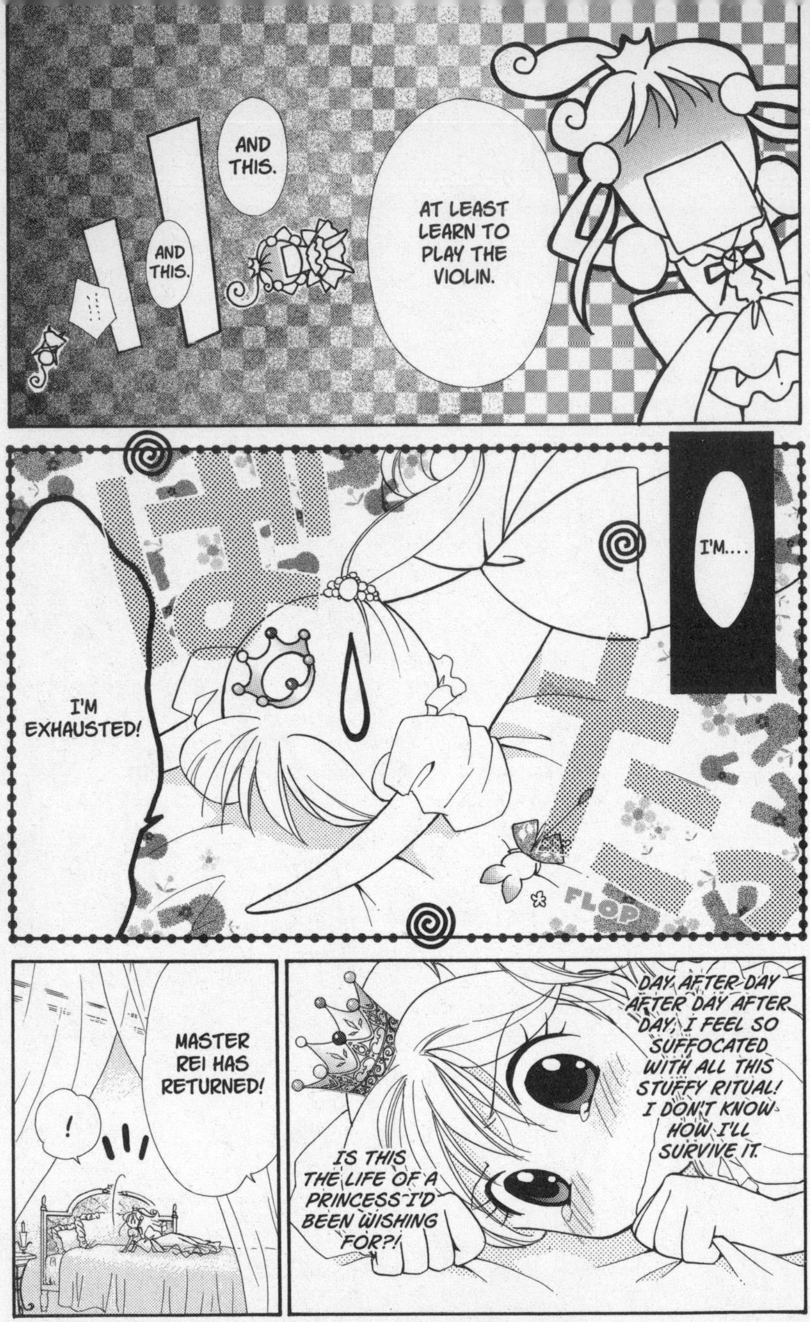
AT LEAST LEARN TO PLAY THE VIOLIN.
AND THIS.
AND THIS.
I'M....
I'M EXHAUSTED!
FLOP
DAY AFTER DAY AFTER DAY AFTER DAY, I FEEL SO SUFFOCATED WITH ALL THIS STUFFY RITUAL! I DON'T KNOW HOW I'LL SURVIVE IT.
IS THIS THE LIFE OF A PRINCESS I'D BEEN WISHING FOR?!
MASTER REI HAS RETURNED!
!

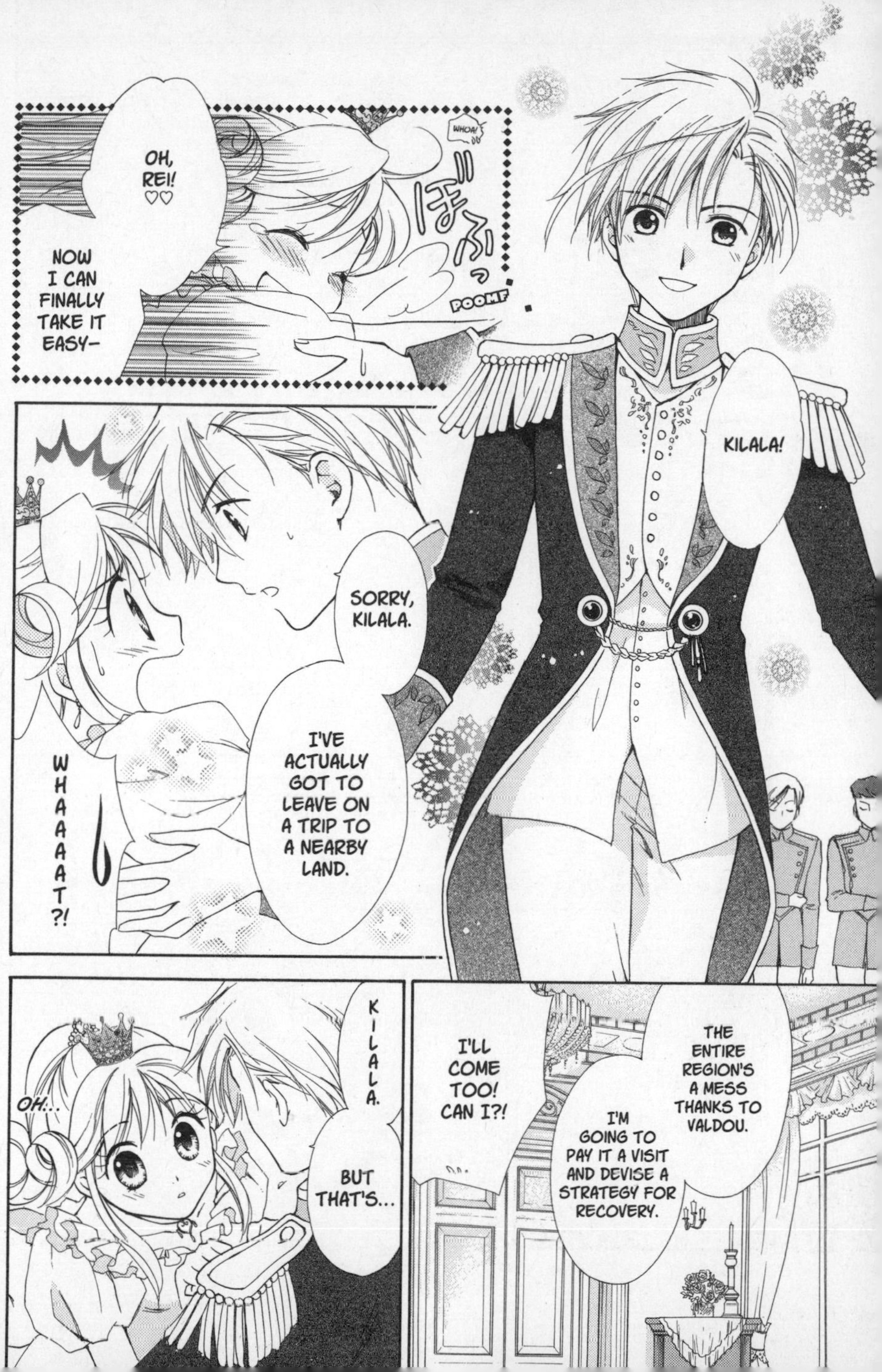

KILALA!
WHOA!
ぼふっ
POOMF
OH, REI! ♡♡
NOW I CAN FINALLY TAKE IT EASY-
SORRY, KILALA.
I'VE ACTUALLY GOT TO LEAVE ON A TRIP TO A NEARBY LAND.
WHAAAAAT?!
THE ENTIRE REGION'S A MESS THANKS TO VALDOU.
I'M GOING TO PAY IT A VISIT AND DEVISE A STRATEGY FOR RECOVERY.
I'LL COME TOO! CAN I?!
KILALA.
BUT THAT'S...
OH...

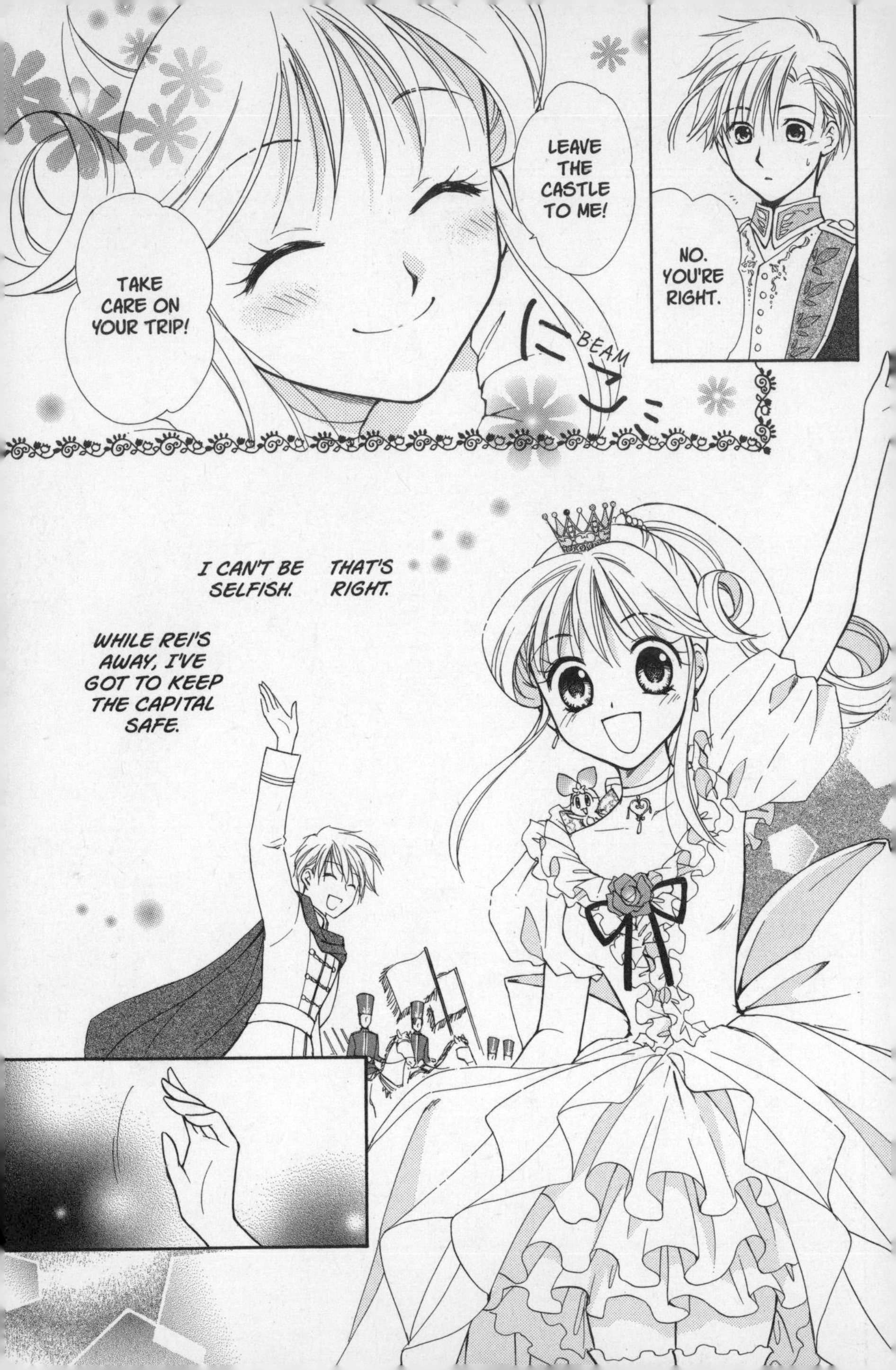
NO. YOU'RE RIGHT.
LEAVE THE CASTLE TO ME!
BEAM
TAKE CARE ON YOUR TRIP!
THAT'S RIGHT.
I CAN'T BE SELFISH.
WHILE REI'S AWAY, I'VE GOT TO KEEP THE CAPITAL SAFE.

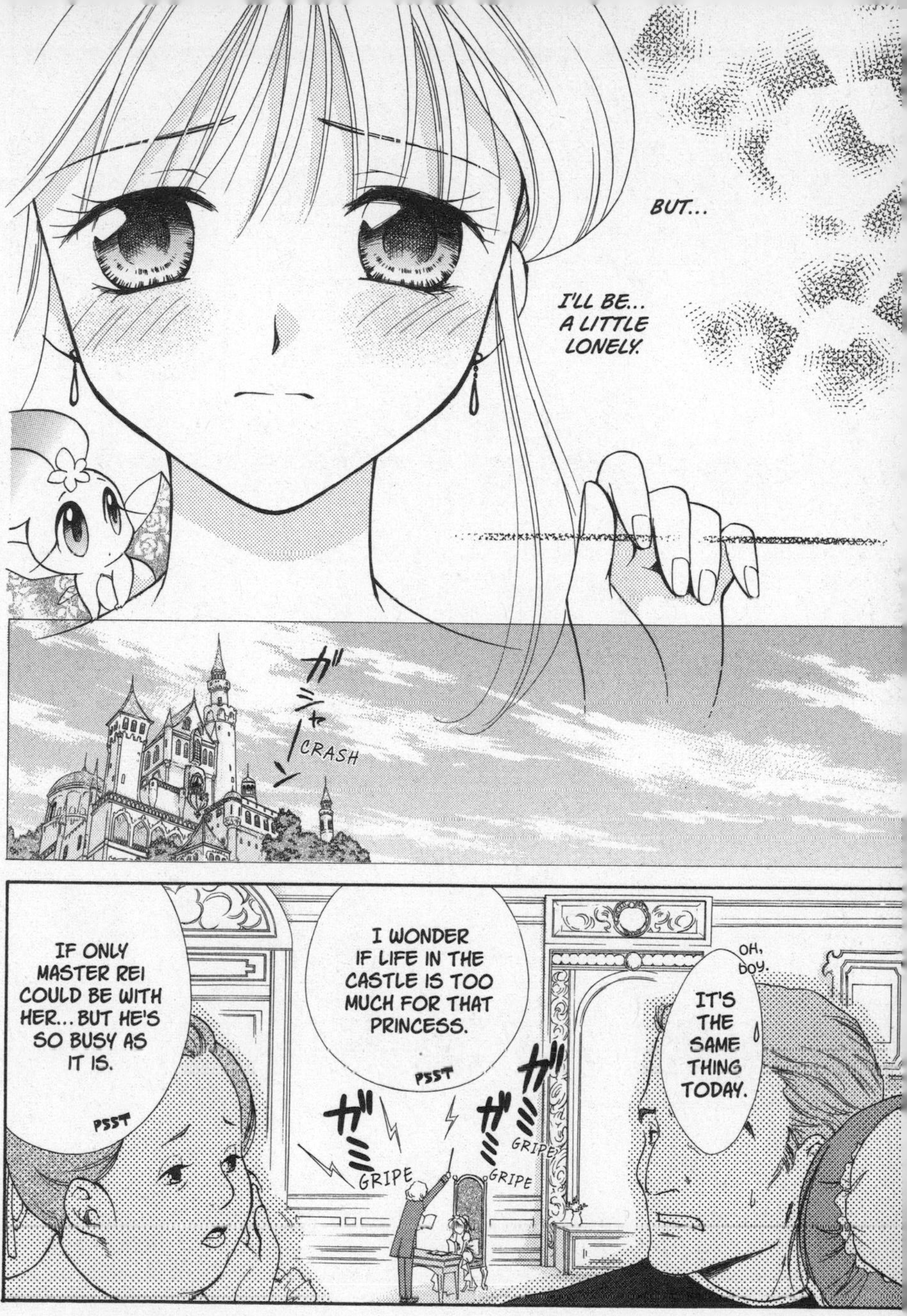

BUT...
I'LL BE... A LITTLE LONELY.
ガシャン
CRASH
OH, BOY.
IT'S THE SAME THING TODAY.
ガミ
GRIPE
ガミ
GRIPE
I WONDER IF LIFE IN THE CASTLE IS TOO MUCH FOR THAT PRINCESS.
PSST
ガミ
GRIPE
IF ONLY MASTER REI COULD BE WITH HER... BUT HE'S SO BUSY AS IT IS.
PSST

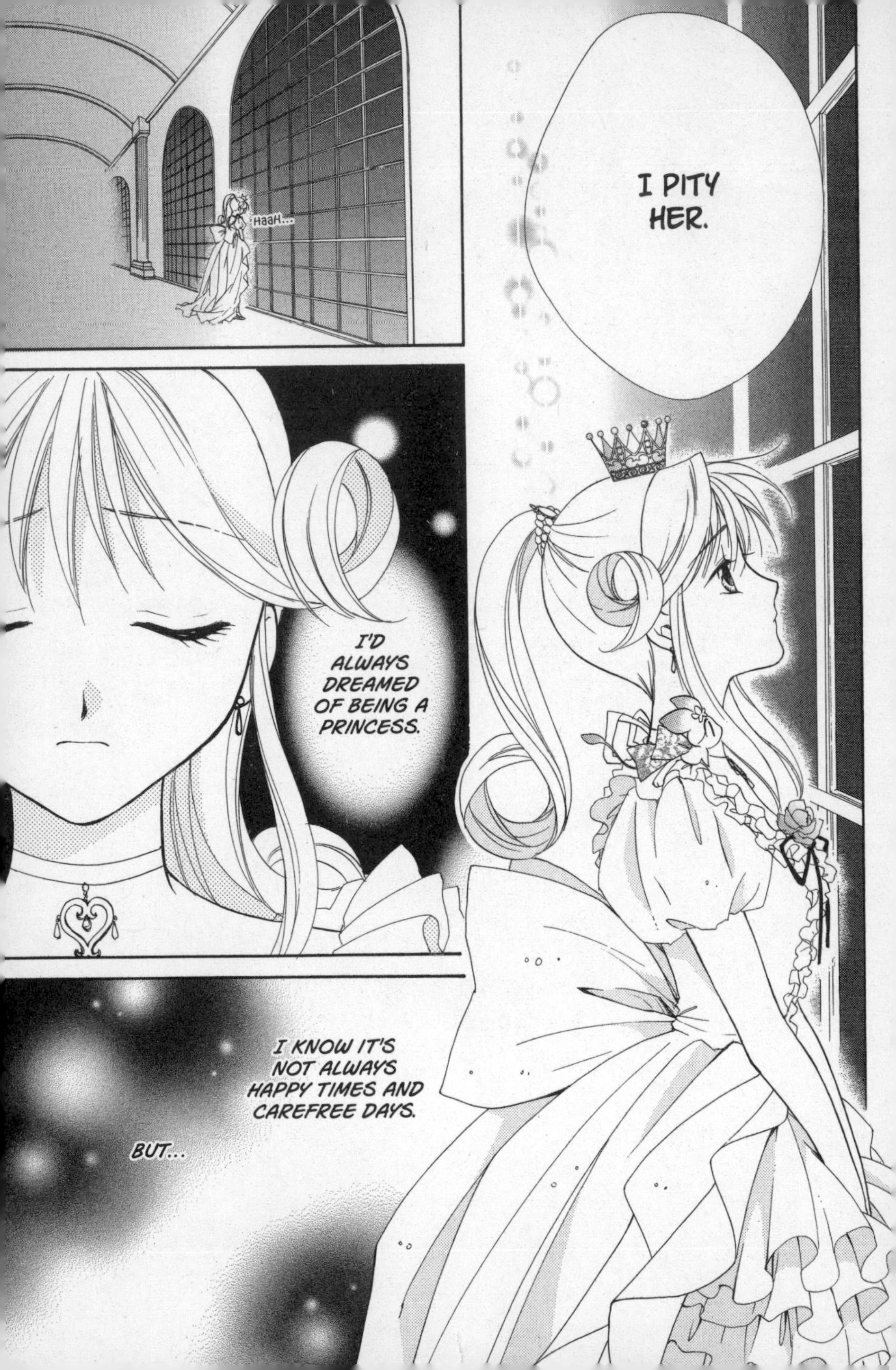
I PITY HER.
HAAH...
I'D ALWAYS DREAMED OF BEING A PRINCESS.
I KNOW IT'S NOT ALWAYS HAPPY TIMES AND CAREFREE DAYS.
BUT...

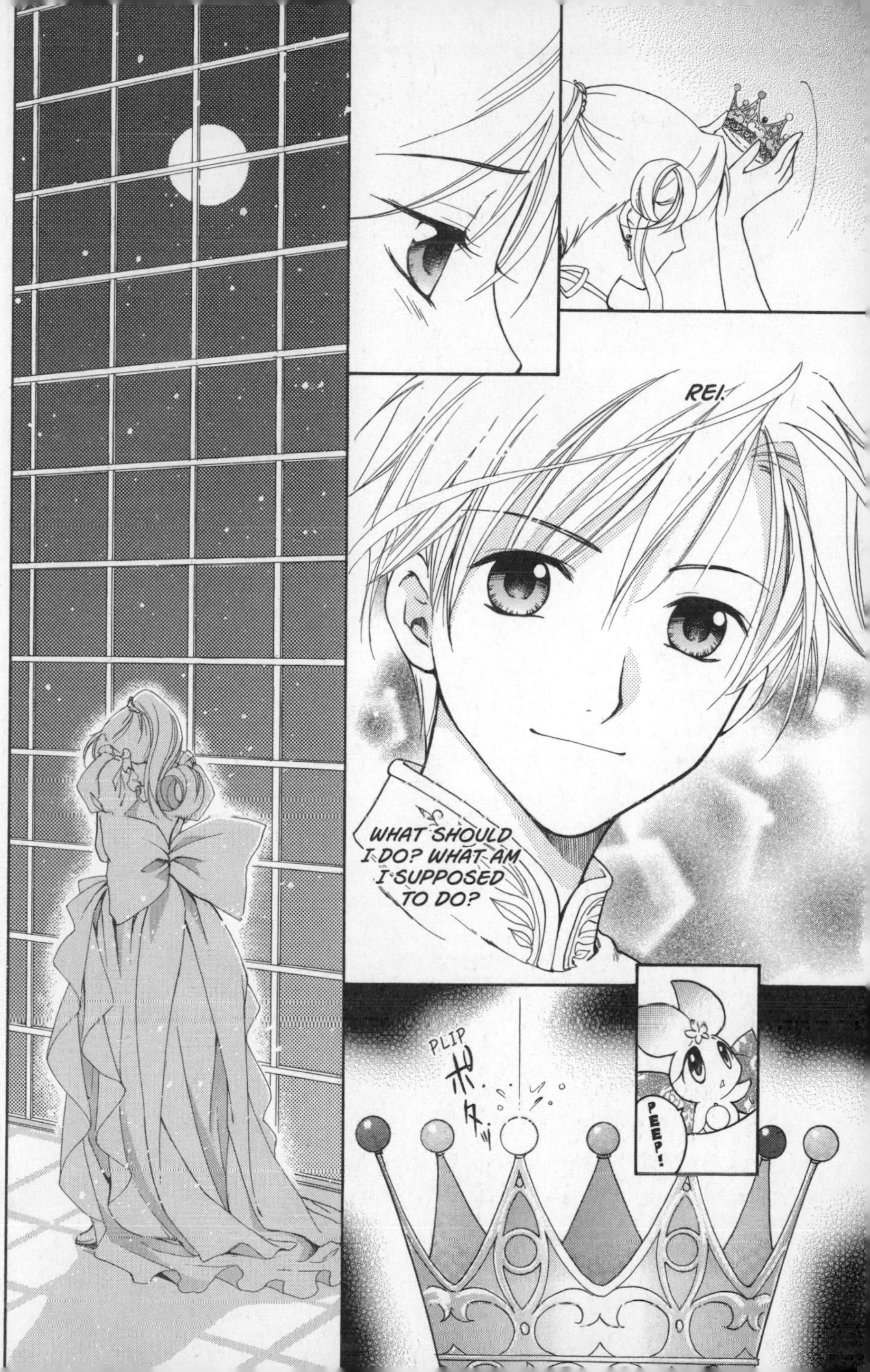
REI.
WHAT SHOULD I DO? WHAT AM I SUPPOSED TO DO?
PEEEP!!
PLIP
ボタッ

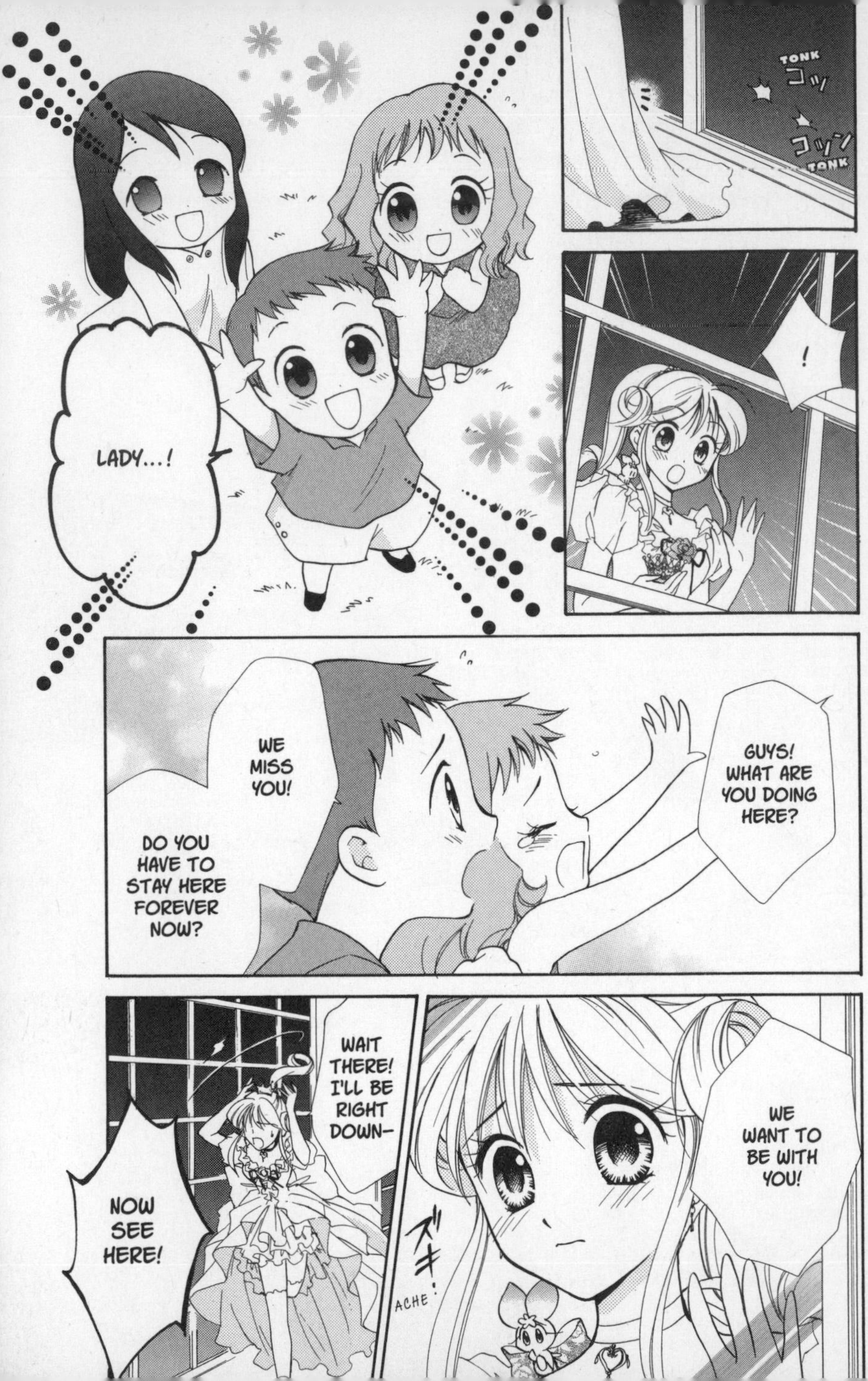
TONK
コッ
コッン
TONK
!
LADY...!
GUYS! WHAT ARE YOU DOING HERE?
WE MISS YOU!
DO YOU HAVE TO STAY HERE FOREVER NOW?
WE WANT TO BE WITH YOU!
ズキ!
ACHE
WAIT THERE! I'LL BE RIGHT DOWN-
NOW SEE HERE!

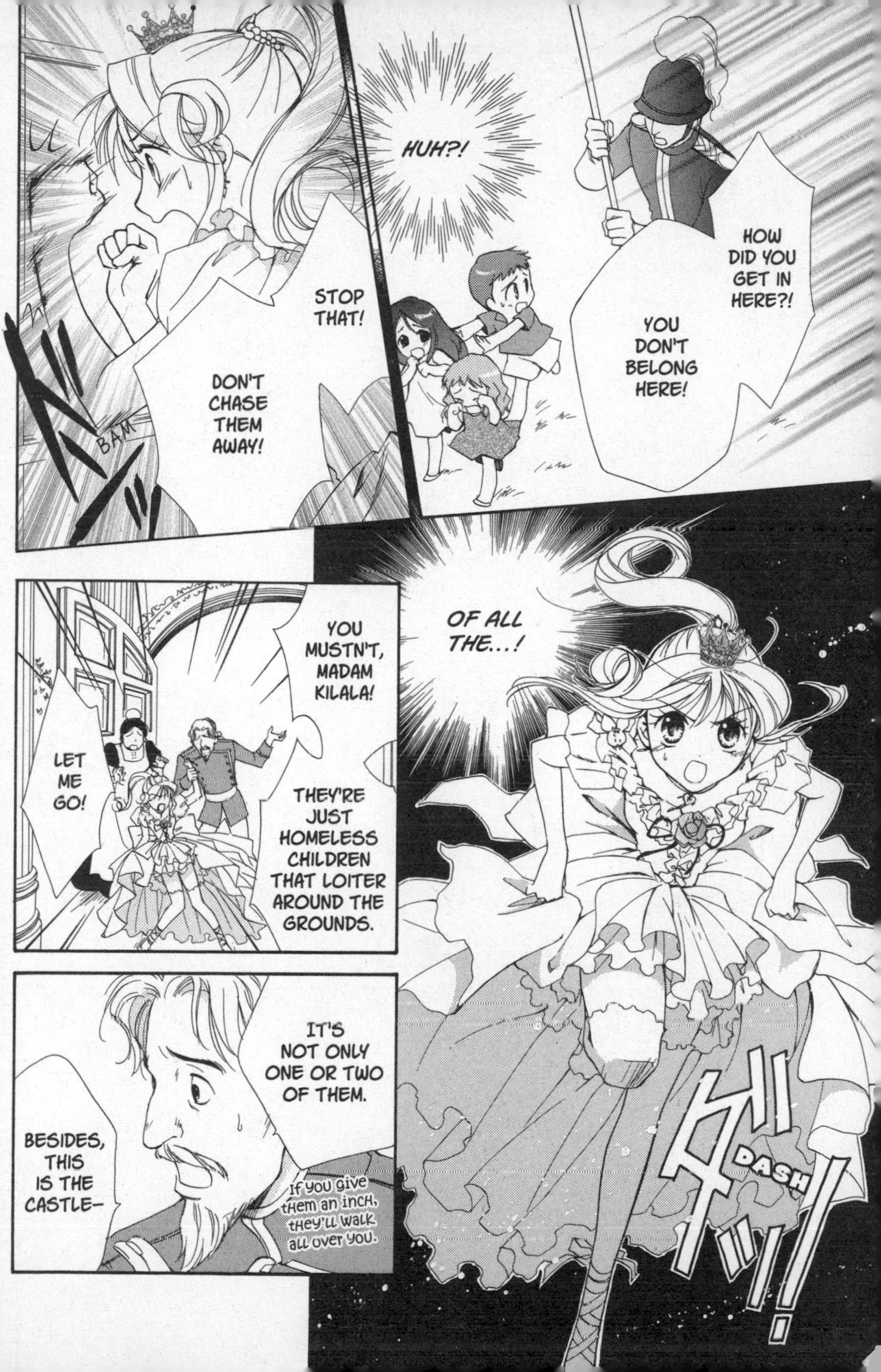
HOW DID YOU GET IN HERE?!
YOU DON'T BELONG HERE!
HUH?!
STOP THAT!
DON'T CHASE THEM AWAY!
BAM
OF ALL THE...!
DASH
YOU MUSTN'T, MADAM KILALA!
LET ME GO!
THEY'RE JUST HOMELESS CHILDREN THAT LOITER AROUND THE GROUNDS.
IT'S NOT ONLY ONE OR TWO OF THEM.
BESIDES, THIS IS THE CASTLE-
If you give them an inch, they'll walk all over you.

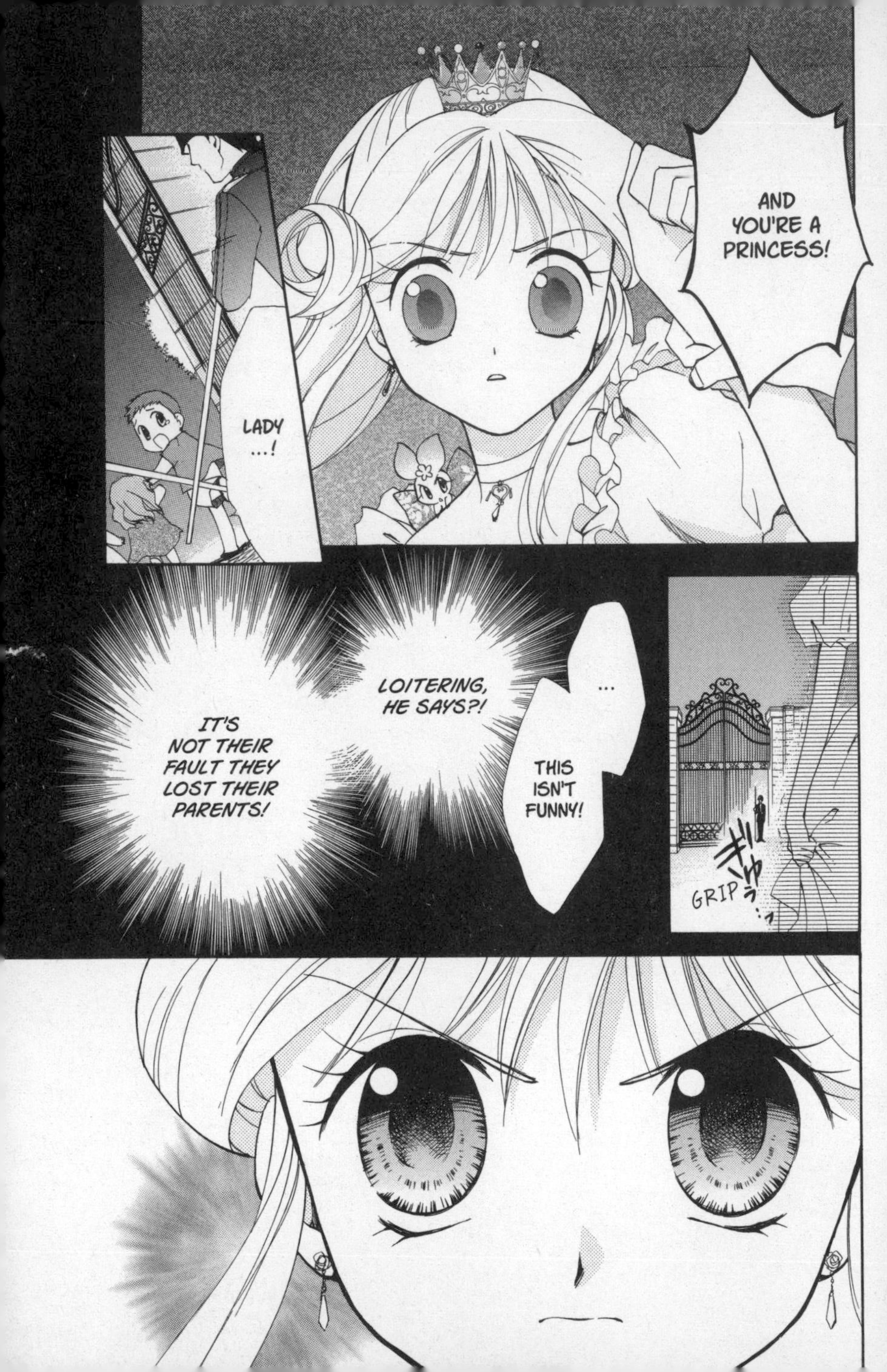
AND YOU'RE A PRINCESS!
LADY ...!
GRIP
...
THIS ISN'T FUNNY!
LOITERING, HE SAYS?!
IT'S NOT THEIR FAULT THEY LOST THEIR PARENTS!

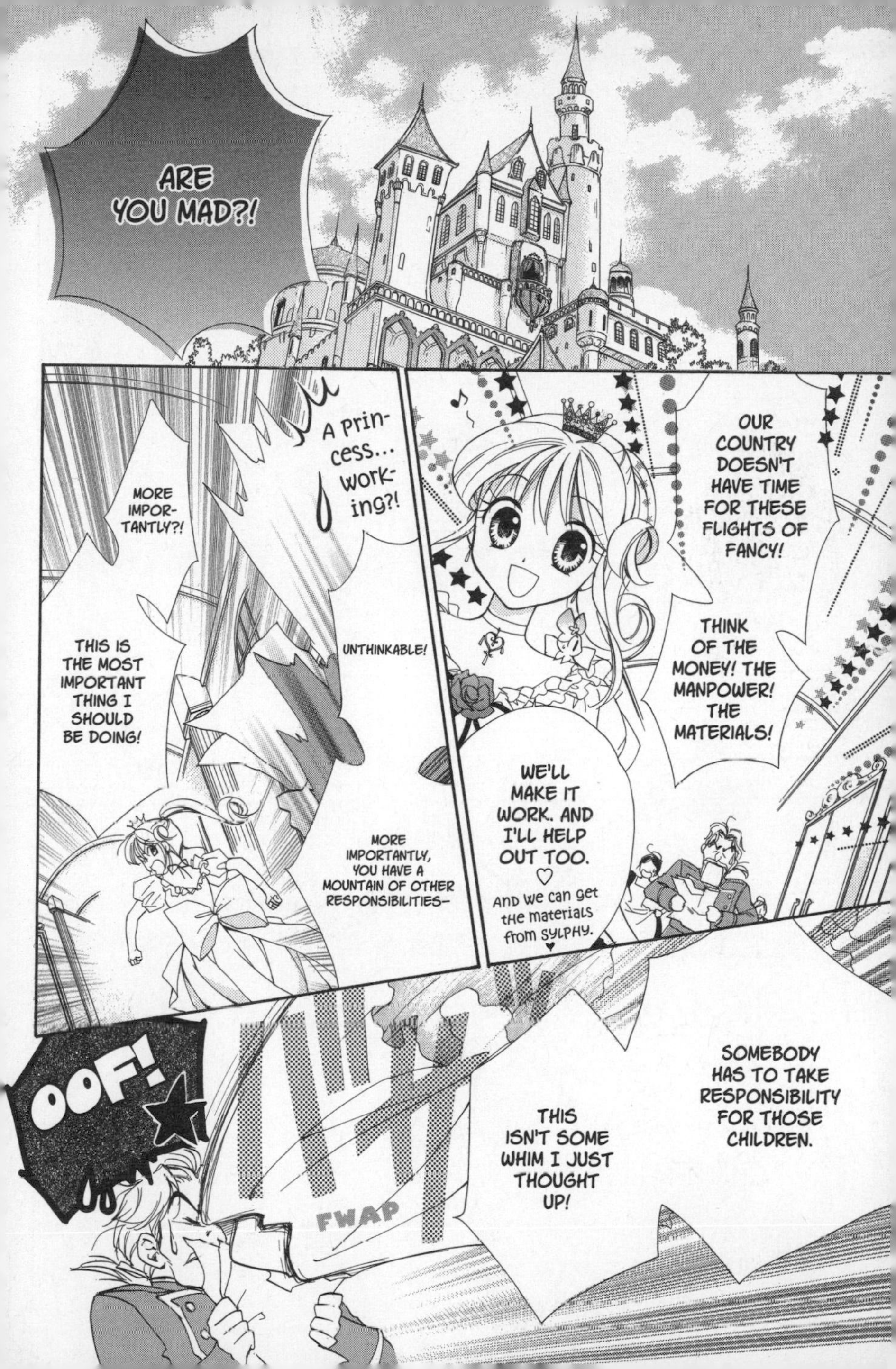
ARE YOU MAD?!
OUR COUNTRY DOESN'T HAVE TIME FOR THESE FLIGHTS OF FANCY!
THINK OF THE MONEY! THE MANPOWER! THE MATERIALS!
WE'LL MAKE IT WORK. AND I'LL HELP OUT TOO. ♡
And we can get the materials from SYLPHY. ♥
A prin-cess... work-ing?!
UNTHINKABLE!
MORE IMPORTANTLY, YOU HAVE A MOUNTAIN OF OTHER RESPONSIBILITIES—
MORE IMPOR-TANTLY?!
THIS IS THE MOST IMPORTANT THING I SHOULD BE DOING!
SOMEBODY HAS TO TAKE RESPONSIBILITY FOR THOSE CHILDREN.
THIS ISN'T SOME WHIM I JUST THOUGHT UP!
FWAP
OOF!

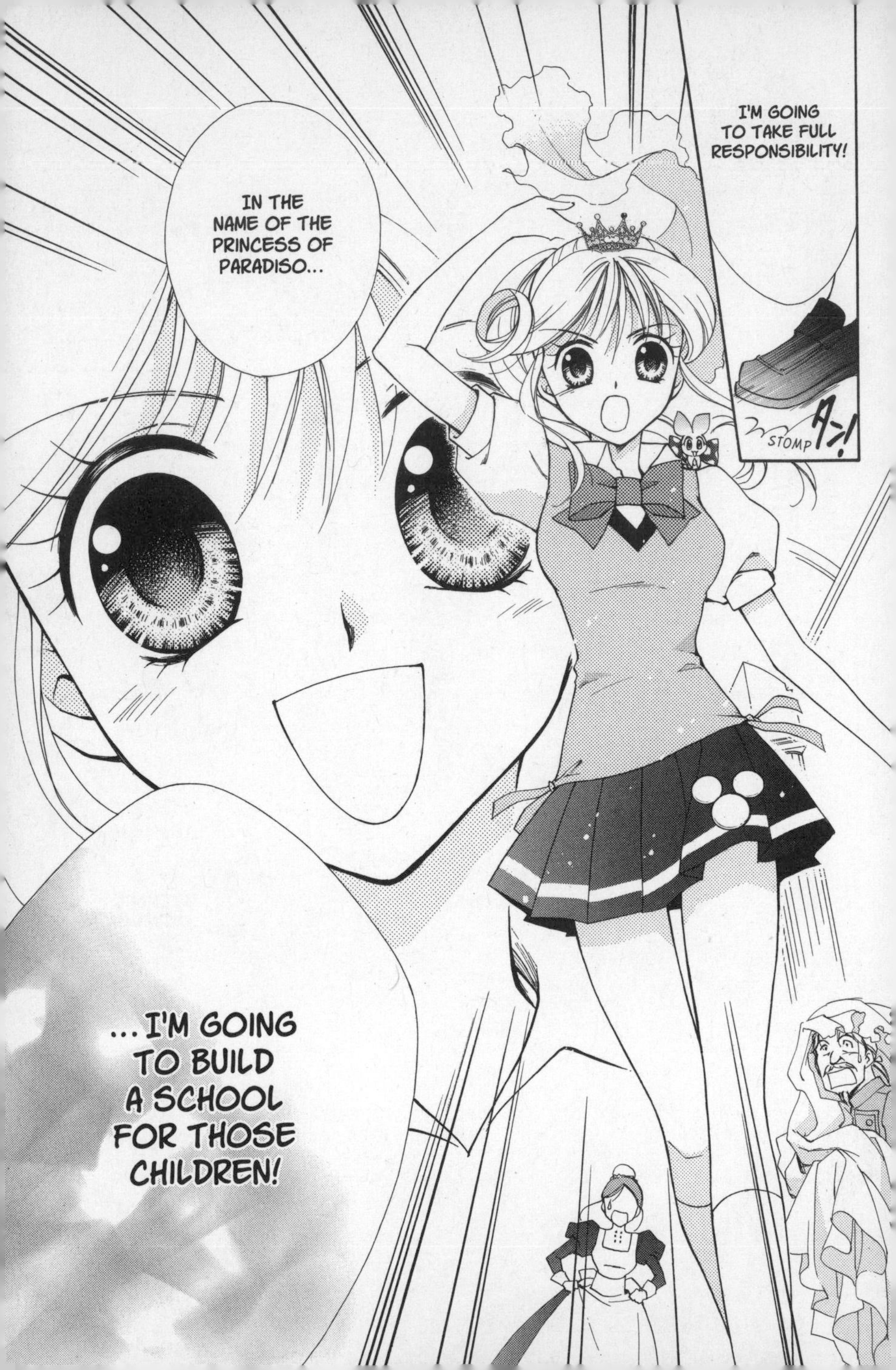
I'M GOING TO TAKE FULL RESPONSIBILITY!
STOMP
IN THE NAME OF THE PRINCESS OF PARADISO...
...I'M GOING TO BUILD A SCHOOL FOR THOSE CHILDREN!

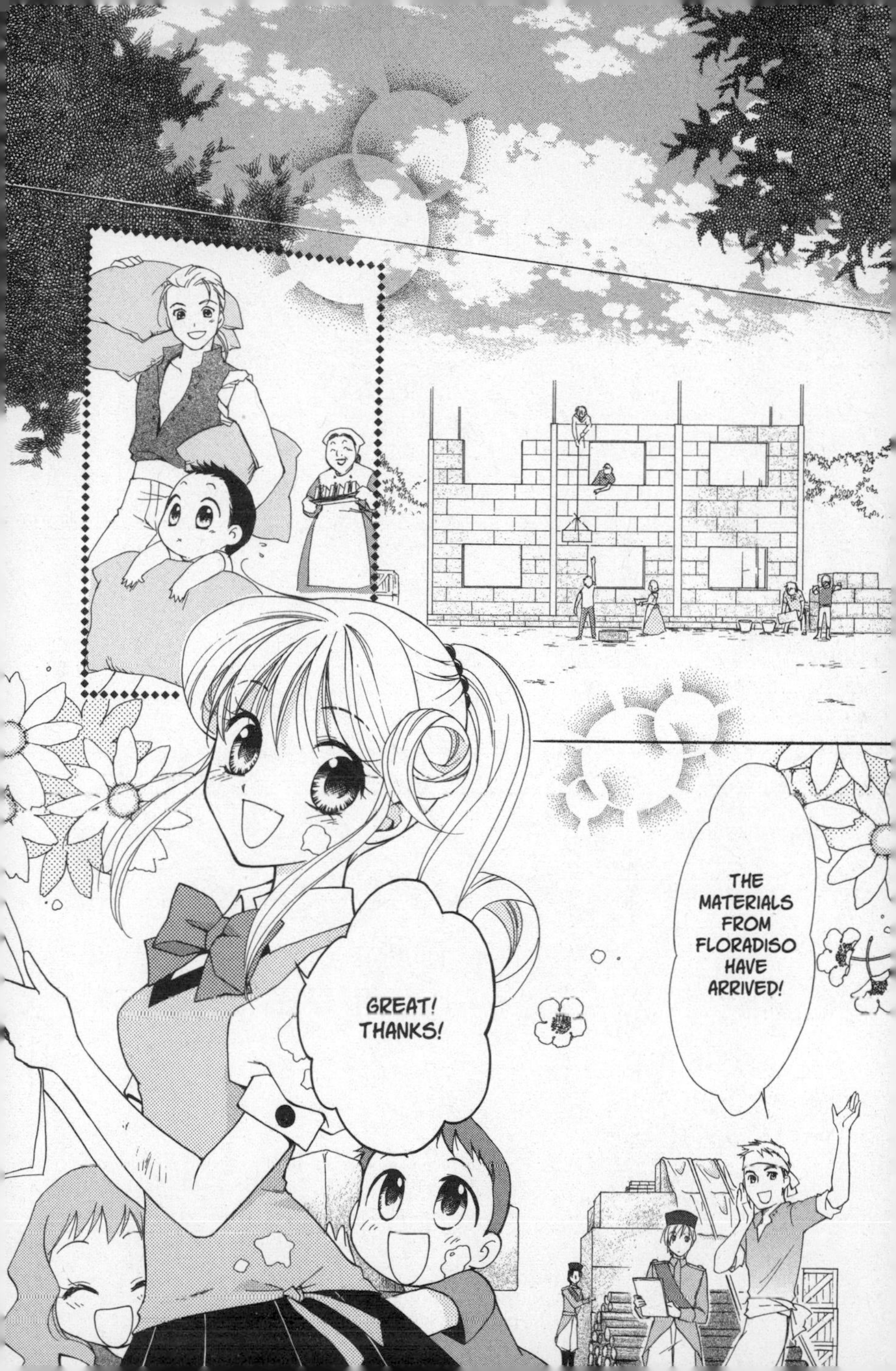
THE MATERIALS FROM FLORADISO HAVE ARRIVED!
GREAT! THANKS!

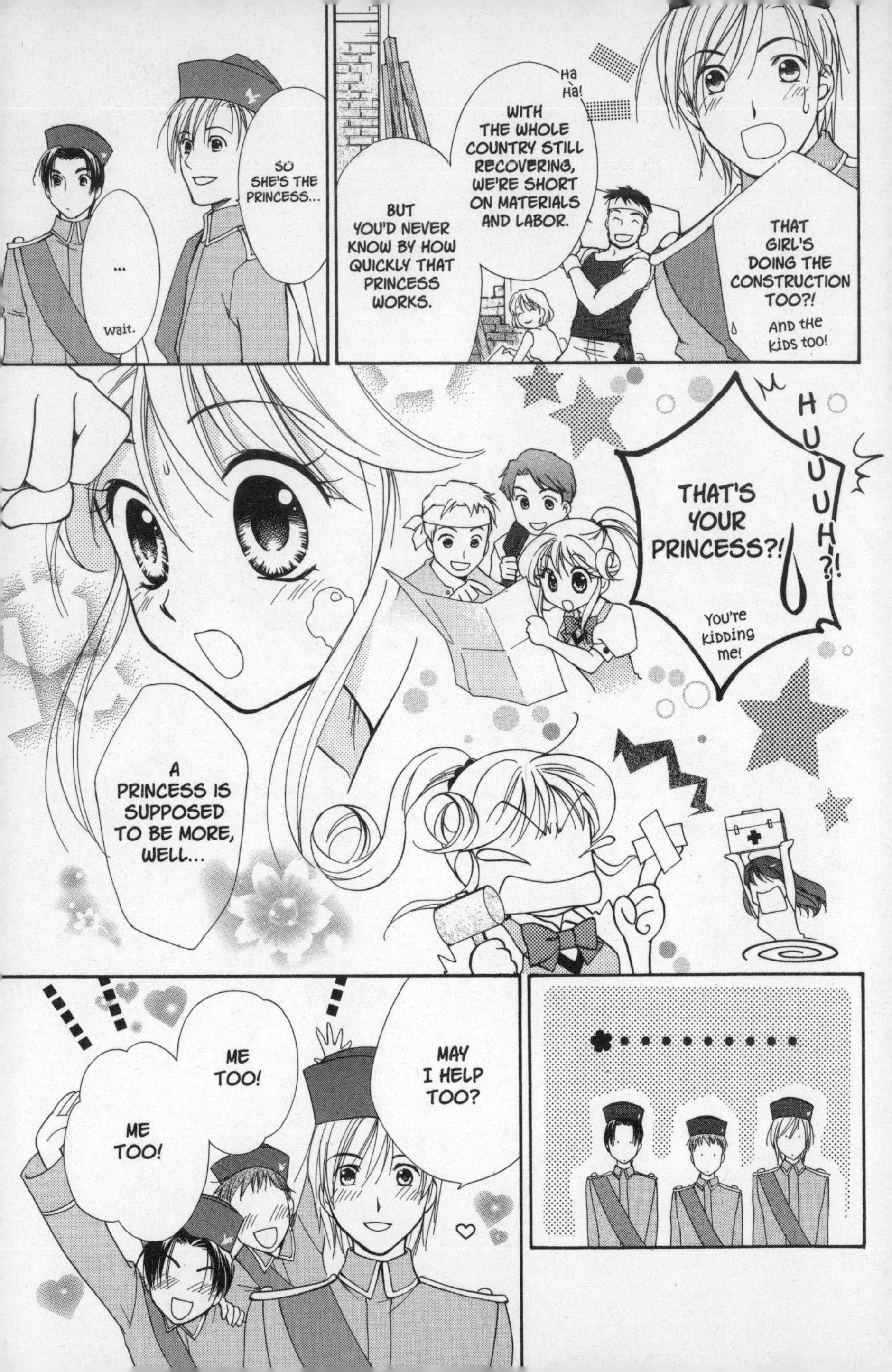
THAT GIRL'S DOING THE CONSTRUCTION TOO?!
And the kids too!
Ha Ha!
WITH THE WHOLE COUNTRY STILL RECOVERING, WE'RE SHORT ON MATERIALS AND LABOR.
BUT YOU'D NEVER KNOW BY HOW QUICKLY THAT PRINCESS WORKS.
SO SHE'S THE PRINCESS...
... wait.
HUUUH?!
THAT'S YOUR PRINCESS?!
You're kidding me!
A PRINCESS IS SUPPOSED TO BE MORE, WELL...
MAY I HELP TOO?
ME TOO!
ME TOO!

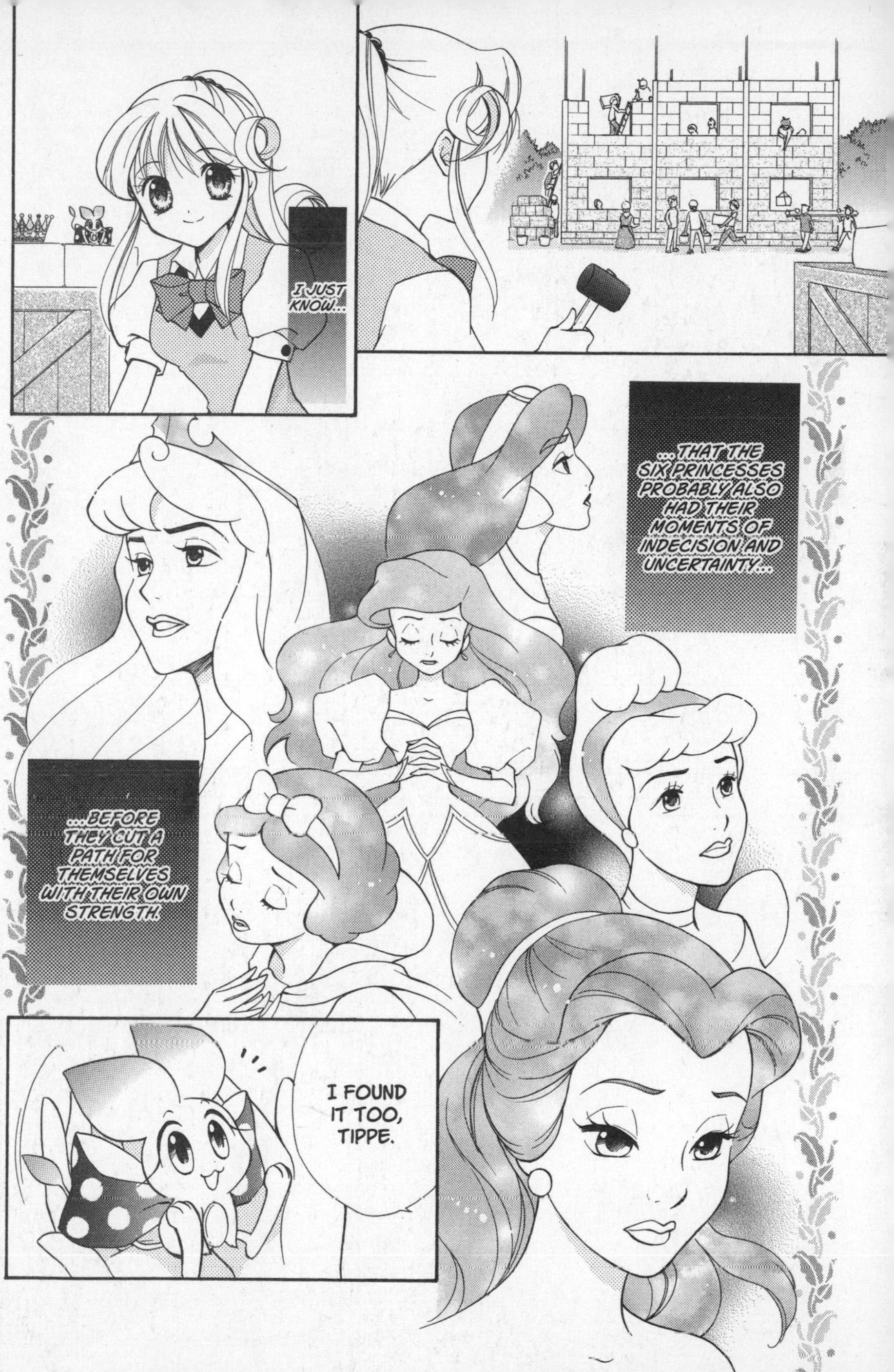
I JUST KNOW...
...THAT THE SIX PRINCESSES PROBABLY ALSO HAD THEIR MOMENTS OF INDECISION AND UNCERTAINTY...
...BEFORE THEY CUT A PATH FOR THEMSELVES WITH THEIR OWN STRENGTH.
I FOUND IT TOO, TIPPE.

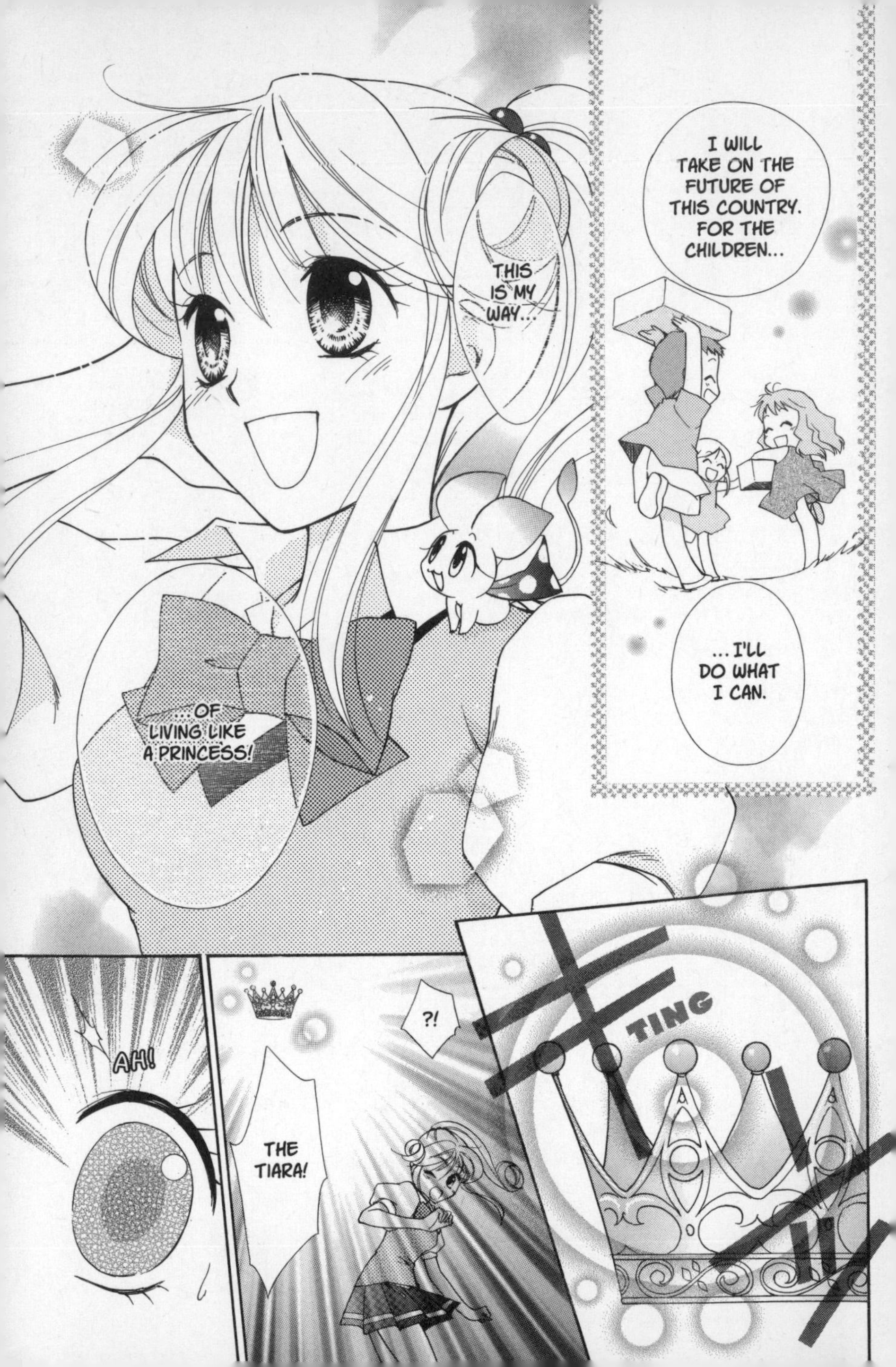
I WILL TAKE ON THE FUTURE OF THIS COUNTRY. FOR THE CHILDREN...
...I'LL DO WHAT I CAN.
THIS IS MY WAY...
...OF LIVING LIKE A PRINCESS!
TING
?!
THE TIARA!
AH!

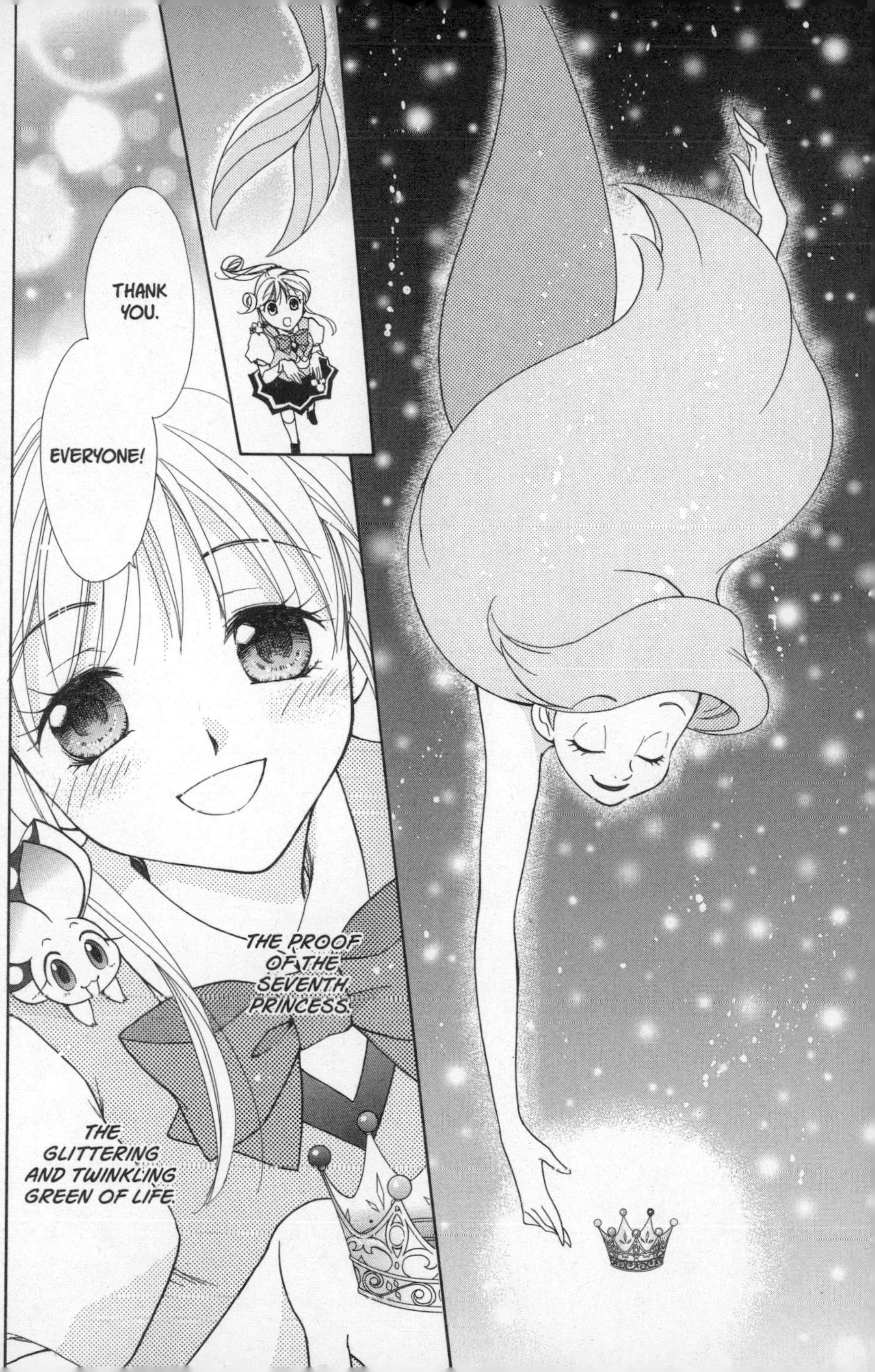
THANK YOU.
EVERYONE!
THE PROOF OF THE SEVENTH PRINCESS.
THE GLITTERING AND TWINKLING GREEN OF LIFE.

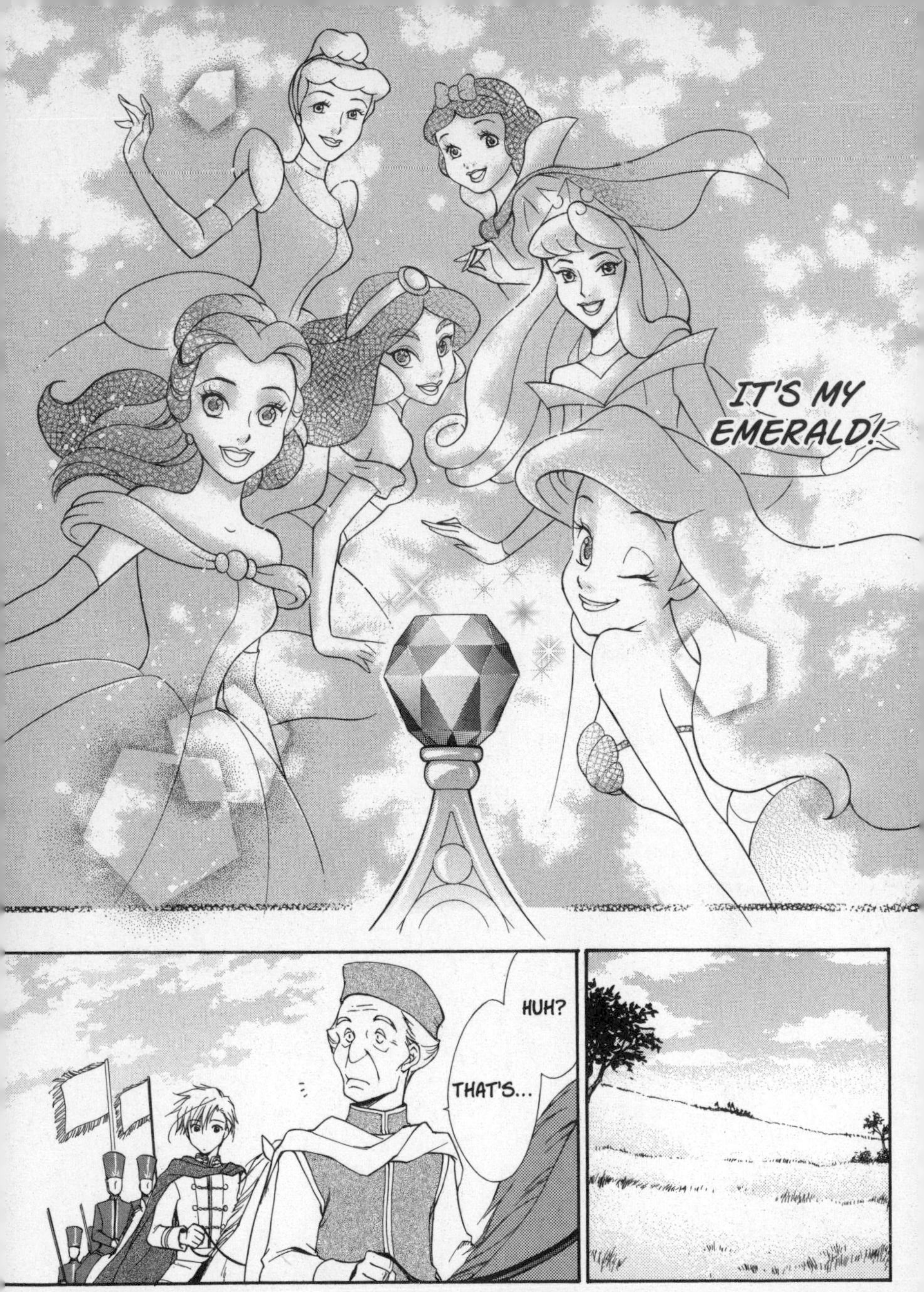
IT'S MY EMERALD!
HUH?
THAT'S...

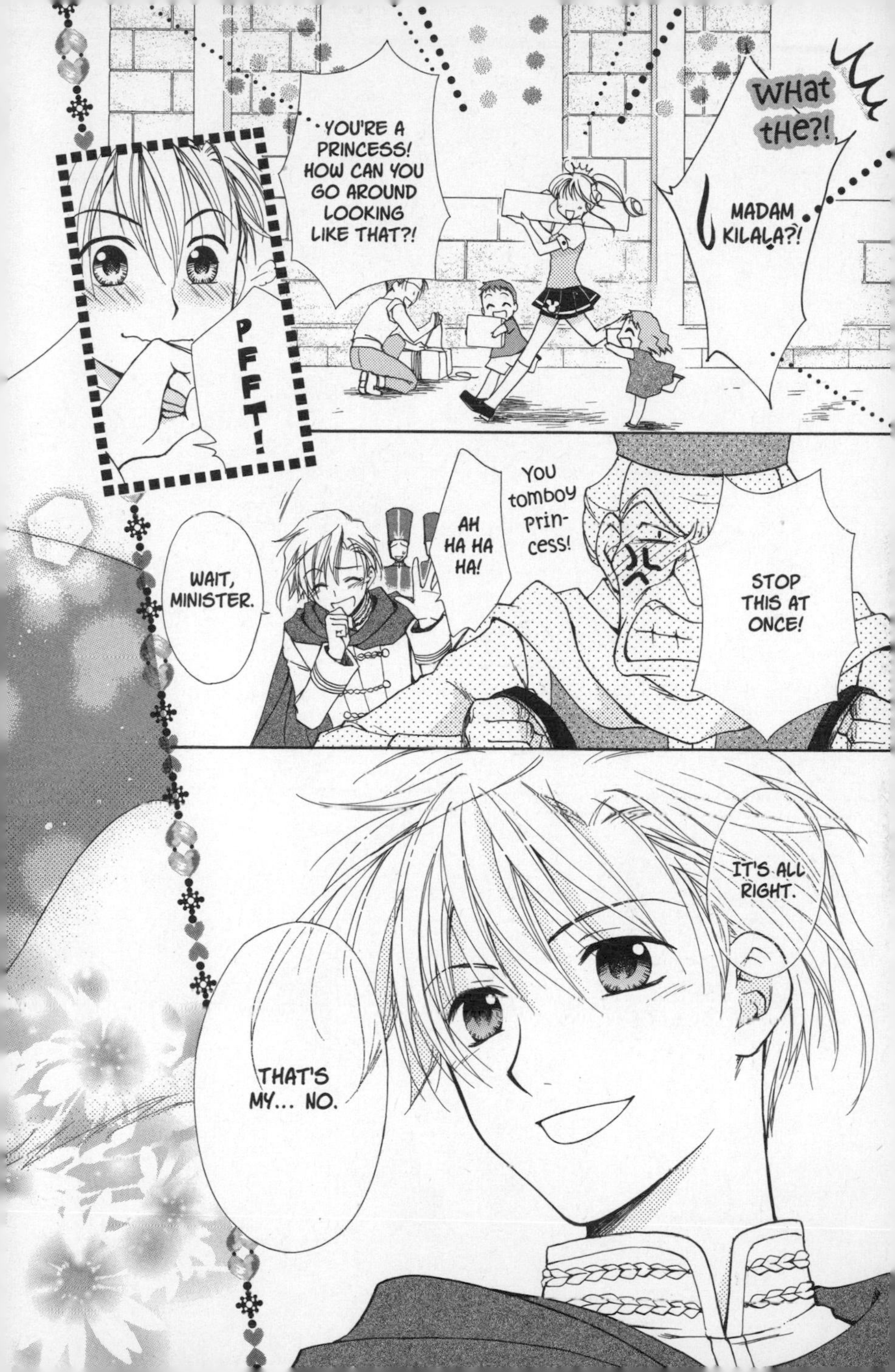
WHat tHe?!
MADAM KILALA?!
YOU'RE A PRINCESS! HOW CAN YOU GO AROUND LOOKING LIKE THAT?!
PFFT!
STOP THIS AT ONCE!
YOU tomboy prin-cess!
AH HA HA HA!
WAIT, MINISTER.
IT'S ALL RIGHT.
THAT'S MY... NO.

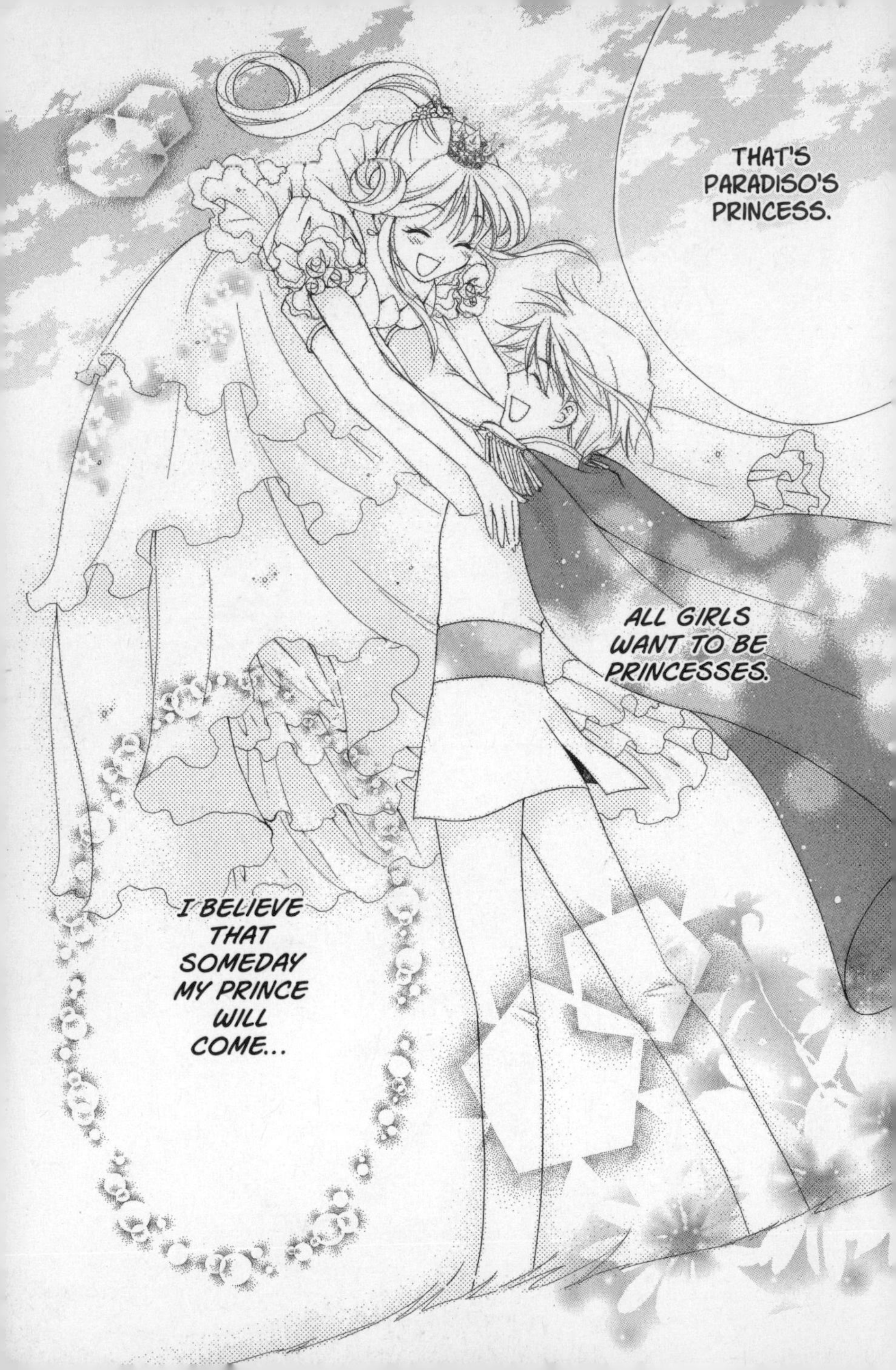
THAT'S PARADISO'S PRINCESS.
ALL GIRLS WANT TO BE PRINCESSES.
I BELIEVE THAT SOMEDAY MY PRINCE WILL COME...

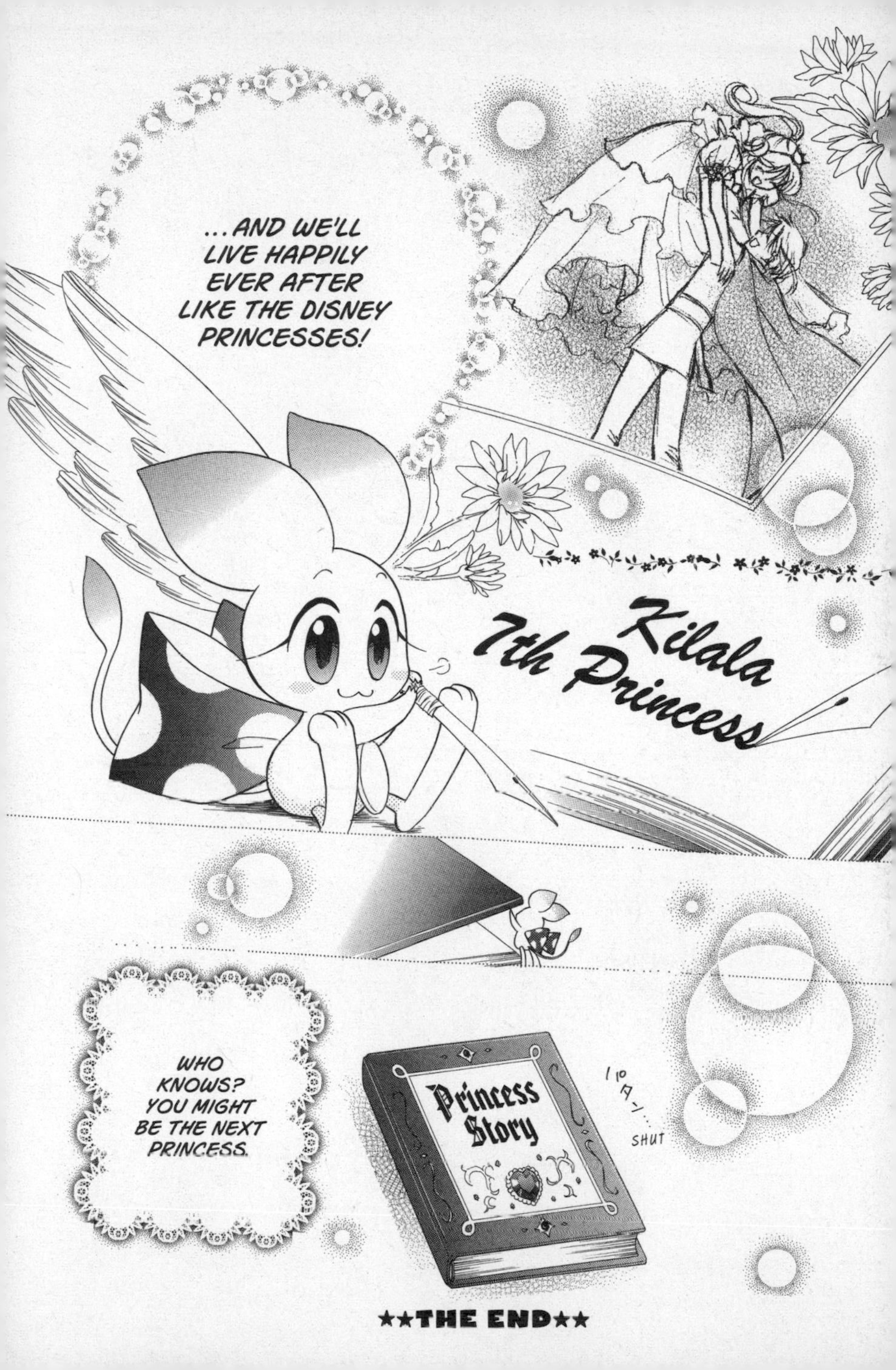
...AND WE'LL LIVE HAPPILY EVER AFTER LIKE THE DISNEY PRINCESSES!
Kilala 7th Princess
WHO KNOWS? YOU MIGHT BE THE NEXT PRINCESS.
Princess Story
パタン…
SHUT
★★THE END★★

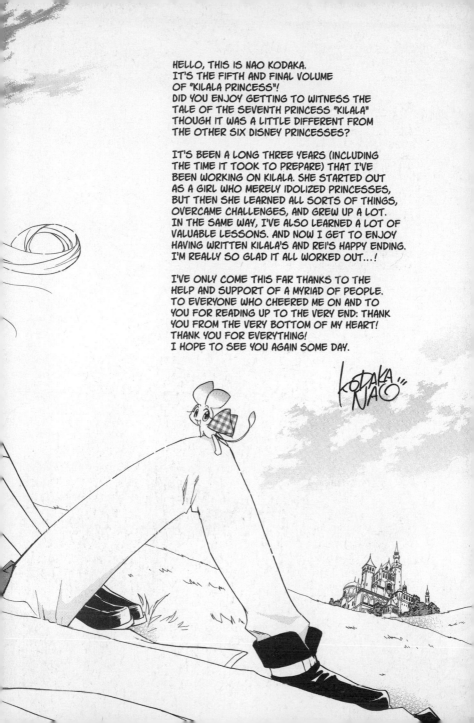

HELLO, THIS IS NAO KODAKA.
IT'S THE FIFTH AND FINAL VOLUME
OF "KILALA PRINCESS"!
DID YOU ENJOY GETTING TO WITNESS THE
TALE OF THE SEVENTH PRINCESS "KILALA"
THOUGH IT WAS A LITTLE DIFFERENT FROM
THE OTHER SIX DISNEY PRINCESSES?

IT'S BEEN A LONG THREE YEARS (INCLUDING
THE TIME IT TOOK TO PREPARE) THAT I'VE
BEEN WORKING ON KILALA. SHE STARTED OUT
AS A GIRL WHO MERELY IDOLIZED PRINCESSES,
BUT THEN SHE LEARNED ALL SORTS OF THINGS,
OVERCAME CHALLENGES, AND GREW UP A LOT.
IN THE SAME WAY, I'VE ALSO LEARNED A LOT OF
VALUABLE LESSONS. AND NOW I GET TO ENJOY
HAVING WRITTEN KILALA'S AND REI'S HAPPY ENDING.
I'M REALLY SO GLAD IT ALL WORKED OUT...!

I'VE ONLY COME THIS FAR THANKS TO THE
HELP AND SUPPORT OF A MYRIAD OF PEOPLE.
TO EVERYONE WHO CHEERED ME ON AND TO
YOU FOR READING UP TO THE VERY END: THANK
YOU FROM THE VERY BOTTOM OF MY HEART!
THANK YOU FOR EVERYTHING!
I HOPE TO SEE YOU AGAIN SOME DAY.

KODAKA NAO

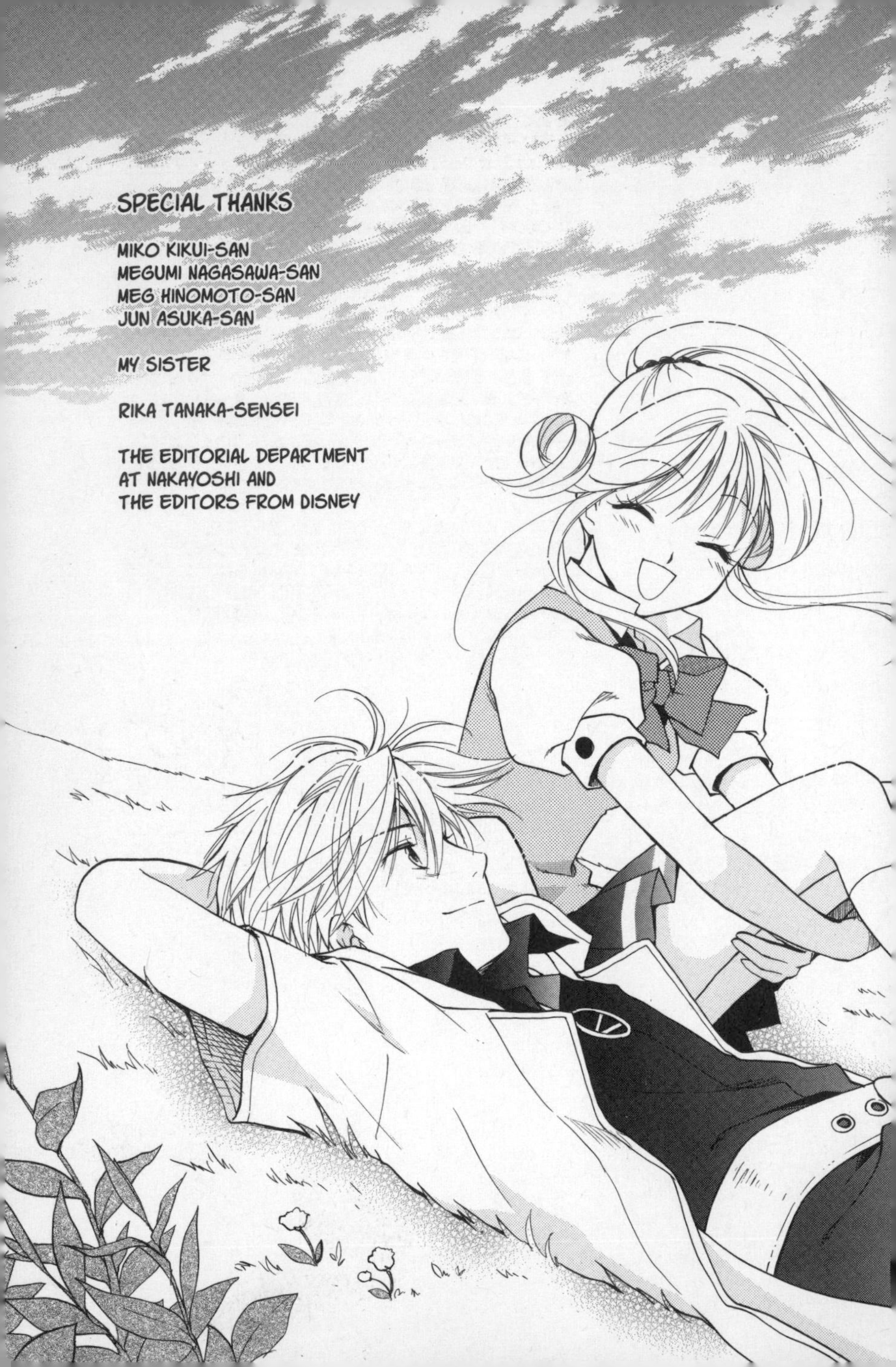
SPECIAL THANKS
MIKO KIKUI-SAN
MEGUMI NAGASAWA-SAN
MEG HINOMOTO-SAN
JUN ASUKA-SAN
MY SISTER
RIKA TANAKA-SENSEI
THE EDITORIAL DEPARTMENT
AT NAKAYOSHI AND
THE EDITORS FROM DISNEY

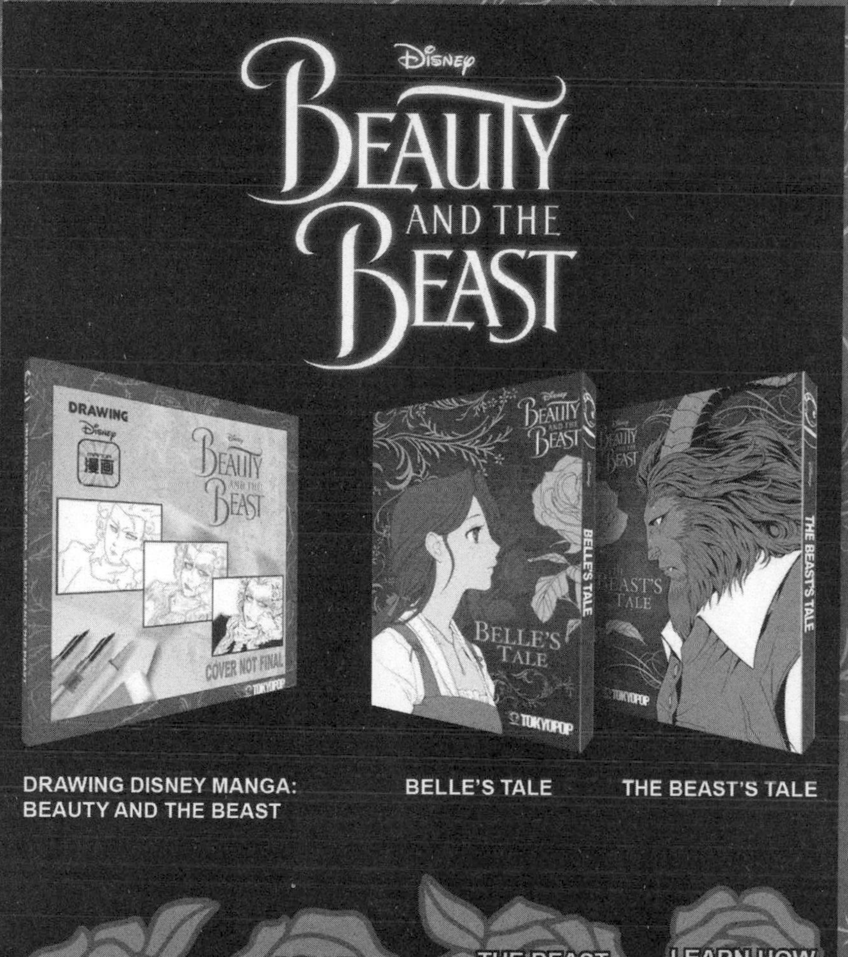
Disney
Beauty and the Beast
DRAWING
Disney
漫画
BEAUTY AND THE BEAST
COVER NOT FINAL
TOKYOPOP
BELLE'S TALE
TOKYOPOP
THE BEAST'S TALE
TOKYOPOP
DRAWING DISNEY MANGA:
BEAUTY AND THE BEAST
BELLE'S TALE
THE BEAST'S TALE
BASED ON THE DISNEY LIVE-ACTION FILM!
BELLE TELLS HER STORY!
THE BEAST REVEALS HIS TORMENTED SOUL!
LEARN HOW TO DRAW THE MANGA!
TOKYO POP
A TALE AS OLD AS TIME,
BROUGHT TO LIFE IN MANGA!
Disney
MANGA
漫画
© Disney

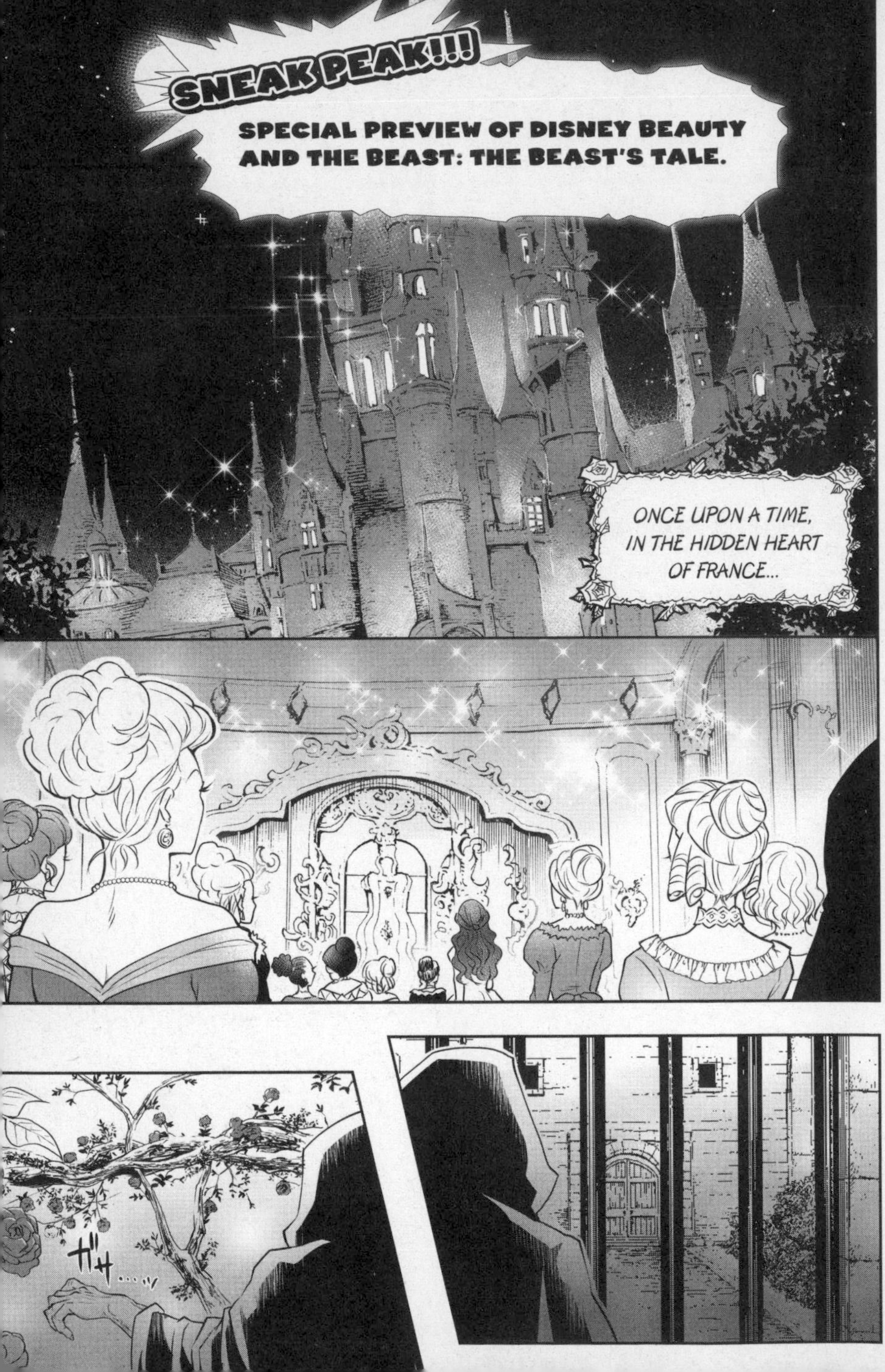
SNEAK PEAK!!!
SPECIAL PREVIEW OF DISNEY BEAUTY AND THE BEAST: THE BEAST'S TALE.
ONCE UPON A TIME, IN THE HIDDEN HEART OF FRANCE...
ガサ...ッ

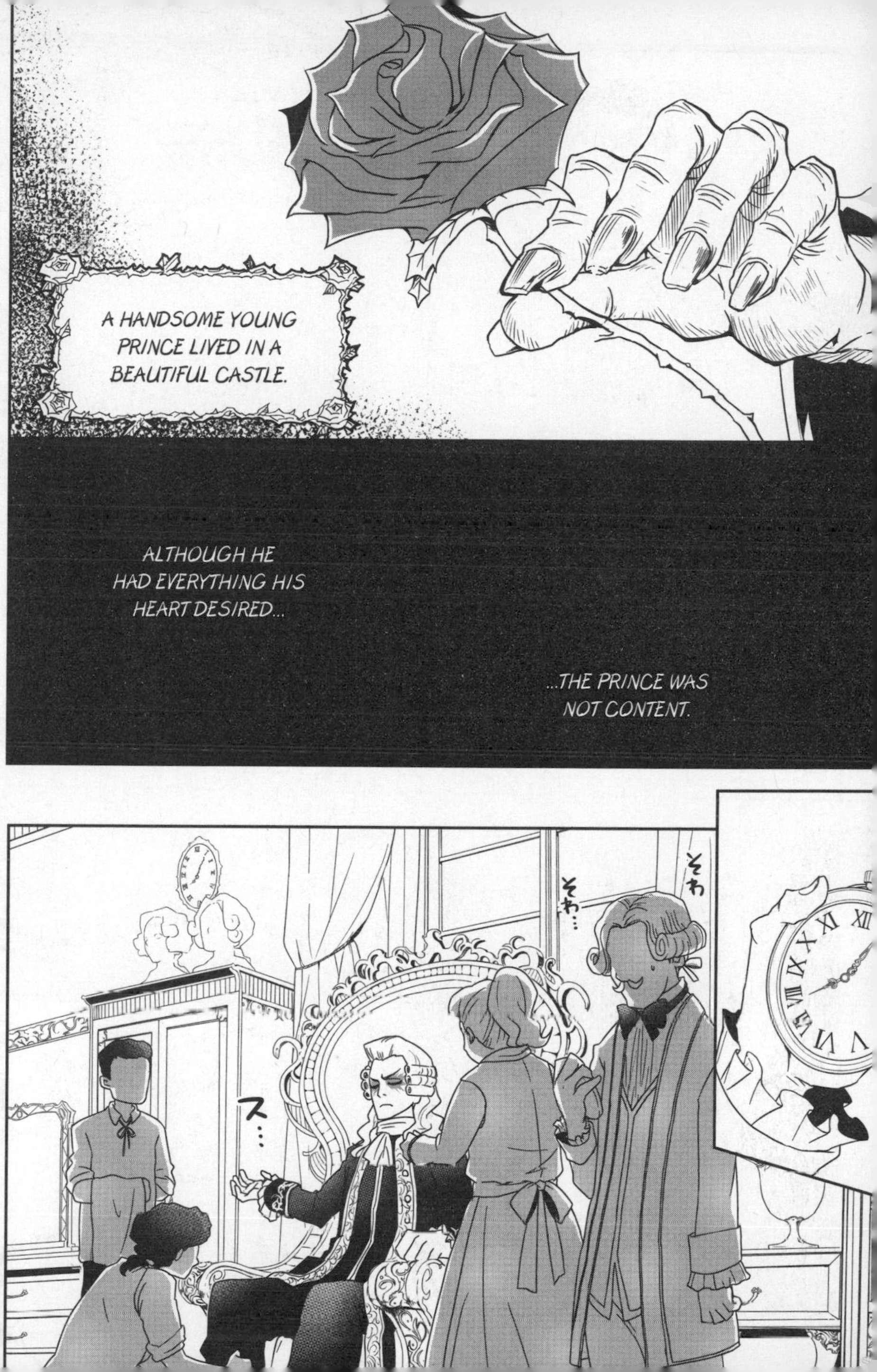
A HANDSOME YOUNG PRINCE LIVED IN A BEAUTIFUL CASTLE.
ALTHOUGH HE HAD EVERYTHING HIS HEART DESIRED...
...THE PRINCE WAS NOT CONTENT.
そわ
そわ…
ス…

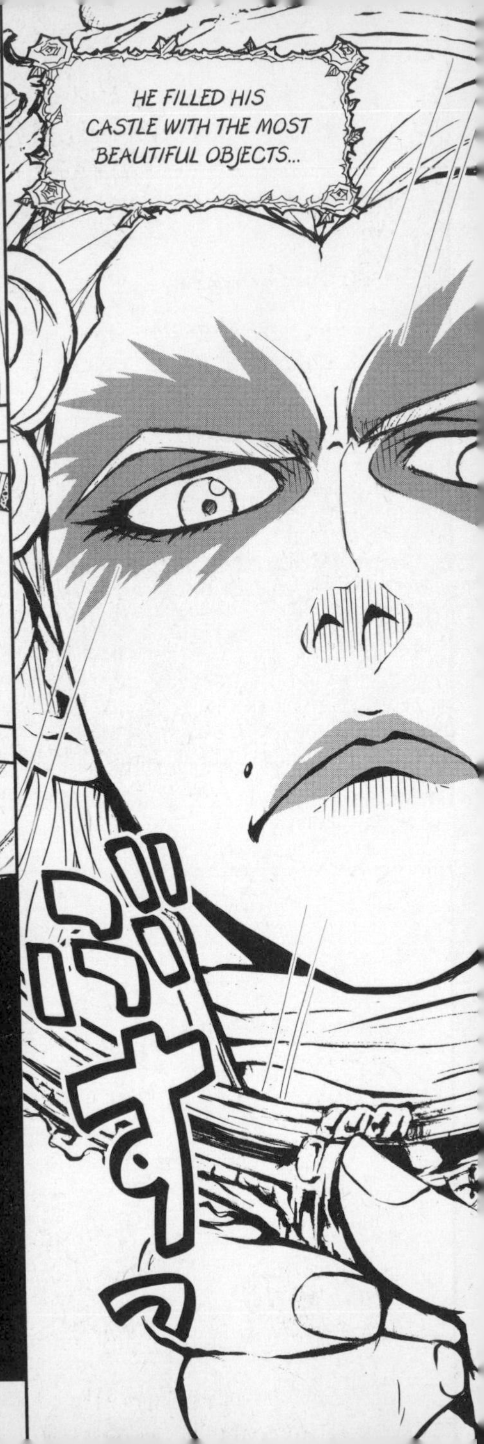
HE FILLED HIS CASTLE WITH THE MOST BEAUTIFUL OBJECTS...
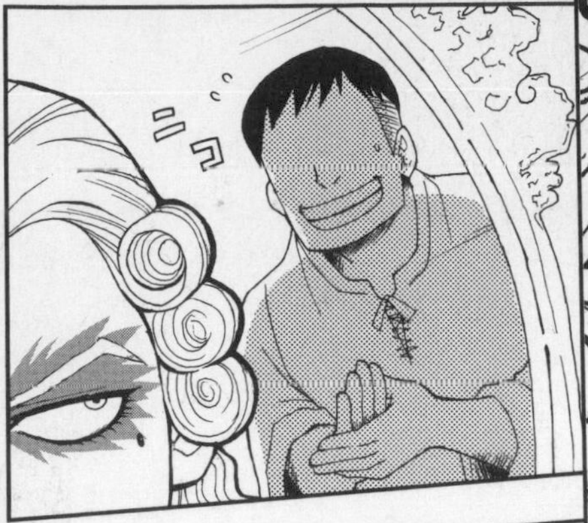
ニコ
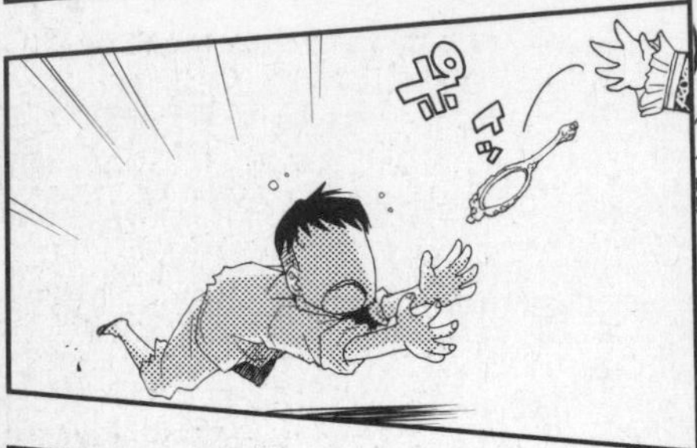
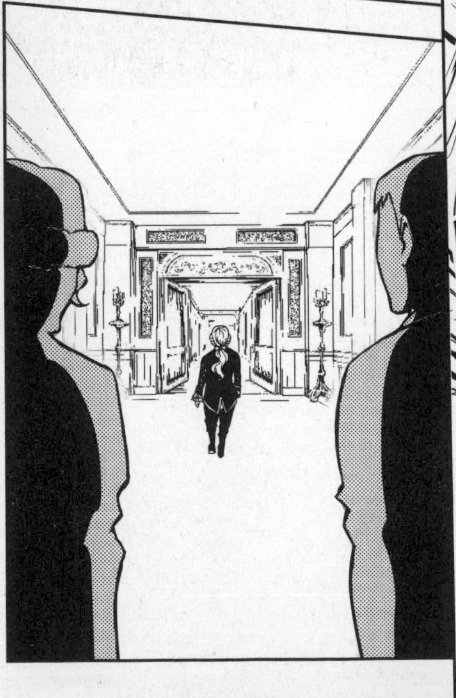

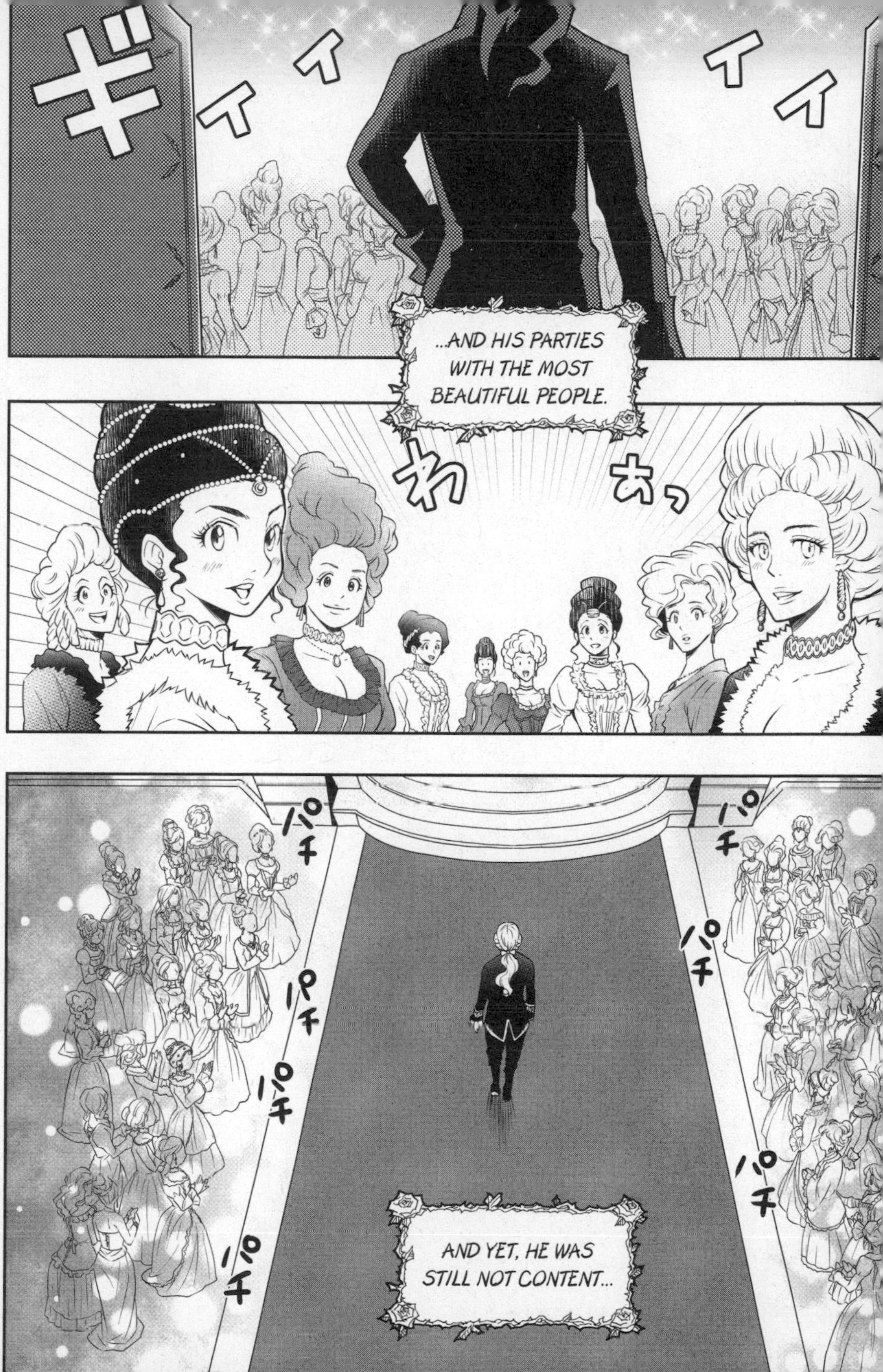
ギィィイイ
...AND HIS PARTIES WITH THE MOST BEAUTIFUL PEOPLE.
あっ
わ
パチ
パチ
パチ
パチ
パチ
パチ
パチ
AND YET, HE WAS STILL NOT CONTENT...

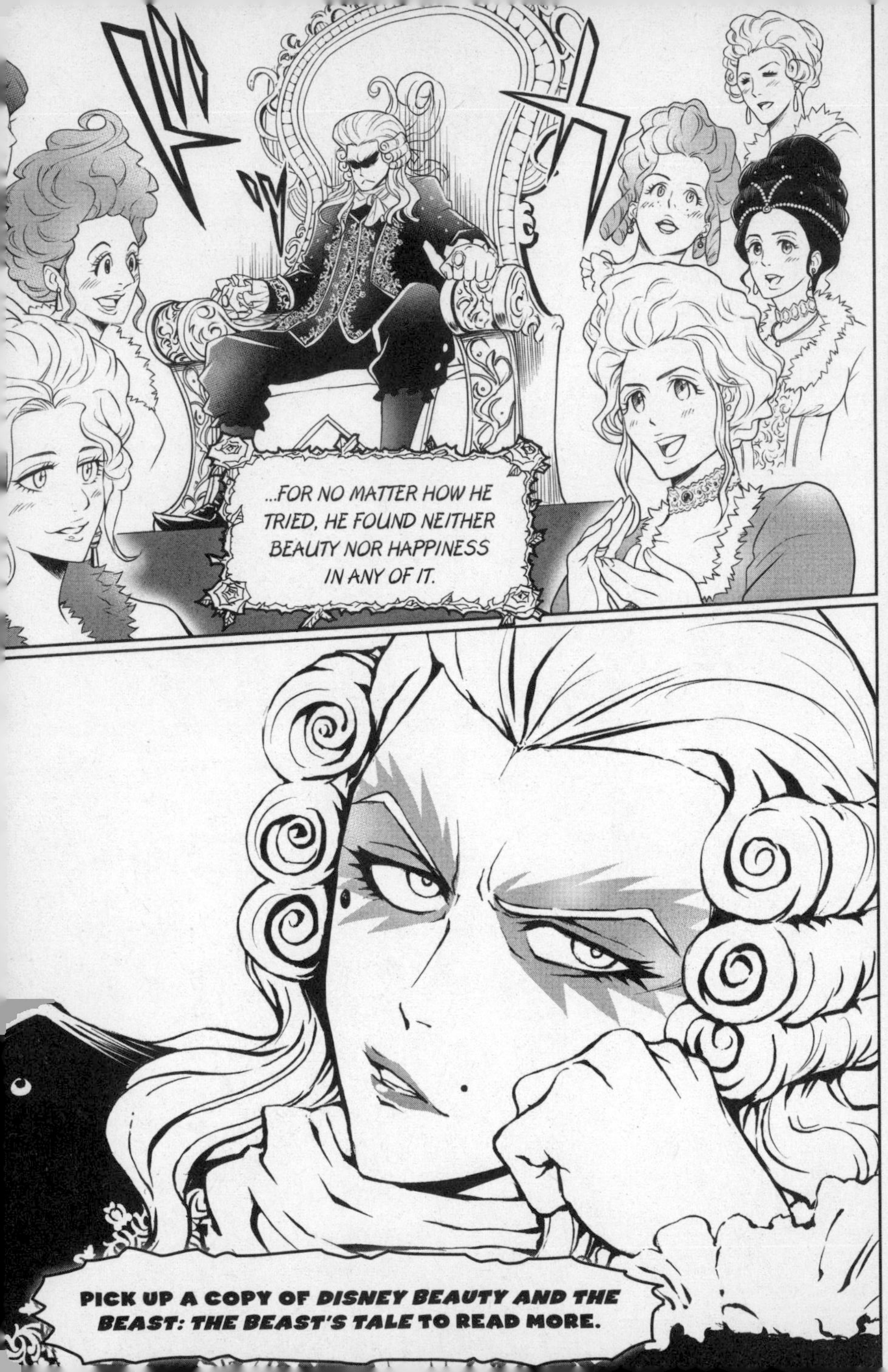
...FOR NO MATTER HOW HE TRIED, HE FOUND NEITHER BEAUTY NOR HAPPINESS IN ANY OF IT.
PICK UP A COPY OF *DISNEY BEAUTY AND THE BEAST: THE BEAST'S TALE* TO READ MORE.

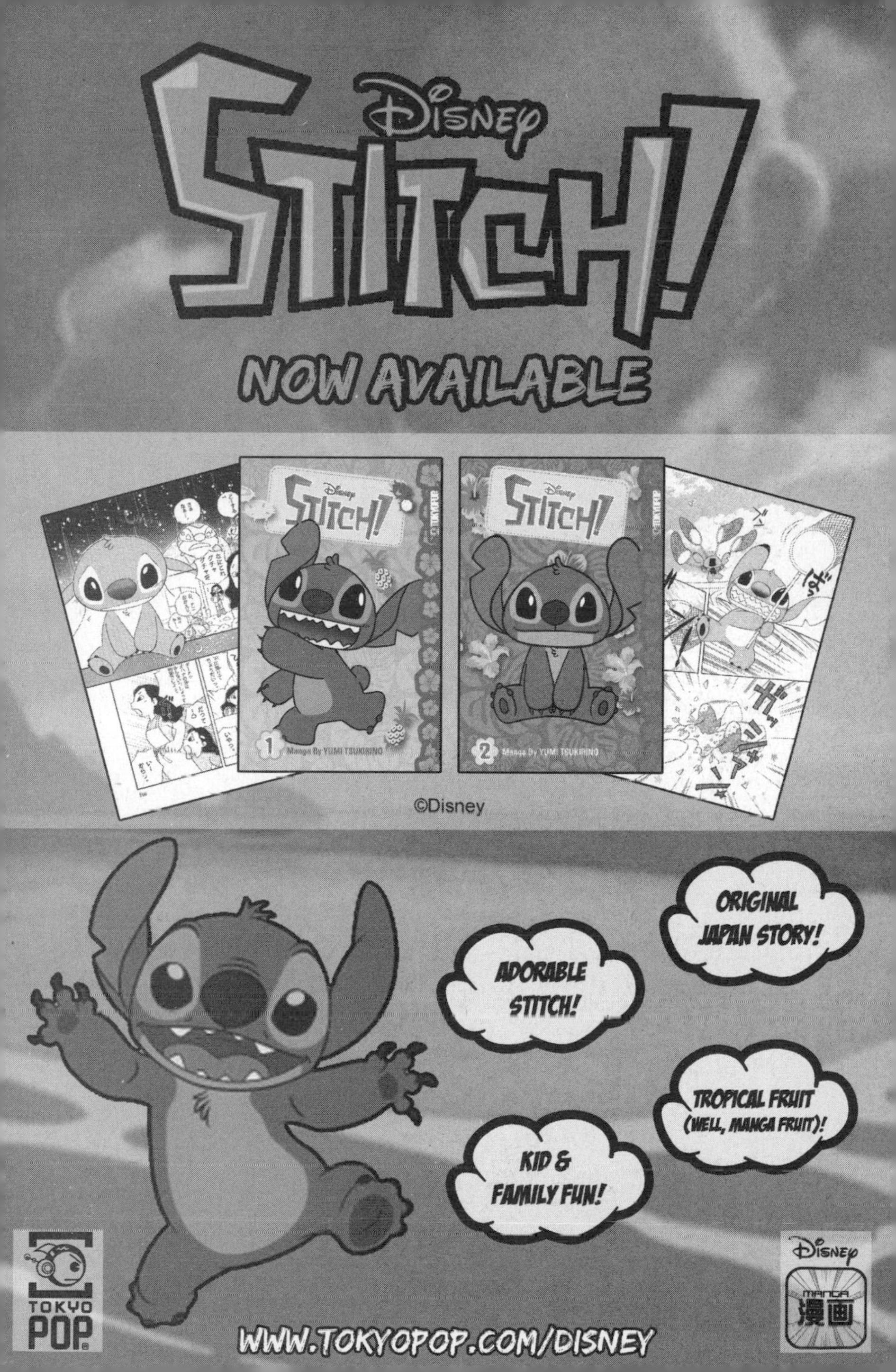
DISNEY
STITCH!
NOW AVAILABLE
DISNEY STITCH!
1 Manga By YUMI TSUKIRINO
DISNEY STITCH!
2 Manga By YUMI TSUKIRINO
©Disney
ORIGINAL JAPAN STORY!
ADORABLE STITCH!
TROPICAL FRUIT (WELL, MANGA FRUIT)!
KID & FAMILY FUN!
TOKYO POP
DISNEY
MANGA
漫画
WWW.TOKYOPOP.COM/DISNEY

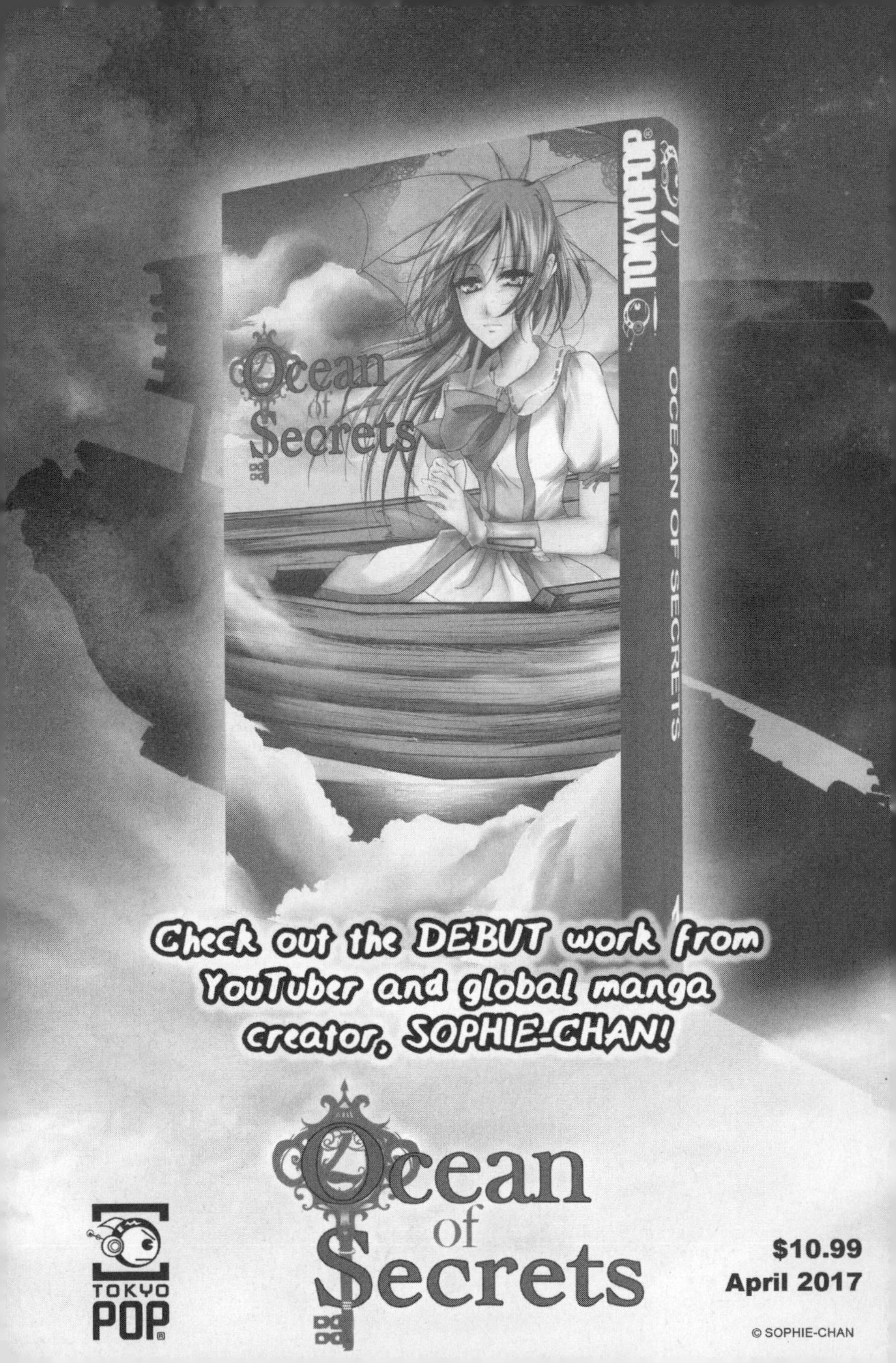
Ocean of Secrets
TOKYOPOP
OCEAN OF SECRETS
Check out the DEBUT work from
YouTuber and global manga
creator, SOPHIE-CHAN!
Ocean of Secrets
TOKYO POP
$10.99
April 2017
© SOPHIE-CHAN

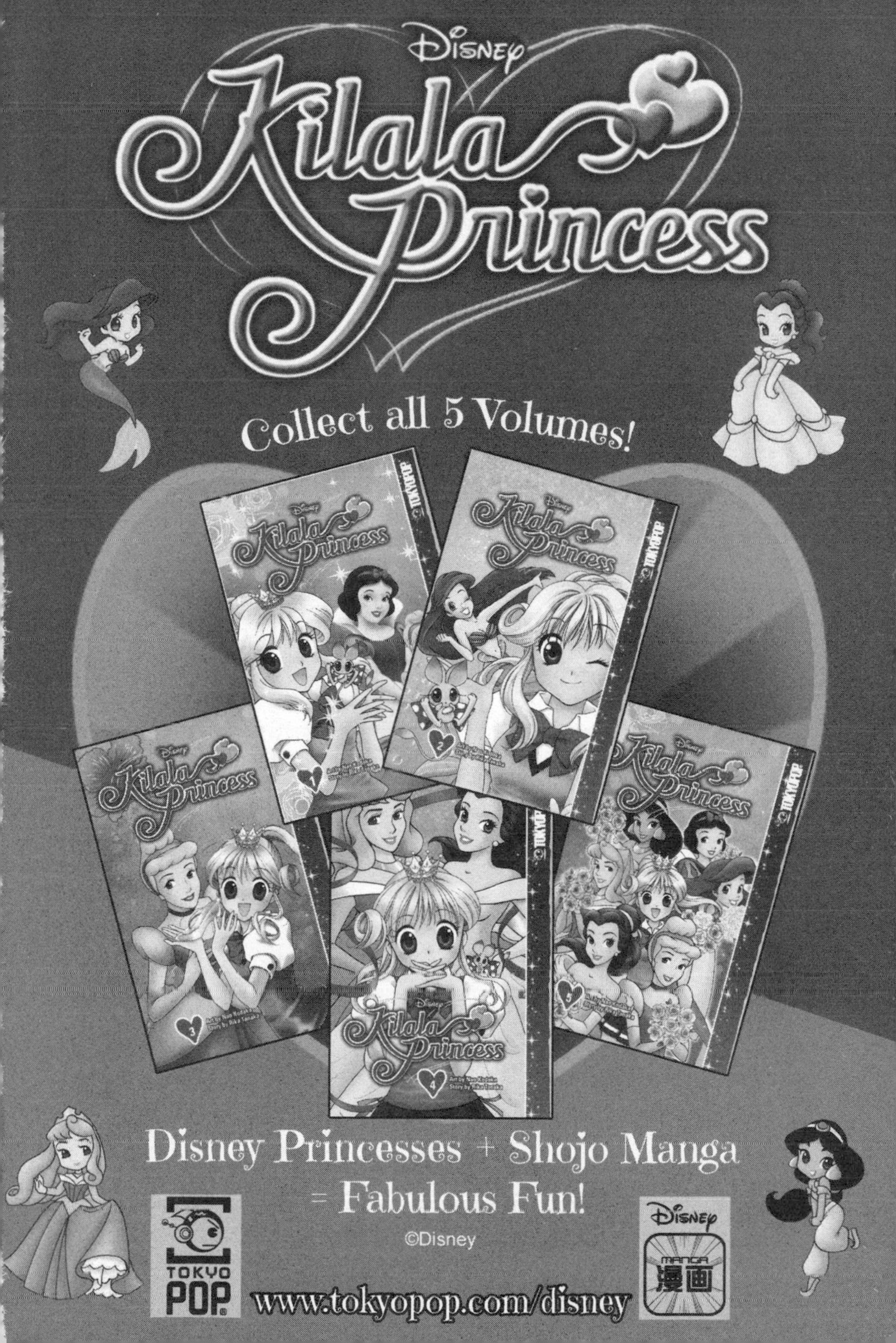

Disney
Kilala Princess
Collect all 5 Volumes!
Disney Princesses + Shojo Manga
= Fabulous Fun!
©Disney
TOKYO POP
www.tokyopop.com/disney
Disney MANGA 漫画

Disney Kilala Princess
Story by Rika Tanaka
Art by Nao Kodaka

Publishing Assistant - Janae Young
Marketing Assistant - Kae Winters
Technology and Digital Media Assistant - Phillip Hong
Retouching and Lettering - Vibrraant Publishing Studio
English Adaptation - Christine Dashiell
Graphic Designer - Al-insan Lashley
Editor - Julie Taylor
Editor-in-Chief & Publisher - Stu Levy

A  Manga

TOKYOPOP and ⟨logo⟩ are trademarks or registered trademarks of TOKYOPOP Inc.

TOKYOPOP inc.
5200 W Century Blvd
Suite 705
Los Angeles, CA 90045 USA

E-mail: info@TOKYOPOP.com
Come visit us online at www.TOKYOPOP.com

⟨f⟩ www.facebook.com/TOKYOPOP
⟨t⟩ www.twitter.com/TOKYOPOP
⟨yt⟩ www.youtube.com/TOKYOPOPTV
⟨p⟩ www.pinterest.com/TOKYOPOP
⟨ig⟩ www.instagram.com/TOKYOPOP
⟨t.⟩ TOKYOPOP.tumblr.com

ISBN: 978-1-4278-5669-2
First TOKYOPOP Printing April 2017
10 9 8 7 6 5 4 3 2 1
Printed in the USA

STOP

THIS IS THE BACK OF THE BOOK!

How do you read manga-style? It's simple! To learn, just start in the top right panel and follow the numbers: